ROC
COMPLEX

The Mickey Hunter Story

TRACEY ICETON

Published by Cinnamon Press
Meirion House, Tanygrisiau, Blaenau Ffestiniog, Gwynedd, LL41 3SU
www.cinnamonpress.com

Print Edition ISBN 978-1-78864-082-4

British Library Cataloguing in Publication Data. A CIP record for this book can be obtained from the British Library.

Designed and typeset in Garamond by Cinnamon Press. Cover design by Adam Craig.

Cinnamon Press is represented by Inpress and by the Books Council of Wales.

The publisher gratefully acknowledges the support of the the Books Council of Wales.

Q. What is the difference between God and a Rock Star?
A. God wishes He was a rock star.

ROCK GOD COMPLEX

Reactions to *Rock God Complex*

'Mickey Hunter was a magus among musicians. This book guarantees him his rightful place in rock mythology.' Roy Grant, editor of *The Four Kings* fanzine and president of The Kingdom of Kings, the Crown & Kingdom fan club.

'While this book may be Mickey Hunter's swansong it reminds readers, critics and fans alike, that the Crown & Kingdom legend is invincible.' Margaret Beubelle, *American Guitarist* magazine.

'There was never a time when Crown & Kingdom weren't part of my life and there will never come a time when Crown & Kingdom won't be a part of my life.' James Ronsarno, son of John Ronsarno, Crown & Kingdom drummer.

'This book proclaims the truth according to Mickey Hunter. But truth is a shadowy concept, darkened by misremembered moments and cloaked in the stubborn belief of what you think you know. All truth is story, but not all stories are true.' Philip Hall, Crown & Kingdom lead singer.

Foreword
False Start

Roy Grant, ed. *The Four Kings* fanzine;
president of The Kingdom of Kings fan club

I was seventeen in the summer of 1972. The Vietnam War was over, at least for the thousands of young Americans who had been repatriated in boxes. It wouldn't ever be over for those of us left behind: the survivors. My brother, Tyler, was killed a week before the Paris Peace Talks opened. He was one of the few 'body not recovered', left to rot in the jungles of South East Asia.

That summer held only the prospect of slogging through another hot July in my father's hardware store with the dim notion that if I saved enough I might, come fall, escape to college and snatch up enough life for myself and Tyler. So I settled down to the drudgery that I thought was my lot.

Fortunately I had friends far less disposed to hard work and one of them, Guy Small, came into the shop and ordered me to down tools (a pencil and order pad onto which I was attempting to calculate the cost of three yards of chicken wire) and go with him to get tickets to see Crown & Kingdom who were playing in Frisco in two weeks' time. I knew I'd get hell from my father if I left the shop. But I didn't care. Something in the day, in the light itself, filtering weakly through the half-drawn shutters, seemed to be calling me to do it. I like to think it was Tyler's defiant spirit.

That undertaking became the single most important of my young life. I was aware of it as we drove through the 'burbs in Guy's beat up '55 Mustang. I was aware of it as we waited in line outside the ticket office, the sun scorching our bare scalps. I was aware of it when, the ticket folded inside my wallet, Guy and I went to a nearby bar and got the most drunk we could for five bucks. I was even more aware of it two weeks later when, my life savings of $23 in my pocket and a rucksack over my shoulder, I walked out of my parents' place, got into Guy's Mustang and made the drive with him, back to Frisco.

The Fillmore was packed out with guys in faded 501s and chicks jangling beads. Guy muscled his way to the front (he a was 6ft 2 line-backer); I followed in his wake. We stared up at the stage. Someone passed a joint down the row. I had my first whiff of weed. The air was charged with this phenomenal electricity. A rumble started up, building to a roar as thousands of young kids who'd been sold out by their elders and betters stamped their feet, clapped their hands and chanted the infamous words that would call down our gods.

And down they came.

The noise of the crowd stopped. It didn't fade out. It just stopped. The lights came up. Mickey, Philip, Pete and John appeared, eyeballing us, getting our measure while we gazed back at them, praying for a miracle. Then Mickey struck a chord. It sang in a clear, pure voice; the miracle was among us and for us and of us.

They must've played three hours that night but it passed in a single heartbeat. What I carry still from that show, like a battle scar, is pure raw power reined in by four master musicians. The beat pounded in my chest, the notes sang in my ears, the lyrics poured from my lips. It was an ecstatic frenzy of passion, pleasure and pain that I hoped would kill me. It made me understand what it means to know you are alive. It made me want to live.

Crown & Kingdom were the greatest rock band ever and Mickey Hunter was their genius axeman but there was so much more to him than a guitar-playing mortal. He commanded the devils of music, conjuring chords so potent they earthquaked my world. He was also someone who knew what life was for and lived it. He was on a mission to become immortal: a legend. He would succeed but only after conquering more in one lifetime than most of us could in a hundred.

When I was seventeen Crown & Kingdom's music was the anthem to my life, my inspiration to live at a time when there seemed little worth living for. I idolised Mickey Hunter, he was my hero; the hero of tens of thousands of others like me. Once you've read this book you'll understand what it takes to be an idol incarnate, what it took to be Mickey Hunter: Rock God.

All hail the king!

THE JOKER

I reach for my gun. Tear it out of the holster. Level it at the man in the black hat. Pull the trigger. Bang.

A revving engine snaps me awake. The bang wasn't me firing my six-shooter. It was that noisy bastard next door slamming himself into his car. I don't care how many fucking goals he's scored he's a right wanker. I wait in the sledgehammer silence for him to crank up the stereo and race off into the night. He obliges and I hear my throbbing power chord matched, and then some, by Philip's angry-young-man singing:

> ♪ The hope of Hell
> And fury of the gods
> We couldn't see the trees
> Hidden by the woods ♫

'Trees of Eden': our anthem.

Listening to John's pounding drums, Pete's steady bass, Philip's wailing vocals and my shrieking guitar throws me into hellish darkness. The sound runs off into the night, fading not fast enough, as Arsenal's top striker tears out of our suburban haven.

I can't close my eyes now. I know I'll have to watch It again if I do. That Night. The one I've tried so bloody hard to blank for three decades. There's no fucking chance I'll get back to sleep now It's reared Its ugly head. My heart thumps. I try to suffocate It, filling my mind with anything but That Night. Did I remind Keira to book the Bentley in for a service? Is it today Meg wants me to take her to Christie's for that Rossetti auction? I ramble on for a quarter of an hour before sacking it as a bad job. I never fucking manage to beat It. I get up, leave of the warmth of our bed and creep across the room without waking Meg.

I shuffle down the marble stairs, they're bloody freezing on bare feet (why did I let Meg arm-twist me on that one?) and go into the kitchen. I sit at the table, facing the night-black window, waiting for the show to start. At first it's only a window. Then it becomes a movie screen. That Night explodes onto it with volatile energy. My own private screening of the feature presentation of my life. Sick to death of reruns but powerless to shut It down I watch, paralytic with fear. This time I've come into the cinema halfway through the film. That's O.K. though, I know the beginning by heart: me, Ronsey and Philip; a few beers and a bit of a smoke; reminiscing over the good times. Then the blow up. The slanging match. Me and Philip clawing at each others' throats. Him yelling; me yelling louder. Us fighting. Me falling. The film plays on. The next scene's this:

I'm on the floor, on my back. My legs are up, on the side table I tripped over in our fisticuffs. I'm out cold and drowning in an ocean of acid. Fucked up. Off-my-tits. Out-of-my-head and soon to be out-of-my-body. Jesus, here I go. With the shimmer of desert sunlight, I split. There are two 'mes' now. The copy, my ghostly twin, hovers a few feet above the original. Both 'mes' have long wavy hair, still dark, and no crow's feet. We're dressed in our period costume of flares and garish magenta psychedelic-print shirt. We are thin and pale, wasted by the chain of high-comedown-high-comedown that shackles our days and nights.

I scan the rest of the picture flickering on my kitchen window, an old cine movie playing on a knackered projector. Philip's his younger self too, his blue eyes burning with anger, his blonde mane tossed back from his stone-chiselled face. Ronsey's the age he'll always be. He tugs at his thick beard and his dark eyes darken as the three of us play out the final act in the Crown & Kingdom opus. For a fraction of a second the frame freezes. I pray the reel in my brain has jammed and I'm spared the final Hamletian scene. But my memory kicks on. The screen flickers again. The figures return to life and start inching towards their tragic fates.

Ronsey goes to Philip, arms outstretched for peace, a ceasefire. Philip, in his blinding anger, pushes him, throws him with all his strength, out and down. Ronsey falls, crashing against the wall, his powerful body demolished like so much cooling stack with so little dynamite. He crumbles into my ten-quid-a-square-yard shag pile with its snarling mouthful of razor sharp glass teeth. He doesn't get up. Nothing moves for an age. Then the real me sucks back the phantom twin with a whirling whoosh. I'm whole again, awake and up. Philip lunges at me. We fight on; fists flailing, fingers tearing, legs kicking. I get him off me and struggle over to Ronsey, shake him, try to lift him. I turn around. Call over my shoulder. Philip is gone.

The screen fades to black night. Imaginary credits roll up my kitchen window: Mickey Hunter as himself. Philip Hall as himself. John Ronsarno, as himself. Finally It's over. For tonight.

So much for the promised soothing effects of camomile tea. I chuck the dregs into the sink. Christ, I miss black coffee. And Scotch. Both are better for the pain. My heart pounds a bass drum beat, each thud a fist punching out the inside of my chest. I wait for it to settle. Lately it's taking longer and longer. After twenty minutes, when my heart's finally stopped trying to fight its way out of my chest, I go upstairs and get in bed next to Meg.

She's still sleeping. Her brown hair with its precious flecks of gold is spread over the pillow. I lie beside her and put my hand out. Her skin's warm. I wriggle towards her heat, hoping it'll melt the ice-hard memory of That Night. I press my lips to the back of her smooth white shoulder which glows in the darkness of the room. She stirs. I want her to wake but I don't want to wake her.

I reach around her with my arm, feeling her chest rise and fall with each easy breath. Her skin, soft and sagged just a little, is comforting. I press my lips harder against her neck. She stirs again. I move in closer, pulling her across me. She says my name into the thick bedroom air and turns to me. I kiss her mouth. Heavy with sleep, she doesn't kiss back. I press into her more and she opens her eyes. Glints of blue flare up at me as she pulls away.

'Mickey, are you O.K?'

I nod and kiss her again. I don't want to talk. I just want to hold her real warm body and forget the past. I pull her over me like a blanket. Hide beneath her. Keep my eyes squeezed shut. Don't look and don't think. Keep It locked out.

When we've made love she sleeps again, in my arms this time.

That Night sleeps too.

The Fool

'Morning, Keira,' I say as she bustles in with the post and her usual stream of obscenities about the ring road traffic. There's no breathless awe, no sycophantic arse-kissing. That's why I hired her. And she's a bloody good assistant.

'Morning, Mr Hunter.' She dumps the post on my desk, narrowly missing my lemongrass tea.

'Careful. You almost spilt it.'

'That'd be a shame, wouldn't it?' she says, 'then I'd have to get you a coffee to make up for it.' Smiling, she reaches for my cup and turns to the door. 'By the way, there's a letter from the National Institute of Musical Excellence. I put it on top.' She pauses in the doorway. 'It looks important.'

I glance at the large, creamy envelope with the familiar NIME logo embossed top left. It's been addressed in pretentious copperplate lettering.

'What do those berks want now?'

'Mr Hunter!'

'Well, they're always asking me to be patron of this or a member of that, expecting me to sit on boring committees with a load of boring old bastards.'

'In case you haven't checked a mirror recently,' she says, 'you are a boring old bastard.' Her eyes twinkle. Thirty years ago she'd have found herself in my bed. Probably more than once.

'Thanks!'

'Aren't you going to open it?'

'Aren't you going to get me that coffee?'

We exchange grinning glares. She laughs and leaves, the panelled door swinging shut on her muttered cursing.

I pull the letter over. They write frequently, saying I should put something back into the industry, implying I owe them: it. But this one's different. Not their usual cheap shiny buff-coloured envelope. I suspect Keira already knows what it's about and, although I've come to prefer being in the dark, there are times when knowing's a necessary evil. I reach for the letter knife and slit its throat. Inside are two sheets of the same full-fat paper, logo embossed and typed in that ridiculous copper-plate font. I scan them.

'Well?' Keira's back with my coffee. She sets it down and drags a chair over, plonking herself in front of me.

I put the letter on the desk, face down, and sip my coffee.

'Didn't you put any sugar in?'

'Mrs Hunter said that was off your menu.'

'She said the same about bloody coffee too.'

Ignoring me, Keira leans forward, clutching the edge of my desk with her thin white fingers. The tips today are green to match her eyes.

'If you're not going to tell me, I'll read it myself,' she jests and reaches out.

I slap her hand away. 'You mean you haven't already?'

'I'd never open your private mail.' She recoils in feigned outrage.

'So all this hopping up and down like a kangaroo on speed is woman's intuition?'

Green eyes flash at me. She grins unabashed.

'I might've heard a rumour.'

'A rumour, that's all, eh?'

'They have, haven't they?' she explodes. 'They've finally got their bloody acts together and given you the life-time achievement award.'

I nod and before I can duck, Keira launches herself at me, shrieking with glee and throwing her arms around my neck. Her lips are warm against the cool white of my creased cheek as she kisses me with over-cooked elation. I pat her on the back.

'Alright, Keira, now get up, please. I might well be a boring old bastard to you but inside I'm still a hot-blooded twenty something and if you insist on jumping up and down in my lap like that I may not be able to control myself. And you're definitely not on Mrs Hunter's diet sheet.'

Keira laughs again but she knows it's only two parts joke. She gets up.

'At last,' she says, 'about time.'

'I'm not bothered. It was all over a long time ago.'

'I think you're wrong. It's only just beginning.' Then, seeing the face I'm pulling, she says, 'You are going to accept, aren't you?'

'It's not up to me. There are others involved.'

'But surely…'

'You think the lure of a prestigious award will be enough to thaw the ice age?'

'Of course.'

'Even Philip?'

'He'd be an idiot to turn this down. I'm going to call his secretary right now.'

'You bloody won't.'

'Why not?'

'I need to think about this. I'm not sure. Can't remember the last time I spoke to Philip, spoke, not shouted. I don't want to repeat our last encounter,' I say.

Keira puts her hands on her hips and pouts her Cupid's bow at me.

'If you don't accept now they won't offer again.'

'Good.'

'It could be your last chance of a resurgence.'

'I don't care.'

'Bullshit,' she snaps. 'I haven't worked for you for seven years without realising how much it still means to you.'

'I don't want the hassle.'

'You won't live forever. Say what you like but everyone wants one last hurrah. Present company not excepted.'

Keira returns to her desk and rifles noisily through scattered files. I shuffle the rest of the mail. The next letter has 'King's College Hospital' franked in the corner. I slip it into my top drawer and peer through the doorway. Keira's shoulders are hunched. She'll sulk as long as it takes.

'Why don't you get me Pete's number?'

She faces me with a broad grin.

'Better start in the baby pool.' I smile weakly.

It doesn't seem like a big deal, making a bloody phone call. But this is how it starts; the train you just caught, the stranger you didn't sidestep quickly enough. The phone call you almost missed.

*

I'm going out, jacket on, fags in pocket. Escaping down the pub for a bit. Anywhere's better than home when she's in. It's far too fucking awkward. Has been ever since it became obvious that I'm the responsible one. How fucked up's that? Barely twenty, never worked a proper job, rocking and rolling for a living, partying like I've weeks to live and I'm the responsible one! I don't like being home at all but I've no choice 'til I get things sorted or find somewhere else to doss.

The phone rings.

Bollocks.

I snatch it up.

'Is that Mickey Hunter?'

'Yeah. Who's this?'

'Pete Smith. We met a bit since. Dave McVie's party.' His

words are rushed and wobbly. I scour my memory. See a quiet looking guy with grey eyes and a cautious smile.

'I remember. Just. That was some night. You're with Skinny Feet, aren't ya? The bass player?'

'Erm, yeah. It's Skinny Legs. But yeah, I'm the bass player. Was. We've called it a day.'

'Oh. Right.' He's after something.

'I heard The Three Bob Band's well… disbanded.'

'Yeah.'

'There's a rumour you're looking to get a new line-up together. Any chance you need a bass player, only slightly used,' he jokes.

There it is.

'Dunno, maybe, I've not really fixed anything up yet. We could meet, I guess. I've not heard you play so…'

'Sure. Any time you like.'

'O.K., tomorrow. Around two-ish.' Her bingo time. 'I'll give you my address.'

At exactly two p.m. the guy from Dave's party rings the bell and I get my first sober sight of Peter Smith. He can only have a couple of years on me but there's something freakily grown-up about him. Least he's dressed his age, faded flares and a fringed suede waistcoat. His light brown hair's long enough to pass for trendy. Just. I hold out my hand.

'Pete?'

'Yeah. Good to see you again, Mickey,' he says and shifts his bass guitar case into his other hand. His grip's strong but not bone crushing. Good thing, too. My fingers are my living, man.

'You need a hand?'

'If you wouldn't mind taking this. I'll nip back for my amp.' He holds out the case.

I reach for it and wait as he walks with fluid steps to the rust-scabbed Ford Anglia parked in front of my yellow Triumph TR4.

Amp in hand he returns. I head down the hall. He follows.

'In here.' I push into the back room and hear a low clear whistle from him as he takes in the set up.

Once her dining room, this is where I live now, where I'm alive, I mean. The only items that could be called furniture are three guitar stools. There are two music stands, three amps (two combis and a proper head and cabs stack) and the rack holding my three electric guitars. They sit upright and proud, the necks of the two Les Pauls lined up and the Strat, with its different profile, a rebel with its own rhyme and rhythm. On the opposite wall hang two acoustic guitars; old faithful, varnished golden as a summer sunset, and my latest recruit in a faded cherry-red finish, full of sweet flavour. The curtains are drawn but even by the half-light I know the room's a fucking awesome sight.

'You're pretty serious about this, aren't you?'

'No point doing it if you're not.'

'Wish I could talk my missus into letting me have a room like this,' Pete sighs.

'That's why I'm not married,' I grin. 'Can't be doing with that shit.'

He laughs. I'm not sure if it's me or himself he's mocking but he adds, 'Actually, I'm pretty lucky. Wouldn't swap mine. Anyway, I've only myself to blame. Every spare corner of ours is littered with kid stuff. It's like a bloody toy shop.'

'Kids?'

'Yeah, two girls. Don't worry. I'm not gonna pull out a load of family snaps. Where shall I set up?'

I watch as he unpacks his bass, pulling it gently, firmly, from the case and wiping over the neck with a special rag. His eyes never stray from the guitar as he makes movements he's obviously made a thousand times.

'This your place?'

'My mother's but we keep out of each other's way. How

long've you been playing?'

''Bout ten years but I've been into music my whole life.' He says it as if a decade might not be enough of an apprenticeship. 'I was having violin lessons when I was five.'

I raise my eyebrows.

'Not my idea,' he adds, 'but it taught me to read music and a lot of the theory I wouldn't have learnt otherwise. It's easy to get caught up in making great sounds but I realised fairly early in the piece that it's not gonna be enough if you want to make it.'

'So you're pretty serious about it too.'

'There's no point doing it if you're not,' he replies, grinning.

All the time I've been watching him, weighing him, Pete's been doing the same. He might think he needs me but he's sharp enough to know it has to be right.

I reach for my favourite Les Paul and plug in. Pete waits. The polite thing would be to have a chat about what music he's familiar with and the stuff he's played before. Instead, I start riffing something I like. An obscure blues number. One I've messed with. The way I do it the timing's quicker and I've add fills and runs. For three bars I play alone. Pete joins me on the fourth, perfectly in time, with a walking blues bass line that, from the way he rocks it, is all his own. His eyes lock into mine. I pick up the pace; he follows. We duel, music surging back and forth like waves of troops advancing and retreating. No surrender; no quarter. I pull into a lead break, a furious succession of notes, playing off and on the beat, stopping to let a note curl through the air like a flung spear before charging forward with another volley. Pete plays through it, the barrage not touching him. I retreat behind the chord-line. When I look up again he's still grinning, his fingers moving fluidly over the frets. The music separates itself from him. It's alive, rampaging with awesome power. This is what happens when an unstoppable force hits an immovable object. I wind down then crank back up for a final flurry, the last assault. We end together on A and I nod approval at what he's done. No musicians were harmed...

'Was that 'Travelling Riverside Blues'?'

'Yeah. My version anyway.'

'I've never heard it done like that before.'

'That's what I'm about,' I sneer, 'I don't want to be like everyone else. I want to be me: Mickey Hunter. Think you can keep up?'

'Yeah, reckon so,' he says without bullshit bravado.

'Let's try another.'

Jamming together that afternoon Pete proves himself more than capable of playing up to me. Aside from his knowledge of music theory he's got the two things that can't be taught: passion and style. He's creative and imaginative, producing something fresh and original as easily as he reproduces something old school.

We knock off the amps. I fetch much needed beers and we decamp to the sitting room. She won't be in for another hour.

Pete waits for me to start. I light a cigarette and toss my pack over. He helps himself.

'Thanks.'

I shrug.

'So?'

'So what?'

'C'mon man, what do you think?' He forces laughter into his voice.

'You don't need me to tell you you're a bloody good bassist.'

'Thanks.'

Even if I turned him down he'd probably leave happy now he's got praise from me.

'I think, yeah, I reckon we could pull something out of the mire,' I say.

'O.K. Alright. Excellent. What next?'

'Find a singer and drummer.' As though it's that easy.

'Got anyone in mind?'

'A couple of possible singers but both've got gigs at the moment. I might be able to lure them away...'

'Are you after a name?'

'Why? Know someone?'

'Not really.' Pete peers into a shadowy corner. 'There's this guy... a mate of mine saw him in some dump in Manchester a while back. Said he'd never heard a voice like it. I've only got his word for it though.'

'Would you trust his judgement, this mate?'

'Yeah, I mean, I wouldn't take advice off him on money or women but as far as music goes he knows his stuff.'

'See if you can find out more about this bloke. If he's performing somewhere we'll go see him. D'ya remember his name?'

'Yeah, Philip Hall.'

THE JUGGLER

Keira slides Pete's number across my desk and smiles encouragement. I pick up the receiver and dial but instantly click to disconnect the call while keeping the phone pressed to my ear. Keira watches but doesn't say anything. It's one of her more valuable qualities.

'No reply.' I shrug. She mirrors my gesture before returning to her work. I open my top drawer. The King's College Hospital letter dares me to read it.

'Keira, would you pop to that new deli and see if they sell gluten-free bagels?'

'Oh. Yes, of course.'

She doesn't move. I tap out a beat with a biro lid.

She looks round. 'Now?'

'If it's not interrupting something important.'

'This can wait.' She dons her coat. A swathe of soft purple leather swings mid-calf. It clashes wonderfully with the red ankle boots and the yellow and blue striped dress she's wearing. She reminds me so much of someone I once knew. She didn't give a damn about what anyone else thought of her either.

I strain my ears for the front door's click, my hearing's not as sharp as it used to be, then count five before checking the window. She's striding along the street, the purple coat lapping at her legs. I grab the letter from the drawer and scrunch it in half. The paper's bulky; I ram it into my pocket, pull on my own coat and am heading for the door when a sudden, ridiculously childish idea pauses me. Why the hell not? I rake through Keira's desk; half used lipsticks, broken hair clips, odd earrings. I know she's got some. The feeling of being a sneaky kid again creeps over me. My eyes catch a sliver of white and gold in the gloom. I pluck out the cigarettes. Lights. But Marlboros at least. Thieves can't be choosers.

Outside I walk in the opposite direction to that Keira's heading down on her bogus mission. My getaway takes me right, left and right again. At first I don't know where I'm going. Distance is all I'm after. But I realise it's not that I need to get away from here; I need to get back there. I keep walking, turning, crossing, hoping I'm going the right way. The streets start to dull down, dumping their colours. It's like walking into a black and white movie.

I don't think I'll be able to find it. The streets look the same, and nothing like they used to. I scan rows of abandoned buildings. A sign hangs loose, 'Wilson's Tobacconist's' suspended by its one remaining nail. Underneath 'Ron's Guitars and Gear' is visible as a faded shadow. I stop at the window, heart throbbing, and look past the reflection of myself, the fine wisps of white hair that curl over my ears and the starburst lines at the corners of my dark eyes. I'm looking for what used to be here: a baby grand, lumps gouged in the mahogany, never in tune, growing dusty in the sunshine; a stack of speakers in the corner, black, shiny and promising volume; spinning racks of strings, bottle necks, plectrums, sheet music and tabs. And the guitar ranks, a musical army waiting for the cry to go up. There's bugger all left except the emptiness of death.

*

I look at my mother. She's dead. Stone dead. Fucking appropriate. One of us is stoned and the other dead. I stare into her eyes. They're blind; a camera with no photographer. The bedroom stands still; I spin in its centre, an axis with gravity whirling me around. I stagger out, reeling and stumbling, push against the door of my room. It folds back on itself. My bed is far away on the other side. I lurch towards it. Fall to the floor and stay there. It's firm: inert. I cling to it. How the fuck do birds sleep in trees?

In the morning she's still dead. That's a bad deal 'cos I'm sober, standing in her room, the remains of last night's booze gurgling in my gut, the stench of death filling my nose. I gag. Rush for the bathroom. Puke into the water-stained bathtub. Sit balanced on the edge, the cast iron cold through my jeans. My legs tremble. I'm shivering. I totter to the sink, run the tap and shove my mouth under it. Water soothes the burn in my throat but only for as long as I keep my mouth under the flow. I creep back to her.

The light, filtered through her bedroom curtains, is dusky pink. The oblong rug, a deep plum colour, lolls at my feet. The white pillow strewn on the floor is a loose tooth waggled out of place. The rank air is bad breath. I'm inside a rotten mouth.

I inch closer. She's been dead, Christ, a day? Two? Three? I stopped checking up on her years ago. Not my job. I retch again and cover my mouth and nose. Not a great combination; hang over, come down and a corpse. Can't say I recommend it.

I scan the scene. Used clothes are chucked over a chair; stockings, like a shed snake skin, coiled on the floor; the wardrobe door's ajar. I kick it closed. It bounds open again. I remember the broken catch. She asked me to fix it. I didn't.

Now there's nowhere else to look but at her. Blood rushes to my face. Her bare white legs are on show and, higher up, the dark patch of hair between them. I see what she really was: a bottle blonde. Like half the girls I've screwed. I grab a cardigan and throw it over her lower half.

Her face is warped, like a wetted ink drawing. Her eyes bulge, the whites large and round. Her war paint is smudged, colouring outside the lines. The red Cupid's bow has bled over her cheeks and chin. A lump of purple flesh, an over ripe plum, protrudes from between her lips. Thin strands of blonde hair are stuck to her forehead. Around her neck is a choker of stripy bruises. She's been strangled. Murdered. I'll have to call the bloody cops. Fuck. Shit. Bollocks.

'What's your name?' The copper's pencil hovers over his notebook.

I shift weight onto my other leg, drag on a cigarette and look around. We're in the front garden. The house is a fucking crime scene. Nosey bitch Henderson from No. 23 gawps on; she cleaned those windows yesterday. She'll get a shock when they bring out the body. I switch my gaze to the revolving blue light whirling on top of the panda car. Be cool for a trip.

'Mickey Hunter.'

'Michael Hunter,' he corrects, 'and the deceased?'

'Is my mother.'

'I see. Her name?'

'Margaret Brown.'

'Brown?' He eyes me over a plump moustache.

'Yeah, Brown.'

'I see. And your father?'

'What?'

'Where is he?'

'How the hell should I know? I never met the tosser.' I'm losing it. Any second now: bang! Blow this dick away and take out cowbag Henderson too.

'Where were you last night?'

'At a party.'

'I see.' He writes. 'Can anyone confirm that?'

Hell, if everyone left in the same state as me they probably couldn't even swear they were there.

'Yeah, loads of people.'

'What time did you return home?'

'Twoish.'

'Why didn't you call the police then?'

Er, I was stoned off my tits and didn't realise she was really dead.

'I didn't know she was dead. I'm well past kissing Mummy dearest goodnight.'

'I see.'

'Do you eat a lot of carrots?'

'Excuse me?'

'For your eyesight.'

He stares. His moustache quivers. A shiver rips through me. The phone in the hall rings.

'You mind if I get that?' Without giving him chance to say he does I sprint up the drive and grab the receiver.

'Hello?'

'Hey, Mickey?'

'Pete.' Thank fuck for that.

'Great news. I've found him,' Pete's voice is lit up with schoolboy excitement.

'What? Who?'

'Philip Hall. He's singing at a club in Birmingham tonight with this band, The Geordie Boys.'

'Tonight might be a problem.'

'What's up, Mickey?'

'I might be being detained at Her Majesty's.'

'I'll come round,' Pete says and hangs up.

'You didn't have to wait,' I tell him as Pete strides over. I'm bloody glad he did, though.

'Hell, I wasn't gonna leave you here. I told them you were at that party last night but they didn't wanna believed me.'

'It must be that shifty look in your eyes, mate,' I laugh as we head outside.

'But they don't really think you strangled your own mother, do they?'

'Nah. They reckon she's been dead since yesterday morning, when I was down the bank. Guess cops are O.K. with alibis from bank managers, if not bass players,' I say.

'And are you O.K.?' Pete studies me, watching for cracking.

'Yeah, man, I'm fine. I could use a drink; I'm still hung over. And a place to doss. They said something about not letting me back inside 'til they've finished investigating. Fuck knows what there is to investigate. She was strangled by a punter. They won't find him.' I catch Pete gawping. 'Look, we weren't close so don't expect me to bawl over her. Silly old cow, I'm surprised it didn't happen sooner.'

'Mickey, what did happen?'

I shrug. 'Dunno. Don't want to. Don't even wanna think about it.'

But that night, in Pete's car, on the way to Birmingham, I do think about it. In reverse. So it ends better.

The pressure's unbearable. A single valve, the weight of thousands of tonnes behind it. She's begging silently. There's no air left for words. She's dead.

She's choking and coughing; gasping. Her throat tightens and her head fills with blood. Her eyes are open but she sees only black. She's dying.

She can feel his mucky lust and his dirty hands as he kisses her face and presses his flesh against hers. He wants her. He slides his fingers around her neck. She's afraid.

She lies on the bed, pats the pink eiderdown with a veiny hand; he sits beside her. He squeezes a breast between his fingers, moulding it. She's pliable.

She smiles at him over her shoulder, girlishly, she thinks. She holds out her hand and leads him into the bedroom. He closes the door. She's trapped.

She takes the money; counts it twice. She flirts like an automaton; lick lips, flutter lashes, pat arm. Pause. Repeat. She's foolish.

She opens the door to him. Bending to pick up the post, her loosely fastened dressing gown falls open, flashing the dark shadow of her cleavage. She's willing.

She sips her tea and glances at the kitchen clock. Then at her face in the cracked mirror on the shelf above the cooker. She's impatient.

She opens the drawer and runs fingers over the satin material, choosing something soft and delicate, a wisp of air. She slides silky fabric over cold skin and feels a trembling inside her chest. She's ready.

She throws back the covers, stands and walks to the mirror. Her fingers reach up and unwind the curlers. It's a new day. She's alive.

'Is this it?' I ask.

Pete's parked across the street from a flat-fronted building with no windows. A single red door breaks the brickwork. A neon sign hangs above the door but it's not on and rendered unreadable by a broken streetlight.

'Guess so.'

We sit in the car, eyeing the foreboding door. Red. Stop. Danger.

'Are you sure you're O.K. doing this tonight?' Pete asks.

Am I? Fucked if I know. My mother's dead face, squeezed and swollen, floats up in front of me.

'I'm fine, dunno if I'll still be after I go in there, though.' I jerk my head towards the club.

'Looks kind of…' Pete gropes for a word.

'I hope he's worth it, this Philip Hall. C'mon.'

The interior is shoddily lit, but not shoddily enough to mask the drab, pokey room. There are lumps out of the plaster walls, ripped posters of last year's bands covering the cracks. The floor is wooden and our feet make the ripping sound of Velcro pulled apart as we cross the sticky beer varnish. The tables and chairs are the cheap plastic kind found in nasty little cafés. The chairs' rubber feet scud across the tacky flooring. Pete and I exchange grimaces.

'I've drank in worse,' he says.

'I've gigged in worse,' I admit. 'Let's get them in.'

The beer's overpriced and watered down. We find a table near the stage. 'Stage' is ambitious terminology. It's a corner cleared of tables and, in the space, speakers, mics and a drum kit have been dumped. The jukebox fires an over-loud Who song at us. The vocals distort through inadequate speakers. I light a cigarette and offer one to Pete. He says something but there's too much chaos for my sharp hearing to tune into any of it. Tinned music crushes against my eardrums. I turn my head this way and that, trying to separate out and draw down single, hearable, sound threads.

It's been a bloody long day. Wish I wasn't here. Where would I rather be? Outside. Where it's quiet. Inside's too bloody noisy, the jabbering of furious monkeys, sound without meaning. But I'm trapped here, in a bubble with liquid walls distorting everything. The room retreats. Her face drifts towards me again, the ripe-rotten tongue ready to explode, the childish smears of make-up, the two sets of purple finger-stripes printed on her neck. I hated her but she was my mother. Now she's lying naked on a slab in the morgue, her mismatched collar and cuffs on show. Maybe he's getting ready to cut her open and rummage around inside. That's what they said they'd have to do: post-mortem. After death. The noise winds up, becomes shrill, shrieky. Goes off the scale. I look at Pete. He's just sitting there. He can't hear it. I press my fingers in my ears. The shrieking doesn't devolume. It's in my head. It's me screaming at her. Why did she let this happen?

A beam of white light stabs me. My eyes search out the source. The screaming stops. My mother's face pops: vanishes. The music from the juke-box is cut and there's some muffled cursing from a figure now standing at the mic. He gestures to something. The shaft of light swings around, landing on him, illuminating the tall, strutting figure of a young man. He points once more at the lights, turns and speaks to, then laughs with, the guitarist who's behind him. His profile is etched in blue light.

Pete announces, 'That's him.'

'I guessed.'

Voices clamour, filling the volume-vacuum created by the jukebox's death. But Philip Hall isn't fazed by his audience of drunken navvies hoping to get laid and tarty hairdressers wanting to get fingered. He chats with the band. Reaches for a bottle of beer. Raises it to his lips, tossing back his blonde mane. Every movement is calm: cool. He exhales blue smoke which whirls around his head in the spotlight's beam. Then he steps up to the microphone, takes it in his other hand and leans in, as if whispering in the ear of that night's best chance for a shag.

'Good evening.'

His voice is mellow, corrupted by only a slight northern harshness. He nods at the drummer who counts in and the guitarist and bass player kick off.

For four bars the music staggers, clumsy dancers. Pete shudders.

'What the hell's he doing to that bass? Strangling it?' He stops, glancing at me in horror.

I'm about to laugh at his unfortunate word choice and subsequent expression of absolute terror when a noise slices the air, a blade surgically sharp, cutting the room cleanly in half. We turn to see Philip transformed. He throbs with energy as he clutches the microphone and screams into it. The note rises higher and higher. It's the sustain I get on top E at the twelfth. For once I don't hear the sound. I feel it as a vibration in my head; the hum of lead crystal, the drone of a swarm: the cry of the wind. It speaks of the future. Tells me what I want to hear. Philip Hall is The One.

The High Priestess

I need to escape this 1950s black-and-white movie landscape. I shove my hands into my pockets, feel Keira's cigarettes in one, hospital letter in the other, and pull away from the reflection of myself, my past, in Ron's shop window. Where's Ron now? Dead, I guess. His guitars sold off. His shop abandoned. His dream dead too. It's a hard thing to bury, a dream, even harder to grieve for. No funeral; no closure. Or maybe he just got old and retired, happy and contented. I should've kept in touch with him. One of a million things I should've done down the line 'cept I was too busy being Mickey Hunter, king of the fucking Kingdom, to do them.

So what if he did go bust? Failure's only the inevitable turn of the wheel. Nature's all rise and fall. The real failure's in staying down: dying. Fucking pathetic. If you accept failure you get what you deserve. Because, yeah, sure, what goes up always comes down. But it goes up again. If you want it enough.

I thought I knew that. Thought I knew everything. Even when I knew fuck all. It's easy to see that now. But things're blurry when you're only six inches from them. What do I know now? That something comes from nothing and goes back to nothing but from nothing something can come again. Something different. Not like before. Something mangled and mashed up? That's what I'm afraid of. The spark that made it so great, does that vanish? Or is it there, waiting, lurking: dormant?

I emerge from the tangle of ruined streets onto a clean, bright main road. The signs above the buildings flash and the paint is fresh. There's no rubbish in the gutters. I've made it back to the Noughties (who the hell came up with that expression?). For all its cleanness there's something dirty about this street. It lies, claiming everything'll be alright. I quicken my pace.

Further on there's a park, an oasis of green in the middle of boiled-dry urban grey. Relieved, I pass through the wrought iron gates and find an empty bench. I gulp air in great lungfuls and try to slow my breathing, steady my throbbing heart.

When I'm recovered I reach for Keira's stolen Marlboros. I play out the bollocking she'll give me later. Fuck it! I light a cigarette. It's been a while since I had one but I remember how empty lights are, like sucking air out of a drained coke can. I inhale, dragging on it with all my limited, old-age lung capacity. Dry heat hits the back of my throat then rushes to my head. They must be making them stronger these days. I close my eyes to the spinning park. It's been a long time since I enjoyed the dizzying rush of a first-time pleasure.

*

'Mickey? Mickey!'

Pete's face comes into focus as I turn from the triumphant figure of Philip Hall outlined in white light and with the mic stand raised overhead like a battle-bloodied sword. My eyes shrink down into darkness. I've been asleep and dreaming for a long time. A fantastic, futuristic dream, not of words or pictures but of sounds. The purest and most sublime sounds. Heaven and Hell in every note. Coming back to the chatter and clatter of the nightclub hurts.

'Well?'

'Woah.'

'Yeah.'

We sit in gaping silence. I light a fresh cigarette; the one I'd forgotten I was smoking has burnt down.

Finally Pete says, 'Christ, their bass player could use a few tips.'

'Fancy setting him straight?' I ask. The room's back in focus now.

'Could do.'

'And if we see him, we might have a word with the singer too.'

Pete grins.

We fight through the crowd, dodging sweat-sticky bodies. The guitarist and bass player are still on stage, sorting through the tangle of cables and leads. Pete asks about Philip and we're pointed to a door leading into the club's back room.

Through the door is a yellow corridor that reminds me of *The Wizard of Oz*. Even the floor is a sickly yellow, trenched up the middle with mud-brown stains.

'Which way?' Pete asks.

To the right are two doors and, standing opposite them, a rail with a mismatched array of clothing dumped over it. Next to the rail, leaning against the wall, is a guitar case. The first door opens. The sound of a flushing toilet rushes out and Philip Hall appears, the yellow casting a sulphuric glow over his face. He tilts his head to one side and studies us. What he's thinking? Yeah, he's wondering what I'm thinking. Pete steps forward.

'It's Philip, isn't it?' He extends his hand.

Philip steps up. Takes it. 'Sorry, man, don't remember you.'

'You wouldn't. We've never met. A friend of mine saw you in Manchester and said you were worth hearing.'

'Was I?' He asks like he's already bored by the answer he knows we'll give.

'We were blown away, weren't we, Mickey?'

'Impressive range,' I say and hold out my hand. He passes the beer he's holding into his other palm and we shake.

'You look familiar,' Philip says.

'Maybe you've seen me play.'

Philip nods.

'That's why we're here, actually,' Pete adds.

'Oh?'

'I'm looking for a singer,' I say.

'For a three-piece?'

'Nah, a four-piece. I'm looking for a drummer too but one thing at a time, man.'

'I might be interested,' he nods. 'Might know a drummer too.' Seeing me about to protest he adds, 'Not this arse; a good mate of mine. Quality drummer. Really powerful. Who did you say you are?'

'Mickey Hunter.'

Philip holds my gaze, struggles to not look impressed. Or desperate. But he knows what it's worth. I can't resist a smug-bastard smile. What's a name worth? Quite a lot when it's mine.

Pete gibbers all the way home. I only half listen but it's infectious, that buzz of energy. It's been too long since I felt this way. Sitting on my arse at home's killing me. I need performance-induced thrills. The darkness outside flicks past the window. There's nothing out there except a whole world of fucking awesome possibilities.

We make it back to Pete's, despite, rather than thanks to, his driving. A near miss with a truck on the A42 is the only thing capable of interrupting his mad-flowing chatter. Now, slouched in the armchair in his front room, he's gone quiet. We're both still coming down from the buzz that grabbed us in the club, at that moment when Philip let out his first wild note. The silence is dangerous. I'm afraid I'll start screaming, for real this time. I blurt out a question.

'Don't you think this is the best bit?'

'What d'ya mean?'

I shrug. 'Got any weed? I could use something to take the edge off.'

Pete doesn't ask what edge. 'Erm, yeah, I think...' He rummages about in the sideboard, plucks out a package. 'Susie's not keen with the girls in the house but as long as they're in bed I guess it's O.K.'

Pete sits, pushes a wave of mousy hair out of his eyes and starts rolling a joint.

'I meant,' I press on, 'like, now there are all these 'maybes' stretching out in front of us. 'Maybes', and 'possibilities' and 'perhapses'. Hope. It's just lying there, waiting to be taken. Waiting for us to take it.'

'That's a bit deep for me.'

'Nah, it's not.' I sit forward.

He lights the joint, drags on it and passes it over. The smell of burning metal wafts across to me.

'It's like, O.K., have you ever wanted anything so badly that wanting it ate you up? It was all you could think about. You breathed it, slept it, dreamt it, lived and died it but when you actually got it, it was a bust, total fucking crap. And the idea, the hope of what having it would be like was better than actually having it.'

'Dunno,' Pete mumbles, 'maybe, when I was a kid. Like looking forward to a holiday and when you get there it chucks it down and the bed's hard and the food's foul and there's nothing to do and it's nothing like you thought it was gonna be.'

'That's what I mean.'

'So you're trying to say you think this band's gonna turn out worse than a wet week in Skeggie?'

'No way. I mean this is the best bit now, when we don't know how it's gonna turn out but we can imagine the possibilities. It's full-blown musical perfection.' I shrug. 'Or a total fuck up. Right now it's both: everything. Once we start doing it it'll be what it's gonna be and that's it. Maybe it'll be better than we think. Maybe it won't but either way it'll be what it is.'

'Christ, stop talking before my head explodes.' Pete laughs as he takes the joint.

'I'm right, you'll see. Store this moment.'

We smoke back and forth. I close my eyes, snap them open when her choked face materialises out of the black.

'What about the, erm, the funeral?'

'Christ knows. Anyway, they're gonna cut her open first, so the copper said.'

'Look, if you want a hand with, I dunno, organising anything, just ask.'

'I don't. But thanks.'

'Mickey, I know we don't know each other that well but I mean it, I'll help if I can. This must be really bloody hard; I can't imagine.'

'Don't. It's not. Leave it. I don't wanna think about it tonight. Tonight's about the future.' I slam the words in his face. There's silence for a while.

'So when'd you come up with this grand theory?' he asks, 'about things being better before they happen?'

I'm grateful for the change in subject.

'Shit, I must've been eleven or twelve. When I first started dreaming about all this.'

The Empress

'Excuse me. Do you have a light?' She holds out an unlit cigarette and smiles. The park's pretty empty; I'm her best chance.

She's young, barely twenty. Younger even than Keira. Her dark hair's cropped close to her head and sits in a row of tight curls on her forehead. Her eyes bubble. The irises are a deep blue, the colour of irises in fact, and she's exaggerated the effect with thick daubs of shimmering purple powder. But her lips are pale. Naked, blue-painted by autumn air. She's thin with sharp cheekbones. She's just my type. Was.

I offer her my lighter. Keira's lighter.

'Thanks.' There's a lilting musical note in her voice that's strangely familiar and a faint Irish accent which is pleasantly foreign.

'Can I join you?' she asks.

'Help yourself.' I shuffle along the bench to make room for her.

She smokes her cigarette and I light another. I've already smoked three but you might as well be hanged for a loaf as a slice. I'll have to buy Keira another pack.

'I have a lighter, actually,' she confesses.

'Oh.' I watch her with growing curiosity.

'I, er, wanted an excuse to talk to you.'

'You did?'

'Aye. You're Mickey Hunter, aren't you?'

'Little young to be a fan, aren't you?' As soon as I've said it I regret it. She's gonna say, 'Oh, I'm not but my da loved every song you ever wrote.' Blah-blah-blah.

Instead she says, 'It's the greatest tragedy of my life: born too late. I never got to see you play live, so I didn't.'

'If that's your greatest tragedy you must've lived a charmed life.'

'Not really,' she replies and there's a twinkle in her dark eyes. 'Would you mind, I mean, could you, if it's O.K., could I get your autograph?'

I laugh. 'It's been a long time; I'm not sure I can remember what to do.' I see wavering and embarrassment in her elfin face and rush to reassure her. 'It's flattering when someone of your age, any age actually, is interested still. Do you have a pen?'

Her smile returns and she rummages in her bag, produces a chewed, lidless biro and offers it to me. I notice the nails on her left hand are short and the tips of her fingers calloused.

'Something to write on?'

She dives into the bag again.

'I can't believe it. I actually had one of your CDs in here yesterday. Now this is the best I can do.' With a groan, she offers me her cigarette pack.

She's not like the fans that used to charge at us, a rampaging army. Glory has its price but sometimes they went too far. She's a world, maybe an entire universe, apart from them. She's into what really counts: the music.

I take it from her, our fingers touching. She smiles but this time with a hint of shyness. Does she really think I'm still Mickey Hunter, legendary rock guitarist?

'Don't worry. Someone once asked me to sign a box of, well, never mind. It was worse than this though. What's your name?'

She laughs. 'My ma would be giving me a proper Irish name.'

'Go on?'

'Aoife.'

'Eee-fa?' I repeat, 'Christ, how do you spell that?'

She laughs again and her voice is alive and melodious. 'A – O – I – F – E.'

I write, unable to keep from shaking my head. 'I'd never have got that.'

'I have trouble myself sometimes. It's worse than bloody Siobhan.'

Our shared despair has a uniting effect. We're easier now. Her eyes are such a deep velvety blue. I remember a girl; quirky, another bright flame, who had eyes as deep, but hers were green. Eyes that I fell into. Eyes that scorched me. I stare at the cigarette packet and twirl the pen. I can't remember what I used to write. Maybe just my name but what the hell's that worth? I should give her the wisdom of someone older and wiser. That's a bloody joke. I shake my head again.

'I don't know what to put.' I feel like a useless old man. Bollocks, I am a useless old man.

'I'm sorry,' she says. 'I didn't mean to put you on the spot. Here you are, trying to grab five minutes' peace. Sure, the last thing you need is somebody hounding you for an autograph.' She gathers her bag.

'No! It's fine. Give me a minute.'

She hesitates then sits again. I put the autograph accoutrements aside.

'You play the guitar.'

'How did you…?'

'I have a sixth sense,' I jest, 'can always spot a fellow guitarist. Have you been playing long?'

'Since I was twelve.'

'You must be good then. Are you in a band?'

'I'm not. I play 'cos I enjoy it.'

'That's the best reason.'

'Do you still play?'

It's the obvious question. I'd ask it if I was her. Her doubt casts the shadow of shame over me.

'Will you when you're my age?' I challenge.

'Aye, if I still enjoy it.'

'I hope you always do,' I say. 'To stop loving something that once meant everything to you, that's a tragedy.' I refocus on the packet. Jesus, I could do with my reading glasses. Squinting, I scratch out, 'To Aoife, love and let love; play and let play. Music is all. Mickey H.' and hand it back. She reads it and nods. It means something to her. That's what I wanted. I expect her to go.

'Would you let me buy you a coffee? There's a stall across the park.'

I glance at my watch. There's time before I meet Meg for lunch. I'm clearly not going back to the office now. I think of the letter, crumpled and unread in my pocket. There's time for that later too.

'O.K.'

We wander across the park. The ground is squelchy but the wind has dried out the fallen leaves and whirls them into mini cyclone-funnels at the base of the trees. I watch enviously as they twist and jive in the breeze.

We order two coffees; Aoife insists on paying. I let her because I think it might transform this dull encounter into a story half-worth telling. Plus I'm not sure how much cash I've got. We sit on another bench and I light yet another cigarette. The flavours of coffee and tobacco tingle on my tongue. Is it simple pleasures that are the best or guilty ones?

'Who inspired you to start playing?' she asks.

'I'd like to say Robert Johnson or someone equally worthy but it was just some tramp I saw busking when I was a kid,' I reply with a grin.

'Ah, sure, go on wid ya,' she lapses into a careless flurry of Irishness.

'I guess you never know who's round the corner.'

*

I'm small, invisible to the naked eye; a schoolboy out early. It's fun being invisible. I can spy on people. I don't even need to hide. Nobody cares what I see. I'm no one.

I come to the end of an ally and peer down it. A bag is hurled over a back wall. A man follows it. He stops in the ally to hitch up his trousers. Then he waves to an upstairs window. I trace the wave to where a young woman in her frilly nightie is holding aside the net curtain and returning his wave. I check the time and jot down the details in my private investigator's notebook. When I glance up the man is staring in my direction. I duck around the corner.

'Oi! What the bleedin' hell d'ya think you're doing? Get outta it!'

Heart throbbing, I press against the bricks and hold my breath. The man rounds the corner after me. He's a tall shit-house of a fella with a blurry tattoo on his forearm. I'll have to note that down later. I dart across the street.

Heading in the direction of town, scribbling as I trot, I note the unusual: her at No. 9 is getting an extra pint; the old geezer walking his terrier is ten minutes behind schedule; the butcher's window has been smashed. A paperboy cycles past, his coat flapping like a cape; he flicks the Vs at me, cheeky sod!

I come to a stall selling teas and butties to workies. A shilling and two half-crowns jangle in my trouser pocket. I cross the road and stretch up to the counter. The man behind it frowns down at me.

'Yes, sonny.'

'One tea, please.' I pull the coins from my pocket. With a grunt he gets the tea pot and pours steaming brown liquid into a chipped mug.

'Sit there.' He points to a low, crumbling brick wall across the road. 'Where I can keep an eye on you.'

I nod and he scoops the coins off the stained counter.

'And make sure you bring the bloody mug back.'

I nod again.

The wall's damp from the night's rain; clammy fingers reach up through the seat of my trousers as soon as I sit. I pull out my PI's notebook and make an entry about the grumpiness of men behind tea stalls at 07:00 hours.

I've about half-way drank the tea when the tramp turns up. I make a note. His clothes are rumpled and mucky. The sole of his right shoe flaps up and down like the jaw of a hungry crocodile, slapping against the pavement as he walks. He wears a shabby brown hat, the twisted brim pulled low, his wiry grey hair sticking out in thick clumps all around. He goes to the stall for a cuppa, setting down the case he's carrying to pay for it. I note that too: a guitar-shaped case. It's battered, like everything else about him. There's a belt of dirty blue twine wound around the middle of it. The case is peppered with stickers from the places it's travelled to. I count them, eight, and make a note. I hope he'll open the case so I can write about what's inside. I've only seen guitars in black and white on telly. I want to know what colour it is.

He picks up the case and moves along the pavement, sets it down again and sips his tea. A couple of workies in overalls start yakking to him. They seem to know each other. One points at the case but the tramp shakes his head. The workie points again and nods hard. His mate joins in and I, from my perch across the street, offer up a silent plea, gripping the mug tightly and clenching my teeth. But he shakes his head. Then one of the workies pulls out some change and jerks his thumb in the direction of the stall. The tramp looks. Hesitates. Smiles, and I catch the words, 'Go on, then.' The two workies shake hands with him. The first goes to the stall and the sizzle of frying bacon wafts over. I step up to the edge of the kerb but chicken out of going any closer.

The tramp kneels down and opens the case. The inside of it glitters, sending out a golden light. He kicks the lid down and the light vanishes. He puts on his guitar. Its body is curved and rounded. Smooth, I think. And silky. The wood is a creamy brown. I forget about note-taking and keep my eyes fixed on him and his guitar. The only music I've ever heard this close is the crappy school choir.

He runs a dirty fingernail down the strings. The sound clatters. He stops. Fiddles with something on the guitar's head. Tries again. This time the sound's fluid. I think of the word 'harmony' and know that's what I'm hearing. He pauses: plays. It sounds like nothing I've heard, sad but not unhappy. Like he's celebrating something sad. I don't understand what it is but I can feel it filling my ears with warm water. The fingers of one hand fly along the neck while those of the other pluck at the strings. He sings as well but I concentrate on the guitar, watching and listening, letting the sounds drip from my ears, down my throat and into my stomach. When he stops my tea's cold.

'Are you finished, sonny?' The man from the stall leers over me, jabbing his finger at my mug. I nod. He snatches it and stalks across the road.

The two workies drift away. The stall-man throws the dregs of my tea into the gutter before climbing behind his counter. The tramp kneels again and replaces his guitar in the case. I try to stop staring but can't make my eyes obey. He collects his bacon sarnie from the counter, turns and spots me. My heart throbs. I freeze. He picks up the case and begins to cross the road. I want to run. I want to stay. I want to run. I want to stay. I stay.

'Hey there.' Up close he smells of outdoor things, fresh and stale. His hair's matted. His clothes grubby. I'm a bit scared of him.

'You liked what I was playin'?'

I nod.

'You have discerning taste, my young friend.' He says each word precisely, like he's posh. Or was once. 'It's the finest music under the whole of God's heaven.' He speaks solemnly, through a mushed-up mouthful of bacon and white bread.

'What is it?'

'The Blues, my young friend.'

My flushing face grasses me up for the ignorant shite teachers are always telling me I am.

Seeing, realising, he explains. 'Music from the heart; music that speaks to your soul. It comes from America, that great land of freedom and repression.'

I don't know what he's on about but I sort of get the bit about the soul. I felt it filling my insides.

'How do you do it?'

'You can't teach someone to play the Blues. You're either born to play it or you're not.'

'How do you know if you are?'

'You want to know if you are?' he asks. I don't answer. 'Well, maybe you are and maybe you aren't. There's only one way to know.'

Cramming the last of his buttie in his mouth, he sets the case on the pavement and opens it. There's no light inside it, just some gold coloured cloth, shiny and frayed. He lifts his guitar out and offers it to me.

'Go on.'

I take it, holding it at arm's length. He laughs.

'It's not going to bite. You have to hold it close. Like this.' He arranges it in my arms, putting the strap round my shoulders. It's heavy. The neck slips as I wrestle clumsily with it. He laughs again. 'Hold it as if it's a beautiful woman. A woman that you want close to you, pressing gently against you.' I flush red hot again. 'Yeah, well, you know,' he mutters.

I get it as comfortable as I can, with a grip that's firm but not tight. I imagine it's alive and fragile.

'Knew you'd get it,' he enthuses.

'Is that it?' I ask, wondering if that's all there is to playing the Blues: keeping hold of it.

'There's a bit more than that. I want you to close your eyes. Relax. Breathe slow and steady. Run your hand up and down the neck.' He puts his hand over mine and pushes it towards the body of the guitar then releases. 'When you feel it, stop and put your fingers on the strings.'

Feel what? I open my eyes. 'Which ones? Where? How will I know?'

'If you're born to play the Blues, my young friend, you'll feel it. You either can or you can't. But if you want it badly enough you will. That's what I've found.'

Stunned and shaking, I do what he says. I pray for a blinding flash, a deafening clap, a heart-stopper that will tell me where to put my fingers. There's nothing. Finally I give up and press my fingers on the strings.

'O.K.' he says, 'with this hand you strum.' I frown so he adds, 'Run your fingers across the strings.'

I do and there's a hideous crashing sound as notes jangle against each other. I move to pull my hands away.

'Now fix it. That's the test.'

I study my fingers, move one down onto the string below and try again. This time the sound is smooth: united. I look up at him but I already know.

'Born to it.' He takes back his guitar.

'What now?' I demand.

'My young friend, get yourself a guitar and play it 'til your fingers bleed.'

After he's gone I write that down in my notebook.

I look at it again. It's only a bloody guitar, second hand, bought cheap from Ron's Guitars and Gear with the money I've been saving and scrounging ever since that old Blues tramp told me to get a guitar and play it. But it's my first; I'm not sure it's safe. I watch it warily from a three foot distance, the most my box-bedroom allows. Today's the first time in the week I've owned it that I've dared drag the case from under my bed, open it and lift the guitar out. Now it's there, propped against my bed, I don't know what to do. I try viewing it from another angle. If it was a fence to jump I'd be figuring how long a run-up to take. The problem with this is I don't know how to get over it. I inch my fingers closer, touching the smoothly varnished wood of the neck before chickening out. Again. I've been stuck like this for ages.

There's a knock on my bedroom door. Mum. Bugger. I cram the guitar back in its case and slide it under the bed then shout:

'What?'

'I've got you something. Can I come in?'

She pushes the door open before I say no. Her hair's pinned up, trying for tidy, but the day's rough and tumble have made a mess of her. She's wearing her dark navy skirt and a white blouse. There is a pale orange stain down the front where she spilt something. She's crap at cleaning and stuff. There is a funny smell on her, makes me think of Alex's crossbreed bitch in heat.

'Here.' She smiles and holds out a flat package wrapped in brown paper. Her hand shakes a bit.

I go over, snatch the package then retreat. The brown paper's rough. I rub it between my finger and thumb, trying to work out what's inside. Feels like a book, but big and flat. Not another *Beano*, I hope. Doesn't she know I'm too old for those now?

'Aren't you going to open it?'

I pull off the paper. *Play in a Day* by Bert Weedon.

'I thought it might help,' she winks at me, 'with what's under the bed.'

Face hot, I mutter, 'Thanks.'

'Good. You can spend tonight looking through it.'

I glance up at her. She smiles, comes a bit closer. 'I know you're dead keen on this guitar business.'

I scowl. It's a new tune for her. 'What happened to it being a waste of money and a bloody noisy racket?'

She tuts. 'Mickey, language.'

'Well, you said…'

'I know, and I'm sorry. I see now I should be encouraging you.' She pats my arm. 'So, after tea tonight, you can come up here and make all the racket you want.'

I pull my arm away from her touch. 'What about you?'

'I've, er, got a friend coming over and I thought, well, you'd prefer your music to sitting with us boring two.'

I glare at her.

'It's an old friend. You don't know him. He's been away but he's back now so I might see him quite a bit, give us chance to catch up.'

I open the book and study at the pencilled price: 1s 6d. Cheaper than sending me to the pictures.

She starts to go but stops in the doorway and turns back. 'You're so grown up now,' she says, 'it's nice to have a man about the house that I can count on. You're a good boy, Mickey.'

She hovers in my doorway. Her face twists slightly, her mouth turning up at the corners. She sways. Puts out a hand to steady herself. Then hiccups.

I drop my eyes off her, turn more of the book's pages. She hangs there for another few seconds but I keep my eyes down 'til I hear the door click closed.

The crisp white pages are covered in neatly ruled lines and boxes. There are circles and dots too. I stare 'til my eyes sting and water. The lines blur into one and the thick black dots grow larger, eating up the space around them. Inside my head two pictures suddenly fit together, one on top of the other. I toss the book on my bed, get the guitar back out and sit cross-legged with it across my lap, the book open in front of me. I know what to do now. Eyes shut, keeping the two pictures in focus in my head, I put my fingers on the strings, matching them up, connecting the dots. Then hit down all the strings in one go. It makes a sound. Not a noise; a proper, musical sound. The A major chord. I try another. E minor. A third. D7.

By the time Mum's saying goodnight to her old friend I've got a dozen chords under my fingertips.

'Are you allowed to take that to school?'

Mum's in the kitchen doorway in her pink dressing gown. It's not fastened properly. I cringe. Look away and shift my guitar case into my other hand, holding it behind me.

'I'm taking it to show my mates.'

'You won't get in trouble, will you?'

'Course not.' I dodge through the door before she can grill me any further.

It's a crisp, cold autumn morning. A smoky smell hangs in the air. I fill my lungs with it. The guitar in my left hand, pulling on my arm, is a friendly dog straining his lead, longing to be set loose to run. Everything is good.

'Good morning, Michael. Off to school, are we?' Mrs Henderson from No. 23 way-lays me.

'Yeah.'

'And what have you got there, young man?' She points a knuckly finger at my guitar.

Mind your own business, you nosey old bag. 'My guitar,' I say.

'I see. So you're going to be the next, oh, what's that young man's name? The one who's always shaking his hips on the television?' She stares at me, expecting an answer.

'Elvis.'

'Yes. Well, hope you aren't going to keep us awake with lots of loud roll and rock,' she says. Her words are jokey but her voice isn't. 'How's your mother? I saw her in town the other day but she was talking to a man and I didn't like to interrupt. A friend of hers, I suppose?'

'I'll be late.' I turn, start walking.

'Have a good day at school, Michael. Give your mother my best.'

In the playground the others flap round me, seagulls to scraps.

'Is that it?'

'Let's have a squiz.'

'Can you really play it?'

'Course,' I say, unpacking the guitar and holding it up proudly.

'Go on, then. Let's hear something.'

I shrug. 'What?'

'Can you do something like that Yank?'

'Who?'

'He means Elvis, you mean Elvis, don't you?'

'No, I don't mean Elvis. I bloody know who Elvis is, dun I?' Alex gives Jacob a shove, 'No, that other Yank, with the glasses.'

'Buddy Holly,' Jacob says, 'that's who you mean. Na, we don't wanna hear that crap. Do something by Elvis. 'Hound Dog', can you play that?'

They're narking me now.

'D'ya want me to play something or are you gonna keep arguing?'

'No, O.K. Play 'Hound Dog'.'

'Yeah, play 'Hound Dog'.'

I hesitate a second.

'He doesn't know it.'

'I bloody do so.' I don't really. But I know enough to fool these buggers. I play a twelve bar blues in E which is close enough. After practising it for hours it sounds pretty good. Bloody good.

And my fingers didn't even hurt now.

'Yeah, that's 'Hound Dog', alright,' Jacob says.

I know I'm showing off. So what? 'Told you I could play.'

'Who's teaching you?' Alex asks.

'Nobody.'

'Get away! You must be having lessons,'

'Am not so.'

'How long've you had it?' Jacob asks.

'Couple of months.'

'How'd you do it then?' Alex demands.

'Practise a lot.' I put the guitar in the case. Leave them hoping to hear more.

'Hunter, come here, boy!' It's Mr Shallow, the headmaster. He strides across the yard. 'What have you got there, boy?'

'My guitar, sir.'

'Who said you could bring that to school?'

'No one, sir.'

'So why did you bring it, boy?'

'No one told me I couldn't, sir.'

Jacob and Alex stand stiff beside me.

His comb-over flaps in the stiff autumn breeze. His top lip quivers, the moustache under his nose wriggles with glee.

'Give me that, you insolent boy.'

I tighten my grip on the handle.

'I said give it to me. Now!' He thrusts out his hand.

'It's mine. You can't have it.'

The moustache rocks violently side to side.

'How dare you speak to me like that? I'll be contacting your mother about this. Get to my office this instant.' He points the way with a jabbing finger.

Bloody hell, 's not like I haven't been there before. I head for the door. Carry my guitar with me.

We pace the corridors towards his office. The floppy soles of my plimsolls pit-pat softly on the hard floor; the stiff leather of his polished lace-ups rap angrily all the way there.

He throws the door open. 'In.'

I stand where I know to, in front of his desk. He squeezes behind it. I study his two chins and the loose, hanging skin of his neck.

'You will not bring that thing into my school again.' The loose flaps of skin start wobbling. 'If you want to learn an instrument you may take up something tuneful, the piano or violin. I am happy to encourage genuine musical talent. But I will not allow corrupting influences in my school. I don't know what your mother is thinking. I've seen these people cavorting on television, these Americans.' He spits the word. 'It's filth. No good will come of it. And I most certainly will not tolerate it in my school, tarnishing the excellent reputation of The William Dickson Memorial Grammar for Boys.'

Everything he says is wrong. I stare at him straight and hard, let him see he's wrong and I know. He pushes back his chair and stands to tower over me.

'You are a defiant and rebellious boy who'll come to no good end.'

He plucks a small brass key from his pocket, unlocks the tallboy behind his desk and selects a cane from his armoury.

'Give me that thing, boy,' he demands, coming round to my side of the desk and yanking the guitar off me, propping it in the corner.

I keep my eyes fixed on it. He swishes the cane through the air, thwacking it down on the edge of his desk. The sound smacks me.

'Hold out your hands.'

I do, palms up and slightly cupped, thumbs tucked down so it'll do less damage. He raises the cane high above his head. Whips it through the air. I hear it coming, feel the sharp tang of it on my hand. It stings. He strikes again. It hurts worse. The guitar case goes blurry but I keep it in sight. He aims for a third strike. Out of the whoosh-whack of the cane I pull a single note, a high C, ringing out clear. I scrabble it towards me and cling on 'til he's done me four on each hand. The pain's running up my arms, across my chest, making me feel properly sick.

'That will do, Hunter. For now.'

I drop my arms. Let my hands drip onto his carpet. He slides back behind his desk, cleans off his cane then puts it away and sits. Picks up a pen and scribbles something. Without looking at me he says:

'Get back to class.'

I don't move.

'Did you hear me, Hunter?' He glares at me

'My guitar, sir?'

'You may collect it from Mr Jackson's office at 4 o'clock.'

Now I can go.

In the corridor outside I inspect my hands. The palms are streaks with red. But he didn't get my fingertips. Maybe I'll properly learn 'Hound Dog' tonight.

The Emperor

We finish our coffees. We've been sitting on this hard park bench far too long for an old git like me with bad knees. Will I be able to stand without staggering? I hate this being old bollocks. My body mocks me: you're not twenty-five anymore. Or even forty-five.

'It's been grand talking with you,' Aoife says. 'Thank you. I'm sure you've got more important things to be doing.'

'Not really.'

She smiles. 'I'll keep this safe.' She indicates the signed cigarette pack. 'You won't see it on Ebay, so you won't.'

'It's yours, do what you want with it,' I tell her, gratitude soaking into me, white bread mopping up beef gravy.

She stands and offers her hand.

'Thanks again.'

I shake but stay sitting, in case my legs show me up. She hesitates for a second then lurches forwards, pecking me on the cheek with her naked blue lips. I stare in surprise but before I can say anything she's dashing across the park, kicking up a trail of golden brown leaves.

What's the time? Shit. If I hurry I can make the restaurant before Meg, just. I stand and sway unsteadily for a minute but my knees hold and I step, one foot then the other. Yeah, I'm O.K. I quicken the pace, cross the park and head onto the main road. Out of breath and short of time, I hail a taxi and direct him to Pierre's.

'Didn't you used to be in that group, mate?' the driver asks.

'Nah, sorry. I get mistaken for him all the time. Must be his double or something.'

'Righto, sorry,' he mutters.

I feel mean but not enough to confess. Because this is how it goes; he'll regale me with a story about the time he saw us play fab in such-and-such shit hole. Or he'll tell me where we went wrong and bust my arse over our break up. Shit I can do without.

We stop at the restaurant and I rake in my pockets. I'm fifty pence short. I can't show him my credit card now I've lied about who I am.

'Don't worry about it, mate.' He shrugs and I scramble out.

I hate Pierre's; would much rather eat at the mock-fifties diner across the river but Meg won't hear of it. Too much cholesterol on their menu. And real chips deep fried? At least they are real, I pointed out once. Meg's response? 'As will be the heart attack you'll have for dessert.' I love Meg too much to fight her. I know this obsession with my health is because she loves me, wants me around forever. Christ knows why. Now it's cardio and yoga three times a week, low fat, low sugar, low salt. No caffeine. No smoking. Thank God for studies into the benefits of drinking red wine. In moderation, of course. This is the small print I didn't bother to read; the T&Cs of marrying a younger woman and a nurse.

'Mr Hunter, welcome sir. Can I take your coat?'

I hand him my jacket. 'Thanks, Pierre.' I know his real name is Paul but I like playing along.

'The flowers you ordered for your wife are here, sir.' He gathers a huge bouquet of roses from the counter. He knows I didn't order them but he too is happiest playing the game.

'Thanks.' I scrabble them from him.

'Your usual table is ready, sir.' He leads me across the room. 'Would you like some wine? We have a superb Merlot.'

I long to say yes but I might be in enough trouble already. Not that Keira would report me AWOL but Meg's got a sixth sense about me after all these years. Mostly I'm grateful. Without her I'd probably, no, definitely, be another name on the rock tombstone: Keith Moon, Phil Lynott, Jimi Hendrix, Mickey Hunter.

'Just water, please.'

Pierre pulls my chair out with a camply grand arm-sweep. Heads are turning. I dump the flowers, sit and stare blindly at the menu, trying to wrestle the specials into focus. Pierre bows and retreats.

'Try these.' Meg thrust my reading glasses under my nose.

'Darling, thanks. Where did I leave them this time?' I stand to kiss her. She dodges.

'In the office.' She plonks down opposite.

I know I'm in for it. I wait meekly. Pierre rushes over.

'Mrs Hunter. Please, let me take your coat.'

In her rage she's failed to offer herself up for the mandatory fawning. She tugs off her silk jacket and practically throws it over Pierre's head. He catches it inelegantly and, sniffing, turns.

'And you better bring us some wine, please.'

I raise my eyebrows. We normally don't drink during the day. Or during the week. Or if there's a full moon. Or no moon.

'It might get rid of that cigarette reek.'

Damn! Busted. Good and. We sit in constipated silence. She reads the menu; I listen around the restaurant. A couple two tables away are flirting, him telling jokes and her giggling. An elderly gent behind keeps stabbing his knife into his plate with a painful plunk. His wife chews with sloppy wet jaws. A waitress marches between the tables with jack-hammer high-heels. It's making my ears hurt, the pain that runs through the middle of your head when you wake up with a hangover on a brilliantly sunny day. I long for a soft steady hum to blur it. Pierre returns with wine.

'Would you like to taste it?'

I shake my head and wince as he pops the cork and up-ends the bottle. Claret gurgles into my glass. A spark bouncing from some highly polished surface, pierces the liquid and spills a dash of blood red light on the white table cloth. It's so rich it throbs. Then I realise it's my heart throbbing, the sound reverberating through me, while I wait for Meg to bawl me out.

'Are you ready to order?' Pierre asks.

'Darling?'

'The goat's cheese and the salmon.'

Would a salad redeem me? Un-fucking-likely. If I'm condemned I might as well have a decent last meal.

'Pâté and the steak.'

Pierre waits for approval. Meg snaps her menu closed. Pierre nods and goes.

'I got you some flowers.' I offer her the crumpled blooms.

'You mean Keira did.'

I shrug. No sense denying the bloody obvious. I wait. That's Meg's way. Let me stew, build up the stress until it peaks, begins to subside. Then, when I think I'm safe: boom. Take no prisoners. Offer no quarter. I glance at my watch. The longest she's ever held out is seventeen minutes. Bet this'll be a new record.

'So you're just going to sit there not saying anything?' She's using her 'restrained rage' voice, the one reserved for public rows.

Wow, only eight and a half minutes. This new tactic throws me off balance. I stagger towards a response.

'I'm sorry.' Pathetic, man. Try harder.

'Mickey, where've you been all morning? Keira and I've been worried. What on earth possessed you to disappear like that? I thought something awful must have happened.'

I laugh. 'Like what?'

'Oh, I'm glad you think it's funny. While I've been pacing the office, trying your mobile every fifteen seconds, imaging you lying in the street with tyre marks over your chest you've been what? Laughing it up somewhere or God knows.' She rants out the rapid torrent of scalding words.

'I went for a walk.'

'Uhuh. I see. Presumably to the nearest tobacconist's?'

'Actually, no.' I reach into my pocket and pull out the remains of my stolen bounty. 'I borrowed these from Keira's drawer.' I put the cigarettes on the table between us; Meg glares at them as though it's their fault.

'Mickey, how old are you?'

'Old enough to smoke.'

'For God sake! Ten years and you decide to start again. I hope you can still laugh when you've only got one lung.'

'Meg, darling.' I reach across the table and lay my veiny hand over her manicured one. 'I know how much you love me.' She tries to speak but I cut her off. 'And I know you want me to be here forever but wanting it isn't going to make it happen. I'm more than a few years older than you and I expect to die first. In fact, I hope I do so you'll have chance to find someone who doesn't need bloody baby-sitting.'

Her blue eyes fill with tears. She looks old and tired. It's wearing her down, this battle with time. She yanks her hand away and digs in her bag for a tissue which she dabs to the edges of her eyes, careful not to tear the delicate flesh or smudge the mascara.

'Mickey, don't.'

'Sorry. Look, I plan on being here for a while yet. I'm certainly not going before I've finished my steak.' I lean back and the bulky envelop in my pocket jabs my chest.

She breaks into a wan smile. The starters arrive and we talk about the NIME award and other stuff. On the surface things are smooth again but underneath, in the darkness of my inside pocket lurks the shadow of something all teeth and talons. Is the devil you do know better or worse that the one you don't?

*

Pete and I are waiting for Philip and this drummer mate of his to show up.

'It's bloody freezing.' Pete blows into his hands and stamps his feet for the fortieth time.

'I said I knew a cheap place we could rehearse, not a warm place.' It's not the cold that's driving me insane me; it's the bloody waiting. 'What time is it?'

'Ten past.'

'Fuck.'

'Give 'em time, man, it's only ten minutes. Philip seemed keen, didn't he?'

'Said so when I spoke to him yesterday.'

'Did he tell you much about this drummer he's bringing?' Pete's wound-up. Drums and bass are salt and pepper, they've got to work together or there's no flavour.

'He's some bloke Philip's known for years. They've been in a few different line ups together.'

'What's his name again?'

'John Ronsarno.'

'That's unusual, isn't it?'

I shrug, finger a few chords then check the tuning.

'What's the time now?'

'Quarter past.'

'I'll give them five more minutes.' I put my guitar on the stand, perch on my amp, light a cigarette and huddle round the glowing tip.

'They probably got lost. It's a bitch to find.'

'You managed.'

'That was luck. I mean, it is kinda out of the way,' he says.

'Yeah, well, I told you, it's cheap.'

The warehouse is a decent space, deep and wide but with a low ceiling giving good acoustics and down by the docks so no neighbours; we can play loud. If they ever get here.

Outside brakes screech. I jump up.

'Maybe that's them,' Pete suggests.

The door is thrown open. Philip's tousled head of curls is rammed through.

'Hey, fellas,' he grins, 'sorry we're late. These bloody places look the same; this is, like, the ninth one we've tried.' He calls out, 'Hey, Ronsey, this is it.'

He comes to me, hand extended. I give him mine and say nothing about waiting.

'I'll give him a lift with the kit.' And Philip's gone before either of us reply.

Pete slaps my arm. 'Told you they'd come.'

The door swings open once more and a bass drum enters in a chaotic clatter, gripped by thick forearms that belong to a tall, stocky bloke with an industrial strength beard who could only be a drummer or a navvy. He strides across and sets the drum down. Philip follows with a snare and a high hat.

'You need a hand?' Pete offers.

'Nah, man,' the drummer says in a heavy northern accent, 'I've got it.' He sticks his hand out. Barks, 'You Pete or Mickey?'

Pete draws back. I smile. At least he's no bullshitter.

Philip cuts in.

'Pete,' he says, 'and Mickey,' pointing at each of us. 'Fellas, John Ronsarno, brilliant drummer, shite manners.'

I finish my cigarette while Philip plugs in a small PA and Ronsey sets up the drums. It's a scaled down kit, only one tom, and I wonder what it's going to sound like. I feel over dressed at my own party with my studio quality amp and genuine Gibson guitar.

'O.K.' Philip says, 'looks like we're ready. What we gonna do?'

They wait for me to deal.

'Does everybody know 'Baby, Let's Play House'?'

Philip frowns then nods. 'Think I've got it.'

'O.K.' I say and look to Ronsey.

He counts in and we launch, arse-up, into our first performance. The take-off falters but the force of the music lifts us skyward. We fly. As I play I glance around, watching the others working together. Pete moves closer to Ronsey and they feed off each other while Philip loses himself in the beat, the vocals exploding from deep inside him. I want to hold this moment forever. I know with absolute fucking certainty this is our only possible future. Together four in one, four as one.

We stop at the end of the song. I see my own awe, surprise and relief reflected back. A rash of crazy grins breaks out. Philip whoops shrilly, a wild, victorious cry of ecstasy.

'Let's do another.'

We rock through the afternoon, each song flying higher and further than the one before, anything and everything from Deep South Blues to West Coast Psychedelia, stopping at all points along the way. It's late when Pete says:

'I gotta go, lads, Suse's working tonight and I've gotta get the girls from her mother's.'

'I think we're done here anyway,' I reply.

'So?' Philip says.

'So what?'

'Are we doing this?'

'Can you think of a reason why we shouldn't?' I ask him.

'Nope.'

'Right, then.'

John Ronsarno's said fuck all. He's just thumped out rhythm after rhythm, a doubled up fist, pounding and smashing through every song, his drums speaking for him.

'What now?' he asks.

'I'll get Don to draw up some contracts, we put together some material and get ready to hit the road.'

'Don? Who the fuck's he?' John demands.

'Don Wiseman, my manager. Our manager now.'

'Manager?'

'Yeah.'

'How the fuck do we know he's on the level?'

'Because I say he is.' We eyeball each other. What's his problem…? Jesus, these two are so green they've never had a manager and they're bricking it.

'Trust me,' I say, 'Don's straight up. I've been with him since the Three Bob Band. He takes care of the legal shit and makes sure we get what's fair. I don't do anything without Don. I won't do anything without Don. You want to join me Don's the package.'

John stares at me for a second or two. I hold my breath, praying he's ready to jump. Eventually he shrugs.

'Whatever.'

'I'll speak to him in the morning, get the paperwork started. Let's meet, say next Monday; I'll sort it, send you his address and a time and we can go through everything.'

Philip nods. 'Sounds good, man.'

Pete agrees.

We pack up and Pete heads off with a jaunty wave. Well, Philip was his shiny idea.

John loads his drums into the van. I'm already packed. I lean against the bonnet of my car with a cigarette on the go. Philip strolls over, thumbs hooked in his belt loops.

'You think we've got a chance of making it?' It's the first glimmer of doubt I've seen in him. Could it be that his cock-sure performance is just that? 'I mean, really making it 'cos I gotta tell you, I've come close before, man, and each time I thought, 'Wow, this is it,' and it never was. If this doesn't work out reckon I'll have to get a proper job.'

'That's up to you but this is all there is as far as I'm concerned.'

He drops his gaze.

'Do you have to get back tonight?' I ask.

'Not 'specially. Why?'

'Crash at mine, if you like. We can talk about music and shit. I've got some wild ideas about this gig, maybe you'd feel better if you heard some of them.' I laugh. 'Then again, maybe you won't.'

'Cool. I'll just have a word with Ronse. He's gotta get the van back to his cousin.'

I watch as Philip reports to John. They laugh at a shared joke. Ronsey playfully punches Philip's stomach; Philip acts up, doubling over only to grab Ronsey around the knees, threatening to topple him. They part with a bear hug. Philip comes back to me.

'Let's go,' I say.

I pull up outside my place. As we're unloading Mrs Henderson from 23 appears with a black bag in her hand. She makes a big show of dumping it in the bin. I keep her on the edge of my eye-line.

'Mickey,' Philip says.

'What?'

'That old lady across the road is waving at you.'

'Bollocks.'

'She's coming over.'

'Shit. Take this in the house.' I thrust my guitar on him and wait 'til I see he's inside, out of earshot, before I face her.

'Michael.' She's wearing that sour-sweet smile. 'Are you alright? I heard about your mother. I am so sorry.'

'Right.'

'She'll be missed.'

'You mean the show she put on'll be missed. What the hell are you gonna do for gossip now?'

'Michael! Your mother was a dear friend of mine.'

'That's a bloody good one.'

'I saw the police cars. Do they know what happened?'

'No, but I'm sure you can tell them.'

'Michael, I was only…'

'Piss off.'

I snatch my amp and leave her in the road, the wind rattling her curlers.

Philip's loitering in the hall.

'What's that about?'

'Nothing. Nosey old bitch. In here.' I take the amp into the music room and Philip follows. In the doorway he stops and stares.

'Cool.'

'That goes there.' I point to the guitar rack. 'You want a beer or something?'

'Yeah, please. Where's your khazi?'

'Upstairs, second left.'

I grab two beers from the fridge and go into the lounge. Philip appears a minute later and I hold one to him before lighting a cigarette.

'Thanks. What's with the tape over the door up there?'

'Long story.'

'Sounds interesting.'

'Hey, leave it, O.K.?' I snap.

'Shit, sorry, man.'

Philip grimaces like I just kicked him in the balls. Christ, it's not his fault.

'Nah, I'm sorry. It's fucked up. Trust me, you're better off not knowing.'

'You O.K.?' He's pulling the same face as Pete when he picked me up at the cop shop. Jesus, I think he's seriously concerned.

'Yeah. Fine, really. I'm gonna change, why don't you go through that lot and pull out something to listen to?' I point to the record cabinet and leave before I crack, tell him everything and cry like a right wanker all down his donkey jacket.

Upstairs yellow tape seals shut the door to the room that was my mother's. In one quick movement I yank the tape, screw it into a knot and hurl it into a dark corner. I'd feel better if I could be sure I didn't wish for this. But I can't. Get as far from it as fucking possible. That's the way.

Back in the lounge Philip's on the floor, records scattered. He's a kid on Christmas morning, wondering what to play with next. Stripped of his stage act that's what he is: a kid, an outline only. I can colour him in any shade I want. I hover in the doorway, frozen in the moment, power pressing me from behind, as Philip sits amongst the records, turning them over with childish glee. I'm hypnotised by the way his curly hair falls forward as he bends over a Joni Mitchell LP, the angle made by his arm, the orange glow cast over everything by the dying sun. I've seen this before in some fucked up way. Maybe far off in a parallel universe there's another me, another Philip, further down the line, already famous, playing to packed concert halls, cutting albums, shagging groupies. Time isn't a one way street; I've come back to a point I've already been to. It's awesome déjà fucking vu. Sensing me standing behind him, Philip turns; the moment's broken.

'Hell of a collection, man.'

'A work in progress, there's a lot more I'd like.'

'More? Man, you've got everything here; Robert Johnson, Bert Jansch, Hendrix, Baez.'

'I have eclectic tastes and that's what I want for this band. I don't wanna be doing the same old crap song after song. Each and every one of those LPs, they've got, like, a slot to fit into. I don't want us to do that.'

'Go on.'

I sit on the sofa cross-legged, some kind of wise master with the young apprentice at my feet. Fuck sake.

'You know the uproar when Dylan went electric?'

'Yeah.'

'Why was that?'

'People thought he'd sold out.' Philip repeats the pat phrasing of a dozen unoriginal music journos.

'Why?'

''Cos he was doing something that was a total departure from his usual stuff.'

'So what was the real problem that Dylan had?'

'That he upped and changed.'

'Nah, his real problem was that he'd done the same old shit too fucking long. If every album had gone somewhere new, fans wouldn't have thrown their arms in the air and booed him off; they would have applauded some frankly fucking brilliant music. But they didn't because they couldn't see it for what it was. They were too busy blowing their minds over what it wasn't.'

'And?'

'I'm going to make goddamn well sure people can't label us like that. We won't be a blues band, or rock 'n' roll, or folk or whatever. We'll be us. We'll do songs we wanna do and fuck anybody who can't keep up.'

'Sounds good to me,' Philip replies with a grin. 'One question though, what we gonna call such a diverse and wide ranging musical enterprise?'

'A name's just another label. The music should speak for us. That's what I'm interested in.'

Philip nods understanding but I feel like a bloody charlatan. We do need a name.

Maybe it's because of that weird feeling I've done this before but sitting up 'til silly o' clock talking to Philip is easier than it has any right being. He doesn't hold any part of himself back. I gape, not so much at what he says but at the fact that he's saying it, telling me how his parents are against him getting into music (it's not respectable enough), how his bird dumped him 'cos he wouldn't settle down with her, how he's been broke enough to go out digging roads between gigs. I feel the need to trade off with him but some things have to be kept behind locked doors. I dredge up hairy stories of live performances that have gone spectacularly wrong. He tells me a few of his own. After the one about the time he and John were playing a club in Glasgow when some guy got up on the stage and yelled that he was looking for a particular so-and-so, and, on having said so-and-so pointed out to him, ran into the crowd and knifed the guy, I know I've had it easy. At least, I've not had to watch the worst of it unfolding in front of me during a Howlin' Wolf cover.

About three a.m., after six bottles of beer, two shots of Scotch each and a joint he ask me the big one.

'How'd you know this was for you? When did you realise this was what you were gonna do with your life?'

'Dunno.'

'But you're like, totally committed; this is all there is and all there ever could be. That kind of dedication and devotion, man, it has to have a deep root.'

'Kinda like a weed.' I laugh.

'I'm serious,' Philip says.

'This is the only thing I'm any good at.'

The Hierophant

After lunch with Meg I return to the office, opening the door a crack and glancing around with a, hopefully, apologetic expression. Keira looks up. Meg's right. I should know better. She says nothing but marches over and holds out her hand. I return the cigarettes then flash her my most sheepish smile.

'You might need to buy some more,' I say, 'maybe regulars next time, instead of lights?'

This draws a smile.

'I hope you got into lots of trouble.'

I laugh. 'Yeah, and I deserved it.'

'Too right you did,' she says, flopping into her own chair, back to me.

'I had to do some thinking. About this award business.'

'If it bothers you that much, don't do it. I've drafted a refusal. It's on your desk. Sign it and I'll post it tonight,' Keira huffs. This is really why she's pissed at me.

'I've decided I will do it.'

Her shoulders drop; she faces me, grinning.

'You're right, I do need one last hurrah. And I'm not the only one.'

'Philip and Pete?'

'Nah. Well, maybe but I'm thinking of the fans. There are still some out there. I met one today. She was so, I don't know, nice: genuine. And she can't have been more than twenty. It got me thinking. People are still listening.'

'Of course they are. That's what this award means.'

'Bollocks. It means those knobs at NIME couldn't think of anyone else to give it too this year. Probably everybody who matters already has one,' I snap, 'but I don't give a damn about that. If I do it, it's for me and the fans and,' I pause, 'for what was, what is and what should never be.'

Keira frowns. I'm glad she doesn't understand. You don't think about how it's going to sit when you're living it. But time stretches, refusing to snap. Today a decade with Crown & Kingdom is only a sixth of my life. The longer I live the smaller a percentage it gets but the heavier it is because I'm weakening. Would I have been better off as Michael Hunter, grocer, or Dr Hunter? Nah, that's guilty fucking coward talk. But there are others who'd have been better off if I'd never become the legendary Mickey Hunter, rock guitarist.

'You better get me Pete's number again,' I say, 'I can't find it.'

'I'm not surprised, state of your desk,' Keira mocks.

'But yours is so tidy.'

She grins.

'And see if you can find Philip's number as well.'

'You're going to talk to him?'

'Well, I'm gonna call him. Whether or not we can talk is another fucking matter. But I have to try.'

*

I turn my TR4 down the road towards Pete's, my guts in a knot. I'm more twisted up today than I was waiting in that draughty warehouse for Philip and Ronsey to show. It's been nine years since I stood, a wet-behind-the-ears fifteen year old in Davy Wilson's front room. I've knocked around plenty since, with Wilson and with the Three Bob Band. Hell, I've cut records, toured the States, the whole shebang, so why do I feel like I'm gonna puke my cornflakes?

It's this name business. Once you name it, it lives. This is my band: my baby. It has to fucking live. And the name's gotta be something that represents what we are, what we'll become, our triumphs and glories but what that is I've no fucking idea. I pull into a bus stop, wrench open the door and spew on the tarmac.

I park outside Pete's. He's at the window holding up one of the girls. He sees me, points and waves. After a bit of prompting she waves too. I trudge up the drive. Philip opens the door.

'Hey, man. How you doin'?' he asks.

'Good, you?'

'Happy as a kite on a windy day,' he smirks.

In the front room Ronsey is on the sofa, Pete's eldest on his knee. He's reading to her, tracing the lines with a thick finger and saying each word low and slow. It's weird seeing this strong, rough geezer with a small, delicate cherub on his lap. Goldilocks and a grizzly. He stops reading as I enter.

'Hey, Alice, who's this?' he asks her.

She shakes her head.

'Haven't you two met?' he demands.

'Sure they have.' Pete comes over from the window cradling the other one. 'Alice, you remember Uncle Mickey? He stayed here before.'

Alice thinks for a minute, nods and says, 'How do you do?'

It's a bloody good impersonation of a grown-up. Hell, she's better at it than me.

'I'm fine. How are you?' I ask, copying her.

'Very well, thank you.'

'That's it for small talk.' Pete sets down the younger child and crouches in front of them, fixing his calm grey eyes on them. 'Alice, take Katy into the kitchen. You may get yourself and your sister a glass of milk and one chocolate biscuit. And remember, I know how many are in the packet so I'll know if you take more than two. Then go upstairs and play. Daddy has to work so be quiet.' He presses his finger to his lips.

'Yes, Daddy.' Alice slides off the couch, pulling her sister by the hand. We watch them skip from the room.

'Lovely,' Ronsey says when they've gone.

'Thanks.' Pete beams.

'Kids are great,' Ronsey continues. 'Having James blew me away. One minute your old lady's flat on her back, screaming bloody murder and the next there's this tiny person in your arms, clinging to you and you know that's it, the best a man can feel. Fucking awesome. Hey, maybe we should do some matchmaking when they're older, your daughter and my son. James is about Katy's age. That'd be pretty groovy, huh?'

Pete laughs. 'Yeah, keep it in the family.'

I roll my eyes at Philip. Big deal. Anyone can make a baby. Philip returns my grimace with a cocky smirk of agreement.

'So, how we gonna do this?' Pete asks.

'Dunno.' I say. 'Anybody got any brilliant ideas?'

There is a unanimous shaking of heads.

'C'mon, dads, how'd ya pick names for your kids?' I ask.

'Alice and Katy are named after their grandmothers.'

'So we'll call ourselves the Four Old Ladies,' Philip quips.

'We got James' name out of this book, *The Big Book of Baby Names*,' Ronsey says. 'It's Latin, I think. There was something about the king, James I. He was a patron of the arts or something.' He shrugs.

We sit in static silence, stuck in neutral.

'Got any books in the house, Pete?' Philip prompts

Ronsey holds up the one he was reading to Alice, *Peter Pan*. We laugh but it's crazy enough to work and next thing we're standing in Pete's dining room, scanning the shelves of his bookcases looking for fuck knows what.

We waste an hour skimming closely-typed words, turning dry, yellowed pages and calling out half-baked ideas. Alice comes in half way through our search to scornfully announce that Katy has wet herself. Pete goes to deal with it. I'm onto the bottom shelf of my bookcase. I sit on the floor and run a finger over the ripple of spines. I remember a man once telling me how to find inspiration by trusting my instincts: 'Relax, close your eyes. Run your hand up and down the neck of the guitar. When you feel it, stop and put your fingers on the strings.' It worked too, sort of. What the hell? I take one deep breath. Hold it. Let it go, exhaling cigarette smoke and beer fumes. I close my eyes at the moment the air is gone and run my finger back and forth over the regiment of books, hoping to fuck none of the others are watching. I tune out the room's mutterings and rustlings. Tune into the silence in my own head. There's something else there, a whisper of sound, wind through rushes. I pull it down. This the hardest I've ever had to work at listening. Gradually, it forms words. The voice is not mine. 'Know thou thine own will?' I stop, open my eyes. My finger is resting on the cracked spine of a faded brown hardback, pulled like a sliver of metal to a magnet. Philip and Ronsey are still there, on the other side of the room, each flicking through a book.

'Did one of you say something?' I ask.

'Nope.'

'Nah, man.'

I take the book from the shelf. Inside the fly leaf it says *Divining the Future: The Holy Qabalah and Its Application to the Tarot.* I riffle the pages.

'You got something?' Philip asks.

'Not sure.'

He stands behind me, reading over my shoulder. Ronsey follows. Pete reappears.

'What's that?' he asks.

I hand him it.

'Looks like something Suse bought at a flea market. She's always going to those and coming back with junk,' he moans.

I hold out my hand and he returns it to me. I feel air tightening around us. My ears are never wrong. This book fucking spoke to me.

''S it O.K. if I sit in your garden?'

Pete waves empty hands. 'Help yourself.'

'Thanks. Keep looking, fellas,' I add but I know the answer is somewhere in the pages of this faded brown book.

The garden is small and bare. A narrow patch of lawn extends a few yards to a row of trees bordering it at the far end. Scattered shrubs dot the beds surrounding the lawn. Most are brown and wilted. I sit on the greyed grass. Start to read, eating the words. The light fades. Ronse brings me a beer.

'You getting anywhere?'

'Maybe. How's it going inside?'

'We've given up. Pete's cooking tea. You want some?'

'Whatever.'

He leaves me to it. I stretch out on scratchy grass, the book open in front of me: 'Chapter 7: The Tree of Life and it's correspondence to the numbers of the small cards'. It gets darker, violet shadows veiling everything. The beginning was nothing, absolute zero, according to the book anyway. Pete comes out.

'Tea's ready.'

'O.K.'

He goes back in. I keep reading.

'Kether: the Crown, the first Sephiroth (number) on the Qabalistic Tree of Life, is the initial manifestation of a point, an idea or reality out of nothing. Malkuth: the Kingdom, is the last Sephiroth, number ten of ten, the end of the line for the initial point that started out at one and has finally become all it can be.'

I close the book and stroke the anonymous cover. There's a lot of deep stuff hidden in it. I don't get it, yet, but it's important. 'Know thou thine own will.' I thought it was asking me a question. I turn again to the page where I've already seen the full quotation. Read it once more to be sure I've understood it:

'Love and Will united create all. Know thou thine own Will. Wander alone bearing the light of creation. Keep silence in all ways.'

It means I have to work out what it is I want and that I'm responsible for getting it or not. The last bit is a warning. The knowledge in this book is a sacred secret, how the magician pulls the rabbit from the hat. And I can't tell it to anyone. Not that I would. A talking book? Hello, white-coated quacks.

Inside they're sitting at the table, empty glasses and plates littering the Formica. I hover in the doorway.

'Think yours might be cold,' Pete excuses.

'That's O.K.' I sit and they ogle me but I'm not ready to give it up yet.

'You want a beer?' Pete asks.

'Thanks.'

He passes it to me. It fizzes on my tongue. This is the moment when it starts for real.

'Well?' Ronsey demands. 'Are you gonna fucking tell us?'

'Crown and Kingdom.'

They exchange raised-eyebrow glances.

'Sounds like a fucking pub,' Ronse barks.

'Does it?'

'What does it mean?' Pete asks.

'Nothing, really,' I lie, 'but it sounds cool.'

'Crown and Kingdom.' Philip digests the phrase. 'Yeah,' he nods, 'I like it. Yeah, think of what those words mean, man.' His face glows. 'The power and the glory, the absolute and the unchallengeable. It's perfect.' He hoots in triumph and punches the air.

We've got a name. We're real, no more a cock-eyed picture in my mind. After busting my balls so long I've got what I've always wanted. Fucking yes! I want to whoop and spin around like a lunatic. Instead, I surreptitiously pocket the book and drive home in the dark with it on the passenger seat, feeling its presence in the air, the warmth of another living being. I don't buy into supernatural bullshit normally but I know as I drive with that book beside me that I'm not alone. The weird thing is that it's not weird; it's like sitting with an old friend in an easy silence. I laugh out loud. The sound of my voice breaking the quiet frightens me. I let it die away.

That other voice speaks up, reminding me to keep the secrets I read lying on the grass in Pete's bare garden.

'Speakest thou to none of truth.'

Christ, this is crazy. Nah, it's not. Otherwise I would've told them what it really means, Crown and Kingdom. But I didn't. I won't. Can't.

'For silence breaks into rapture.'

I know.

'Calculate well the formula of thy way.'

I have: Crown and Kingdom: from our lowly start to our triumphant finale and whatever the hell it's gonna take to get us there. Crown and Kingdom. With '&' instead of 'and'.

'Love all and let all love thou. Rejoice without shame. Give forth thy light to and never doubt. Find thyself in every star; achieve thou every possibility.'

That's what I want, what I've always wanted.

The Brothers

Keira places a scrap, torn from the green notepad she uses, on my desk. Two phone numbers are scrawled on it.

'Thanks.'

'I'll make coffee.'

'Good idea.'

I wait until she's gone, then start dialling. With ridiculous bravado I punch in Philip's number first but click the catch on the cradle, disconnecting before it rings.

I try Pete instead. A brief buzz in my ear then the repeated echo of the phone ringing down the line. It rings for a long time but I don't hang up. I need to make it through one of these calls. I feel a right twat. I used to be a conquering hero. Now I'm a doddery, gutless old man afraid of talking to a good friend.

'Hello?' It's a woman.

'Er… is Pete there?'

'Mickey? Is that you? It's Susie.' She shrieks, 'Pete was going to call you. Isn't it wonderful? I mean, about time, but still, it's wonderful.' She means the award.

'Erm…'

She saves me from having to say anything else.

'I'll give Pete a shout, he's downstairs practising. First thing he did was get his bass out of storage.'

I hang in space while Susie fetches Pete. What the fuck am I gonna say to him? It's been too long. I meant to keep in touch. Managed it for a while but it was over and I couldn't be arsed pretending it wasn't. Speaking to him like it was 1975 not 1995 became impossible, because '75 was dead, cremated and the ashes sprinkled over my guitar. Now we're even further down the line. The memories are frayed at the edges.

'Hey, Mickey.' His voice is warm. Pete was always a generous bloke. Thank God.

'Pete, how are you?'

'Good thanks. You?'

'Alright. The usual pensioner's aches and pains.'

He laughs. 'Comes with the territory.'

'Yeah.' Well, that's that. I clear my throat. 'I, er, gather you got the same letter as me?'

'Seems so.'

Neither of us wants to ask; it's too reckless. But I rang him. Plus, I want to do this, so it has to be me.

'What d'ya think 'bout it?'

'I think it's about damn time.' He's only half joking. 'What about you?'

'We should front for the award.'

'That's a given. What else?'

'Dunno. I was wondering what you thought?'

'It could be fun, and if we're going to now's the time. If my back gets any worse I doubt I'll be able to carry my bass.' He laughs again.

'Your back and my knees. But what about...' His name tastes foul on my tongue.

'Philip? Have you spoken to him?'

'Not for, Christ, twenty years.' I rummage my brain, the pain of time hitting me below the ribs. 'You?'

'We get a Christmas card off him, that's it,' Pete says. 'We had drinks maybe seven years ago. His heart wasn't in it. Not without Ronsey. Do you think he will?'

'I don't know but if you're keen I'm prepared to try. If he doesn't then he doesn't. It's that simple.'

'It's anything but simple. There'll be interviews, re-releases, maybe a few gigs; people will expect things. We can't do it without Philip.'

'But we can without Ronsey?'

'We haven't any choice,' Pete says. 'Anyway, we know what John would want us to do.'

'But will it work without him?'

'We'll have to get another drummer in, I suppose,' Pete muses. 'Any ideas?'

'Let's deal with Philip first.'

'O.K.'

Truth is we were a machine that needed every part in working order to run smooth. Together the four of us conquered the world. Now, without John Ronsarno, there's a good chance it won't start again. There's only one person I can think of who could, maybe, take John's place and make the engine turn over one last time. But it's a fucking shot into space.

*

We're ready for this. Yeah, the repertoire's limited, but we've got enough for this first gig and there are two weeks 'til the next. If we can get fifteen songs to performance standard in a week, we should have forty-odd before the next gig. No problem. If we get through this first one.

Pete's up front next to me, stiff with nerves. His usual stream of fast-flowing gabble has ran dry. The van jolts over a manhole cover; he bumps into me, pushing me again Lenny who growls low and deep, reaches for the gear lever and shoves me over towards Pete. Next time I'll take the window seat.

'You sure we're ready for this?' It's about the thousandth time he's asked since Lenny and I picked him up before collecting Philip and John from the station.

'Course.'

'We've only been playing together a week.'

'The audience don't know that. We can do it, that's what counts.'

'I'm not sure about that medley at the end,' Pete moans. 'Don't think I've got it right even once.'

'You'll do it when it counts. If you get lost watch me and, I dunno, it's all in G so jam something.'

Pete nods but his mouth is pressed into a pin-thin line.

'You think they're O.K. back there?' He jerks a trembling thumb towards the rear of the van where, jumbled among guitar cases, amps and drums, Philip and Ronsey are being jarred and joggled.

'It's the best we can do for now. Once we make a few quid we'll have two vans and they can ride up front. We'll have two Lenny's as well, won't we mate?' I pat the thick bicep of the gorilla Don has supplied as driver-come-roadie-come-security guard-come-fuck-knows-what. He grunts. 'Yeah, don't think there can be another like you,' I mumble and Pete throws me a warning glance as Lenny swings the wheel and the van skids into Henley Street, the Two Blues club up ahead on the right, the neon sign flashing against the inky sky.

'Check, check one-two, check. Christ.'

Philip fiddles with the treble knob on the vocal channel.

'Mickey, do me a favour and whack the first verse of 'C'mon Everybody', will ya?'

I shoulder my guitar. How much fucking longer is he going to take over this? I pound out the chords as Philip throws a handful of words into the mic before stopping mid-sentence.

'Can I get a bit more on this monitor?' he asks the club's sound guy.

'It's maxed out, man.'

'Shit. Well, that's as good as it's gonna get.' Philip leans away from the microphone.

'You happy now?' I smirk.

'Hardly.' He wrinkles his nose at the mic, cursing the pissy sound. I don't know whether to admire his attention to detail or be narked at his fannying. He's got a nerve grumbling about the set up, jumped up wanker. Hope I've done the right thing. His singing's faultless, it's putting up with the rest that bugs me and that's only gonna be easy on alternate days. Or if he's had his Weetabix. Or whatever. Philip crosses to Ronsey who asks for a light and in the green glow of the club's lighting rig I notice his hand shaking. It hits me that this is probably the biggest venue he's played in. Hell, it's the biggest I've played in for a while but at least I've headlined here enough times to be an old hand. Shit, hope I've got the patience for mollycoddling him.

Pete comes over.

'I could do with a drink.'

We head for the bar, leaving Philip and Ronsey on stage, bent together in conflab. Pete puts his hand in his pocket.

'Drinks are on the house.' I order us two beers.

'How d'ya swing that? In fact, how d'ya swing this gig at all? It's a pretty big venue for a début performance and I don't just mean the capacity,' Pete says.

'Mutual back scratching. I played here pretty often with the Three Bob Band and got to know the manager. When we spilt he was left hanging so I promised him a freebie when I got my next line up together. Then it turned out he knew my mother too. Can't imagine why he never told his missus he was knocking the back out of some old slapper. Anyway, he appreciates a good thing, does Eric, so he offered to pay us generously, you know, being such a patron of the arts and keen to support talented musicians.' I wink at Pete and raise my glass. 'Here's to back scratching.'

He lifts his glass. We drink. People filter in. Pete watches the audience swell and merge. I light a cigarette.

'Maybe we should go backstage.'

'If you want,' I say but make no move to go.

Pete clears his throat. 'Did you hear anything about what happened to your mum? I mean, did the police find who...' Having embarrassed us both he gives up.

I keep my eyes away from his. The sight of her naked lower half and the stench of rotting flesh flash up at me in 3-D. Christ, why did he have to fucking bring that up?

'The inquest's down for next month. I have to go, apparently, 'cos I found her. Fuck knows what good that'll do. They won't find him. If they're even looking.'

'But surely they'll try.'

I don't want him to ever ask me about this again. 'An old whore on the game strangled by a punter? I think it's pretty fucking low priority.' I glare at Pete. 'I don't give a shit. I told you we weren't close and when you're dead, you're dead. There's fuck all you can do about it so why waste time stewing on it?'

'Stewing on what?' Ronsey demands as he and Philip join us at the bar.

'The dead.' I'm spoiling for it now.

'Who the fuck's dead?'

Pete opens his mouth. I don't give him chance to cram in his other foot.

'My bloody mother. But as I was saying to Pete, so the fuck what? When you're dead, you're dead. The end.'

Ronsey says, 'Nah, man, I don't buy that. You're not gone, not really.'

'Shit, you're not from the God Squad are you?' I ask.

'It's not that.' He struggles for the words. 'We all leave something behind.'

'Such as?'

'This is how I see it, right. My boy, he's part of me. When I'm gone he'll still be here. Pete, you've got kids, you get it, don't ya?'

'But he'll be dead one day too,' I say.

'But if he has kids of his own…'

'He might not.'

'There are other ways,' John insists.

Now I want, need, to know the answer. Is he really going to tell us, here? Now? I'm calling his bluff because I can't believe he's got a hand to play. And the magic word is… written on the back of your own head. Surely he's not the mirror?

'Such as?'

'Like, people like, you know, Shakespeare and that. They're not gone are they? People are still reading his bloody plays. I've even read one at school. And what, he's been dead for a couple of hundred years or something?' Ronsey says.

'Try four.'

'Whatever. The point is people still remember him. How can you be dead if so many people know you? It's your what's-it, i'n't it, that matters.'

'Legacy?' Philip prompts.

'Yeah, legacy. What you leave behind for people to remember you by. If you're like Shakespeare and do something that people are gonna love for a long time after you've kicked the bucket then that's it. You've done it,' Ronsey says.

'Done what?' I demand.

'Cheated death. Life everlasting, that shite they go on about in church. I mean, that's why we're doing this, ain't it? To be great; to be remembered.'

At that Philip bursts into raucous laughter. 'Nah, man,' he says, 'I'm doing it for the chicks.'

We all laugh now because it's the appropriate response but Ronsey's right. Shit. He's fucking right. His words are a blood vessel exploding in my brain. If I think about it it's un-fucking-believable; standing at a bar of all bastard places, beer in hand, for

Christ sake, I've had the meaning of life explained to me by a common-as-arseholes drummer, not a species known for their ability to get philosophical about life and shit. What's more, I know it's true because I realise now I knew it all along. That's why this means so much to me. Cheating Death. The ultimate hustle.

While I chew over this mind-blowing truth, Philip continues to unwind his thread on women.

'So blonde, brunette or red head?'

'Got to be blonde,' Ronsey says.

'Well, the girl I love's got long, black wavy hair so I'll have to say brunette. Susie'd never forgive me otherwise.'

'Mickey?'

'Don't really care. It's not their heads I'm interested in.'

There's a round of smutty giggling; I'm not joking.

'You must have a preference,' Philip insists. 'C'mon, look around. What tickles your fancy, man?' He waves his hand at the room.

I shrug but look, to shut him up. The room is a hideous Picasso daub, hit and miss dashes of colour thrown here and there, moving and twisting into patterns like coloured glass beads when you rotate a kaleidoscope. I notice her because she's black from toe to top, not in glorious Technicolor, and wearing trousers. Mini-skirts are in but I like trousers, tight, with legs that lead somewhere. Her hair's dark too and cut like Twiggy's. She's standing in the middle of the room with a small circle of space around her as though she's raised an invisible force-field. She revolves slowly on the spot, taking in the view. While her back's turned I point her out to Philip.

'She's O.K.'

'Ladies and gentlemen, we have a winner. The man says, 'Brunette'. Personally, I think you're all wrong. Give me a feisty red head any day, or night, and I'll show her a good time. More than once.' He grins and nudges Ronsey.

'Alright, Casanova.' I pat him on the shoulder. 'Let's get back stage before the birds here lay siege to you.'

As we leave I scan the crowd for her tall, slender shadow but she's gone.

There are only a few minutes before we go on. Eric's been round twice, checking we've got everything. I get Philip to kick up a fuss about the crappy PA, not because Eric'll do anything about it (I know he won't; he's too much of a tight-arse) but to see him squirm and sweat. He fingers the stiff collar of his pin-striped shirt.

'Nice duds, Eric,' I say, cutting Philip off mid-complaint. 'Sandra buy that for you, did she?'

He bristles at his wife's name, makes some piss-weak apologies then disappears like a rat, back up his own polyester trouser leg.

Meanwhile, Pete's working himself into a frenzy, prepping by threatening himself with a fate worse than death if it goes to shit. Philip has retreated inside himself, the mask of bravado washed off. He's sitting there, staring at an unlit cigarette. Ronsey is the only one who stays calm. He sits on a plastic chair and thumbs his way through yesterday's *Daily Mirror*, beer in one hand, cigarette in the other, his moving speech about legacies forgotten.

My mind tracks back to another night in a much tougher club, when I was a kid with borrowed gear, something to prove and people to prove it too. I'd thought it wouldn't ever feel as desperate as it did then. But it does now. This has to be my legacy because it's mine, my group, my idea: my dream. There's never going to be another shot at it. Not like this.

The clock ticks down to zero hour. Eric's on stage. I listen for the words I've wanted to hear my whole life: the words that introduce my band.

'Ladies and gentlemen, Crown & Kingdom.'

The Chariot

I say 'bye to Pete and hang up. Fucking fool, what've you agreed to? A young thing with a pretty face asks for your autograph next you're jumping off the ledge? A wave of fear soaks me. How in hell on earth can I resurrect the me that was so full of it he believed it himself, got everybody else believing and made truth from nothing?

The letter is still crumpled and unopened in my pocket. I smooth it out on my desk, the shield in the King's College Hospital logo battle-bent. It says what it says whether or not I read it. Before there were reasons for not knowing. Now there's a reason to know: so I can bring it on home.

I rip at the seal. Scan down the paper. The letter confirms what we discussed at the consultation as Dr. Sangha sat relaxed, hands folded on his oak desk, and I perched on the swivel chair, straining every muscle, tendon and nerve to keep myself from swinging childishly side to side. Three times the fingers of my right hand wandering to the ring on my left, twisting it round and round. *Bedknobs and Broomsticks* popped into my head. They needed something they could rotate to escape on the flying bed. That and, 'There's no place like home.' Wrong movie. But the two fitted. Each time I pulled at my ring and snapped my hands back onto my knees, Dr. Sangha's eyes followed but his own hands remained resting on top of my file. He said the words, 'chronic heart failure'. I twisted the ring again. Stopped, again. Asked what that meant. He reeled off some facts, tried to sound optimistic, listed several treatment options.

'If it does turn out to be this chronic thing,' I said, desperate not to use the words heart and failure in the same sentence, 'is that it?'

'Aside from the medications and surgical procedures there are things you can do it terms of lifestyle change; eating healthily, exercising, not smoking. If it does turn out to be chronic heart failure, but I must stress we won't know for certain until we get the test results back.'

'But is this it? Is this what I'll die from?'

He hesitated; I thought, 'Come on, get some balls, you bloody shit, and tell me the truth,' while I twisted my ring again. Stopped, again.

'There's no cure for this condition and, though modern treatments are effective, prolonging the lives of patients considerably, it is likely that…' Our eyes met. I flashed him a grateful smile. 'Of course you never know, you might leave my office today and be hit by a bus.' He winked at me.

'Bus? Down here? More likely a doctor racing to the golf course in his Roller.'

He chuckled.

'I'll write to you when we know for certain.'

And he has. The words, 'diagnosis confirmed' and 'follow-up appointment', leap out at me.

Keira enters with coffees. I slide some papers over the letter and sip the coffee. It's only lukewarm.

'Is everything alright?'

'Abso-bloody-lutely fantastic. Jesus Christ, this coffee's fucking stone-cold.'

'Give it here, then. I'll make fresh.'

'Don't fucking bother.'

'Give it here.'

'Leave it, will you?'

She stamps out.

Damn it. 'Sorry, I'm sorry, I'm just bloody…' What? Bloody dying, that's all.

She leans against the doorframe.

'I guess this reunion is bringing it back. I can't imagine what it must be like and I'm not asking you to tell me, either,' she adds, 'unless that'll help.' She pauses. 'You must still miss John.'

That's it, the true reason why I'm turning myself inside out.

I should tell her she's right. Tell her everything else. But I can't. My lungs are lead-weighted.

'Are you alright, Mr Hunter?'

'Give me those cigarettes.'

'I don't think…'

'Fucking hell, give me the bloody cigarettes before I sack you.' I bang a fist onto my desk. Wince as pain thumps through my hand, up my arm.

Keira wrenches open her drawer and flicks the pack over. It lands on top of the paper pile hiding the fatal letter. I snatch it out from under, screw it into a ball and hurl it at the bin. It misses. I get up. Stride to the bin. Kick it. Twice. Keira flinches.

'Go home.'

'It's only half past…'

'I said, go home.' I cross back to my desk, stand behind it like it's a blast shield and I'm the unexploded bomb. She rustles some papers. I face the window, watch her reflection in the tinted glass. She puts on her coat, grabs her bag, snatches a file, wipes at her eyes. The door bangs behind her.

I sink into my chair and light a cigarette. There are only five left. I decide to smoke them all. I need a drink too. I think of those crappy police dramas Meg watches where the old hack copper keeps a bottle of noxious blended Scotch in his filing cabinet for the night the murderer kills again. I'm not that prepared but check the cupboard on the off chance. Some of the die-hards still send me stuff. Never profess to a liking for something in an interview. Keira sorts through it but there's usually a backlog of unwanted junk waiting to go out. I pray for whisky or brandy. The best I can do is a bottle of mead sent by a fan from Holy Island.

I throw the cold coffee out the window and sling the honey-dripped liquid into my mug.

I do miss Ronsey. But that's not the problem. I'm afraid. Fucking terrified. Because I don't deserve a second chance. Not at this, not after what happened That Night, the one Ronsey died. But I'm in danger of getting one. I'm afraid because I don't know how it's gonna turn out this time.

*

I'm fifteen. In three days I leave school. I have to figure out what to do with my life. There's only one thing I want to do: be a guitarist. Me and a thousand others who've bought a guitar, slogged through the CAGED chords, wrestled with the minor pentatonic in all five positions and learnt to play a twelve bar in any key. I lie in my narrow bed thinking of the last three years spent learning to play. I'm good but that means sod all if I don't make it. In the darkness, with the weight of my empty future crushing me, I know if I want to be alive, there's only one thing for me to do. If I don't do it I might as well be dead.

I turn onto my side. There's another voice in my head, the voice of an old man. He asks angry, bitter questions I can't answer. His knuckley finger jabs me in the chest. What'll happen if I try and fail? What will you do when your dreams are ash in the grate? I squeeze my eyes shut. It won't happen. I can't let it.

It's dark when I open my eyes. A light breeze brushes my face. I stare into the nothingness, trying to stab through it for signs of life. The sky turns bluish and, as my eyes adjust, I see the darker outline of blue-black clouds creeping silently, hiding and revealing stars as they go. I'm on a dirt road in an empty land. I lie down, face in the dirt, and spread myself on the ground, feeling its warmth and solidness holding me up.

I stay like that a while. Maybe I sleep because I feel like the jarring ring of my alarm clock wakes me. But that's not it. The ground under my spread-eagled body is shaking. I stretch my arms, clutch at the ground, trying to dig fingernails into hard-packed earth, straining muscle and bone to keep attached to something I'm not part of. My brain rattles inside my skull. It covers up my screams.

My right hand finds a crack. I wedge my finger in but the ground is dry, crumbling between my fingertips, disappearing like ice shavings. I claw at earth. More chunks disintegrate at my touch. The surface splits down the middle. A deep crack crawls towards me, the shaking earth forcing it to run wider and deeper. I can lie here waiting to fall into the crack. Or I can get up and run.

I stagger to my feet and sprint. Power surges through me. I can outrun this. My legs start to burn. My chest is tight. I keep pushing. The ground spirals uphill. I lean into the curve. If I stop I'll die. The ground gets steeper. Pain and heat spread through my body; blood beats in my ears. The air is dry, thin: empty. I run higher and higher. There's nobody to tell me I can't so I can.

The ground levels out. I'm up a height, a safe distance. It's light now. On the horizon is the red glow of an early sun. The ground below is a brown mass; whipped, churned and beaten. But the mountain I've climbed is solid. I jump up and down to check. Yeah, rock-solid. I should be safe here. But it's a long way down. What if I fall? The only thing holding me up here is me. My stomach flips over. My head is dandelion-clock light. I sway in a threatening breeze.

Thunder claps. Rain pours down, drenching me. Water starts rising around my mountain. It reaches my feet, washes over my shoes and climbs my legs. When it reaches my waist I think I'll drown. When it's up to my chest I remember I can swim. I push off into it and float away on the frothy surface.

'Mickey, get your backside out of bed.' She's banging on my bedroom door.

I sit up. My room's filled with bright yellow light. It's late.

'You haven't left yet,' she shouts.

'I'm up. Piss off.' I hear her muttered curses as she stomps downstairs.

I swing my legs out of bed. Sit looking at my feet, remembering them being covered by rising water. I get dressed and go down.

She's in the kitchen, drinking tea and wearing last night's clothes. On the yellow Formica tabletop is a roll of pound notes. She follows my gaze and, a frog snatching a fly from the air, grabs the money, hiding it in her cleavage.

'Where's your uniform?'

'In the wash.'

'At least put on a proper pair of trousers. You can't go to school in those.' She waves a dismissive hand at my jeans.

'What are they going to do about it? Expel me?'

'Mickey, for God sake.'

She's pathetic.

'What?'

She sighs grey smoke.

'What are you going to do with yourself?'

'I've got it sorted.'

'You better have, young man, I'm not working my fingers to the bone to keep you while you waste your time playing that bloody guitar.'

'Be nice if you did work your fingers for a change, give your,' I wrestle the word up and out, 'cunt a rest.'

And I'm gone.

The bell above the door tinkles as I push it open and step inside. Ron's Guitars and Gear is officially my favourite place.

'Hello, Mickey,' Ron says from behind the counter. 'No school today?'

'No.'

He winks at me. 'You looking for anything in particular?'

I want to say, 'Yeah, my future please, and if it comes in bright red that'd be smashing.'

'Not really.'

'Well, let me know if you need a hand.' He flips open his newspaper.

I move between the aisles lined with guitars, amps, music stands, drum skins, sheet music, and thread my way towards the back where the notice board lives. It's Ron's cunning plan; if you want a squiz at the board you've got to go through the shop and hopefully you'll see something irresistible on the way. I try to avoid clocking it but I've seen it too many times to ignore its glow on the edge of my vision, a beckoning lighthouse. I promise myself a quick-fix look at the cherry sunburst Les Paul on the way back. Business first.

I scan the thumb-tacked scraps of dog-eared paper. Panic blurs their whiteness, dazzling my eyes. I look away. Take a breath. Start again, avoiding the middle where everyone else looks, hoping for something unthumbed. Not too much competition.

'Rhythm Guitarist wanted for rock 'n' roll four piece. Up to £10 per gig. Steady work GUARANTEED. Contact Davy Wilson for details. Must have own equipment.'

I tear the ad from the board.

Back at the counter Ron glances up.

'Did you find it?'

'What?'

'Whatever it was you were looking for.'

'But I wasn't...'

'You were on a mission,' he teases.

'Yeah, O.K. Ron, can I ask you about this notice?' I slide the paper across the counter. 'Do you know him?'

He scans it.

'Oh, aye, Davy Wilson, he's in here almost as often as you,' Ron laughs. 'He's got a skiffle group or something. Nice lad, hard worker. Last time I saw him he was fired up about a regular gig down at the Smithsonian Club, two nights a week, he said. He was talking big break, record deals, touring, the full whack.'

'Do you think that's gonna happen?'

'Who knows? It's a fickle business, this, Mickey. If you're not prepared to take the drops with the catches you'd be better getting yourself a steady apprenticeship, be a plumber or something.'

'No.'

He studies me. 'You're interested in it?'

'Yeah but...'

'So go for it, lad.'

'But they want someone with their own gear. I've only got an acoustic.'

'Then it's a good thing you're in a guitar shop,' Ron jokes.

'I don't think I can afford anything. I've a bit saved but not enough.'

'What about a deal? I'll lend you a guitar for the audition and, if you get the gig, you can give me what you've got as down-payment and pay the rest weekly from your earnings?'

'Really?'

He nods. 'Reckon you deserve a break and, who knows, if I'm the one to give you it I can take the credit when you're pulling bigger crowds than the Beatles.'

'Thanks.'

'Got your eye on anything special?'

My head swivels in the direction of the cherry sunburst Les Paul.

Ron allows himself an amused chuckle. 'Steady on, lad. That might be a bit much, even for someone of my generous disposition.'

Before I can blink it's done. Ron lets me make the call from the shop phone; I get straight through to Davy Wilson. Faltering and stammering, I arrange to meet up with his band and play for them. Ron presses a second hand Stratocaster on me, it's a bit scuffed but good enough for now, and a fifteen watt amp. The sound is tinny until I tweak all the knobs, finding something fatter and fuller. I play through a couple of songs, ones where I've worked out the lead breaks from listening to the records over and over. I think I can make this work. Ron's expression says he thinks so too. We sign some paper work. I promise I'll be in first thing in the morning whatever happens. I don't know what's more terrifying; getting it or not getting it. Then I'm standing on the pavement outside the shop, guitar in one hand, amp in the other, terrified and exhilarated.

Davy glares at me through a cloud of cigarette smoke.

'How old are you, kid?'

I gulp. 'Sixteen.' Give or take six months.

His eyes narrow.

'You better play us something.'

With trembling fingers I set up my new gear, trying to mask my fumbling. When I'm ready to face them Davy's stretched out on the sofa like royalty, flanked by Bill, the drummer and Walt, the bass player. The singer, Tom, hasn't bothered showing up. I strum a chord, expecting a blast of sound but am greeted by the weak twang of unamplified strings. Silence clashes around me. I wince.

'Christ's sake,' Bill mutters.

Davy scowls. 'Works better if you switch it on, kid.' He leans forward to snap the wall switch for me. I flinch again and feel the pins-and-needle prickings of sweat on my forehead.

'This better be worth it,' Bill growls.

I try again. This time the sound bellows out. I look up defiantly and blast my way through my three best songs including the most elaborate solos I can manage. With the energy of terror coursing through me I race to the end, stop and pant breathlessly, not caring about anything other than the fact that I did it. Whatever happens, I bloody did it.

'Shit, kid can play,' Davy mutters, sitting forward.

'That's all well an' good, playing rehearsed stuff but can he do what we do?' Bill asks.

Davy studies me. 'Think you're up to it, kid? You're playing with the big boys now, ya know.'

'Course.'

'Let's see how full of it you are.' Davy springs, catlike, from his chair. 'Walt, talk him through the set list while I get changed.' He sweeps from the room, leaving me stranded and with the dread feeling I've swum across a crocodile infested river to find the opposite bank swarming with lions.

'What's happening?' I ask.

'You're on,' Bill says. 'Try not to piss yourself, O.K.' He laughs and follows Davy from the room.

Clutching my guitar like a shield, I look to the bass player. Walt smiles.

'Don't worry about those two. They always give the new lads a hard time. That's why we get through more rhythm players than new strings. As long as you do O.K. tonight, you'll be fine. And from that little performance, I'd say you'll manage, no problem. If you get lost, cast your eyes my way. I'll play some root notes to get you back on track with the progression.'

'Tonight?' I'm sure I'm about to throw up.

'Yeah,' Walt says, 'we're on at the Smith's: 8 p.m.'

The Smithsonian is a working men's club. I've been past but never inside. She used to come here 'til they twigged she was prowling for punters. We're in the dance hall, the poshest room in the club. At least, the one without sawdust on the floor. Also, the only room which lets in women. A gangly array of them have gathered. Their colours are garish: violent pinks; bloody reds; bruised purples; icy blues and acid greens. The oranges are the worst, staining everything they touch. Against the drab background, these women are poison weeds. They repel me more than the dull, dark men that hover around them like wasps. I don't like the game they're playing.

'Hey, kid, you ready?'

I yank my head back through the doorway.

Davy's there in his stage costume; blue jeans, red shirt, white tie: cocky smirk. His hair is brushed back and I can taste his aftershave. It makes me gag.

'Don't think he's gonna survive it,' Bill says, peering over Davy's shoulder.

'Yeah you are, Mickey, you're O.K. aren't you?' Walt tries reassuring us both. He cares because the music matters to him.

'Dunno,' Davy says. 'He looks kinda pale. You're not gonna pass out on us, are you, kid?'

Before I can defend myself Bill jumps in.

'Let's give him a beer, that'll help.' He offers me an opened bottle. I've never drank beer before.

I take it and swig the way I usually slug back cherryade. The taste is bitter, the pith from oranges. My tongue curls back on itself but I swallow.

'Thanks,' I say and, disappointed that I didn't spit it out or pull a face, they turn away.

'Where's Tom?' Walt asks.

'He'll be here,' Davy says.

The door behind me swings open, slapping against my legs, bumping me forwards and jerking the bottle in my hand. Brown liquid fizzes up and sprays out all over me. Bill roars with laughter.

I swipe beer foam from my chin with the sleeve of my shirt. In the doorway is an older lad, blonde hair cut into a smooth round bob. He's wearing a purple and yellow checked shirt and black trousers. A large white cowboy hat is crumpled in his hand.

'Who the fuck's standing behind the F-ing door?'

'Tom, 'bout bloody time,' Davy snaps, 'I said eight.'

'Shit, it's only…' he looks at his wrist and laughs, 'ain't got me watch on.' He holds up his bare arm as proof. 'Musta left it at Sally's or maybe Laura's.' He winks at Bill.

'Alright, we get it,' Davy barks, 'you got some. Well fucking done. We're on in five.'

Tom shrugs. Notices me. Cocks his head.

'Who's this?'

'New rhythm guitarist,' Davy says.

'This the best you could do?' he sneers then, seeing me scowl, adds, 'Hey, no offence, mate.'

I force myself to bite back. 'You shouldn't wear that shirt, then,' I say to which Bill roars again.

We take our places out front. There's no stage, just a cordoned-off area of the dance floor filled with our equipment. My hands shake. Sweat glues my shirt to my back. I need to piss. Tom and Davy straddle a mic each. Walt and me line up behind, on opposite sides. I half-face him so I can follow his playing. He throws me an encouraging smile. Bill sits astride his kit, sleeves rolled up, cigarette dangling, pint in easy reach. My stomach threatens to express-return the beer. I glance at the door, think about legging it, remember Ron's faith in me, and don't.

Bill counts us in. I miss the first bar, picking up the second on the beat. Only Walt notices. After that I focus on the music, chanting each chord in my head as the progression marches on. The audience lunges towards us, a wave trying to breech the seawall. I wait for them to crash over us but they stop and begin twisting and turning on the dance floor, flopping fish beached by the tide. I press harder on the strings than I need to. My arm, tense with effort, aches but I keep going, concentrating on what I'm doing, watching the shapes my hand makes as it presses the strings, holding here, releasing there. I lose time. Each song runs into the next so there's an unbroken stream of sound. Finally we get to the last number. Davy stretches it out, repeating the chorus too many times. Only now can I relax enough to watch him. He's basking in the audience's applause. And they're not just cheering him. Some are cheering me, too. They like this; wish they could do it. Tom arches his neck. Shrieks the words into the mic, causing a huge spill of feedback from the PA system which is overloaded with our instruments and Tom's vocals. He stops singing to press his hands over his ears in mock despair before winking at a pretty blonde in a pink mini-skirt who's waggling in front of him. Davy scowls at Tom. He doesn't realise what's happening. I do but can only watch as Davy's top E string quivers and contorts, reaching breaking point as he strikes it again and again. I open my mouth to call out over the din. The string snaps. Whips up over Davy's hand like a lash.

'Ow! Fuck.'

Bill drums relentlessly. Walt's solid too. We make eye contact and he mouths, 'Keep going,' but the audience know something's wrong. I pick up the lead part where Davy left off. He scowls at me but as I start to get it right, his frown fades. With modified fingering, he takes over the chords and we limp to the song's end.

The crowd cheers. Tom brings the mic to his mouth.

'We've been wonderful, thanks very much to us.'

Davy signals me to bow; I jab myself in the shoulder with the headstock as I bend over my guitar. Someone switches on the juke-box. It's over. I made it. We unplug. Davy comes across.

'Nice save, Mickey. Let's get a bloody drink, lads.'

At the bar Davy orders me a lemonade.

'No booze out front 'til you're eighteen. Can't afford to get ourselves thrown out of a gig for giving beer to a minor.'

'Does that mean…?'

'Unless anybody's got any objections?' Nobody does. 'You're in, welcome to the Davy Wilson Quintet.'

Adjustment

I'm drunk now, the mead effectively numbing parts other alcoholic beverages can't reach. Good. Drunk I can maybe get as far as the phone ringing. I pick up the receiver. Dial Philip's number.

It rings twice before there's a click at the other end.

'Hello?'

The voice is an echo of something that's long gone. I put my hand up. Rub my cheek, smearing sticky wetness over the crinkly surface.

'Philip?' I croak his name.

There's a hollow silence. I expect him to hang up. Pain's all we have in common now. And who the fuck wants to share that?

'Mickey.'

'Hello, Philip.' The name sounds more solid this time. I force jollity into my tone, 'How the heck are you?'

'Better than you, I suspect.'

We know each other too well to bullshit.

'You get a letter recently?'

'Yep.'

'And?'

'I think sleeping dogs are best left dreaming.'

'Don't you think the fans would…'

'I've got my own fans. I'm not interested in sharing yours. If there are any left. Those with any sense'll have wised up years ago. The rest are dead. Like Crown & Kingdom. It's all gone, Mickey,' he taunts.

We used to fence like this; once Philip had realised he was my equal he wasn't afraid to attack. We'd fight for the things we wanted for the band, for ourselves. We were, are, both shit at losing. Perfection's the goal. But we had a different vision of it. That's what held us together, 'til it drove us apart. It was worth the struggle. Still is.

I draw my sword. 'What's the matter, Philip, afraid you can't hit those high notes anymore?'

'Believe me, that won't be a problem. I haven't polluted my body with chemicals, addled my brain with drugs. What I'm afraid of is you making fools of the rest of us. I've got my own career now; I don't need you fucking it up. Again.'

I feel the sting of his words, hitting where I'm weakest. Philip's the only one of us with 'active' status. Pete and I were decommissioned years ago but Philip, he hadn't had enough, hadn't got what he wanted. What the fuck is he still trying to achieve? But it's not that he's more famous than me now that pisses me off.

'Can't you think of anyone other than Philip Hall, you selfish fucking bastard?'

'Who would you expect me to think of? You?'

'Pete, actually. It'd be a bloody shame if he lost out because you egoistically decided that there was a danger you'd look bad standing in my shadow. 'Cos let's be honest, that's what's really freaking you. That and worrying about whether or not you'll cut it in tight denim.' I've thrown it down to him. Philip will do whatever he wants. Like he always has. 'You owe it to Pete,' I press, 'he was the one caught in the crossfire when it blew up.'

'He wasn't the only one.'

Does he mean Ronsey? Nah, course he fucking doesn't.

'You? That's a real bad case of Lead Singer's Disease, you got there, Phil. Maybe you should get some therapy.'

'Maybe you should go to hell.'

'Been. Got a season ticket and frequent flier points.'

'There's no reason for me to agree to this,' he says. What he means is there's nothing in it for him. Twat.

'I dunno know 'bout that. There are the old reasons of course; money, glory, women.'

'I'm fine, thanks.'

'What about the good old days? Happy memories?'

That's got him, the tosser.

'I'm not fronting up for some poxy award and that's it.'

'Don't you fucking dare hang up on me. You'll be sorry if you do.'

'What the hell kind of threat is that?'

'My silence has been cheap, free in fact, for what? nearly three decades, but the price has suddenly gone up. Inflation's a bitch, Phil.'

'You gonna shop me for smoking weed thirty years ago?'

'Not that.'

'Christ, I've had enough of this.'

'I never said anything about it but that doesn't mean I've forgotten.'

'Forgotten what?'

'You being there.'

'Being where?'

'At mine. That Night.'

He knows. I know. We both fucking know so now what?

'I kept you out of it. You owe me for that. Do you really want it raking over?'

I expect the click-buzz of him hanging up. It doesn't come. I strain into the earpiece. Hear him holding his breath. Neither of us wants to get any closer to the truth tonight. For now it's enough that he knows I haven't forgotten. It's probably better if I keep one in the chamber for later. Yeah, that's what I'll do. Save what I saw, what I know he did, for when I really need it.

'I think it'd be good if we met up. Talked this through,' I suggest.

'Fine.' He's remembering too. But he thinks he's safe.

Knowledge is power.

'Fucking marvellous,' I say, returning to my sham joviality. 'Tomorrow. Café Minstrels. It's the Italian on Henley Street,. I'll book us a table for two o'clock.' I don't give either of us chance to back out. We're long overdue this reunion.

*

'The conquering hero returns.' Ron stretches across the counter, knocking over a box of guitar strings as he reaches for my hand.

'Hey, Ron, how's business?'

'Not bad, thanks, Mickey,' Ron says. 'So what's a star like you doing in this shithole?'

My cheeks are burning. 'Come off it, star's a bit much,' I protest.

'You've done alright though,' Ron presses.

'Yeah and I owe you for most of it. I haven't forgotten what you did to help me get started.'

'I know, lad. Those regular-as-clockwork payments told me so. What are you up to next? I heard a rumour Davy Wilson's pulled the plug on you lot.'

'Yeah, he wants to go solo.'

'A nice way to thank you lads for propping him up long enough to make his name,' Ron snaps.

'It's a fickle business,' I remind him. 'Anyway, it's not just Davy with the name since we started sharing lead guitar duties.' Sharing? Well, 70-30 to him but I'm counting it. 'I've a few ideas about my next move. Actually, that's why I'm here.'

'Not gonna check the notice board again, are you?' Ron laughs.

'No. I've come for that.' I point to the cherry sunburst Les

Paul. I'm ready for real dragon slaying now.

Ron grins. 'Always thought you'd be back for it. You want to try it first?'

I don't need to but it'd be nice for Ron to be the first to hear me play it, here in his little shop up a dead end in a dying town.

'Yeah, let's have a whack at it.'

He sets up an amp and checks the tuning before handing me the Gibson. The maple neck feels silky in my palm. I run my hand over the swollen curves of the body. It's even more perfect to hold than to behold. I slip a plectrum from my pocket and strike each string in turn, letting them ring, savouring this first taste. The notes are pure. They perfume the air. I glance at Ron; he nods. I play the opening riff of the song that's been our encore every night for more than two years. As I play it morphs, the picture changing before my ears. I hear what I play but don't know how I'm playing it. It's magic. The notes soar before plummeting down to swoop back up, eagle-like, avoiding fatal impact at the last second. I didn't make this guitar but I am the one bringing it to life.

'A match made in musical heaven,' Ron says as I let the last note float away.

I pay and Ron packs it into the case for me.

'Where to now, lad?'

'I've got an audition later, outfit called the Three Bob Band. Hope that's not what they're paying.' Ron chuckles as he slips the bill for the Les Paul inside the case. 'But first, I'd better go home.'

The shop bell tinkles behind me. Misty drizzle swirls in the air, seeping into my clothes and hair. I open the boot of the brand new Triumph TR4, bought with earnings from our knackering, non-stop gigging, and load the Les Paul, wedging it amongst the bags and cases stashed there. Two-and-a-half years on the road and I've stockpiled more crap than is good for me. The plan is to dump the unnecessary baggage at home, crash there 'til things are fixed up then get the hell out.

I thought about not going back at all. I could just keep sending her money and absolve myself of responsibility. But she is my mother. Maybe it'll be better now I'm older. But there's something about the place you grew up that sucks you back. No matter how much it might have fucked with you. It's a scab to be picked at. Plus, I do need somewhere to doss; the car and the Les Paul have cleaned me out. Not that there was that much to clean out. We've been ripped off for a lot of gigs. Fucked if I'll let that happen again.

I park opposite the house. It looks unchanged. The front gate squeaks a familiar greeting. It's early afternoon so I reckon she'll be in. Alone, hopefully. I twist the tarnished brass handle but it's locked. I don't have a key. Threw it at her the night I left, along with some foul, truthful insults. I'm reduced to ringing the bell at my own front door.

It buzzes apathetically and I listen through rotting wood and cracked glass. Hear the clicking of my mother's footsteps on the tiled hall floor. She opens the door. Her blouse is undone one button too low. Cheap scent clouds about her. She's expecting someone. Not me. I don't know what to do. She's my mother. I should feel something. Something that doesn't churn my guts.

She recovers first. 'Mickey, what are you doing here?'

'I need a place to stay.'

'I'm expecting someone. A friend.' Her attempt to maintain the pretence is feeble and amusing. 'Now's not a good time.' She reaches inside her blouse and pulls out a pound note, 'Why don't you go down the road and get yourself a...' It used to be sherbet lemons from the corner shop. 'Drink and come back later. When my friend's gone. About four-ish.' She pushes the money on me, smiles falsely, waits for me to go. As I walk down the drive, Mrs Henderson gawps from her garden.

'Hello Michael,' she calls. 'Have you come home at last?'

'Piss off and mind your own bloody business.'

I slam the car door and tear away from the pavement, the pound note screwed up in my hand. Round the corner I throw it on the passenger seat, drive to the nearest pub and sit smoking through a pack and sipping one pint, not thinking about my mother and her 'friend'.

At four I try again to go home. This time she's ready for me, greeting me at the door, the buttons on her blouse all fastened. She kisses my cheek. She reeks of aftershave and shagging.

'I'll put the kettle on, shall I?'

'Whatever.'

In the kitchen I sit at the table. The place is cleaner than I remember. There's a new electric toaster on the counter, bright-patterned curtains, a wall clock shaped like a teapot.

'Looks different in here.'

'Thanks to Mrs McNamara.'

'Who?'

'My cleaner,' she says, 'a real find.'

That's not what my money's for but I can't be arsed debating it with her.

'Look at you, all grown up. Is that your car?' She sits opposite me and pushes a china cup and saucer over.

'Yeah.'

'You're doing O.K., then?'

'So far.'

'How long are you going to be home for?'

Let's rattle her cage. 'Dunno. The band's split up. Not sure what I'm gonna do. Might be a while 'til I sort things out. That's O.K., isn't it?'

'Of course.' She pats my hand. Her nails are long, red and false.

'I'll bring my stuff in, then.' I go out, start unloading the car, hiding my smirk when I see her peering through the front window at my bags and cases. I leave only the Les Paul and my amp in the boot.

I go to my room. Sit on the bed. It's smaller than I remember. The mattress groans under the weight of my adult self. I can't sleep on it. From my rucksack I pull the sleeping bag, bought for nights kipping in the car, and chuck it on the floor. I'll camp. I don't bother unpacking.

Back downstairs I head for the front door. She appears in the hall.

'Have you left something in the car?'

'I'm going out.'

'When will you be back?'

'Later.'

The audition's in a church hall.

'You Mickey?'

'Yeah.'

'Richard,' says the lad who greets me on the step. 'Davy Wilson says you're pretty hot. Shit, I hope that's true.'

'You'll find out in a minute. Where can I set up?'

'Over there. Neil should be here soon.'

'There's just the two of you?'

'Yeah, I'm on bass and lead vocals; Neil drums. Our guitarist dropped us in it last week and we've been looking for someone pretty frantically,' Richard explains. His thick, curly hair is frizzed out all over his head. His paisley shirt is rumpled. His eyes are cloaked in dark shadows. He's not lying about the guitarist.

'He get a better offer?'

'One he couldn't refuse. From Her Majesty,' Richard frowns. 'I said he was asking for trouble messing with a married chick but he wouldn't have it. Her old man caught them, there was a hell of a fight and he gets brought up for violent assault.' He shakes his head. 'Waste of a decent guitarist. Hope you've got more sense.'

'Anything longer than one night's a pain in the arse if you're asking me.'

Richard chuckles. 'Sounds like a motto.' He plugs in his bass.

I set up my amp. Neil arrives and they throw the drum kit together. I lift the lid on my guitar case and gaze in at the Les Paul. The golden glaze on the body gleams in the hall's dim light. Richard creeps up behind me.

'Is that a real Gibson?'

'Yep.'

'How long you had that?'

''Bout three hours. Let's find out if I can play it, eh?' I put it around my neck like a chain of office.

Neil scrambles in amongst the drums. Richard gets his bass.

'What d'ya wanna do?' he asks me.

'How about 'Let it Rock'?'

'You mean that Chuck Berry one?'

I nod.

'It's not what we usually do but reckon I can probably get it going.'

Neil counts us in and we're off. But slowly. They are leaderless, in disarray, the last two chess pieces on the board when the game's already lost. They play for safety, pulling each other up with an easy beat and a groove that flat-lines in the ear. I count ahead, planning my moves. We play out the song like that. Richard and Neil look at me expectantly.

'Can we try it a bit differently?' I suggest.

'What you got in mind?' Richard asks.

'Maybe up the tempo. What d'ya think, Neil, do it half as fast again and maybe with a fill between each repeat?'

'Like this?' He pounds through the same rhythm but this time it races somewhere.

'Perfect. And Richard, could you do a similar fill on the bass to match that?'

'Yeah, I'll work in twos and use the octave note.' He tries it out as he talks.

'Shall we have another go? I might do a little bit of a lead thing this time, too, so keep on the progression 'til I come back in.'

We go again but this time I make an effort to drive the thing, cranking the tempo up and thumping it out; they dog-trot along side me. Richard loses the lyrics in trying to keep pace and we have to regroup.

'Sorry, man, it's just 'cos I'm not that familiar with it,' he excuses.

'You'll get it,' I say. 'Again.'

This time we make it through to the lead break and I let the Les Paul tow me above everything. What I'm doing's too much for the song but I need them to see what I'm capable of. I've seen what they can do; it's piss weak but that's what I'm after. So I have to convince them they want me.

I fall back to the rhythm. Richard comes in with the final chorus repeat x2 then end.

'That was some pretty wild playing, man.'

'Blame the new axe. It carried me away.' I grin at them.

'No, I mean, wow, it was great, really great,' Richard says, 'Neil?'

'Yup.'

'Does that mean I get the gig?'

'Reckon so,' Richard says.

'Great, what else can we do? I was thinking about 'Summertime Blues'. There are a few others I'd like to try that I've never done before, too.'

'Sounds good,' Richard says.

Yeah, it does, 'cos it sounds the way I want it too.

The Hermit

Café Minstrels: I wouldn't normally eat here but I want to see if Philip'll remember. The waiter parks me at a corner table, out of the way. My palms are damp. I rub them on the thick white table cloth, trying to wipe away sweat that keeps oozing to the surface. A feverish chill coils inside my guts. Every few minutes it shivers, sending a wave of nausea through me. It's the hangover, that's all. Last night alcohol-related moderation was out the bloody window, a necessary precursor to calling Philip but I'm paying for it now. I expect to pay more later.

I avoided Meg's earful this morning by pretending to be asleep. Childish but effective. She stood over me, sighing loudly. She wouldn't wake me but if I happened to wake as she was standing there, well, fine. She knew I was faking but she'd never say so. After a two minute stand-off she sacked it and left. So there's that to face later. Sometimes I think she's built a museum around me, given herself the ball-aching job of curator, trying her damnedest to preserve me. As much as I love her I can't help her do it. If you're the exhibit you can't also be the custodian.

There's Keira too. I cringe as I remember yelling at her. She was trying to help. They reckon women pick husbands that remind them of their fathers. So men must pick secretaries that remind them of their wives.

The waiter comes over again. He's about twenty and clueless so I'm not in danger of being recognised. He tops up my water from a jug. Probably tap water and I'm paying a quid a glass for it. He offers to tell me the specials again and asks if I'd like to order yet. I tell him, again, that I'm waiting for someone. He doesn't understand why that stops me from ordering. He goes away, narked. I sip my water. The python in my stomach tightens its grip on my innards. I look for a clock but there isn't one. I think about calling the waiter back to ask the time but decide not to give him the satisfaction of knowing that I'm getting impatient too. I want this to be over but it hasn't even started yet. The seconds before going into battle are the undoing of a man. Hope I don't piss myself.

The door opens. Philip steps into the restaurant, a mystical being from another planet climbing through an astral portal. He stands in a premeditated pose, framed by the oblong of light, to scan the room. He's tall, but not as thin as he used to be. He's not young anymore but all he's lost is self-doubt. It's a bloody impressive entrance. He was always good at that. But, like me, he's only an imitation of himself. His eyes fix on me. He closes down the space between us. I brace for impact.

As he nears me I study his face. The outline is as I remember it but the details are shabby and worn. Time's cruel enough to leave a trace of what used to be to remind you of what it's stolen from you. I want this to be civilised so stand to greet him. We're in public, and, ignorant twenty-something waiters aside, it wouldn't take long for the papers to get hold of it. **Former Crown & Kingdom rockers in lunchtime punch-up.** Not what I fucking need right now.

'Philip.'

'Mickey.'

He takes my outstretched hand but drops it quickly. We sit. The waiter buzzes over, presents Philip with a menu and recites the specials. I could have saved him the trouble. We order. I ask for wine. With a smirk of superiority Philip plumps for mineral water. I don't care. I need the hair of the dog, a great shaggy old English sheepdog.

Philip's eyes wander round again.

'Feels like I've been here before but I can't remember…'

'It was the twenty-eighth of August, 1969. We opened with 'Long Tall Sally' and finished with 'Johnny B. Goode'.'

He stares at me, trying to pull that moment to the surface. Shakes his head.

'Living in the past is pointless.'

'It's better than pretending it never happened,' I reply. Because it did happen, right here.

*

Across the stage from me Philip is bathed in the unearthly aura of the spotlight. He stretches out his arms to embrace the audience: the birth of a god. The young girls who've been standing at the front since Eric announced us surge forward and hold their hands up to Philip, begging for his blessing. His final note dies. Determined not to give him the last word I bang down on the chord once more, before muting it with my palm. The End. In that moment of silence Philip, the victorious knight, bows low.

He might have struck the killer blow with his high wailing voice but I led the army into battle. I glance to Pete and Ronsey. They're grinning. We all feel it: we won. Together we stand; divided we fail. That's the way it is now. That's what this moment means.

I step forward, wave at Pete, getting him to join me. We stand beside Philip, looking at the audience. I feel the rush of heat that blasts from them. Their smell is salty sweat and sweet perfume. Philip grabs my wrist on one side and Pete's on the other, dragging us down into another triumphant bow. Determined not to miss out on the glory, Ronsey clambers onto his drum stool and, precariously balanced, whacks his sticks together high overhead. I could stand here all night.

The stage lights flick off, throwing us into blackness; the house lights come up and tinned juke-box music blasts us. I pull away from Philip and set about unplugging myself.

Ronsey gets down from his wobbly roost and struts over.

'Let's get a drink. I'm as dry as a fish in the desert.'

'You go ahead. I'm gonna sort this lot out.'

'Leave it,' he says, 'we deserve a drink.'

'In a minute.' I coil a lead.

He shrugs. Heads to the bar with Philip. Pete hesitates. Abandons his bass on stage and goes to join them. Lenny appears and begins dismantling the drum kit. He'd be at the bar too 'cept he's being paid to work.

I'm traipsing back for my amp when she waylays me. The girl in black from the dance floor.

'Hello.'

Do I know her? Maybe I screwed her and can't remember. It's like she knows me. Her eyes are brilliant green. No. I'd remember her, I'm sure.

'I'm Anna.' She holds out her hand.

'Mickey.'

'I thought you were good.'

'Not too shabby. We haven't been playing together long.'

'It doesn't show.'

Now it's my turn again.

'You want a drink?'

'O.K. But not here. I don't like this place.'

'What're you doing here then?'

'I was meeting someone but I guess he had better things to do.' Her lightly musical voice says she's not bothered about being stood up.

'Alright. Gimme a minute.'

I wander to Lenny. Tell him the score. He checks Anna out. Nods.

When I go back to her, she's standing like she did earlier, in a circle of space. Around her people are dancing, bumping into each other, pushing and shoving. She keeps still, separate from them, hands hanging at her sides, looking around as if she's gazing at a proper curiosity. She's untouchable.

'Hey.'

It's as if I've woken her from a dream. She smiles.

'Where're we going? It's pretty late, I'm not sure there'll be many places open.'

'It's cool. I know somewhere that's always open. It's not far from here.'

She leads.

The street's quite, deserted. I'm thrown out of sync after the inside din. My ears search for a sound to follow. Our footsteps echo, keeping a steady rhythm. I listen to her walk, purposeful but not quick. There's no rush. We walk for twenty minutes. Narrow, gloomy, three storey terraces loom over us but Anna's slow, ambling gait makes it seem like we're strolling in a sunny meadow on a summer's day. Perhaps in her mind we are. She doesn't speak. Thank fuck for that. I hate small talk, especially with birds; it's full of mantraps. But it's weird. I should say something. One of us should. I gulp cold night. No words come.

'Here.'

She turns into a side street, stops at a brown door. Knocks. The door opens a crack. I peer through. The dry, fragrant aroma of incense escapes through the chink. A face appears in the gap. The chain has been left on. It cuts across the face, below the nose, a metal moustache.

'Yeah?'

'It's Anna. Hurry up, let us in. It's cold out here.'

'Anna who?'

He's only a foot from her. Why doesn't he recognise her?

'Ade, you freak, stop pissing about, it's me,' she says with a dancing laugh.

The door closes. I hear the chain being slid off. The door reopens. Anna steps through. I follow.

We're in a narrow passageway. There's not enough room for the sentry to pass without bumping into us. He puts his hand on my shoulder, turns to Anna.

'Who's this?'

'Mickey,' she says, 'new friend.' Then to me, 'Say something to Ade, Mickey.'

I glance at her. She nods.

'Hi, Ade.'

He turns to the sound of my voice. His chin and cheeks are unshaven. His dark hair is matted, stuck in clumps over his ears and across his forehead. His nose has been broken, more than once. His eyelids are sealed shut by a long thin scar that runs from high up on his forehead, across both eyes and ends on the opposite cheek. It's nothing more than a faint white line of raised skin but the result is a perfect seam searing shut his eyes. He's not much older than me, I think. Christ, to be blind so young…

'Mickey.' He's hooking my name to my voice for future reference. 'Alright, Anna.'

'Thanks, Ade.' She tugs on my sleeve, dragging me along the passageway.

We go through another door and down steep concrete stairs.

'What is this place? Who's he?'

'Don't mind Ade, he's cool,' she says. 'This place is his. Down here he makes the rules and keeps the profits.'

'Profits?'

'Welcome to The Opium Den. Don't worry, Ade likes to move with the times; you can get any poison you want here.' She smiles. 'Some of them are even legal.'

She pushes on another door. It folds back, revealing a long thin basement room. Pungent fumes sting my eyes and burn my throat. At one end there's a bar, beer pumps lined up along the top and a row of spirit bottles hanging upside down on the wall behind. Some assorted armchairs and half a dozen tables furnish the room. But most of the patrons are slumped on cushions and pillows strewn over the stone floor. The air is heavy, hot and arid; the lighting suitably dim with a hellish red glow. It's a nightmare world. I can't wait to get high so I can enjoy it.

'Let's get a drink,' Anna says.

We step over the bodies of a young couple, ravelled up together on the floor, their legs twisted into a Gordian knot. Anna orders and pays at the bar. We find a table and sit. She scrutinises me. By what I do next she'll make her mind up about me.

'I've been to some crazy parties but I've never seen anything like this.'

'Cool, isn't it?' she says.

In the red light of the room her green eyes gleam as though there's a light behind them.

'You come here a lot?'

'It's the only place I know where you can be anything you want.'

'You should be whatever you want all the time.'

'The problem is I'm never what other people think I should be. Every now and then I need to come somewhere they can't get at me. Often I don't even bother getting high. Just being here does it.'

I don't get what she's telling me. Or why she's telling me it.

'You're lucky,' she continues. 'If you don't know what I'm talking about it means that you don't let them get to you. There is a problem with that too, though.'

'Go on?'

'No island is an island.'

'What?'

'You've heard that saying, haven't you? No man is an island. I always thought it was a fucking stupid phrase. It makes more sense if you say no island is an island.'

'You've lost me, darlin'.'

'If you think about islands not being islands then you get what it means: nothing exists in isolation. An island is only an island because it's surrounded by sea, therefore, it's not isolated; it's got the ocean surrounding it. Even in deep space, there's not nothing because even nothing is something. All I mean is that you can't live cut off from every other human being anymore than an island can exist without the sea on its beaches.'

I laugh.

'What?'

'You. Jesus. You don't say anything the whole way here and now you're trying to blow my mind with philosophy.'

'Never mind philosophy, I know something more effective.' She holds her hand out, palm up, uncurls her fingers. Two round white tablets lie nestled against soft pink skin.

'You don't have to,' she says and, of course, I do.

I take one of the pills. Wash it down with a mouthful of vodka and coke. I don't see if she takes the other.

I've found myself. Thank fuck for that. Been looking for ages. Dunno where I've been 'til now. I'm not where I thought I'd be, though. Fuck knows where I am.

It's hot. Bloody roasting. Sun hung in empty blueness. Good thing I brought a hat. Was I wearing a hat before? I put my hand up. A grubby white Stetson comes away in it. It's not my hat. I used to know who it belonged to. That lad, what was his name? Him with the purple and yellow shirt. He'd lost his watch. Must've lost this too. Oh well, that's his tough shit. I put it back on.

Stretched out in front of me is a long, wide street. The land is so flat and the street so long I can trace the line of buildings as they narrow, merge and disappear over the horizon. I'm at the mouth of the street. Behind me is nothing. No, that's not true. There's not nothing. Nothing is something. Who told me that? Flat brown desert, never-ending, washes away from me. Christ, I don't like this. I'm an upright target on a flat plain. Too visible. I walk towards the shelter of the street.

A loud bang.

I freeze. The street is empty. I strain my ears. Get the faint whispering of wind. My mouth is dry. I need a fucking drink. Along the street is a hand pump. Dunno how I know that's what it is. Never seen one before, have I? I walk across to it. Pump the handle. Clear water gushes from the tap. I put my other hand under it, catch and scoop. Water runs through my fingers. I try again and again. Each time when my lips kiss my palm it's empty.

Another bang.

I whirl around. See him. A man in the middle of the street, a brown door behind him, swinging in the wind. He lifts an arm, points at me. I move forwards. So does he. We bear down on each other, two forces converging on a single baring. He's wearing a cowboy hat too. But his is dusty black. It throws his face into shadow.

We're close now. He stops. I stop. The wind whispers to me again, words I pull easily to me.

'Ready thyself for any fight.'

I reach for my gun. Yank it from the holster. Raise it. Sight along the barrel. Fire. He's still drawing his. I shoot first. I shoot last. He falls backwards into the road. Lies there, making a sand-angel. What a shot! I win. You die.

I kick off his hat. The man is Philip. His smile's crooked. I kneel down. Look closer. The smile contorts into a snarl. The features rearrange themselves. What the fuck...? The face is mine now. I catch my reflection in the saloon's grimy window. It's Philip looking back at me from the glass.

He's me. I'm him.

I return to earth. We're sat in two of the arm chairs. Anna smiles.

'Good trip?'.

I picture Philip's face, shifting into mine.

'Let's go.' I stumble to my feet.

We walk to hers in silence. Against the night blackness I see Philip's face contorted in pain. Feel his agony in my body. It fills me 'til it feels like I'm going to explode. This is her fault.

In the dark hallway of her digs I grab Anna, press her into the wallpaper. She doesn't struggle. Maybe she's still high. But I need a fight: a conquest. I crush against her. She trembles, her heart pattering like a sparrow's. I trail a finger over her cheek. She squirms. I cover her mouth with mine, sucking air from her lungs. She struggles harder. I stare into her wide eyes. I want her to be afraid. Like I am. I close my hand around her throat. She bleats. With my other hand I undo her trousers. She claws at my fingers. I squeeze her throat. She scratches at my other hand, trying to bend my fingers away from her neck but I press in close.

I could kill her so fucking easily.

Shit.

I let go.

I don't breathe, don't think, don't know what to do now. Anna throws back her head and laughs victoriously.

'See, I'm not what you think I am.'

She takes my hand and reels me up the stairs.

Fortune

I gulp down overpriced Chianti. Philip stares. I carefully pour another glass, straining to keep my hand steady.

'Want one?'

Philip shakes his head.

'You haven't changed a bit, have you, Mickey?'

'Dunno 'bout that.'

The food arrives. Philip scrapes the skin from his grilled fish, eats his steamed veggies without butter. I take a large bite of my meat feast pizza, lick grease from my lips and forbid myself to think about Dr Sangha's advice.

'So have you given some thought to this award business?' I ask.

There's a flicker in Philip's eyes. I recognise it as pain and wonder what hells he's been through. Is still going through? I recall the rocky, terrifying landscape I wound up in after Ronsey's death, due mostly to the heroin I was flooding my veins with then. I barely got through it wasted, can't imagine what it would've been like sober and the relentless fear of it is still there, lurking. Fear that I wouldn't come back. Fear I would. Christ, I hated myself. Hated Philip. It hurt like fuck. Hurts like fuck.

'You really want to do this?'

'I think we should, while we've got the chance. Playing together one last time, it could be a good thing.'

'I don't see how.'

'I've got my reasons. You wanna hear them?'

Philip doesn't decline so I outline my plan to offer the vacant drum stool to Ronsey's son. At the mention of John's name Philip drops his gaze. But I don't surrender. Maybe Philip's right; I haven't changed. Am still that selfish bastard who hurt people to get what he wanted.

'Why?'

'He's trying to make it as a drummer. This'd give him a leg up.'

'What makes you think he'll want to do it?'

'He might not, but I want to offer him it. We owe him first refusal, at least.' Considering it's our fault his dad's dead.

'And?'

'What?'

'You said 'reasons'. I'm here; I might as well have it all.' Philip's face tightens. What I said to him on the phone about That Night, it's been gnawing at him. I decide to spare him. And myself. Fucking coward. Let's try something easier first.

'This could be your last chance.'

'For what?'

'You forget how well we know each other. C'mon, you've slogged your guts out for the last what, ten? fifteen years? with this solo stuff but it's not lived up to your expectations, has it?'

'What makes you say that?'

'If it had, you wouldn't be doing a new album every other year and fifty shows up and down the country every six months. Come back now, satisfy yourself with a memory.'

'You're wrong.' He raises his voice. The couple on the next table glance over. 'I'm still doing it because, unlike you, I can. There are people out there who want me to do it.'

I tack into the wind. 'What's the biggest gig you've played in, oh, I dunno, the last five years?'

Philip's folds his arms and pulls a face like a baby refusing to take nasty medicine. Yeah, there it is: he's kept going because he thinks there's a bigger, better prize to be had. Better than what he got from Crown & Kingdom. He hasn't found it yet, though, and he knows it. Knows I know it.

'Fine, but Mickey...'

'What?'

'What you said on the phone, about me being there when John...'

'I couldn't think of what to say to get you here but I shouldn't have mentioned it. Forget it.'

'You said I owed you.'

'Do the ceremony and we'll call it even.'

He frowns, twirls his glass then taps his fork on the edge of his plate. 'Fine. But after this that's it, O.K.? We're agreed there's nothing left between us.'

'What the fuck happened to us, Philip? Didn't we use to be mates?'

*

I stand on the stage, gazing around the Royal Albert Hall, a venue fit for kings: for us.

It's like being inside a giant raspberry blancmange, the kind made in a fancy mould, majestically domed, served at swanky banquets. Crimson velvet seats and scarlet-curtained boxes are swirled together with strawberry jam carpets, the whole thing decorated in gold piping cornices. Maybe it's more like a cake. Whatever, it's rich. Craning my neck, stretching back, I view the scooped-out ceiling, gilled like the underside of a mushroom, festooned with floating silver-cream discs that hover, seedpods ready to burst and scatter their juicy load over us. They're designed to improve the acoustics, I'm told. Yeah, man. I scan each level, from the arced and pillared top layer that crowns the gods, over the dress circle and luxury boxes down to the rows of seats set out on the oval floor. The place reminds me of some Roman amphitheatre. Fuck, hope we're not throwing ourselves to the lions.

I feel arms around my neck, a sudden weight on my back as

Anna pounces from behind, her scent giving her away before she speaks.

'Hey,' she whispers in my ear, 'you O.K.?'

I shrug her off, swing her round in front of me. 'Yeah, darlin', now you're here.' I slip my arms around her. 'Thought you weren't coming 'til later.'

'Nipped out of work for a bit,' she says, 'to make sure things are cool here.'

'That mean you're not staying?' I pout.

'I'll be back later, for the gig,' she promises with a smile.

I grin, am about to drop my mouth onto hers when a movement in the wings distracts me.

I glance up, see Philip swaggering towards us. Anna cranes her neck to look. I slacken my hold on her as she turns back to me, grabs the front of my shirt in both hands and crushes us together, forcing her mouth over mine. I lose myself in her touch.

Philip coughs fakely. I pull away from Anna, catch him smirking at us. She stays at my side, one hand wedged deep in the back pocket of my jeans. Philip flicks his eyes over her, thinking something for a second then throwing the thought away as a fresh one overtakes him and he whirls round, challenging the empty theatre.

'Bleeding grand, ain't it?' he says.

'This isn't some shitty little blues club,' I admit.

'I know. Hell, I can't believe it though. How'd we get here so fast?'

'Hard fucking work,' I point out, recalling weeks and months of flagellation, stumbling from poxy student bars, back-of-beyond nightclubs and rain-drowned festivals where we made do with daylight sets, the after-dark slots reserved for the tried and tested. None of who played as hot as us. And, Christ knows how, between the treadmill hours of travelling, setting up, playing, packing up and travelling on we got the first album down and watched 'Crown & Kingdom vol. 1' rampage up the charts, annoying the fuck out of too many snooty-nosed music journos who thought we'd never be as much as the Three Bob Band, who were average on a good day, present company excepted. Naturally.

Anna shakes her head against my chest. I look down at her.

'Fate,' she says.

Philip snorts. 'You what?'

'Fate,' she repeats, the word intoned precisely. 'Life is what it's meant to be,' she adds.

Philip shrugs at me. I raise my eyebrows in reply 'cos whatever got us here I don't really fucking care. It only matters that we are here. Hot on the coattails of the Zep boys. We sold out faster, though, sending them scurrying back to their mammies.

Then Philip springs forwards, arms outstretched to embrace an invisible audience that, in a couple of hours, will be plenty visible, all three fucking thousand of them.

'Good evening, London,' he screams to no one. 'Are you ready to rock?'

Equipment set up, checked and rechecked, we loll backstage on directors chairs and a plush leather settee. Lenny, in his new black T-shirt sporting the words 'road crew' in white letters, leans against a wall, dragging on a cigarette. His recently hired helpers, two young lads dredged from the dole queue to limply manhandle our expanding rig, huddle together, sickly with silent awe, while we swig the champagne Don bought to mark the night when we'll take our thrones at the court of British rock. It's taking the edge off the nervous boredom that's rattling us. Wish Anna hadn't gone back to work. Wish she was here now. Wish she'd hurry up and bloody get here.

Ronsey scans the curved corridor that mirrors the Hall's oval shape.

'What's up with this fucking pink?' he asks, flapping a hand at the paintwork which is vivid fuschia.

I shake off wanting Anna to answer him. 'It's cool.'

'Aye, how'd ya figure that?' he barks.

'It's the same colour as the cover of Cream's *Disraeli Gears* LP.'

Pete straightens up, staring at the walls. 'Knew it reminded me of something but I couldn't place it.'

'It's too fucking girlie,' Ronsey moans.

'So we're not having it on 'Crown & Kingdom vol. 2'?' I tease.

'Are we fuck.'

Don refills our glasses. He grins at me. We know what tonight means: respect, recognition and royalties.

'Relax, lads,' he advises. 'Enjoy the moment, the first of many more.' He raises his own glass and toasts us with a wink.

Pete gulps his drink. 'How long 'til we're on?'

I glance at my watch; Don answers.

'There's plenty of time. Have another, Pete.' He goes to top up Pete's glass but Pete covers it with a trembling palm.

Philip stretches on the sofa, yawning like a Roman emperor.

'Where'd Anna flit off to, Mickey?'

'Work. She's coming back later.'

'You wanna watch it with her,' he warns, 'or she'll have you wanting to marry her.'

'Nah, man,' I laugh, 'not Anna's style. Or mine.'

'Nothing wrong with being married,' Ronsey says gruffly, 'is there, Pete?'

Pete jumps at the sound of his name. 'What?'

'I said... shit, never mind,' Ronsey mutters, slumping in his seat.

Philip throws a mouthful of champagne down his throat, tipping his head back so his wild blonde mane spills over the arm of the sofa. 'I mean it, Mickey, she's hooked you.'

'Bollocks,' I say, grinning.

Philip just stares at me. He doesn't believe me. Do I believe myself? Fuck it, this is getting too serious.

'Let's play a game.' I jump up. 'Hide and seek. Pete, you're it. C'mon, girls.' I slap Ronsey's shoulder, haul Philip up by his tie-dyed t-shirt and crook a finger at Lenny. 'Count to twenty. Nah, make it fifty,' I tell Pete before bolting down the right hand curve of the corridor, disappearing into the blackness.

Behind me Philip's boots rap on the parquet flooring, echoed by the slapping of Ronsey's and Lenny's in-sync tennis shoes. The corridor is lined with doors. I bypass the first two and throw open the third to reveal a storage room, boxes banked high. I stumble in. Philip jams up in the doorway. I turn and, grinning, shove him out.

'Find your own hidey-hole, you cheeky prick.' I taunt, slamming the door on him. He hurtles away down the dim twisted passageway, throaty laughter bouncing off the walls after him.

I scout the room, wriggle in round the packing crates and hunker down to hide. A minute later Pete is opening doors further up. He reaches mine. A shaft of light stabs the junk room. His shadow cuts it up the middle. His footsteps creep towards me. I hold my breath: wait, wait… spring up.

'Boo!'

'Jesus.' Pete staggers backwards, tangling his ankles in a stepladder and falling on his arse. 'You nearly gave me a heart attack,' he moans, clutching his chest.

'You hide; I'll be it,' I gasp through snorts of laughter, clambering over him and setting off in search of the others.

Twenty minutes later, sweaty and giggling, we collapse back into our chairs, glasses recharged ready, and quench childish thirsts with adult pop.

'Ready to have some real fun now?' Don asks.

'Been ready for this my whole fucking life.'

We take the stage at nine p.m. Houselights down, the hall's fire-red interior is darkened to the colour of venous blood. The air pulsates with anticipation as we slide into our appointed places, take up our instruments and brace for the spotlight. A five second pause then the white beam splits the hall, carving up the blackness. Torn wide open, the hall throbs with sublime, ecstatic pain.

'Good evening, London, let's rock and roll,' Philip yells, snatching the mic stand and twisting it on its side, a stiff dancing partner.

Notes fly off my guitar, strings thrumming with raw energy that courses through my fingers, up my arms and across my shoulders to burst behind my eardrums. I look at Pete. He plucks bass notes sweeter than ripe cherries, his eyes closed, his hand guided from within by the music. Ronsey thunders behind us, hurling beats, a giant tossing megalithic stones at the audience, crushing them like Gulliver's puny Lilliputians. Philip wails words with passion; a diatribe, a cacophony: a command. We etch our music into their souls, lines that score and scar, hurt and heal. We are not the Christians in the Coliseum; we are the lions. I stamp on the overdrive pedal; my guitar roars and rages. Power and sweat stream off me, flung in scalding droplets from my face as I pogo-hop along the length of the stage, matching Philip's two-step with the mic, swinging my guitar overhead, raking the strings in glorious disharmony, the crowd cowering from and rushing towards me all at once. I don't want to ever stop.

We play in a frenzy, time sucked into a black hole of sound, consciousness drowned by audio pleasure. The songs attack, swooping over the crowd, dive-bombing like spitfires, dropping atomic rhythm explosions; dum-dummer-dum-do-de-de-dum-dummer-do. Each note is a friendly bullet finding its mark in the throng that is so close I can pick out individual targets: a pretty blonde on the front row, her black roots showing under the sweeping spotlight; a speccy, beardy lad further back punching his fist in time with the music; a couple with matching bandanas and beads, pawing each other in a box stage right; three kids with C&K T-shirts who wave a bed sheet banner from the gods. We hit them, slay them, gratify them, give them life's mojo. Us, we do it. Me, my band: I create a new world with every strum, greening the grass with my vibrato, bluing the sky with my tremolo, reddening the poppies with my hammer-on/pull-off and yellowing the sun as I slide from C to D to C.

I step back. Close my eyes. Drag desert-scorching air into my lungs and plunge into the inferno, skipping among the flames, fanning them with fresh notes, stoking the blaze with another tune. We finished the set-list ages ago; now we're jamming through every-fucking-thing we can remember; songs heard way back, half-forgotten, hauled to the surface, tangled in weeds. We clean them up and set them aside, gleaming like unburied treasure; Long Tall Sally, Whole Lotta Shakin' Going On, Johnny B. Goode, Jailhouse Rock, Somethin' Else, Roll Over Beethoven, That's All Right Mama, Great Balls of Fire… the medley stretches, rolling off into infinity, chased hard by the audience who scream in orgasmic pitch.

The beat switches from four-four to sixteenth notes. I throw Ronsey a look. He's chucked his sticks aside, is pounding the drums with his palms, a demented witchdoctor calling down demons. He nods at me and leaves off the beat. Philip's throaty cry peels off, rising to the quivering-jelly roof, shaking the hovering flying saucers. Pete keeps a steady root note rolling. I jump into the void with a rapid-fire solo, notes ripped from E minor pentatonic, a flurry, feathers bleeding into air as an albatross is shot down. Ronsey replies with another slam-slamming of skin on skins. It's move and counter-fucking-move. The crowd trembles, willing both of us to win. I toss them an over-the-shoulder glance and see hundreds of pairs of wide bright eyes staring back, unblinking, afraid of missing the tiniest flutter of my fingers. I stride across to Ronsey. He's grinning madly. Yeah, me too.

'C'mon, you bastard, keep up,' I crow, flicking notes at him.

He pounds back and for five minutes the song disappears as we dual with guitar and drums, egged on by our own insanity, the crowd's insanity, every insanity in this insane fucking world. As I peel back another score of shimmering sounds, I catch Ronsey signalling to someone in the wings. Lenny rushes on with fresh sticks. Behind him, a darker shade of grey in the shadows, I see Anna watching it all. She waves to me. I nod back, fighting to keep the stream of notes flowing fast. Lenny whips past me, skidding over to Ronse.

'You win, Mickey,' Ronsey bellows, winking at me, adding, 'this time,' as he snatches the sticks and falls back to the original beat.

I drop into the chord progression. Philip, caught out by the sudden collapse of our musical boxing match, darts for the mic and gabbles out, 'Rock, rock 'til broad daylight.'

We finish 'Rock Around the Clock' with a clatter, the last few bars buried under applause so loud the ground shakes, the world thrown off its orbit. The lights snap out but the raging torrent of clapping, whistling and cheering keeps the room bright, our glory glowing. I stagger under the weight of it, towards Philip, and throw my arms around him, my guitar wedged between us, crushing my bollocks.

'Jesus, man, look what we've done,' he says as we slap each other on the back.

Pete comes over. Ronsey climbs free of the drum kit and we cling to each other, shaking, sweating and gasping, blood pounding in our ears, our hearts dancing.

'This is it,' I say. 'We've fucking done it.'

The house lights come half-way up. The Albert Hall's regal

interior is restored to oxygenated red. Fists thump the air, feet hammer the floor. The crowd start a chant. It builds from the front row, rippling backwards then rushing forwards, breaching the fourth wall. We take our bows, gorging on the swell of euphoria and walking off to their new mantra: all hail the kings.

Lust

'How was lunch with Philip?' Keira asks as I stroll into the office.

'Fine. You got my message, then?'

'Yes, I was at the post office when you called.'

'Sorry I missed you.' I try for a light tone. Keira's the same as she was yesterday, before I started freaking out, yelling at her. Should I say something or not? Do I wanna rock the boat, risk sinking?

'Coffee?'

'Better make it a herb tea. Nothing too pink though,' I say and she nods.

'Feeling more like yourself today?'

'If you mean am I feeling old then, yeah. And I forbid you to make even so much as a sympathetic sounding sigh because, God knows, I don't deserve it after yesterday.'

'I'm just glad you're feeling better,' she says. 'Oh, Mrs Hunter called. I told her you'd be in this afternoon. I got the impression she wanted to speak to you urgently.'

Payback time. 'Thanks, Keira.'

While she's making tea I dial Pete's number for the third time in two days. He's out. I leave a message with his secretary saying Philip has agreed and asking Pete to let me know when he's available for a meeting. When Keira returns I tell her to start making arrangements for the award ceremony.

'So you're going?'

'Yes.'

'All of you?'

'Yeah. I suppose we better prepare a statement or some bloody thing. It's been so long I can't remember what to do,' I sigh.

'That's why you employ me,' she says. 'You'll need a new suit, I'll ring the tailor's on Bridge Street, they're good. And a speech, but I can help with that. Oh, I guess I should contact NIME first.' She covers her mouth, horrified at the uncharacteristic oversight.

'Yeah, do that. Find out what they expect.'

'The letter said they hoped you'd play at the ceremony.'

'Then you better get the number of a good guitar tutor,' I say and Keira is still rolling her eyes at me when the door opens and Meg enters.

'I'll make these calls outside.' Keira grabs an armful of papers and scurries off.

Meg stands beside my desk, towering over me. God, she's beautiful. A soft beauty; creamy skin with a faint pink blush, peachy lips, warm blue eyes. Her hair, honey blonde, curls in wisps around her ears. I like it cut like that, short, but not too short, the natural wave in it making it bounce when she moves. A peaceful beauty. Honest. Real. It's what saved me. Keeps saving me. I stand. Go to her, take hold before she can start bollocking me, and kiss her warm mouth. She stiffens at first, her anger struggling to the surface, but I press her to me, breathing in the smell of orange blossom shampoo, letting her know that I love her and I'm sorry. I do and I am. Fuck. How does she manage it? She makes everything safe.

*

'You've flown before, haven't you?' Pete asks. 'These things are safe, aren't they?'

Anna uncurls herself from my lap, stretching coiled limbs with no purpose than to turn around and get comfy again. She answers Pete.

'Nothing's truly safe. That's what makes life worth living.'

'British Airways flight 418 to New York JFK is boarding at gate number eleven,' reports the nasal-voiced tannoy.

Pete cringes. He's packed all possible disasters for this trip: the plane might crash; our luggage'll go missing; the guitars'll arrive smashed; the gigs won't have sold any tickets. They won't like our music. The last disaster is the only one I'm certain won't happen.

Philip bounds over.

'That's us, let's go.' His hair has grown longer and wilder in the six months we've been playing together. Now it bounces around his face as he leaps towards us, hopping up and down like a daft puppy.

When Don told us that he was booking a US tour Philip practically bayed at the sun, a wolf out of sync with everything and loving it. His fears that we wouldn't be good enough vanished after the Albert Hall triumph. Now he wants it all and knows he'll get it.

Anna winds herself around me. Fucking glad I talked her into coming with us. I hold onto her, absorbing her warmth. Beyond Philip, Ronsey is hunched up on the hard plastic airport seats, solid as a gargoyle.

'He alright?'

Philip casts a glance over his shoulder. 'Maybe he didn't hear the announcement.' Philip heads over.

'He heard it,' Anna says, 'he just didn't want to.'

I sit away from her to get a better look. What's her deal? Wish to Christ I knew. She freaks me sometimes but it's like she said; danger is joie de vivre.

'C'mon.' I pull her up and we move towards the line of people trailing across the chequered carpet, a thin column of smoke winding its way into clear blue.

The engines' thrust pins me in my seat as the plane's speed builds and we charge down the runway. Anna opens her book, starts reading, feet curled under her. She could be at home in the faded wing-backed chair, the one with the rip in the upholstery, for the notice she takes of the plane as it leaves the ground. New or old, each situation rolls evenly over her. Whatever sparks her candle is a fucking mystery to me. And that's how she likes it.

Out the window the land begins to shrink. Oblong buildings and ribbon roads are set out like a toy village. Before we get too high I catch a glimpse of Wembley Stadium then everything blurs into colour blocks. Things stop being individual objects, become part of the whole. All is one and one is all. For us too.

'Budge up, will ya?'

Anna drags her eyes from her book to glare at Philip.

'I want a word with Mickey, move will ya?'

She gets up without a word and takes Philip's empty seat; he plonks down next to me.

'What ya bring her for? She's gonna get in the way.'

Cheeky twat. 'Not when she's in my bed she won't.'

Philip continues as though I haven't said anything. 'I had a word with Ronsey. He's O.K. Just not too happy 'bout leaving his old lady at home with the lad. Shit, he loves that kid but I reckon he'll get over it once we start shaking the world up on the other side of the pond.'

'Hope so. I don't wanna waste this chance. If we blow it there might not be another.'

'We won't blow it,' Philip says. 'It's us. When've we ever blown anything?'

'Just 'cos something's not happened doesn't mean it won't.'

'You're sounding more uptight than Pete.' Philip jerks his head at the row behind where Pete is in the aisle seat, gripping the arm rests, eyes screwed shut.

'Can I have my seat back?' Anna reappears, book clutched to her chest.

Philip eyes her but makes no move to go.

'Anyway, it's cool,' he says to me. I expect him to leave now. Instead he leans over me to study the view, 'Where'd ya reckon we are?'

'You're in my seat and I'm standing here like a prick,' Anna snaps, her temper a struck match. She arches her neck and laughs. Her elegant white throat is exposed to the nasty florescent lighting.

Philip gets up but doesn't move aside for her.

'What ya reading?'

'*The Tibetan Book of the Dead*.'

'What's it about?'

'Life.'

'Oh.'

'You can borrow it if you like.' She winks at me. 'Then we can discuss it.'

'Yeah, O.K.'

Philip's in deep now. Serves him right. He goes. She reclaims her seat.

New York emerges from the blackness, a grain of sand: a distance star. I stare with fascination and fear as we hurtle towards it. The engines wail and judder as we start the descent. The plane lurches forwards and downwards. We're falling. I close my eyes. When I open them I'm outside the plane, falling towards the light. Falling and falling. I fall onto the light. It's a disk, white, flat and oval. It looks solid but that's an illusion. I fall through it and drop down on the other side.

'Mickey, good flight?' Don crosses the arrivals hall.

'O.K.' I say. 'Good to have a friendly face waiting for us. Better than that time you sent me out here with the Three Bob Band and we had to spend ten hours in immigration because some twat hadn't got the right visas.'

Don shakes off my wrist-slap. 'We're all keen for this to go well. The six Ps, that's the secret.'

Ronsey hovers nearby. He hasn't spoken since we landed. Seeing Don doesn't cheer him up.

'The six Ps? What the hell are they?'

Don winks at me. 'Confidential. Top level management protocol. I couldn't possibly divulge it to a mere drummer.'

Scowling, Ronsey clenches his fists.

'Relax, John. The six Ps, you know. 'Proper Planning Prevents Piss-Poor Performance'. He's winding you up. Don, hadn't you better see to the luggage?' I say.

'Er, yes, of course.'

Philip sidles over. Sweeps the scene with a glance.

'Man, we made it,' he enthuses.

'Yeah, thank God for that.' Pete joins him. 'I thought when we hit that turbulence we were goners.'

Ronsey and I start laughing at Pete's pessimistic interpretation of Philip's triumphant statement.

'We haven't made it yet,' I remind them.

'But we will,' Philip declares.

'Yeah, we will,' I say and Ronsey finally catches the fervour of the moment.

'Onward, lads,' he yells, a general ordering the charge, 'our destinies await.'

We're celebrating. It's what we do every night. 'Cos there's so much to celebrate. Crown & Kingdom: welcome to the party. Thrown by me, in my own honour, to celebrate the fucking awesome success of my band.

The room's full of people; I know hardly any of them. I've been here before though but different band, different time. Different everything. Carried on a cloud of marijuana fumes and champagne bubbles, I drift towards a corner where there's space to view the spectacle from. Merging colours flicker back and forwards across the room, forming patterns with a millisecond life span. I blink like a camera's shutter, trying to capture each scene before it's gone forever. But each time I blink, burning one image to film, I miss another. I save as many of these moment as I can.

Don, sharp-suited and impeccable, is circulating in his pro capacity. Several strippers, birthday-suited, are also circulating in their pro capacity. Too many scruffy journalists circle like sharks. Lenny watches them like a harpooner. Good old Lenny, worth his weight in coke. That Margaret chick from *American Guitarist* hasn't shown up this time. Probably best, what with Anna here. Ronsey's by the bar, bottle of champagne in one hand; juicy, smouldering joint in the other. Pete's with him, talking ten to the dozen and flapping his arms. Shit, is he high? Philip's here too, somewhere.

Don's gone for weird décor tonight: balloons tacked up in the corners; paper chains draped from the light fixtures. We should be playing pass the parcel. Or postman's knock. No, coalman's knock. Same but dirtier. More appropriate. It's a safe bet the strippers'd be up for it. Or down on it.

A skinny blonde chick in pink hot pants emerges from the crowd to rub herself against me. Between her fingers a fat joint is balanced. I look for Anna but can't see her black outline against the spectrum of colours. I take a drag. Blow smoke at Pinkie. Return her joint. She skulks off. A moment later I watch her wander towards Ronsey and Pete, attaching herself to Pete, a limpet to a rock in a rough swell. What's Mr Responsibility's gonna do with that? The crowd closes around them, blocking my view.

I slip onto the balcony. It's a warm night. We're on the fifteenth floor. The view is fucking trippy, flashing signs and streaking headlights. Too good to waste. I drop the tab of acid Lenny gave me. It melts on my tongue. I lean over the railings. It's a long way down. That'd fucking hurt.

'So Mickey, how does it feel to be back in the States pulling in bigger crowds than last time you were here?' It's one of the dickheads from *Rolling Stone.*

'Pretty fucking good.'

'No regrets about dumping the Three Bob Band?'

I teeter perilously on the edge of acid-induced insanity. 'Who says I dumped 'em?'

'The decision to split was mutual?'

'In the end we felt...'

'Isn't it true that Richard and Neil wanted to continue but you believed they were holding you back?'

'Nah, man, no way. They wanted to go in different directions.'

'What directions?'

'How the fuck should I know?'

'I understand Neil is a garbage collector while Richard is living off welfare. How do you feel about that?'

A sharp chemical tang hovers in my throat. Things're getting hazy in the middle.

'I've made my own way. It's up to everyone else to do the same.' A plume of smoky acid fogs my brain.

'So you're a subscriber to 'every man for himself' no matter what the cost to others? Gee, I guess it's hard to concern yourself with the problems of others when you're surrounded by wanton excess.'

'Hey, wait a minute...'

The acid drowns me.

He's... Shit, what's that? Fuck, I don't like this. What the hell is that thing? Shit, it's coming at me. Fuck. I've got to stop it. Christ, it's coming at me. I've gotta stop it. Just get hold of it. I don't want to touch it. Bloody Hell. I'm gonna have to. O.K. Now, get it over the edge. Push it over the edge, throw it away, get rid of it. Then it won't be able to come back. What if it flies? It might fly back up. No, it won't. Surely it won't. Push the bloody thing over the edge. Fuck, it's a strong bastard. Get a better grip. That's it, almost. A little more. Come on, Mickey, you can do this.

'Shit, Mickey. Mickey, stop it.'

Words hit me and bounce off. I spin round. See Ronsey rushing over. He shoves me and grabs me. I fall. He's pulling a white-faced man off the balcony railings. The man slumps on the floor opposite me. We gaze at each other. He looks kinda familiar. Where do I know him from?

'John, what's going on?' It's Don.

I stay on the floor. So does the other guy. Ronsey goes to Don. Says something. I feel really off.

'Bollocks.' That's Don again. 'Get him out of here.'

Ronsey squats in front of me.

'Hey, man, you alright?'

I nod.

'Come for a walk.' He hauls me up.

We wander through the party.

'I need a drink.'

'Yeah, alright. Oi, Lenny,' Ronsey bellows, 'I'm taking Mickey next door. Bring some brandy or something, will ya?'

Next door is Ronsey's room. It's quiet. Quieter. He sits me on the bed. Lights a cigarette and gives me it. Lenny must come in 'cos next Ronsey's giving me a bottle to swig from.

'For Christ sake, Mickey,' Ronsey says. He starts laughing.

'What's up?'

He laughs harder. 'Nothing. Jesus. Nothing. Do us a favour, eh? Stay here 'til you finish tripping, will ya?'

He goes out again. I drain the bottle and lie down. Psychedelic swirls paint the ceiling. After a while I sit up. Remember Ronsey's laugh. And everything else. I laugh too as I head back to the party.

It's later but everyone's still here. The record on the turntable runs out and a witchy screech splits my ears as the needle scrapes over the centre of the LP. Jarred from drug-induced stupors, people gawp about the room. It goes quiet. Ronsey jumps onto a tabletop, king of the castle. He waves a champagne bottle overhead, spraying his subjects with a sticky mist.

'Ladies and gentlemen,' he slurs, 'I'd like to say a few words.'

Someone restarts the record player.

'Oi, turn that fucking thing off, ya cunts,' he yells, 'I'm making a fucking speech here for fuck sake.'

Drummer's privilege: being the loudest. The music is stopped.

'Cheers. Now, I wanna start by telling you what I think of your country. We've been here now for, what? Ten weeks?'

Don, who's nearest, says something to him.

'Twelve, I'm reliably informed we've been here twelve weeks. And what conclusions can be drawn after twelve weeks?' The champagne varnishes Ronsey with freaky poshness. 'Let me tell you a few of my observations of the good old US of A. Firstly, it's too fucking big. Five and a half hours on a bastard bus and you haven't left the city you started from. Why the fuck do you buggers need so much space? I say, squeeze everything together; it'll work better, trust me.'

With these words he presses the palm of one hand against the champagne bottle which he still has by the neck in his other hand.

'Secondly: the food. I like it; it's simple, uncomplicated, hell, I'd even go so far as to say a bit scruffy. And I mean that sincerely.'

He thinks this a compliment. Don creeps closer. Kneels on a chair, trying to get Ronsey's attention.

'So yeah, good food. But what the fuck is that brown piss you keep passing off as tea? I know some of you might have a problem with British tea. Some shit about a party on a boat, but fucking get over it. Get some decent tea, some Tetley's, Christ.' He pauses to tip champagne down his throat and over his shirt. 'There was something else… Yeah, I remember. What the hell is this shit in Vietnam about?'

Stop.

'Christ, I dunno Jack-shit about political bollocks but seems clear to me that decent lads are dying for nothing.'

Jesus, stop, Ronsey.

'Hell, you might as well line 'em up and shoot 'em yourselves, save the cost of flying the buggers out there.'

Fine, don't stop. It's your lynching.

'Anyway, cheers, here's to the United fucking States of America.'

John raises the champagne bottle to his mouth but it's empty. As he peers forlornly into its green depths, one of the listeners blows off.

'You're nothing but a Commie bastard.' He charges towards Ronsey.

Someone else yells out.

'He's a fucking humanist. You fascists are the real problem, sending young guys to their deaths,'

From the opposite corner the second speaker begins to hack through the jungle of bodies, also making for Ronsey who's still on the tabletop, trying to wring a drop more bubbly from the bottle.

Don's now frantically tugging on John's trouser leg, a faithful dog worrying its owner for attention. Ronsey lashes out with his foot. Catches Don's nose with the toe of his boot. Red ejects from Don's nostrils and sprays up Ronsey's jeans. He doesn't notice 'cos the two armchair politicos or signed-up patriots or draft dodgers or whatever the fuck they are have reached the table and are grappling with each other. Ronsey, not a fucking clue what's happening, rears up over them, roars like a grizzly and smashes the bottle on their heads. Glass shatters. Flies off. Screams ripple out. The noise pierces my head, running from ear to ear. Cries clamour across the wave of people. Panic follows; the wave swells and the pier, with Ronsey on top, is flooded by bodies. He disappears from view, sinking under the writhing murder of people. The scene is chaotic and funny. Arms and legs thrash like tentacles and somewhere, in the midst of it, Ronsey is being digested.

I wish the acid hadn't worn off. This'd be an awesome trip. Pete appears alongside me, the pinky smear of a bruise-to-be on his cheek.

'Mickey, Christ, what the hell are we gonna do?'

I lean against the wall. 'Get some popcorn?'

'Where's Anna?'

His question crushes me. I rake over the teeming mass in the centre of the room, shifting through the purples, blues, greens and silvers for Anna's black silhouette.

Bang.

Freeze, mother fuckers.

Lenny is posed in the doorway, a handgun raised over his head like a cowboy in a wild west showdown.

'Where the hell'd he get that?' Pete says.

'Probably one of Don's ideas.'

The monstrous mob untangles itself. Battered figures separate out. Begin drifting around the room, dazed. I dive forward, panning through debris for Anna. She's not there.

I'm sitting on our bed, in the dark, waiting for Anna. I was gauging the time with shots of whisky but I've lost count now. In my ears is the wind-rushing sound of silence. It swishes round inside my head. I light another cigarette. It's my last one. There are some more on the dressing table but I can't reach them without standing up and I've drank so much my legs are numb. I press my spine, rod-iron straight, into the headboard and lean my head back for extra stability. The night is one blurred nightmare and I'm still sleeping.

The latch clicks.

Anna materialises at the foot of the bed. She smiles but doesn't come over.

'Where've the hell've you been?'

'Walking.'

'Where?'

'Round the city.'

'Alone?'

'Yes.'

'You shouldn't.'

'Why not?'

'It's dangerous.'

'Good.'

That's it. Row over.

'You missed the fun.'

'I gather. I saw Pete on my way up. Nice shiner.'

'I thought you might be hurt.'

'I'm not,' she says. Could have beens don't mean shit to Anna.

She floats into the bathroom, an oblong of yellow light grazing the floor. I listen to the tinkling of water, the fuzzy sound of her brushing her teeth. She reappears in the block of light to undress. I watch. She sits on the bed next to me. Takes the cigarette from my fingers so she can drag on it. Something's missing. Christ knows what. If I could clear the fog in my brain I might have a chance of seeing it. She stubs the cigarette out. Dying curls of smoke waft up from the ashtray. Anna coils around me, her bare skin thawing me. What was I just thinking about?

The room is greyed with early morning light when I open my eyes. On the pillow beside me is the impression of Anna's head. Thrumming water reveals she's showering. And that I have the mother-fucker of all hangovers, a right ear-splitter. I stagger out of bed. Grab my jeans off the floor. Have to sit again to keep from toppling over. I pull them on one leg at a time as far as my knees. Debate standing for a full two minutes. Get up. The room lurches left and right. I sway with it, staying upright long enough to fasten my trousers. Like a drunk spaceman, I flop across to the dressing table. Trail my hands through the jumble of objects until I find some cigarettes. Swooping them up, I go onto the balcony.

Outside the cold sucker-punches me. I gag. Light a cigarette. Stare at the soothing expanse of colourless clouds. Peering over the railings, I check for a human outline in chalk and a police-tape cordon. There's nothing. 'Cos that only almost happened. Shit, the rumble. I don't even know if Ronsey is O.K. Or Philip. Was he there or not?

The phone gives a one-trill ring. Anna answers it. Comes onto the balcony.

'That was Don. He wants to know if you're joining them for breakfast.'

'Oh.'

'I said you were.'

'Right.'

She watches me, head on one side, a curious bird trying to pluck up courage. Then she pecks me on the cheek and goes inside, leaving behind the scent of hotel shampoo. I watch, dizzied, as she pads around the room, drying her hair, pulling on her knickers. That's what I missed last night: a smell, the cold sooty smell of city air on her skin.

Breakfast is more subdued than usual. Hangovers are the norm but today the figures in the breakfast room wouldn't be out of place on a bomb-torn battlefield. Pete has a cracking purple bruise on his cheek. Don's nose is a swollen bulge. Ronsey looks like a prize fighter who was KOed in the fifteenth. Staring at him I feel a throbbing sympathy pain behind my left eye (his is welded shut) and another nerve-jangling twinge in my mouth. He glances up from his breakfast beer. Forces a grin. His upper right canine is missing. How did I manage to get off unhurt?

Don perches at the end of the long table; everyone else

slumps. The hotel manager, a spindly guy with a sharp suit, stands, grim-faced, next to him. Don signs a cheque, tears it off, stands and holds it to the manager.

'That should cover it,' Don tells him, voice robotic from his blocked nose. Damages paid for, Don stalks from the room.

I slide into an empty seat opposite Philip, who's talking to Lenny. Lenny's knuckles are scraped and scratched but his face is unmarked. He nods me a hello but carries on talking to Philip, recounting the riot in blood-soaked detail. His words drift over me but Philip catches every one.

'Man, I can't believe it,' he screams. The noise slices me. I glare at him with slitted eyes. 'Sorry man, you got a bad head or something?' He doesn't sound sympathetic.

The waitress comes for my order. I request black coffee; she retreats to the kitchen. We're making the other guests nervous.

I search my pockets.

'Have one of mine.' Philip pushes his pack across the table. 'Lenny's been telling me. Man, what a night. Heard you nearly pitched some reporter off the balcony.'

'Yeah.'

'Was that before or after the riot?'

'Before.'

'So where were you when that kicked off ?' Philip asks.

'Ringside,' I say through lips clenching a cigarette, 'you?'

'I ducked out for a bit. Can't believe I missed the fun.'

Pete, who's a couple of seats down from me glances up. ''S'not my bloody idea of fun.' His face is pale; the darkly shadowed bruise stands out, a lipstick stain on an otherwise guiltlessly white collar.

'Aww, c'mon,' Philip says, 'no one got hurt. Not seriously.' He laughs and while his attention's on Pete I inspect him. He's got a nice tan. And some not so nice dark rings under his eyes. We all could use more sleep. His tosses his head back as he laughs, throwing long curly hair off his neck.

'Get a little action last night, did ya?' I point out the red blotch on his throat.

'What? Oh, yeah.' He puts a hand up, covering the mouth shaped blemish that pouts there. 'Some chick. Dunno who she was.'

''S that it?' Ronsey's coming round. He leans over on Philip's other side, lisping words past broken teeth and bloated lips. 'C'mon, give us the juicy: what was she like?'

Philip laughs again. It sounds hollow. My stomach dives due south.

'The usual, ya know.'

'We would if you'd give up this bullshit chivalry and tell us,' Ronsey says. 'Man, did you hit your head last night?'

'What's that supposed to mean?' Philip's tetchy. I know what Ronsey's getting at, though.

'Normally we can't get you to shut up about it, long after we've stopped giving a damn how hard she sucked,' Ronsey says.

'Hey, I don't have to tell you everything,' Philip snaps. 'You're not my fucking mother, ya know.'

He pushes his chair back. Stalks from the room. The four of us stay sitting. No one looks at Ronsey. Lenny clears his throat, trigging a coughing fit.

'Christ sake, have a fag.' I shove Philip's abandoned pack towards him.

'Cunt,' Ronsey mutters and gets up too, heading for the French windows that open onto the garden.

Pete moves up to sit next to me. 'What was that about?'

Yeah, what? 'I don't wanna know.' I really don't.

Five minutes drag out in icy silence. Lenny slurps his cigarette, coughs some more. The waitress reappears with my coffee. As she puts it down Pete grips my arm. Her hand trembles; some of the dark liquid slops onto the white tablecloth. She mumbles an apology but I can't be bothered with it, or her, and turn away. Pete's eyes lock into mine in horror.

'What?' I demand.

He makes some cryptic gestures with his head in the direction of the waitress who's retreating again, full throttle.

'It's her,' he says.

I picture her in pink hot pants. 'Oh, Christ, Pete, you didn't?'

He drops his gaze.

'Alright, Pete. Remembered how to use it finally?' Lenny whacks him on the shoulder.

'I didn't mean to,' Pete pleads, 'but after what happened, she was terrified. She came over, shaking and crying. I wanted to make sure she was O.K.'

'Forget it,' I tell him.

'But Susie…'

'Is not here and doesn't know anything about it.'

'But I know. When I woke up this morning and saw her lying there I thought, 'Oh shit'.'

'After what went down last night, I don't think it matters. Christ, I nearly killed someone,' I say.

'What?'

'Never mind. Look, you can't undo it, so forget it.'

'Forget what?' Don joins us.

'Nothing,' I say, catching the alarmed expression on Pete's face.

Don shakes his head as if trying to flick water out of his ears.

'I've got this terrible ringing,' he mutters.

'It'll pass,' I say not knowing if it will.

'Anyway, we're squared up. Time to go. We've outstayed our welcome, lads.' With that Don heads off.

Lenny follows him, leaving me and Pete. He continues to whinge about last night; I fade him down. What you can't take with you should be dumped at the roadside. I stare into my coffee. It winks at me as the overhead light flickers on its slick surface. I feel sick. If I drink it I'll puke.

Who was Philip shagging last night?

Ronsey returns from the garden.

'Where's Don?'

'Probably packing. We've leaving soon,' I reply.

Ronsey stomps out. His interruption forces me into retuning Pete's self-bollocking.

'Do you think I should call her?'

He means Susie.

'And say what? Look, leave it, eh?'

I've had enough of this place.

As I cross the lobby the manager fires a warning shot at me with his pin-prick eyes. Another time I might have gone over, reminded him how much money we've dropped here these last two nights but right now I just wanna leave. Wanna go upstairs, grab my guitar and rucksack and flee, head to the coast, where the air's deep. But we're a Big Top show now, dragging the whole bloody circus with us. In the lift, the numbers flick round; each part of the count-down.

The doors open on three floors before mine, prolonging the agony as people quibble about getting in or out. On my floor at last I squeeze past the fat, highly patterned arse of a middle-aged trollop. The doors close behind me. Philip comes down the corridor. Stumbles as if he's unsure whether to stop or keep walking. He does stop, at the last minute, nearly trips because of it.

'Mickey.' His face is flushed.

'You alright?'

'Yeah, I, er, I came up the stairs.' He indicates the fire exit at the end of the corridor. 'I'm sorry about before, downstairs.'

'You don't need to apologise to me.'

'Was he pissed off?'

'Yeah.'

'Fuck it. I was, oh, I dunno. Sometimes I feel like I've no space to myself. You know what I mean?'

Yeah, I do. But fucked if I'll help salve his conscience.

'We've been spending so much time together these last few months; playing, recording, partying. I just need some space,' he continues.

'You'll get plenty of that if we don't make it.'

'What ya talking about? We've made it, man, we're here.'

'Remember what Ronsey said about legacy. That doesn't happen quickly.'

His eyes flick over me and away down the hall. I think of our first gig; the way the he held the white spotlight in the palm of his hand, holding it up as the winning trophy. He thought that was it.

'I'm not saying we haven't done really fucking well but there's more. Out there and in here.' I tap the side of my head. 'And in there.' I point at his. 'We can't take it easy now. You've got to look for the peak that's higher than the one you're on, see where you're going next.'

'Where d'ya think that is?'

'On to bigger things, the biggest. We are gonna make it but you'd be wrong to think there's one single time when we'll be able to say, 'Yeah, that's it, we've done it,' 'cos there'll always be something better. I'm not gonna settle for half-arsed when we can go all the way.'

'You're right. Think I've been suffering a bad case of road fever. Cheers. I better find Ronsey.' He strides off again.

In our room Anna's packing. She knows exactly what she's doing though it doesn't look like it. I watch as she darts about. Faster than a sparrow nest-building, she gathers up our junk. It's a freaky sight, Anna doing something domesticated. I don't expect it's something I'll see that often. I enjoy it.

'Aren't you going to help?'

'Nah, you've got it.'

'Thanks. Philip was here before,' she says, her head in a suitcase.

'Oh.'

'He was looking for you.'

'I saw him outside.'

'I thought maybe you missed each other.'

'Nah.'

'Right.'

She flicks past me on the way to collect another load of knickknacks. I grab her arm.

'What?'

I stew over Philip's bad case of road fever. That blotch on his neck. Anna being AWOL last night. Am I going fucking mad? 'I dunno. Nothing.'

I pull her to me, pinning her arms to her sides. Kiss her mouth. It tastes the same. Her lips open. She kisses back but it's not enough. I push her into the wall. She arches her spine, throwing her head against the patterned paper. I move my hands up to her neck, unfasten the buttons of her high-collared renaissance frilled blouse. What'll I do if I find it, that telltale red mouth mark on her skin? I bite her lip. She moans and presses against me.

'Mickey.' My name is the wind whispering through dried rushes.

Her neck's unmarked: pure skin-white. My heart throbs. I stop. She opens her eyes. Stiffens against me at this unexpected timeout. I kiss her again, force my tongue inside then pull away.

'C'mon. Don wants us to go.'

I turn my back so I don't have to see the lust in her green eyes.

It's the last show of the tour. We're waiting to go on. A hard knot is lodged in my gut. Every note has to be perfect tonight; we have to leave them craving another fix. Pete huddles next to me, shivering.

'It's bloody freezing. Do they need the air-conditioning on so high?'

'You'll warm up out there,' Ronsey says.

Philip tosses a fag end onto the floor. Crushes it under his boot. Takes a final swig of beer. Hands the bottle to a grim-faced Lenny who grips the bottle by the neck, weighing it in his hand, judging how handy it might be later. He's already had to eject two young lads he found skulking backstage without passes or excuses. Not that he would've wasted much time listening. These gigs are getting too big for him and his spotty, dweeby apprentices. Don's already suggesting a bigger road crew for our next tour.

The steady buzz from out front moves up a notch as the compére announces us. We step stage-side. I let Philip go first. Watch as he dives into the pool of light. The buzz becomes a roar, enraged, reckless and howling. When it reaches my ears the knot in my stomach throbs. I follow him. Take up my stance at the front of the stage. A minute later Ronsey and Pete are also in place.

Philip leans into the microphone with his usual greeting.

'Good evening. Here's one you'll know.'

I strike the chord. Like a blacksmith hitting red hot metal, sparks fly off into the darkness. The crowd bays at us, hungry wolf cubs wanting their first taste of warm, blood-soaked meat. As their starved cries rush in from the darkness I fly at the strings of my Les Paul, flinging notes for them to feast on.

We play two, three and well into the fourth hour before the crowd begins to stagger under the weight of its own gluttony. Every time I look at Pete he's hunched over his bass, fingers like lightning flashes striking the frets, adding fills and runs where before he would have made do with one steady note. Ronsey matches him. Side by side their pounding of drums and bass becomes the crowd's heartbeat as they run faster and more keenly towards the cliff edge.

Philip wails vocals in agony and ecstasy, passing through fear, rage, hate, love, fifteen times a bar. He cries words, drinks deeply when they are shrieked back to him from the euphoric audience. His microphone is a weapon. He wields it with ferocious energy, battering the audience. They refuse to submit, driving him higher, each note cutting above the one before until he shatters the roof.

I rise up with him. High above the auditorium we battle. My guitar calls him to order. He answers defiantly. We lock horns, two stags in rut, grunting, sweating, steaming, fighting to break off the other's horns before the tune plays out. The pain of combat is drowned in the adrenaline-dowsed moment of battle. Every blow he strikes I fend off, swiping and slashing, cutting and cleaving notes, welding them together, splitting them again. Nothing matters 'cept the music. Nothing can stop it. Stop us. It's un-fucking-endable.

The audience lay drained at our feet. Still locked in a death grip, Philip and I slide back down: show over. I look at him; he bends into the light to take another bow. We survived. He thinks he won. I think we both lost.

Don fires the cork from the bottle's neck and splashes champagne into waiting glasses. Ronsey grabs another bottle, opens it with a violent jerk and sprays us with the foam. Pete giggles. They're unaware of the on-stage war between me and Philip. But he's not. Throws himself into the celebrations with full-of-it enthusiasm, wanting me to know what he knows; under the pressure of my full force he didn't buckle. Isn't this what I wanted? A power equal to mine. One I could play off and draw from? We cancel each other out, a half and two quarters. But there's a fatal flaw: we can only carry on together by making equal and opposite shifts in energy and motion. It's Battleships. If he ever starts winning it'll be game over.

'Mickey, have some champers.'

Philip comes over. Drapes his arm around my shoulders, thrusts a glass to me. I take it. Swallow a mouthful.

'That was a hell of a...'

Punch-up? 'Yeah,' I say, 'best performance so far.'

'Agreed,' he says, 'and ya know, what you said the other day, you were right.'

Yeah, I'm still the fucking king here. 'Oh?'

'About reaching higher 'cos there's always more. There is more and I don't wanna stop 'til I've got it all.' His words drip total self-belief.

C'mon, then, you son-of-a...

'Alright, girls, have you finished?' Ronsey roars up to us. 'There's a bloody party.'

Anna comes across the room in that deliberate way of hers, hunter stalking prey. As she kisses me I breathe in deeply but all I smell is her. Above us a banner, suspended between two sparkling chandeliers, reads, '*Vendi, Vidi, Vici*' in foot-high blood-red lettering. Soon we're deluged by people, slapping my back, pumping my arm, howling praise at me. I tighten my grip on Anna, left arm round her narrow waist, hard edge of her hip pressing into my side as a hurricane of journalists and photographers blows over us.

Don flickers around the room, speaking to all the right people, setting things in motion for next time.

Philip is herded alongside Anna and cameras snap in our faces, supernova explosions of stars going nuclear. She tries to pull away as the flashes pop.

'Mickey, let me go,' she says, her lips brushing my ear.

'Nah, you gotta stay, darlin'.'

The three of us turn: three heads, one body.

'Squeeze in, please,' one of the photographers instructs.

Philip moves closer to Anna.

'A little more. Put your arm around her. I'm sure she doesn't bite,' the photographer teases.

Philip does as directed. I feel Anna squirm.

'What will you be doing now you've achieve phenomenal success with your shows here?' a reporter asks.

'Getting a bloody drink,' Philip says.

This raises a chuckle.

'And after that: the world. Isn't that right, Mickey?'

'We'll be getting back into the studio pretty quickly,' I say, 'getting the next album down.'

'So you've got some new material?' the journalist asks.

'One or two things,' I reply.

'Will you be co-writing the next album?' another enquires.

This is directed at me; Philip buts in.

'Before I was happy letting Mickey do the writing; he was more experienced than me but now I'm in a position to contribute, lyrically and musically, to the next album.'

The room lurches away from me. 'We'll all be working together on new material,' I add.

Don buzzes over.

'Gentlemen, I think that's it for questions. Shall we adjourn to the bar?'

He manoeuvres them into the adjoining room. Lenny covers the door with his solid oak shoulders.

I turn to Philip but before I say anything he pulls away from Anna and strides off. She clings to me, shivering.

'What the hell does that say?' I point at banner, her handiwork.

'It's Latin, 'I came, I saw, I conquered'.'

'Hey, Mickey, wake up.' The voice creeps in, water seeping through wool.

I open one eye. Pete stands over me.

'Here.' He offers me a mug. 'Coffee.'

Cautiously I open the other eye, sit up and squint around. I'm at the mahogany dining table we were snorting coke off last night. Strewn around me is the evidence of a bloody good night; empty bottles, dog ends, coke crumbs. A grass-haze hangs in the air and two half dressed groupies loll like floppy rag dolls on the puffy peach sofa.

I sip the coffee. It's only lukewarm. 'What time is it?'

'Five-thirty, a.m.'

'Jesus.' I push the coffee away. 'Gimme a smoke, will ya?'

Pete finds a pack. Sits opposite me and we smoke thirstily.

'Good bash last night,' he says.

'Yeah.' Dazed, I try to pull pictures from the static buzz in my head.

'Great way to end the tour.'

The fingers of my left hand start to fizz with pins and needles. Must've crimped a nerve lying slumped across the table. 'Yeah.' I rub my palm.

'Did you think it would be like this?' he asks.

I shrug. Rub my hand again.

'Still, it's been good.'

'You sound as though ya think it's over,' I accuse.

'You think there's more? I mean, can we keep this up?' he asks.

'I can if you can.'

'Yeah, course.'

Silence bellows in my head. The room swings out of and back into shape.

'I'm off to bed. See you in the morning.' I say and stand, legs trembling beneath me.

'It is morning.'

'I mean tomorrow morning.' I pat his arm and stagger for the door.

In the corridor is the fallout of a nuclear holocaust; junk and bodies waiting for the wind to blow them away; I navigate around cans, bottles and two crumpled party-goes. The chick is only wearing knickers. Her flesh is goose-pimply, a goose plucked for roasting. The light is too bright.

Snow-blinded, I stumble towards my room, through my door and into soothing darkness. I let the coolness of it wet my parched senses. My eyes adjust. I listen for Anna's soft breathing. Hear a different sound: heavier, deeper.

What the fuck…?

My brain snaps on. My heart stutters. I press against the door, paralysed by panic. I wanna be out in the too-bright corridor but if I open the door I'll find myself back in this dark room. You can check out but you can't fucking leave. I creep forward.

Thick curtains are drawn across the window. I kick over to them, a drowning man trying to break the surface, and yank the curtains open. Light rushes in, forcing me back under water. I gulp for air. Turn round. See the bed. Anna. And Philip.

Water closes over my head. I sink in a bottomless ocean.

The Hanged Man

The reunion's on. But we're down a drummer. With Pete and Philip's agreement I head out to the cemetery to see if I can do the impossible.

John's buried in the family plot in the churchyard of the small village his folks are from. It's off the A68, in the Pennine foothills: a long drive made longer by the fact that I can't remember the way and get lost. Twice. This is 'cos I've only been once before and it took half a bottle of Scotch to get me up to the wrought iron gates. This time isn't going to be any easier. I'm sober plus Dr. Sangha's diagnosis makes me feel less like a visitor and more like a potential buyer.

Doesn't look as though James is here yet. I cross the road and crunch along the gravel path that winds through the churchyard, zigzagging around the graves, obstacles to be avoided. One day that's all I'll be.

I stumble around, scanning worn inscriptions, trying not to notice the narrow strip of life marked on some of them; age forty-three, age fifty-six, age fifteen, age twenty-seven. Age thirty-two. This one's John's. I was spared having to watch them dump him in the ground. Family only for that. Here lies England's most powerful drummer. It seems odd that, here, in the quietest of spots, sleeps the loudest of men. But he could be quiet too, John. For some fucking reason it hurts more remembering him that way. I read the inscription:

'Beloved father, wonderful husband, missed every day, make them rock up there.'

The world turns misty. The church bobs about in my sightline. Something's missing, like I've forgotten to bring it with me.

It's John. He's not here, is fuck knows where now. I'd like to believe he's still around me, a feather in the wind, but that's bullshit. He was too solid for any of that crap. Night after night he pounded his drums, the thick muscles in his forearms contorting as he hit harder, faster, louder with every beat. Hearing him was like standing on the edge of a waterfall listening to the bellowing torrent battering rock. Gravity only works in one direction but it keeps going in that direction forever. It can't be stopped. Neither could John Ronsarno. Or so I fucking thought.

I turn from the headstone, groping in my pockets for cigarettes that aren't there and see a man coming towards me. His gait has the rolling rhythm of waves rising and falling on a beach. Hypnotised, I fix on him as he walks. It's John. He's not dead. It was all a fucked up mistake. 'Cept it wasn't and he is and I dunno what the fuck is happening now. I back away; he bears down on me, muscular arms swinging at his sides, giant stride swallowing the ground between us. Closer and I see a thatch of thick dark hair sweeping across a broad forehead. He glares at me, dark eyes squinting into the bright sun. I knot my hands into fists; sweat prickles across my back, my mouth dries up, fear thunders in my ears. I can't believe it. Don't want to believe it. But do want it to be true. John…?

'Uncle Mickey, how are you?'

I don't reply. Can't.

'Uncle Mickey? Are you O.K? You look like you've seen a ghost,' James says, grinning.

Christ, even his voice, his accent…

C'mon, get it together, man.

'James, it's, I didn't expect… you're so much…' I stop. Try again, 'How are you?'

'Fine.' He tugs his goatee beard, a hereditary gesture. 'Sorry if

I spooked you.'

'For a second I thought...' He must've heard it a thousand times.

'People're always saying I'm his double,' he shrugs, 'but not for much longer.'

'What d'ya mean?'

'I've already got a few years on him. Soon I'll be too old for there to be any likeness left.'

'I guess.' It's hard to accept, though, 'cos in front of me is John Ronsarno; he hasn't aged at all while I've grown older, closer to death. Now I'm the corpse and there he stands, young and fresh, shouldering life. Ready to rock the world.

*

Richard and Neil take me to meet Don. His office is shabby: one window boarded up; leather armchair coming unstuffed; carpet pile flattened into a matted layer of swirls and suspicious stains. Not the backdrop I'd pictured for this moment.

'You must be Mickey. Richard says you're a real wiz on the guitar.' Don Wiseman comes towards me on patent leather shoes and holds out his hand.

I try not to step in any of the more incriminating stains.

'He's right 'bout that.'

Richard warned me about Don, 'He's not what he seems,' and I get what he meant. A shade over five foot, clean shaven, pale watery eyes, neatly trimmed hair, thin lips, tiny hands and feet, dressed in a light grey suit; everything about him says Don is a little man. He grips my fingers with precisely controlled pressure, just enough to threaten. He's an iceberg; his low-key exterior masks danger.

From his desk he selects a leather-bound folder, opening it with ceremony.

'I think you'll find everything in order.'

He takes a fountain pen from his breast pocket and offers me it.

'Sign on the line.'

'I'd prefer to read it first.'

'There's no need.'

I hear eons-harden granite in his voice. 'If I want to read it then there is a need: my need.'

Don eyeballs me. Fuck him. I stare back. Don breaks with a chortle.

'Quite right; I never sign anything legally binding until I've scrutinised every word. Take it with you. Bring it back when you're happy.'

I snap the folder shut. Don reclines in the too-large leather chair cramped behind the too-small desk. From a drawer, he takes a bumper-value box of Henri Wintermans, extracts a thin cigar, lights it then turns the box round.

'Help yourselves, boys.'

Richard and Neil grab cigars. I retreat and light one of my own cigarettes. Don watches.

'So, expecting that everything will prove satisfactory,' he indicates the folder under my arm with the glowing end of his cigar, 'we should start planning. I've a list of gig dates here, for your approval, naturally,' he adds, smiling at me, 'and if all goes O.K. I've, provisionally, of course, booked studio time. After that I'll see the Three Bob Band off to the States. That's where the action is. And the money. How's that sound, Mickey?'

'Pretty good.' Just remember: you work for me.

The studio is steamy. A trickle of sweat runs between my shoulder blades. I roll up my sleeves, brush hair from my eyes. It's airless in here. I'm suffocating.

'You O.K., Mickey?' Don's voice over the intercom is shrill, with a tinny whistle to it.

No, I'm fucking not. We've been trying for three fucking hours to get the rhythm track for 'Mean Woman Blues' down for the album. The drums were sorted yesterday but there's still the vocals to do and the lead breaks. It's going to take another two bastard days to get the album sorted if we keep working at this pace, slow enough bore a snail to death. Not sure I'm gonna make it.

'Come on, let's get this fucking finished,' I mutter.

Richard presses his lips into a tight line and nods. It's his fault this is taking so long. He keeps cocking up in bloody stupid ways; starting in the wrong key, playing the bass line from a different song. He glares at his bass; I glare at him.

'O.K.,' says the engineer behind the glass, "Mean Woman Blues' take thirteen.'

I count us in then tear into the chords, my desperate need to get the fuck out of this tin box driving me hard. Richard feels the rage in the music's roar. Fear or fury, I don't care which, forces him to pull it together, playing the right notes in the right places. At fucking last. Four minutes and thirty-one seconds later we've done it. But there are six more tracks to get through. I unload my Les Paul. The neck's hot and slick from my hand, the strings greasy with sweat. I snap a towel off the table and rub it down before setting it on the stand.

Don wheezes over the intercom again, 'Take a break.'

I head for the door without saying anything to Richard, his eyes following me with that kicked-kitten look. Fuck him.

Outside it's subzero. Ice frosts the pavement. Flecks of snow swirl, settling on my bare forearms, pricking like fine needles. I gulp mouthfuls of cold air, feeling it rush down my gullet, dousing the fire.

Don emerges, the stub of a thin cigar clutched between his lips. His brow's pinched into a frown but, seeing me, he relaxes. I haven't done a runner. Yet.

'Can I join you?'

I nod. It's cool. We've sussed each other out: he's got the balls to do his job; I've got the talent to do mine. We're after the same thing: success. Yeah, he's O.K.

'It's pretty rough in there today.'

'I'm bloody sick of being cooped up. When're we gonna get out on the road?'

'I'm in the middle of making arrangements. Once the album's finished and off to the pressing factory we can go.'

'How long?'

'A month, six weeks.'

'Fuck sake.'

'Mickey, you don't want to be three thousand miles away, letting some pimp engineer mix and edit your beautiful work.' He's trying to get me where he thinks I'm weak. He's off target though. Right now I couldn't give a shit about the album. I wanna get out there: gig again.

'This is part of it, you know,' he reminds me.

'Not the part I like.'

'It'll be worth it when you've got that black disc in your hand, your name printed on the sleeve.' He's working me over; jab, jab, uppercut. I say nothing.

'How're things at home? How's your mother?'

'How the fuck should I know?'

'So this tantrum doesn't have anything to do with what happened last week, your home life?'

He's asking me to talk about shit I don't even want to think about. He's making me think about it by asking. It's a runaway train pelting downhill…

They're any normal, middle-aged couple out for Saturday night drinks. She's done up to eleven; war paint, hair curled like a movie star, high heels. He's in his second best suit, sharply pin-striped but the lining's ripped under the arms. He offers her another drink.

'Are you trying to get me drunk?' she asks.

'Do I need to?' he replies.

She giggles. Flutters her eyelashes.

They drink up.

'I should be going,' she says.

'It's late. Let me drive you,' he offers.

'I don't want to put you out,' she says.

'You're not,' he insists.

They leave the pub. Climb into his car. It's cold; she sees her own breath as puffy white clouds. They're both tipsy.

'Where to, love?' he asks.

'Skinner Street. Do you know it?' she asks.

'Oh, I know it, love,' he says.

They drive in the correct direction for two miles. Without warning he turns the car left instead of right.

'Silly, it's up there,' she teases.

'Is it? I'll find somewhere to turn around.'

He pulls into an alley. Switches off the engine.

'What are you doing?' she asks.

'I know who you are, love,' he says.

She laughs clumsily.

'I thought we were just having drinks.'

'We both know where this is going,' he warns.

'Take me home,' she demands.

'Not until you've put out,' he says.

'I'm not some cheap whore who does it in alleys. If you want me you'll have to come to the house and pay up front like everyone else,' she snaps.

'I've paid enough already, all those Babychams you've guzzled,' he snarls. 'Now be a good girl and play pretty.'

He grabs her. She slaps his face. He hits her back, harder than he needs to. She screams so he hits her again, grabbing her wrists in one hand and smacking her with the other.

'Stupid bitch,' he yells.

He tears her blouse open. She screams again. He gives her another slap then clamps his palm over her mouth.

'Shut the fuck up, bitch.'

She bites his hand, drawing blood. Scrambles out of the car. He chases her. Catches her before she makes the end of the alley. He drags her to the ground. He's on top of her. She's struggling but he's heavy.

'I know this is what you do,' he says, 'so why are you making it hard for me? Do you like it rough, is that it?'

He thrusts his hand up her skirt. Rips down one of her stockings. She jams her knee into his groin. He rolls away, groaning. She gets up and runs. Makes it onto the main road. Her hair's a mess. Her blouse is torn. She's only wearing one stocking, missing a shoe and she's left her handbag in his car. She keeps running. Gets lost in the tangle of terraces. There's only one thing she can do. She tides herself up.

The first car doesn't stop. But the second does.

She bends to the window. Is recognised by the vice copper patrolling in the unmarked car and arrested.

They call me at home. I fantasise about leaving her to rot. Silly old cow. Then get in my car and drive to collect her.

The desk sergeant gives me the grubby details, his fat round face shining under the station's fluorescent lighting. Fucking superior bastard. Like he doesn't keep a copy of *Playboy* behind the cistern for his morning wank.

An iron door clangs in the belly of the station. A WPC with saggy tits brings my mother to the desk. There are black tracks down her cheeks from crying, her lip is swollen and split by a red jewel of crusted blood; her blouse is torn and her hair dishevelled. I fix on the paperwork, her bail bond. The sergeant tells us they may decide to press charges of solicitation; we will be notified about any required court appearance. I sign. We leave.

In the car she says nothing. There's nothing she can say. I glance down while changing gear. Her hands, resting in her lap, are clasped like she's praying. Too fucking late for that. Her skirt has ridden up over her knees. She's only wearing one stocking. She reeks of cheap perfume and sweat. I can taste the smell of her in my mouth as we drive. It makes me gag. I want to throw up in the gutter. I want to throw her up in the gutter, get her out of my stomach, my brain: my life. Instead I fix on the empty road ahead, drive us home in silence.

I park opposite the house.

'Mickey.' She reaches across to me with a shaking hand, the scarlet talons raggedly broken.

There's nowhere for me to pull back to.

'Get out.'

'Mickey, I'm sorry, I didn't mean to… it's not true, what they said, it wasn't like that.'

'For Christ sake, get out of my fucking car.' I reach across her, fling open the door, shove her out and drive off.

I slept in the car that night. It was fucking freezing but better than sleeping where I could smell her. It's not any better now I'm older.

'My home life's not your fucking business,' I tell Don, glaring at him. 'I want to get back out on the road again, that's all.'

He doesn't believe me. He's not the only one. Sleeping in my car's a ball-acher of a fix.

'O.K.,' he says, 'well, five more minutes then we'll get back to it, eh?'

He chucks his cigar butt into the gutter and goes. I watch the embers cool from red to black.

'O.K. boys, I've got two things for you. Both of which, I

guarantee you are going to want to kiss me for.'

We're back in Don's office. It's night and the shades are pulled low. The garish electric lighting shows up cracks in the ceiling, rips in the wallpaper and the shadows of cobwebs. I sit in the armchair I've taken as mine and pick at the exposed stuffing.

Don's jammed behind the desk in his oversized leather chair. I can't see because the desk is the kind that comes with a modesty panel but I bet his feet dangle midair when he's sitting on that chair. He's a porcelain midget in a giant's doll house. He stands and, like a slightly malevolent elf, comes to each of us, saving me for last, giving us two envelopes; one large and square, the other narrow and floppy.

I already know what's in the square one so I open the smaller of the two first, slide out the contents and devour the words. British Airways. London, Heathrow to JKF, New York. Next Monday's date and, Jesus, 6.30 a.m. But at fucking last. Three thousand miles between me and her. And gigs to play; lots of bloody amazing nights doing what I love best. Don has lingered near me. He catches my eye. I nod my thanks.

'I'll have your itinerary typed up by Friday but the venues are booked and tickets are going well. Of course, that'll help.' He points at the unopened envelope in my lap.

I slide the record from its sleeve and flip it over to examine in the cover. Richard and Neil cluster round me, bursting to share my non-existent excitement. I stare back at myself from a black and white shot of us posing with our instruments framed by psychedelic orange and purple swirls. Is my hair really that long? I put a hand up to check.

'Looks good, doesn't it?' Richard beams.

'Yeah, great.' I try sounding like I care about a grooved piece of plastic but it comes out more sarcastic than sincere as I scan down the track list, remembering angsty days, Richard fucking up, me storming off, Don placating. I force something more genuine into my voice. 'Yeah, really great. I'm dead pleased. It was worth it.'

'Definitely,' Richard says.

For fuck sake, he's forgiving me. But then, I am doing them a favour. Hell, before I came along they were pissing about with the lights off, missing the mark more than hitting it. With me here they can see the bloody target at least.

I replace the LP in the envelope. Time to pack up and head out.

Death

I study the headstone one last time. Don't think I'll have the balls to come back again. James stands patiently until I turn away.

'You wanna get a beer?' he asks.

We go into the Black Dog. Order two pints. I pay. We sit in a quiet corner. It's a proper village pub. I miss pubs like this. John would've liked it.

'So what're you doing these days, James? Keeping out of trouble?'

'Aye, the odd gig here and there. I was at uni for a while but jacked it in.'

'Why?'

'Too bourgeois,' he says, 'I wasn't learning anything real; it was bullshit to keep the masses quiet.'

'I didn't figure you for a Commie, James.'

He laughs. 'I'm not, really. But I didn't see the point in spending three years learning how to live when I could be out there doing it.'

'How's your mother?'

'Fine.' He flips over a beer mat, tapping the table with it. 'She told me about the award,' he adds.

He must know this is why I called, asked to meet. Can I really right the past by rewriting the future?

'Yeah.'

'Well?' There's suppressed ferocity in his voice.

'And we plan to collect it in person.'

'Are you going to be playing at the ceremony?'

'Yeah.'

'Who's gonna drum for you?'

Steady. Don't bolt the horse.

'You, I hope.'

His dark eyes hold mine; they're not brown but a deep shade of grey that's almost black. There's a long pause. I sip my beer. James drums on the table with his fingertips. What am I waiting for? Fuck sake, I don't have the luxury of time anymore.

'Well?'

'Didn't think it would take you this long.' There's anger in his reply.

'Sorry. I should've called when I first heard but there was some stuff I had to sort out and...'

'I don't mean that. You promised you'd come and see me so we could play together. When you said it might be a while I didn't think I'd be waiting this fucking long.'

What's he on about?

'I don't rememb—'

'After the inquest.'

Shit, I fucking forgot about that. Bloody bollocks. 'Jesus. James, I'm really sorry. I wanted to, honest, but I didn't think I'd be welcome. Then, after a while, it was too hard to do it, everything coated in a dust I didn't dare disturb. That's no excuse, I know. But I'm here now and I really want you to do this. We all do.'

He studies me, working out how long he should torture me. Christ knows I deserve it.

'No one can drum like my dad.'

I feel the knife twist. 'We know that. We're not expecting you to be able to... I mean, I'm sure you can, but it's not why... You know the songs like no one else does...' I'm tying myself in knots. James doesn't help. Why the fuck should he? 'Do you remember that time we played together, you and me, in Don's office, you must have been about nine, ten? You started drumming on the table with two old biros and I did a bloody tricky progression but you kept the rhythm going perfectly. Your dad was dead proud. Jealous too, I think. He could see then that you were already as good as he was. You shouldn't waste that.' Am I pushing too hard? But he needs a kick up the backside. With John gone I've a proxy right to do it.

James clenches his hands into fists, powerful and threatening. Then he relaxes his grip, fanning his fingers out in a fluttering motion. I recall John sitting with one of Pete's girls on his knee, stroking her hair like it was silk.

'I remember,' he says. 'You made me work it out for myself when I couldn't get right.'

'Because I knew you could. And I know you can do this. It's got to be you, James. Your old man'd want you to do it. He always said you were his legacy.'

James swallows a mouthful of beer. I watch it stick for a second, blocked by the knot in his throat before he forces it down.

'O.K. I'll do it.'

'Great.'

'Is this just for the award ceremony?'

I can't answer 'cos I don't know myself. I think, with heart pounding, of rehearsals, recordings, gigs, parties: things as they were for one last time. But that's a mirage. And I'm an idiot for heading towards it. Things can't be as they were because it's not then. It's now.

Then I had control.

*

The room's full of people; journalists, photographers, promoters, execs from the record company: scary big knobs waiting to set about us. I scan the party for Don. He promised he'd be here.

'Where is he? Where is he?' Richard pleads at my side.

'Dunno. But we can't stand here like turkeys at Christmas.'

A chick breaks away from the flock and heads towards us. She's tall and thin with hair pulled into a bun and glasses perched on the end of her nose, the frames angled into cruel points. She smiles.

'Bloody hell, where is he?' Neil demands. It's the first time I've heard Neil swear.

She gets closer. Brings her notebook and pencil up like a gun, training the sights on us.

'You must be Mickey. Margaret Beubelle, *American Guitarist.*' She's a witch promising gingerbread reviews. She holds out her long slender wrist, her hand dangling at the end of it, her fingers relaxed, coaxing.

Can she smell fear? Only if I reek of it.

I flash my most charming smile, take her hand and press my fingers around hers.

'Margaret.' I hush her name and stare into her heavily painted eyes. 'It's lovely to meet you. Can I get you a drink?'

Magazines are crumpled in the foot-well of the limo. The results of long hard nights spent arse-kissing the press.

'This one's not bad.'

'Let's see.'

'It says, 'The Three Bob Band are England's latest export and offer a welcome change from the modest pop music that has tended to drift over the pond in recent years. Is this the next wave of the British Invasion?',' Richard reads.

'This one's better.' Don straightens out the latest issue of *American Guitarist*, and reads from the centre spread. "The Three Bob Band are certainly worth more than their name implies. Cutting edge music spawned from traditional blues, these boys play and sing like they mean it. More of it please, guys!'.'

Richard clocks my smile.

'Was that that Margaret bird you disappeared with?'

'Might be.'

'Whatever you bloody said to her it worked.'

I shrug. 'Didn't say anything. Didn't have to.'

Don catches my eye. I wink at him.

'Be carefully, Mickey,' he warns, 'hell hath no fury etcetera.'

'It's my new hobby, I'm gonna collect journalists, well, female ones anyway.'

He scowls but, shit, I'm entitled to some playtime.

The car pulls up outside tonight's venue, a New York theatre. Its purple neon sign boasts it's the hottest spot in town. Next to the gaudy flashing colours is our poster, the picture from the album cover in the centre and our names written underneath each grey face. It looks like a wanted poster but it's fucking working; there's a queue three deep coiled around the block.

Richard presses his face to the window.

'Christ. Are they waiting for us?'

Don tosses the magazine onto the heap at his feet.

'Yep. We're sold out here.' He grins. 'It's onward and upward, boys, home and abroad, to the moon and back: the whole damn universe.'

March 30: Anderson Theatre, New York
April 8: Thee Image, Miami Beach
April 9: Thee Image, Miami Beach
April 10: Thee Image, Miami Beach
April 12: Action House, Island Park
April 13: Action House, Island Park
April 14: Action House, Island Park
April 25: Allen Theatre, Cleveland
April 26: Cincinnati Convention Center, Cincinnati
April 28: Brown University, Providence
April 29: University of Massachusetts, Amherst
May 3: The Grand Ballroom, Detroit
May 4: The Grand Ballroom, Detroit
May 5: Hullabaloo, Mentor
May 10: Earl Warren Showgrounds, Santa Barbara

May 11: Melodyland Theatre, Anaheim
May 23: Fillmore West, San Francisco
May 24: Fillmore West, San Francisco
May 25: Fillmore West, San Francisco
May 31: Shrine Exposition Hall, Los Angeles
June 1: Shrine Exposition Hall, Los Angeles

Night after night we charge the stage, exploding with the full force of our music, blasting audiences that scream and gyrate, clamouring for beats that throb inside their hearts, riffs that roar in their ears and the rapture of rhythms kick with life. They raise their fists, pounding the air in supplication. We fire out licks and lyrics like prayers. We feed them, thousands of desperate, starving kids, not with loaves and fishes: with notes and chords. I feed them. My raging guitar wails and shrieks, a beast possessed by its own power. The buzz of electric sounds and elated crowds vibrates through my body each night, taking longer to fade. I lie awake until two, three, four, six, eight a.m., wallowing in the hum of pleasure. It's the most perfect high I've ever had and I surrender myself to a lifelong addiction.

Another gig, at the end of another tour, my fifth with the Three Bob Band, our second in America. Another crowd anticipates our arrival on stage. Maybe the same one as last time we were here; maybe a different one, lured by our latest Top Ten album. I slip away from the wings.

In the dressing room Richard is nervously twisting the machine heads on his bass, tuning, de-tuning and retuning it. Neil is in the bathroom and Don's roaming somewhere, probably checking on door receipts. I sit down, light a cigarette. I used to keep busy before gigs, playing the songs through in my head, fingering the solos against empty air. Now I know the stuff inside out. Hell, I should; I wrote most of it. So I'm just sitting here, bored shitless 'til it's time to go on.

Jesus, when did this happen? When did I start boring myself?

Before or after we toured Europe, scored four number ones and started cashing three figure royalty cheques? Isn't this everything I wanted? So why the fuck isn't it enough? I eyeball Richard, who's bent over his bass. Because he's not enough. Or Neil. They're solid, steady. Capable. But not talented. The music is stagnant. This thing we've become has gone as far, got as big, as it can. It's time for me to step down. Off. Up.

The dull note of Richard's unamplified bass strings twangs in my ear.

'I can't get the damn thing in tune,' he mutters.

'I'm not surprised the way you've been arsing around with it. If you spent as much time working out some new grooves we might actually be going somewhere with this shit.' I jump up. Snatch the guitar off him. Tune it and hand it back. He stares at me. I should apologise. Fuck that.

Neil strides in. Don materialises behind him.

'Right, boys,' he claps his hands, 'are you ready?'

'Suppose so,' Richard says.

'Yeah,' I say more firmly.

'Well, lads, let's take stock.' Don forces us into a huddle. 'It's been a fantastic four months over here. We've topped ticket sales from last year's tour, the new album's still climbing the charts and you're playing to the biggest audiences of your careers with tremendous bloody responses from the kids. This is the last gig so blow them away.'

I pull out of the huddle. Stalk away down the corridor.

'Mickey?'

Don's followed. I stop.

'What?'

'Is there a problem?'

I snort. 'Can't you see it? Hear it?'

He lays a hand on my arm. 'We'll have a word after the show, eh?'

'Fine.'

We take up formation on stage. Lights flash. I draw a breath. Hold it, hanging on to the moment before the start of the end. Neil counts us in. I exhale. Let go. Lash out with the first chord.

Number after number we soar and dive above the crowd that rhythmically ripples below us. I feel alternately that I'm above everything, looking down, watching myself play, and that I'm in the audience, looking up at me thrashing my guitar. The music washes over me but it's like I'm behind glass; I hear the wave coming but don't get wet.

Don stands in wings, as he often does. I feel his eyes searching me, trying to fix me in place. He's invested too much to let me leave. Two years, three UK/Europe tours, writing and recording two albums, the States twice, four number ones. He's not dumb; he'll follow the talent. And the money.

The final notes die away. The compére steps up to the mic.

'Ladies and gentlemen, the Three Bob Band.'

Applause batters us. Richard claps my shoulder. Neil comes down from his drum stool and stands beside me. Lined up as if for the gallows pole, we make our last stand together.

Later Don comes to my room.

'We'd better have that chat, Mickey.'

'Guess so.'

I sprawl on the bed and start rolling a joint. Think I'm gonna need it.

Don tuts loudly.

'What?'

'Don't you think you've had enough?'

'Yeah, but not of this.' I light up and drag heavily on the weed. 'I want out.'

'You can't be serious.' A deep groan lies buried in his words.

'You know we've come as far as we can.'

Don perches on the armchair. 'I only know that's what you're telling me.'

'If that's what I'm telling you then it's the truth.'

'You're not being fair to Richard or Neil. They're both competent musicians.'

'Competent? Fucking hell, Don, how much further d'you suppose we're gonna get on competent? I'm not gonna settle for average. That was never the plan. What did you expect me to do?'

'I expect you not to run out on everything I've given you because of a few reviews raving about how bloody great you are. Reviews you get by screwing the tarts that write them,' he rages.

'Fucking bullshit. I get those reviews because I play shit hot. I earn every fucking word, on stage not in the bedroom. That's just a hobby. You're right about one thing, though, it's my praises they're chorusing, not Neil's or Richard's. Now I'm telling you I'm leaving, not asking for your fucking permission. If you've got any brains whatsoever you'll support me.' I sit. Swing my legs off the bed, like I might get up and go right now.

'Why the hell should I support you if this is how you're going to thank me for two years of hard slog, running around after you and getting you this far? Without us, you'd be a nobody going fucking nowhere.'

'And without me that's exactly where you'll end up.'

He knows I'm right. I can see the pound signs cavorting behind his eyes.

'There are no guarantees once you walk away from this, Mickey.'

He's not happy but I've twisted his arm, the one he uses to bank our cheques.

'The only thing guaranteed if I stay is that I'll fucking die of boredom. I need to be working with musicians who have vision, talent, can do something new, be creative: original. I've carried these two long enough; I need someone I can feed off now.'

Don folds his arms. 'Fine, if that's what you want. Do whatever the hell you like. You will anyway,' he says. 'I hope to God you have a plan, though.

'I do.'

'Are you going to share it with me?'

I lie back on the bed. Take another soothing drag on the joint. 'I'll put my own line up together. Hand pick musicians that can do what I need. When I've sorted that, I expect we'll need a ballsy geezer to run the show for us.'

'Be careful, Mickey,' Don warns, 'you might be in danger of getting what you want.'

We face off. I shrug. He slams the door on his way out.

I decide the weed's not enough and ring room service for a bottle of Scotch.

When I open the door it's not the bellboy. It's the receptionist bird.

'Your whisky, Mr Hunter.' She presents the bottle.

She's not a reporter but she'll do.

'Thanks.' I take it. 'Where's what's-his-name that usually does this?'

'It's after midnight. There's just me and the night-porter, sir.'

'Must be pretty bloody boring sitting down there 'til morning.'

'It's my job, sir.'

I glance down. No ring. Not that I care, but it means there's a decent chance of me getting her into bed.

'You get breaks, though?'

'Yes.'

'You due one now?'

'I really don't think...'

'Come on, you're not going to make me drink this whisky all by myself, are you, darlin'?'

She bites her bottom lip. I wonder how old she is; seventeen, eighteen? Hell, she's gotta grow up some time.

'It's a lonely life, you know, a touring musician's, on the road, hundreds of miles from home.' I cast my eyes down, shuffle my feet.

'I could take five minutes,' she admits.

I smile at her. 'Great.' I hold the door open and stand in the doorway so she has to squeeze past me to get in.

When I've fucked her 'til she screams I feel better. She gets dressed. I lie on the bed and open the whisky.

'You want a drink?'

'I better get back to work,' she says.

'Suit yourself.'

She leaves. I drink two-thirds of the bottle and smoke the rest of that joint before I'm ready to sleep it off. There's no room for regrets.

The morning light is a pale, cold pink. I stand at the window. The sun sits on the horizon. The sky is an angry orange that heats up to red before cooling down to mauve the further out it spreads. I push the window open and the LA drone comes in; steady traffic whir, punctuated by random horn blasts. I close my eyes. Let the calming hum fill my ears. Wonder if Don's told them yet.

I don't go down for breakfast. Or answer the door when someone knocks. After they've gone I hang the 'Do not disturb' sign on the handle. I ring Don and tell him I'll take a taxi to the airport. 'Fine,' is all he says before hanging up.

I stay in my room 'til the last second.

Downstairs the reception bird is finishing her shift. Her boyfriend's come to meet her. She catches my eye and blushes. I wink as I drop my key on the desk. I'm half way across the lobby when I hear him.

'Where'd the hell you get that from, Jackie?'

He's spotted the love-bite on her neck. Wonder how she'll talk herself out of that? I push the door open. Step into the late morning sun. Feel its heat on me. I stretch and my new-grown wings unfurl, drying in the breeze.

Art

Here we are, three survivors and James, sitting round a too-big table. There's a fruit bowl in the middle of it; apples, bananas and a single tangerine. Or maybe it's a satsuma. There must have been others. Who ate them?

I wish Don was here. Curses on the cancer that killed him five years ago. Mind, he'd have got us the award long before now. What'd he think of this? He'd be on my side, too fucking right he would, making sure I get what I want. But he'd be proud of us all and taking his share of the credit. He'd handle Philip for me, too. After bottling it at our last meeting, I'm ready to puke my guts today. It's too early and the day too grey for confrontations.

I force my eyes up from the fruit bowl and glance around the table. Pete's much as he was, that grown up air fits now he's had time to fill it out. His brown hair is sprinkled with grey, cut short and neat. He was never happy out on a ledge, preferring to blend in with whatever's going down around him: standard M.O. for a bass man. Philip's still clinging to his younger self, fair hair longer than he can get away with at his age, falling into his eyes, allowing him that arrogant head-toss to throw it back. I'm pleased. It must mean he's also crapping himself at the thought of getting old: dying. Using the mirrored window opposite I study myself. The old man who stares back is me but he's also a stranger, no longer sure who he is, where he's going. I always knew. Or thought I did. He smiles and his eyes disappear into a mess of creases. He's offering me what's left of his courage, a wounded hero on the battlefield, urging me forwards into no man's land. Fucking cheers.

Then, among us three old bulls, is James, a young buck. He's not old enough to have anywhere near the baggage we're lugging around. But he's got more than he deserves. He carries a dead man's weight.

Philip has brought his lawyer, a hard-eyed fella whose suit probably cost more than my car. Pete has Susie with him, literally holding his hand. James came by himself. I wish I had his balls. We're waiting for Keira, who's deliberately late. My idea, a ploy. It's only a pretence of control but better than nothing.

The door bangs. She rushes in, purple leather coat flapping around her knees which are exposed by the short green skirt she's wearing. James' eyes are drawn to her as she flies across the room.

'Sorry I'm late,' she manages to not sound even slightly sorry. 'I was waiting on a fax from NIME.'

She plonks down next to me and I introduce her.

'Keira Martin, my PA.'

James is the only one who stands and offers her his hand.

She clears her throat unnecessarily and passes round sheets of paper.

'NIME have sent this provisional running order for the ceremony. They'd like you to open with one of your big hits, something energizing, there'll be sundry other awards and yours will be last. They'd also like you to close the ceremony with a set.'

Everyone stares at the papers.

'How long a set?' Philip asks.

'Up to you. There's a limit to the broadcast time for scheduling reasons but if you want to go beyond that they assure me it won't be a problem. The venue is booked for the night and provisions are being made to record the show for possible release on DVD later.'

Hard-eyes jumps in. 'We need to give the details a look-see.' By which he means check the bottom line.

'Info regarding Ts and Cs is on page two,' Keira says.

Hard-eyes flicks over and scans down. The slight upward movement of his eyebrows indicates he approves of the 'details'.

'It would be nice to do a decent set, at least thirty, even forty-five, minutes,' Pete says.

'I agree,' I reply. 'There's no point setting up for two songs.'

Philip, who's been bent in conversation with his lawyer, glances over now.

'James, what are your feelings on this?'

I see James look first at Keira, then me. 'I agree with Uncle Mickey. Dad wouldn't want you doing a half-arsed job so if you're doing it in his memory there's even more reason to do it properly.' It's not bullshit.

'O.K.,' Philip says after a pause.

'If you're all in agreement,' Keira continues, 'NIME want you to sign this document. After all,' she laughs lightly, 'this event's costing them a fair bit; they can't have things changing at ten to it kicking off.'

She passes a second sheet of paper to me. I scrawl my name in large, bold lettering and hand it to Pete. He signs too and gives it to James. After James there's only Philip.

'This is just the award ceremony we're signing up for?'

'There has been renewed interest from the record company,' Keira says. 'They'd love you to put together a collection of your back catalogue. The timing, from their perspective, is perfect. You could get it together quickly, a bit of remastering maybe, some thought about what to include, the order etcetera, come up with cover; it could be the way of bringing your music to a whole new generation of listeners.' She stops breathlessly. 'A generation of listeners who've had to make do with a load of saccharin pop crap for too long.'

She's pushing Philip's buttons. Vanity was always his Achilles' heel. Time for one last stand?

'If you go ahead with that and it's well received, who knows?' She leaves the golden promise hanging in the conference room's synthetic air: the temptation of our crowns reclaimed and donned with pride.

Pete and I exchange grins. Susie lets a little sigh escape. James's hands are clenched into fists. Keira smiles at him.

Philip leans back. His eyes fix on mine. I grind my teeth. He moves the pen seamlessly over and under the fingers of his right hand. Fuck it, I should have unloaded both barrels into him over lunch. Ambushed him with the fact that I saw him kill Ronsey. Got him doubled up in agony when I had the chance. But at such close range the gun would've recoiled, taking me down too. Shit, it's no more than I deserve.

'If you're gonna sign it, just bloody sign,' I snap, 'or I might have to retract the fucking generous offer I made you over lunch the other day.'

As my cryptic threat circles the table, poison sushi, eyes drop, hands fidget and throats clear. None of them are Philip's.

'Hey, man, take it easy,' he says.

Philip leans forward. Adds his name to the piece of paper. Joins the party.

*

Anna is gone. I'm alone. With no fucking idea what to do about Philip, the band; I've cut myself off. It's in a right shit state. I can't even think about it because it's salt in a deep cut. I need sleep so I get a quack to give me pills. I swallow a handful, lay back and am out. But it's not a quiet sleep.

I'm scaling a mountain. Loose rocks roll away at my touch and fall endlessly; my feet scrabble over uneven ground. Nothing changes. I've no idea how far away the summit is or how far I've already come. The pink sky is streaked with blue wisps that wind themselves around me like sticky cobwebs. I climb on.

I don't know how long I've been climbing. I may have to climb forever. There's nothing else. My legs burn; my head throbs. I've climbed so far. Further than I thought possible. Above me the clouds mass into a shape, circling the misty mountain top in a neat ring. I must reach it. I keep climbing. As I get nearer I feel the ring pulling me. The rocky mountainside becomes glassy. There's nothing to hold onto but the ring hauls me up, a magnet drawing iron filings.

I'm there: the peak.

I stand on the blue ring. The centre of it fills with a hot light. I narrow my gaze against the glare. The light bursts. I see a goat, grey and vague. I creep closer. Note features: two long horns spiralling up to the pink sky; a thin face with a ragged beard; mouth curved into a knowing smile: three eyes. The central one blinks at me. I blink back.

'The way is twofold. Create all for thyself under thine own will. Accept all that is created by others.'

The voice comes from the third eye, transmitting words like radio waves. It's a voice I've heard before, ages ago, when this was first starting.

The goat taps a hoof on the glowing ring. The surface is pierced by a long blue shaft topped with a winged globe and a two-headed serpent. I reach for the shaft. It's cool, slips through my hands as I glide down it, back to the centre of the earth.

I wake. Look around. I'm home. Everything's normal. No, it's fucking not 'cos she's not here. I shiver. Hear that weird goat again: 'Accept all that is created by others.' So fucking what? It was a dream. No surprise that my brain can conjure something totally fucked up and totally real. It's got nothing to do with anything. It's just a dream.

But I dream it again the next night. Wake to the feeling of falling as I slide down the blue shaft. I flick the bedside light on.

Everything's ordinary, in place. But I'm not bloody convinced so race through the house, turning on lights, even leaving the fridge door open and turning the oven on so it too lights up. In and out of every room I'm trying to work out where it's coming from, this dream. I know it's from something real. I retrace all the trips I've had. Nah, that's not it. Maybe the goat is in a painting I've seen, a picture in a magazine. Or a book. I'm in the living room now. A book... I charge to the bookcase. Tear over the spines. See it; small, brown, anonymous, on the bottom shelf. I prise it from its slot. Flick pages.

'Chapter 13: The twenty-two Atu (keys) of the tarot and their attribution to Hebrew letters.'

I sift the words until one grabs my eye: goat. I read slower.

'Atu XV: The Devil. This card is attributed to the Hebrew letter Ayin, translated as 'eye' and represents creative energy in its most potent, material form. The card depicts a goat, leaping in ecstasy upon the summit of the world. The goat represents not only Capricorn of the Zodiac but also the god Pan, the all-begetter, and Set, the ass-headed Egyptian god. The formal interpretation of this card is the complete appreciation of all things in existence: 'He rejoices in the rugged and barren no less than in the smooth and fertile.' Creative energy at its most masculine pervades this card and engenders the impulse to create without logical, rational foresight or reason. It's ultimate message is to create all for oneself under one's own will while accepting all that is created by others.'

That my twisted brain remembered reading this the day we named Crown & Kingdom, stored it to torture me now is too fucked up for control. I slam the book shut. Hurl it across the room.

But it won't leave me in peace. I try shutting it up with booze. When that fails I try uppers and not sleeping but, after staying awake for three days, my body begs for mercy and when I let it sleep the dream's waiting. I go back to the quack. He gives me different pills. I sleep for twelve hours and dream the dream twice. In the morning I flush the rest of the bottle and let it come instead. I pull myself out of it, watching it like a TV show. I'm there and not there. I split. There are two 'mes' in two places at once; each is an escape from the other. I don't know which is real. Maybe neither.

One morning I wake up, dress, go into the kitchen, open the curtains, look out on the sunny dawn, light a fag and am waiting for the kettle to boil before I realise it: the goat dream didn't come last night. I'm ready now.

Time restarts for Crown & Kingdom; for me and Philip. I call Don, arrange a meeting. On my way to his office I take my Les Paul to a bloke who does wood carving and get him to etch on the back of it, 'Accept all that is created by others.'

'This is your fourth album together. Do you find it easy coming up with new material even after you've been writing together for five years?'

Philip answers, scattering words and cockiness.

'There's always something new to write about.'

'In the early days you did most of the writing yourself, Mickey. Has it taken some of the pressure off, now you and Philip write together?'

I open my mouth but my brain's empty.

'Mickey's always happy to share,' Philip jokes, 'especially when it comes to work. But seriously, since I started writing I feel that's helped us go in new, exciting directions.'

Get it together, you daft twat. I glare at Philip. He ignores me.

She scribbles in her notepad. 'And how does it feel to be here for your seventh tour of the States?'

I jump in. 'Pretty good, darlin', now you're here.'

I wink at her. She drops her eyes to her notepad, her cheeks flushing. My hobby's pretty fucking notorious now. I'd like to add her to my collection. She's got that sacrificial virgin thing going on.

Philip retracks us.

'We're always glad to get back here. I mean, for me, I was so young when I first came over it feels like I practically grew up in the States, it's home, ya know. Plus, the audiences are fan-fucking-tastic.'

What a load of bullshit. I start sniggering.

'One final question: after all your achievements what's next for Crown & Kingdom?'

Philip opens his mouth but I'm determined to beat him.

'I'm hanging out for them to make fucking tasty music journos an Olympic sport. Sure I'd be a gold medal contender in that.'

'Darlin', you're killing me here. Get off.'

I shove her to the side. She lies limply, her dyed blonde hair staining the white pillow. Her make-up is smudged from our fucking and her eyes look swollen and bruised. I hate her. She's number… shit, I've lost count.

'If you're gonna fuck me at least have the fucking decency to do it right.'

I roll her onto her front, grab hold and drag her up onto all fours. Her back arches away from me. The knobbles of her spine rise under tissue paper skin, a mountain ridge. I push inside her. She yelps. I push harder. I wanna make her scream. I dig the long nails of my right hand, kept sharp for finger picking, into her shoulder, pulling her down onto me. Her head drops below her shoulders. She's an inhuman shape. I bang her harder and harder. The headboard thumps off the wall. I ram into her until I feel my body burning and long to have icy water thrown over me. Every fibre and nerve is stretched taut, ready to snap. Fire scorches me.

She raises her head. Screams gargle in her throat. I let everything go. The fire moves on. A cool wave of blissful pleasure dowses me. I pull out. Slump into the crumpled twist of sheets. She's moving on the bed next to me but I don't look. Sacrificed? Yes. Virgin? Not fucking likely.

'Fucking lie still will ya.'

She freezes. I let myself drift off for a few empty seconds of euphoria before plummeting earthward.

'Fuck off.' I kick her over the edge of the bed.

She lands with a flump on the fluffy carpet. I feign sleep while she moves about, banging into things in the candlelight. When I hear the door creak I open one eye. Her thin, shivering shoulders tremble beneath the sheer fabric of her blouse. Her feet are bare. The bony legs sticking out from her mini don't look as though they're strong enough to hold her up. She turns. Looks at me. She's crying, silly bitch. I stare back. She opens the door. Leaves. Don't think she'll be writing this up. Don't give a fuck if she does.

When she's gone I go into the bathroom. There's only enough left for one more line. Shit, I'll have to find Gomez. I scrape the white power into a neat row and snort it back. It buzzes through my head, a deranged wasp, before settling in my chest as a steady hum. I glance in the mirror above the sink. I don't see anything.

In the corridor, hunting for Gomez, I run into Philip. I'm still pissed at him for his performance in that afternoon's interview.

'Hey, man,' he says.

'Seen Gomez?'

'He's somewhere abouts.'

I shoulder-charge past Philip.

'What's up with you?' He grabs my arm.

'Get your fucking hands off me.' I pull away.

'Cool it, will ya,' he snaps.

'Cool it? Me? You're the one needs to cool it.'

'What you on about?'

'That interview.'

'What about it?'

'That shit about you taking the band in wonderful new directions.'

'I didn't say it like that.'

It's slipping. I grab for a hold. 'You'd do well to remember who's fucking band this is.' I turn. 'And if you're looking for that chick from the magazine you're too late. I banged her and kicked her out.'

I stagger down the corridor.

The crowd screams its collective insanity at us. Philip kneels at the front of the stage, the mic raised to his lips for the final words to be poured into it. I thrash out the last chords, strumming furiously, diluting his vocal majesty with my six-string magic. The Gibson bellows. I envy its recklessness, how it blinds and deafens without fear of consequences. There will be consequences. I yank the lead from the jack. The music cuts off, leaving Philip screaming into a musical black hole. Power, malicious and malignant, surges through me as I replace my Les Paul on the stand at the edge of the stage and strut off. I'm always first off. Last back on for encores. A second later Pete and Ronsey join me in the wings. Philip stays onstage, blowing kisses to the crowd.

'I've got the final numbers: 45,693,' Don announces.

'Fucking hell,' Ronsey yelps.

Pete purses his lips to let out a low whistle that can't be heard over the shrieking audience.

'Not bad,' I say.

Philip hooks himself off stage and appears next to me, draping an arm around my shoulders.

'Fucking brilliant.'

'I was aware,' I say.

'Over forty-five thousand's in there, ya know,' Ronsey brags.

'Really? That should get up Jagger's nose.' Philip lets go of me and starts hopping up and down.

'I'd rather it got up my nose,' I say. 'Where's Gomez?'

'In a minute,' Philip begs. 'C'mon, one more song, two maybe. Listen to them, man, they want us.'

'They've already had us,' I reply.

'But more, man, they want more.'

He goes back out. Like he always does. Ronsey follows first, then Pete.

Let the bastard wait.

'Go on,' Don says. 'It's you they're bloody screaming their heads off for.'

I grin. 'Yeah, I know.'

The sound of my strings ringing flat to pitch to sharp to pitch wails out of the headphones, filling my ears. I bend over the neck, fingers poised. There, right there, you son of a bitch. I fly at the strings. Press down. Draw back. Slide and bend. Hammer on. Pull off. Pre-recorded rhythm and played-live lead wrap around each other endlessly. Four more bars. Three more. Two. Last one. Stop. The high E screeches to its death. The rhythm fades in through the headphones before it too vanishes into the vapours around me.

I pull off the headphones. Sit up, stretching my back, flexing cramped fingers.

'That was perfect, Mickey,' the sound engineer says over the intercom.

I hold up one finger.

'You don't need one more. Honestly, that was it.'

I reinstate my one finger.

'O.K.,' he sighs.

I replace the headphones. The howling chords come through. I run down the lead notes once more, chasing after them. They thrill and spark, scattering and jostling each other as I play. It's good. Fucking awesome. I wanna keep listening to it the way you stare at a rainbow before it dissolves.

'O.K.,' the engineer says, 'that's it.'

I nod. It'll do. For now.

The door opens. Philip strides in.

'You done?'

'Yep.'

'Want a drink?' He holds a beer bottle.

'Cheers. What time is it?'

'Gone midnight. Not too late for a party?' He grins.

'Never too late for a party.'

'Yeah, I'm sure a couple of music gods like us can find some action,' he says.

I sit my guitar on the stand. Swallow a mouthful of beer, trying to wash down his arrogance. It's that sweet American piss Ronsey hates. Why the fuck does Philip drink it when we're home? He could get some decent ale in.

'Ronsey'd go mad if he saw this.' I wave the bottle.

''S O.K. I got some Newkie Brown for him,' Philip laughs.

'Where is he? And Pete?'

'Man, they went home hours ago,' Philip says, lighting a cigarette and offering it to me.

'What're you still doing here?'

'Wanted to make sure you finished it without killing yourself. You've been in here for, like, two weeks solid.'

'We all have.'

'No,' Philip says, 'not the way you have. When did you last sleep, man?'

I shrug. Fucked if I can remember. 'Anyway, it's done now,' I say, 'there's the mixing but I'll give it a few days.'

The soundman pokes his head through the door.

'Any chance of me getting home while it's still dark tonight?'

'Yeah, I'm done,' I say.

He nods gratefully and retreats to the control booth. A second later the lights flash off. I pack my guitar and coil the leads before bagging everything.

'Think I'll head home too. Gimme me a hand to the car with this, will ya?' I ask Philip.

'Sure.'

We lug the gear outside. It's pissing down. I fumble for my keys, panicked about rain leaking into the amp's circuits.

Philip scowls at the sky. 'We have people to do this for us now.'

'Yeah, where the fuck are they?'

'All in bloody bed.'

'You didn't have to sodding well stay.'

'Can't let you do all the work; you might think you can take all the glory too,' he says, only half joking.

I slam the boot lid. We skulk in the dark, the rain soaking our T-shirts.

'You don't fancy that party?' Philip asks.

'Nah, I'm gonna chill for a bit.' Jesus, I can't keep walking away from him like this. I suck in a breath. 'Join me, why don't you? Think I've got some party supplies stashed away. We could both do with unwinding.'

Under the yellow glow of the street lamp, Philip's eyes gleam like a tom's, stalking its prey. I haven't properly seen him for a long time. Because I was afraid to. Now I realise he's changed. Doesn't match the image I've held in my head. Dunno who he is anymore. I'm worried he's me and I'm him, that we're switching places: roles. I'm not ready to give it over to him. I can taste the sourness of fear in my throat.

'Yeah,' he says, 'hell, we work too fucking hard. I could use a night of laid-back, weed-smoking pleasure. You can give me the grand tour of your new pad.'

The car crunches over the gravel drive that lies twisted round the front of my newly acquired three storey Georgian manor house. We get out. Philip admires the mansion, its floodlit turrets, gothic architraves and double-fronted oak entrance.

'Nice.'

'Every king needs a castle, eh?' I joke.

'Your own private Kingdom, capital K.'

But I don't give him the tour. The sight of my life in packing crates is not majestic. Instead we settle down for the night, what's left of it, in the drawing room, huddling around the stone inglenook fireplace. I draw the heavy brocade curtains against the black rain, light the fire and some candles.

'Haven't you heard of this new discovery? Call it el-ec-tri-city,' Philip teases.

'No bulbs,' I lie. I like candles better. They throw reassuring shadows into the corners.

Philip stretches out on the velvet-covered Chesterfield.

'Man, you need a new car. That heap of yours is not comfy. Get your name down for one of those new Aston Martins; Ronsey's in love with his.'

'Dunno. Mebbe. Got history with my old Triumph.' Nights spent kipping in it, days spent escaping in it montage through my memory. I brush them aside. 'Drink?' I offer him one of the two shots of whisky I've poured.

'Cheers.'

I sit on the floor in front of the fire, feeling the blaze on my skin, and start rolling a joint. My fingers fumble. I haven't had to roll my own for a while. Philip watches. Sees the tremor but doesn't say anything. I light the joint and take a drag. The metallic smoke is soothing and warm. Then I have to pass it to Philip.

He smiles at the first breath.

'This is good.'

'Turkish. Not that cheap crap Gomez palms us off with on the road.'

'You should tell him. We're bloody paying him enough.'

'Doesn't really matter. It's just to top up the buzz out on the road.'

'True.'

We smoke back and forth in silence. I remember doing this before but it was so long ago I can't be sure it was really us. Philip reclines on the sofa. I stay on the floor, feeling the solid seventeenth century floorboards beneath the carpet, hundreds of years old and still sturdy. Down here I can't fall.

'What's been your best moment so far?' Philip asks, propping himself up.

'Of what?'

'All this, you dick,' he says, laughter on the edge of his words.

'Dunno.'

'Come on. Six years of fame and glory. The adulation of thousands, maybe millions. Money coming out of our bloody ears.'

'It's all been good.' Liar.

'Yeah, but the one thing that, if this went away tomorrow, you'd mourn? What would it be?'

I think back. See a blur of images, flicked over so fast I can't tell one frame from another. The flicking only stops when I'm right at the beginning.

'The first time we played together.'

'You mean that shitty blues club north of the river?'

'Nah, the first time we played together.'

'Christ, that draughty warehouse?' Philip sees it too.

'We did 'Baby, Let's Play House'.'

'All I remember about that was driving around for three hours, trying to find the damn place,' Philip complains, 'and being abso-bloody-lutely terrified.'

I snap my eyes onto his. 'Why?'

'Jesus, I wanted it so badly and it felt like that was my last chance at it but you and Pete had already done so much; I was worried I wouldn't be in your league.'

'If I'd thought you weren't I wouldn't've asked you.'

'I was too dumb then to think logically.' He laughs at the memory of his younger self. 'So why is it that?'

'Hope.'

'What?'

I shake my head. 'Don't think I'm gonna explain this well.' I struggle up off the floor. Reach across the table, sling more whisky into our glasses. 'I knew then that we had it. I could see it, hear it: feel it. I knew we were going to be… this… fuck… whatever it is we are. This amazing potential unrolled at my feet, stretched way off. I saw us standing on the edge of a wide green field that went beyond the horizon, knew we could walk the whole way across it and there wasn't a single thing to stop us unless we stopped ourselves.'

Philip's face is pouted into a frown. Slowly it relaxes.

'Yeah.' He breathes the word all the way out, pressure escaping. 'I've got it.'

We don't say anything else 'cos there's too much to say. As the silence presses into me I feel a familiar dull ache in my chest. It's that Anna-shit. Danger creeps towards me, low to the ground, only half hidden. Mebbe tonight I should stab at it, see if it bleeds. It might be my last chance to put things properly right between us, before we plunge over the cliff together. I open my mouth a couple of times. Nothing. The fire crackles and pops. Flames dance to music in my head, a tune that's been going round and round in there for a long time, trapped on a carousel.

'Man, it's quiet here,' Philip says.

'You want some music?'

'Whatever.'

I fetch my old acoustic from the other room. Philip raises his eyebrows. 'Aren't you sick of playing?'

'Nah. Make yourself useful and roll up again.' I perch on an armchair, check the tuning and start to finger-pick a handful of notes. They come gracefully, a melodic blend of honey-sweet sounds with a gently rising tempo. After four bars Philip turns his ears to me, the unlit joint abandoned. I let the music build, taking the notes higher, making them sing, picking double strings, rolling a low burbling open E that provides a soothing drone. I've played this through thousands of times but never found my way to the end, the notes always vanishing like melting ice. But this time, after I pass the last familiar point, from somewhere outside of me the rest of the song emerges. It rises and rises, pitching up, fine rich flavours melding together on my auditory taste buds. I stop picking. Start strumming, harder and faster, the notes crammed together, crushing against each other. I climb on. And on. And on. Reach the top. Slide slowly and fluently back down. A familiar voice in my head that's not mine and that has been mute for a long time speaks up.

'Accept all that is created by others.'

Philip's eyes shine.

'Have you got some paper and a pen?'

I find some. For twenty minutes he scribbles. He hums the tune I've only played for him once as he writes. Three pieces go into the flames; four others survive. He finishes with a flourish.

'Ready?' he asks.

I cast Anna from my mind. Maybe this is the real way to fix things between us. I play it again. Philip sings. The song is born.

The warehouse has shrunk. I don't know how it's gonna contain our music this time. Wind rattles the windows, a storm seeking refuge from itself.

'You O.K., man?' Philip rests his hand on my shoulder.

He's as wound up as me but he holds on, steadying me,

anyway. That's how it's been since that night at mine, when we sat around, getting high, breathing new life into our relationship: making our song. There's a stronger connection; we're one single piece without joins: indestructible. Energy and substance welded together

'Yeah.' I smile at him.

'Christ, it's wild out there,' Ronsey moans as he forces the door shut against the wind. 'Dunno why we couldn't do this some place with an indoor bog. Aren't we better than this now?'

We've each got homes with rehearsal space; there are any number of high-tech studios we could've booked. If we wanted it Don'd get us the fucking Royal Albert Hall. Again. But I needed to come back here. 'Cos we need to go back to the beginning and start it again but this time dodge the bullets, duck the low bridges, dowse the flames before the fire takes hold.

'You've got no appreciation for the sentimental, man,' Philip accuses.

'Bollocks,' Ronsey says as he sits behind the drum kit and grabs his sticks.

'What is it you want us to do?' Pete asks.

'Listen and play whatever comes to you,' I say.

'How do you know something's gonna come to me?' Pete demands.

'It will,' Philip says. I nod. We've already done it so we know it's doable.

I perch on my amp. Philip sits across from me on an upturned crate. There's nothing left but the music. I'm looking down at the world from space, ready to jump, hoping the parachute opens again this time. I caress the first notes. Philip murmurs the opening lyrics. We've leapt and now we're falling, floating at first, as the tender harmony of my guitar and his voice drift downward. The music gathers momentum; forces we can't control plummeting us. We could fall to our deaths like this, the two of us, leaving everything behind. But I want to pull Pete and Ronsey with us. Together we stand; united we fly. I don't want to leave them. Ronsey's snare snaps time; he's made the leap. Pete chases him, catching up breathlessly in the next bar. We're together. I pull the cord; the chute opens. Billows out behind us. We ride air currents and land safely.

Silence settles amongst us. I'm relieved: ecstatic. So's Philip. The connection between us is holding.

'Bloody hell, that was good,' Ronsey says.

'Was that what you had in mind?' Pete asks.

'I didn't have anything in mind; I wanted you to play what you felt you should,' I say.

'But was it O.K.?' he persists.

'Fucking brilliant,' I say and he starts beaming.

'How long've you two twats been sittin' on that?' Ronsey demands.

'We came up with it at Mickey's the other night. He started playing it. I got the lyrics right away and that was it.'

I don't tell them I've been sitting on it a hell of a lot longer than that.

'What are we going to call it?' Pete asks.

''Trees of Eden',' Philip says, the title we've agreed on.

'Is it going on *Return of the Kings*?' Ronsey asks.

'Why not?' Philip challenges.

'Is there time?' Pete asks.

'Course,' I say.

I can do anything I want. I'm the legendary Mickey Hunter.

The audience is quiet. The collective hush of a world that knows the apocalypse is coming. Fifty thousand people stand at my feet, breaths held, hearts stopped. Behold the four kings. Philip goes to the mic stand, replaces the mic in the cradle and leans into it.

'This is a new one, I think you'll like it. It's called 'Trees of

Eden'.'

I sit on the waiting stool, the newly acquired Telecaster across my knee, my foot by the footswitch, ready to stamp on the overdrive at the song's apex.

Philip twists round to me. 'Ready?' he mouths.

I nod. Start picking the opening refrain. I'm not afraid of playing it now. There's no rising panic as my fingertips stroke out the first few bars. I can't believe there ever was. The fear that I'd go to play it and it wouldn't be there has gone. This song is mine, mine and Philip's. It'll always be there.

Philip sings, his voice crooning to match the delicate notes I pluck from the guitar. Ronsey and Pete wait. They know this bit is ours. I let the vocals carry me blissfully downriver on a warm summer's day.

The music ramps up. I'm on my feet now, the guitar kicked into overdrive. Pete and Ronsey wade in, pounding drums and pulsating bass. Philip screeches the words in ecstasy. That rising crescendo of notes erupts and overflows. Our whole selves are in this song. I'm free-flying, hurtling skyward, a space rocket in take-off. The song burns hot and bright. It fizzes then burns out. I return to earth. The buzz hums inside me.

The audience is quiet. The collective hush of a world that has survived the apocalypse. Fifty thousand people stand at my feet, roaring at us, applause cascading. Behold the four kings. I feel my heart freeze. Feel Philip's heartbeat stopped too. I bathe it in.

We're on the road again, bigger, better and ballsier than ever. 'Trees of Eden' skyrockets up the charts. We're gods reborn, an evangelical sun of music shining from our arses. The world is good, better than good, fucking unbelievably awesome. We roll into L.A., rock royalty in a stretched-out V8 chrome carriage, crowds gathered to wave and cheer, clamouring for a glimpse of long wild hair, a wiff of armpit sweat, a gob of spit, anything to claim personal contact with the almighty ones. Ronsey whooshes down the limo's electric window, swigs the last mouthful of lemonade from his can and pitches the tin at the horde. Girls claw each other, tearing hair, ripping blouses, just to get at that crumpled 7 Up can that will, years from now, be a holy relic. Flowers are flung at the motor as we speed to the hotel. A white rose flies in through the open window, landing on Ronsey's lap. Philip snatches it, leans across Ronse, and waves the rose triumphantly at the gabbling groupies. Their shouts of adoration and desperation crash into the car, massive breakers threatening to wash us away; we surf it with ease. Yeah, we're that fucking cool. Jesus could only walk on water; we dance on it.

The cavalcade of cars hauls up at the hotel's glittering entrance. Giant guys in suits and shades form a human fence to hold back more screaming banshees, hysterical in fuck-me boots and mini-skirts.

'Man, look at that lot,' Philip moans. He nudges me, sharing the promised excitement of conquests to come and coming on the conquests.

I plump back against plush leather, my mind buzzing with coke and hype. Paralysed by unadulterated exhilaration that's so real and so fucking unreal, I can't get out of the car when the door's opened by a spotty teenager in the hotel's sharp dark livery.

'Mr Hunter, welcome to the Hyatt House,' he gushes. 'It's a pleasure to have you staying with us.'

Too bloody right it is. This fella's never had anything so magical touch his puny WASP life; the Stones, The Who, Led Zeppelin: screw 'em all. We're the top bollocks now. Pete prods me.

'You getting out?'

'Yeah.' I pull out of the daze and step into the LA heat.

At the sight of us the roar redoubles. The suits strain against the crowd's throbbing weight as it surges forward. Muscles ripple and buttons stretch their threads, damming the tide long enough to get us through the glass doors into the cool marble lobby where wealthy businessmen and their model mistresses stare at four English boyos who've knocked the world on its arse.

Checked in, Lenny and Gomez usher us to the lifts and we glide to the penthouse, our home for the next few weeks of rocking and rioting. Barricaded in my suite I go to the window and, hidden by velvet drapes, peer down. Fans have settled in the road like starlings. Some have shinned up telephone poles, climbed onto neighbouring rooftops or stand spread-legged on car bonnets, anything to be nearer to their gods than thee. How the fucking hell did we summon up this? It's… supernatural. I feel the grin aching my face. Here we are, World, come and fucking get us.

That night Don hosts a spectacular to launch our thirty-night tour. Rock's hoi polloi flock to us, hornets around honey; Ronnie Wood, Jimmy Page, Roger Daltry, Don Henley, Eric Clapton. They all look big 'til they stand beside us. Champagne is quaffed; canapés nibbled. Nameless, humourless minders fringe the room, their backs to the doors, marking their charges like football defenders. Only the rich, the famous or the pretty are admitted.

Bob Dylan inches round the buffet table, his bone china plate dotted with two spring rolls and a crab puff.

'What's his problem?' Ronsey asks me.

I shrug. 'Whaddya mean?'

'Tried to say 'how'd ya do' to him and he looked like he was gonna shit himself.'

I snort on a mouthful of champers. 'It's probably the state of you. He musta thought you were a roughneck about to beat shit outta him for his anti-war singsongs.'

'Nah, that can't be it,' Ronsey muses. 'Everyone knows I'm a great big softie.'

'With a crusty exterior.' I wave a hand over his tatty T-shirt that has some orangey substance dribbled down it.

'Aye, but look at him.' Ronsey points to where Dylan is cowering away from Jack Bruce who's spouting about something, gulgs of cigar smoke punctuating his words. 'He's afraid of his own shadow. If that's what fame does for you I don't fucking want it.'

I sweep the room with my arm. 'Sorry, mate, but you've already got it.'

A waitress in a black ra-ra skirt and a sequined bikini top struts over, a tray of champagne flutes balanced on her upturned palm. I swap my empty glass for a brimful one. When she drifts off again Dylan and Bruce have been engulfed by the swirling crowd.

Later, mebbe an hour but, Jesus, it could be five minutes, Ronnie Wood staggers to where me and Philip are holding court with twin blondes from Phoenix and a redhead from Albuquerque. Wood is pissing himself laughing, eyes creased and wheezing chortles.

'Fuck sake, you've gotta hear this, it's an absolute corker,' he gasps, falling in a heap across the redhead's lap.

She pushes him up.

'Sorry, sweetheart,' he mutters, wiping cry from his cheeks, fighting to compose himself.

I grin at Philip who smirks back. We're both thinking, 'What's the fuck's eating Ron?'

Ronnie squeezes himself on the couch between us. 'So I'm over by the bar and your manager is trying to chat up one Mr Dylan. He goes, 'I'm Don Wiseman, Crown & Kingdom's manager,' and dear old Bobbie suddenly gets this bad smell up his nose. He looks your man up and down like, 'what the fuck?' and he says, face deadpan, 'Shit, man, that's some fucking bad karma you're dragging around with you.'.' Wood breaks down again, howling, slapping his thigh, mine then Philip's, shrieking, "Bad karma!' It's priceless. You blokes.' He shakes his head.

'Our infamy doth proceed us, me thinkest,' I say to Philip, winking.

'Too fucking right it does,' Wood says, pulling himself together now. He glances around the room. 'Thought Blackmore and crew'd be here.'

'Nah,' Philip says, 'we don't invite riffraff to our shindigs, do we, Mickey? You're lucky we let you in, you pussy.' He elbows Ronnie off the couch, into the redhead's lap for a second time. She scowls, prissy little madam, and shoves him off before batting doe-eyes at me. Yeah, I'm the one she wants; no other fucker's good enough to touch her up.

Ronnie scrambles to his feet, grinning inanely. 'You wanna watch ya don't get too big for those crocodile skin boots of yours.' He wags a finger at Philip's handmade footwear, the scales gleaming under the 100 watt lighting, then strolls off, shoulders shaking with renewed fits of laughter.

'Did we even invite Deep Purple?' Philip asks when Wood's out of range.

'Dunno. Left that bullshit to Don. Probably didn't wanna been seen in our spotlight, 'fraid we'll upstage them,' I say, lighting a cigarette. 'Which we will. Are.'

We'll upstage the whole fucking lot of 'em before we're through. Why the hell not? Someone's gotta be the best. Gives the others a measuring stick to go off, one they can beat themselves with for not reaching our high water mark. We're six foot thirteen and growing.

THE DEVIL

A week's passed since we signed on the solid line, committing ourselves to the award ceremony. A week to stew on it. I'm cooked now. How the hell am I supposed to get through this? Sweat coats my brow. I rub a hand across it for the umpteenth time. The view from the car window flicks by; trees and fields, houses and roads. Greens and greys merge into a dull, lifeless, no-colour colour. If Hell has a colour it's this.

'Where are you? You should've taken junction 9, the A34 for Oxford. Keep on the M40, come off at the next junction and take the A40, go through Oxford and follow the signs. Whitney's the next place on that road. O.K.... About another hour... O.K.... See you later.' Keira clicks off her mobile. 'That was Pete. They've got lost. Think I've put them on the right road though.'

'Can you do the same for me?'

'Are you alright?'

I laugh. If I don't I might lose it, have a subatomic breakdown. Go catatonic. Jesus, I'm a house of cards trying to stand in a force nine.

'Fucking fine. Haven't got any cigarettes, have you?'

Without a word Keira reaches into her bag and hands some over. The cool blue smoke doesn't make me feel any better but at least holding it and flicking the column of ash into the narrow-mouthed ashtray gives me something to do.

'It's fine to be nervous,' she says. 'I'm sure everyone'll be feeling the same. Pete sounded like he was really uptight.'

'That's normal for Pete.'

'At least for you three it's familiar. Imagine how James must be feeling. He's got a lot to live up to.'

'You're awfully concerned about someone you've only met once,' I say.

She flushes and dodges left. 'It's just a rehearsal. Pull yourself together.'

Rehearsals: days before them I'd start itching. I'd stay up night and day, playing through our songs in order, reminding myself how fucking brilliant they were. Are. Then I'd play the new material I'd written alongside the old to check the pieces fitted together. They always did. By the time we had a run through I'd be full of it, us in our greatness, standing victorious on a battlefield littered with the bodies of those who only thought they were good enough. We actually were. Are. Aren't we?

You arrogant shit. You shouldn't be doing this, you fucking stupid old prick.

'Stop.'

'What?' Keira snaps up from the papers she's studying.

'Stop.' I slide the glass dividing us from the driver. 'Can you turn around? I want to go back.' I sound like a sulky ten year old on the way to boarding school. I don't care. I want to go home. Take me home.

The driver meets my eyes in the mirror. 'I can't turn around on the motorway. We'll have to wait for the next junction to come off.'

'Do that then.'

'Don't you dare.' Keira slams the glass partition shut and turns on me with blazing green eyes. 'What the hell do you think you're doing?'

'What I should have done forty miles ago. Shit, what I should have done forty years ago: giving up while that's still an option.'

'You are not.'

'Erm, who's the boss here?'

'We're too far down the line to stop now.'

'Bullshit. I can stop whenever I want to.'

'Fine. We'll go back, if that's what you want,' she says, 'but you've got to tell me why first. Why, after all the fighting to get this together, you're suddenly going a whiter shade of yellow on me.'

It's a pretty reasonable request. But what the hell can I tell her? The truth would be nice but which one? The one about me being terrified of cocking this up, proving that I'm an old has-been in front of forty thousand disillusioned fans? Or the one about me standing onstage looking out at a completely empty auditorium, realising that Crown & Kingdom are dead, cremated and forgotten? Or the one where I despise Philip and Philip despises me and we blame each other for what happened to Ronsey and we're both right and both too cowardly to admit it to each other? She waits for me to say something.

The driver slides the glass back.

'The next junction's coming up. Do you want me to pull off?'

'Yes.'

'No.' Keira glares at me. 'Well?'

'I just don't want to do it.'

'That's not a reason.'

'That's all you're getting.'

'Fine. Keep going,' she orders the driver, and bangs the glass closed again.

'I'm not up to this,' I plead.

'Yes, you are. You're nervous, I get that, but remember, you're a bloody amazing guitarist. For God's sake, man up a bit and get on with it.'

I wince. Somebody once tried telling me how the water that surrounds an island doesn't cut it off; it actually joins it to all the other islands. I need to learn to walk on water if I don't want to end my days cut off: alone. Dr. Sangha's voice whispers, 'chronic heart failure'. Christ sake, don't let me die haunted by the past. I definitely can't tell Keira that truth. The junction, and safety, glide by the window.

*

The hit hits me, an explosion of bliss that devastates and obliterates with apocalyptic perfection. From the inside out, inside my chest and my head, it bowls me backwards. I fall without resistance or fear. I fall higher and higher, whooshed skyward by a sonic boom of orgasmic pleasure that hurtles me through the clouds and right into Eden. I float, bodiless, an ethereal spirit, empty and full, benign and dangerous, peaceful and mighty. A hundred million supercharged atoms buzz through me, surging in every artery, vein and capillary, penetrating muscle and sinew and bone, saturating organs, flickering with the ebb and flow of energy moving through burning coals. I feel every single, miniscule, microscopic synapse tingle inside me as pleasure impulses leap the tiny crevasses. The universe's stardust, a billion years old, golden, ageless and never ending, oscillates inside me. It's fucking awesome.

It goes quieter. There's a faint humming, or mebbe a ringing? in my ears. From the explosion. But that's all. Nothing else. Everything else is satisfyingly numb. I surrender to absolute contentment. I surrender to the absolute.

aaaaaaaaaaaaaaaaaaaaaaaaaaaaaaaaaaaaaaaaaaaaaaaaaaaaaaaaaa
aaaaaaaaaaaaaaaaaaaaaaaaaaaaaaaaaaaaaaaaaaaaaaaaaaaaaaaaaaaaa
aaaaaaaaaaaaaaauuuuuuuuuuuuuuuuuuuuuuuuuuuuuuuuuuuu
uuuuuuuuuuuuuuuuuuuuuuuuuuuuuuuuuuuuuuuuuuuuuuu
uuuuuuuuuuuuuuuuuuuuuuuuuuuuuuuuuuuuuuuuuuuuuuu
uuuuuuuuuuuuuuuuuuuuuuuuuuuuuuuuuuuuuuuuuuuuuuu
uummmmmmmmmmmmmmmmmmmmmmmmmmmmmmm
mmmmmmmmmmmmmmmmmmmmmmmmmmmmmmmm
mmmmmmmmmmmmmmmmmmmmmmmmmmmmmmmm

mmmmmmmmmmmmmmmmmmmmm

who am i? don't know don't care don't need to know or to care . where am i? nowhere somewhere anywhere everywhere . where am i going? nowhere somewhere anywhere everywhere . how will i know when i'm there? can't tell don't need to know why do you care? who are you? don't know don't care don't need to know or to care . what next? go back go forward go sideways stay exactly where you are : come to me . am i dead? am i alive? what's the difference? don't you know? why should i know? you know everything . who told you that? i can't remember . nothing knows everything . everything knows nothing . am i dead? does it matter? no yes i don't know i want to know . it doesn't matter . i thought you didn't know. i don't know everything i know that much . it's more than i know . is it? isn't it? no i am you you am i . oh sorry i thought . . . i know you did i did too . oh . go home come back later i'll still be here . right . look behind you . what? . . don't go. . . hello? . . . come back . . . are you there? . . .

'Mickey. Oi, wake up, mate, room service.'

The nirvanic bliss is dissipating now. Slowly, carefully, I open my eyes to blinding reality. Gomez is standing beside the bed where I'm propped against 100% goose down. He's shaking me. Residual traces of ecstasy sweep gently over me like a rain song. I cling to drying drops of the heroin's harmony, sweeter than nectar, purer than water, better than fucking life.

'Like that, did ya?'

'Yeah.' The word is satisfaction's sigh.

'First time's the best, for fucking sure. Now for dessert.' He steps aside. I see the two girls he's picked for me. A blonde and a red head. No brunettes. He knows better than that. I sink into the pillows, lead dropped from space, the high deserting me.

'Fine.'

'Smashing.' He moves to go but turns back. 'Eh, lock ya door, will ya?' He nods towards the blonde. If she's older than fifteen I'd be fucking surprised.

I drag myself off the bed and stumble behind him on someone else's legs.

As I let him out he whispers in my ear. I catch the shit stench of his breath as he mutters, 'Let me know if you want anything else. I've got a queue downstairs.'

I shut the door. Turn the key. Lock myself in. Or out? Pull the girls into my bed and fantasise about my next hit while I fuck 'em.

On the road somewhere this shit happens:

'Where's Gomez?'

'Fuck knows, haven't seen him.'

'He's in the wind.'

'In the bar, ya fucking mean.'

'Shit. I need sorting out. Have you got anything?'

'Sorry, man if it could be smoked, snorted or shot up I've done it already.'

'Bollocks. Ronsey, you got anything left.'

'Eh?'

'Forget it.'

'Look, send Lenny out, he'll get ya somethin'.'

'O.K. Yeah, Lenny, right. So where the fuck's he hiding?'

'Next door.'

'Lenny. Lenny!'

He swaggers in.

'Ya seen Gomez?'

'Nope.'

'Right. Well, go out and get me some gear.'

'Whadya want?'

'I don't give a fuck, something, anything, whatever.'

'O.K. Right.'

He leaves. Doesn't come back. A nigger with a gun blows his

brains out. It's not my fault. I didn't pull the fucking trigger.

'Your latest album is called *The Slain Gods.* That's an unusual title. What does it mean?' she asks.

The room is tiny and crammed with music press wankers. She's the only chick. Her pen is poised over her notepad. The air is thick with heat. A trickle of sweat runs along her collar bone, disappearing down between her tits. I'll get her number for later.

'It's ironic, darlin',' I smirk. I hoped one of them would ask me that.

'Can you explain that, please?'

'It's 'cos, darlin', despite the shit you lot keep writing about us, you haven't managed to slay us yet.'

'I believe the new album has sold more copies over here than any other album by a British band. How does that make you feel?'

'Like I'm king of the fucking universe.'

Don digs me in the ribs with a sharpened elbow

I jab back. I've stopped giving a fuck about interviews. They only print the same old shit-stained lies.

'We're pleased about that,' Philip adds. 'Of course we'd like to be the biggest selling band ever over here.'

'You mean bigger than home-grown bands?' another journalist with a deep southern drawl asks.

'Why not?' Philip challenges.

'Your latest tour is breaking records; biggest single attendance at a music event, biggest grossing turnover for a British band, most tour dates by a British band ever, longer shows than other bands, loudest recorded outdoor performance by any band,' a preppy-looking fella comments.

'And we're grateful to the fans that make it so. We'd like to thank them for their support over the last eight years,' Don says, heading me off.

'How do you feel about the other records you're breaking?' Mr

Alabama demands. 'For example, there were reports of thirty-five fans being arrested for public order offences queuing to buy tickets in Miami, and forty-seven more were arrested in New York actually at the show, most on drug-related charges. What are you doing about those statistics?'

'That represents a tiny minority of our fans. They're a bit high spirited but it isn't a serious problem,' Don replies.

'In Chicago last week a fan was fatally stabbed actually at the concert,' Mr Alabama drawls. 'Surely you can't claim that's not a serious problem?'

Don doesn't blink. 'You are misinformed. There was, tragically, a fatal stabbing in Chicago last week, on the day of the concert but it was two miles from the stadium and unconnected to Crown & Kingdom's scheduled performance.'

'The killer and victim were on their way to the show,' someone else calls out.

Don's neck reddens.

'You cannot expect musicians to be responsible for an incident like that. Who has a genuine question?'

But Mr Red-Neck, Bible-belt, not-in-the-back-yard-of-my-sweet-home Alabama won't give up. 'How do you respond to the claim that the aggression of the performances onstage and the immoral, debauched behaviour of the band off-stage is causing a generation of young people to act out dangerous, self-destructive fantasies that have ultimately led to the death of one fan?'

'Bollocks,' Ronsey yells before Don can insert a more sedate response. 'We haven't killed anyone. If it's that bad an influence on the audience how the fuck do you suppose we've resisted the urge to murder? Or maybe you believe that shite about sacrificing goats and virgins?'

There's a titter from the more supportive journalists and Mr Alabama turns a hot shade of pink.

I say, 'Each to his own, yeah? What other people do is their shit, not ours.'

'Even if they're following your example?' Mr Alabama accuses.

'What example? Like Ronse said, we haven't killed anyone. I'm pretty fucking sure I'd remember that.'

'But you do live a life of depraved excess and,' he gropes for a suitably polite word, 'fornication.'

'What's the matter, man? You jealous?'

'How'd you guys like front row seats at tonight's Elvis gig?'

The promoter waves a fan of gold-edged tickets. Don, who's hovering at his elbow, having shown him into the suite to brief us on the latest press releases, ticket sales and breakthrough FM play-lists, beams at me. This, his grin says, is your invitation to dine with royalty, lads.

Philip leaps from his armchair, bounds over and snatches the proffered prize.

'Really? Man, you've got to be shitting us?'

'Nope,' promoter says smugly. 'The King's personal invitation. He heard you guys were in town and wants you to come along. He's also asking for you to join him after the show. He'd sure like to meet y'all.'

'Would he, now,' I say, throwing my legs over the chair arm. Fucked if I'm gonna rush forward and fawn over the also-ran.

'He sure would.' The promoter clears his throat and jams two finger inside his collar, tugging on it. 'You guys'll come, won't you? The King'll be mighty disappointed if you don't.'

'We might.' I shrug, dragging on my cigarette. It's high time the Big E P abdicated. We're the new kings in town.

'C'mon, Mickey, you'll go, won't you?' Ronsey pleads. 'It'll be no fun without you.'

I see Don and the promoter exchanging edgy glances. Don kneels beside me.

'I think you should go, Mickey,' he murmurs. 'Elvis just wants to meet the limeys who've bested him at the box office, that's all.'

'Whatever.' I blow a plume of smoke to the ceiling.

Don pats my arm and turns to the promoter. 'Where's the after-show party?'

The two front rows have been roped off just for us; me, Philip, Pete, Ronse, Don and Gomez. Philip feels lousy about the empty seats under the King's nose and sends Gomez to find some skirt to fill the spaces. Gomez returns with a fucked up version of a St. Trinian's school trip; a dozen or more proper little dick-stiffers uniformed in hot pants and halter-neck tops, dewy eyes made up with kohl and lips plumped with passion pink. I don't reckon there's one of 'em much more than sixteen. Don lifts his arse from its plushly padded seat to have words but the lights go down and a spotlight strikes the vacant stages, robbing him of the chance to bollock Gomez for his underage posse.

Elvis swaggers out to a suitably grand cheer. Philip and Ronsey are on their feet, applauding. Presley comes right to the stage edge and nods to us. Philip screams like a frigging girl, delirious at being the god greeted by the King.

Presley takes the mic.

'Good evening, Los Angeles. It sure is a pleasure to be back in your little ol' town 'gain. Before I do a few tunes for y'all tonight I'd like you to join me in welcoming some real special guests who're here tonight to see this humble little show of mine. They're one of my favourite bands and I sure am looking forward to playing for them. Mac, can we get some lights down here?' Presley shades his eyes and peers into the gantry, waving to the invisible lighting tech who obligingly swings a second spotlight on us. 'Folks, let's get a big old Californian round of applause for Crown & Kingdom.'

The steady hum of crowd appreciation ratchets up several notches at the unexpected announcement. Philip drops, face flushed, back into his seat but Ronsey, about as shy as a pig at the trough, about-faces and waves grandly and with both arms to the entire auditorium before spinning back to Presley, climbing on his seat and clapping the King.

After a few moments the applause dries to a trickle and Presley takes the mic. I tune out the schmaltzy love songs, aware that next to me Philip is crooning 'Love Me Tender' in sync with Elvis, to one of Gomez's schoolgirls, now being jiggled up and down on his knee like a toddler. But when Presley comes off the saccharine pop crap and heads down the trail to his blues roots I sit up. He does 'Baby, Let's Play House' and I'm blasted back to a draughty warehouse, four guys shitting their pants over whatever will, and won't come from the next five minutes of whacking around on an undersized drum kit, wailing through a ten watt PA and twanging away on a Fender bass and a one-careful-owner Gibson Les Paul in cherry sunburst finish. The memory crystallizes in too-bright colours that hurt my eyes. Fuck sake, was that desperate bunch of go-nowheres really us? I know it bastard-well was but I can't bloody believe it, sitting here, heat from Elvis's spotlight searing my cheeks. We took off that night and we're still flying, soaring, speeding like light through a vacuum. Heading into the unknown. Making our own universe, creating as we go.

Sitting there, watching Presley's back-up band plod through music that should be diving and whirling through air instead of trudging through sludge I fantasise about leaping up on stage. I'd grab that axe, flail at the strings, rev the rhythm, rip the whole thing up and reignite the blues, playing them like they mean something, mean everything. Philip would catch a stray spark and burst into flames like dry tinder, leaping onstage with his arse blazing, elbowing Presley into the wings and jiving with the mic stand as the lyrics gush outta him. Then I'd look round and Ronsey'd be on the drum stool and Pete alongside me; they'd be pounding and rolling the beat, pushing it downhill at a hellish lick and all these dopey bastards who think Elvis is numero uno would be flagellating themselves for their blind-eared fuck up.

I could fucking do it. Should fucking do it. Do them all a fucking favour. There's nothing to stop me out king-ing the King.

The gig closes with a medley of Presley's big hitters; 'Jail House Rock', 'Blue Suede Shoes', 'That's Alright Mama'. The music empties and fills me. I grip the chair arms, holding myself in my seat, muscles straining, fingers itching to play it myself; better, harder, faster, cleaner, louder: realer. I can't wait for our next performance. Music makes the world go round.

Elvis hosts us at a swanky hotel further up the strip from ours. The room buzzes with rock royalty. Fragile waifs in Parisian high fashion, dresses cut thigh-high, sheer fabrics draped over pert breasts, are corralled by men in suits. Bowie is there, his eyes dark with kohl and glittering with silver powder. He flicks a silk scarf over his shoulder, strolls across.

'I see the King's trying on a new crown tonight.'

'Fuck off, Davo,' Ronsey snarls.

Bowie's mouth curls into a lazy smile. He drifts away, a feather on the breeze.

Don steers us to the bar and, champagne in hand, we settle into the familiar routine of mingling. Each manly arm-pump, every requested autograph, all the flirtatious smiles, remind me this is anything but fucking routine. Except that's what it is for us. Has been for so long. How can it be and not be? Because we are and we aren't.

Presley's no where to be seen.

'D'ya think he'll show up?' Philip asks, his foot tapping an impatient rhythm on the lush carpet.

'Whaddya care for?' I snap.

'He's the King. Christ, what am I even gonna say to him?' Philip moans.

'How's about 'Hello, Elvis'?' I smirk. 'Jesus, he's just some guy who...'

'Check that.' Ronsey nudges me, making the glass jerk in my hand and bubbly slop to the shag-pile.

I follow the line of his pointing finger to a door in the corner. As we watch the door inches open and two eyes shine in the crack.

'What's that about?' Pete asks.

I grin. 'Reckon the King requires sufficient courtiers before he'll be bothered making an appearance.'

The door opens at regular intervals another five times and, only when the room is loaded with hangers-on, hangers-off, hoorayers and hotshots, does Elvis slip through the gap, resplendent in a red silk shirt and black trousers with crisp creases. He brushes off welcomers, a bull swishing its tail at buzzing flies, and makes right for us.

'Uh-oh, he's coming over,' Philip hisses.

'Course he is,' I snap. 'He's the King but we own the Kingdom.'

'How'd you fellas enjoy the show?' Elvis asks, offering me his hand first.

'Great,' Philip gushes. 'We're such big fans.'

Are we in-fucking-deed?

'Shucks, the feeling's mutual,' Elvis drawls.

As if to prove his King-worship, Philip bursts into song with the opening line of 'All Shook Up'.

Presley grins and plays along, singing the second line in a deep warble that mocks his own showy delivery.

Then they sing the next line together, Philip's voice shimmering on the air, drawing stares. He out-Elvises Elvis, without meaning to. It's fucking brilliant.

'Say, there's something I was wanting to ask you guys,' Presley says, his words hurrying us away from the moment that saw Elvis sang-down at his own party.

Philip eyes me nervously. Don steps forward.

'Mr Presley, I'm sure the band will be happy to tell you anything you want to know.' Don shoots me a look that says, 'Don't try any of your usual shit tonight or I'll have your bollocks for earmuffs.' I don't need to though. Just being here I'm sailing with the wind behind me.

'It's this,' Elvis continues, 'I've heard a heap of stories about you fellas. Any of 'em true?'

Ronsey splutters. Don's face pinks hotly. Pete studies his shoes and Philip coughs.

'Only the really far out ones,' I say, winking at the King.

'Sure, that's what I was thinking,' Presley replies, 'and why the heck not? You guys are young so make the most of the good times.'

'We are,' I tell him, and, seeing Gomez waving to me from across the room, I excuse myself and head into Presley's $300 a night alabaster bog to tap a vein.

Five minutes later, swimming in warm, golden brown waters that mellow and energise, cocoon and release, I'm chatting up a promising shag when Elvis, flanked by two minders, ambles over.

'Mr Hunter,' he says, holding out a gold-cased fountain pen and a leather bound notebook, 'my li'l Lisa Marie'd never speak to her ol' pa again if I let you go without getting her your autograph.'

I rest my champagne flute on the edge of the linen-covered table, take the pen and the pad. I'm sorely tempted to write something crude but it's not necessary; the King is asking for my autograph. I write, 'To Lisa Marie, work hard, rest well and do what you're daddy tells you. Love always, Mickey H.' When Elvis reads it I see admiration in his eyes.

'You have yourself any kiddies, Mr Hunter?'

'Not that I know of.'

'Well, you should. You'd be a fine daddy. Y'all must come back and see me again sometime.'

Elvis strolls off, clutching the autograph book. I see him asking Ronsey and Philip to add their names and, finally, Pete, who had been sitting quietly in a corner, basking in the beautiful fortunes we've carved for ourselves.

The King wanted our autographs. Forget Jesus, we're bigger than Elvis.

It's the same routine night after night; set up, gig, party on high, fall into a coma: sleep it off. It's drying me out. I'm getting more brittle every day but there's no way to stop it. Picture being on one of those steep escalators that drop down to the platforms at King's Cross Underground, being on the down one, trying to go up. You're knackered from running against the machine. But if you stand still, even for a second, you'll get sucked in where the stairs collapse and disappear. Maybe I should just go down but that scares me more than staying on. I keep running, chasing the next shot of pleasure before the last one fades. It's not the highs doing for me. It's not even the fucking lows 'cos once you're down you know you're coming back up. It's the repetition: a tune stuck in my head.

The hotel suite is littered with the human trash that is permanently caught in the gravitational pull of Crown & Kingdom, all of them intent on slicing off a piece of our good times. I enter at the end one of Ronsey's long-winded, funny-as-diarrhoea anecdotes. He's got a load of the dedicated around him, most sat at his feet like he's a guru and they the neophytes.

'And then he said, 'Nah, man, that's my mother',' Ronsey shrieks, throwing back his head, his eyes rolling. Madness is infectious.

Ronsey's audience, a ramshackle mix of groupies, junkies, musicians (I pick out Townsend's big hooter and Iomi's stubby fingers) and layabouts don't give a damn if it's funny or not. They laugh along with him. One girl turns her dark sleek bob, looking towards me. In the dim light and smoggy air I glimpse green eyes that freeze me.

What she's doing here? How the hell'd she get in? I've fucking told Gomez: no brunettes. Anyway, she's dead, isn't she? I thought she was dead. She smiles. Is she here for me or Philip? I should ask her...

I beckon her over. She comes.

'Anna?'

'My name's Tori.' She snakes a hand through my arm. 'What can I do for you, baby?'

Up close her eyes aren't green. A lighting trick. She slides her hand down my chest, heading south rapidly. I push her off. Where's Philip?

I find him in the kitchenette, snorting lines off the perfectly smooth marble counter top with three groupies. When he sees me he holds out the rolled fifty. I accept and lean over the counter. In the black glassy surface I have no reflection. I snort the line. The chemical taste of coke drips down my throat. The buzz rushes to my head. Columbian courage. Tonight I'm gonna make Philip tell me the truth, get the song outta my fucking head.

One of the girls, a young face but an old hand at this, sidles up to me. She drapes her thin arms around my neck. I stick my tongue down her throat and my hand up her blouse. Her breasts are warm squishy blobs under my fingers. She's not worth it. I shove her away.

'Get lost, darlin',' I order and she retreats sulkily.

Philip's got his hands full with the other two who are sliding over him like slugs on lettuces. I slap the nearest one's arse. She turns baffled cow eyes on me.

'Oi, Phil.'

He glances up from the other's neck, a tartie red-head with eyes etched in cold blue shadows.

'What?'

'Lose the bitches, will ya?'

He frowns but pushes off the red-head and nods that she should do as I say. The two link arms and slink out, pussies on the prowl. There're plenty of fucks in the next room; might be Tone's lucky night if he pulls out what's left of his fingers. But these girls were hoping for the big one.

'What's up?' Philip lights a cigarette. Rubs a hand over his strained crotch.

Anna. I dunno how to do this. I've left it to long. Can't leave it any longer. I stall.

'Good gig tonight.'

'Yeah,' he muses, replaying it, 'though I was starting to think you were never coming back in with the rhythm after the solo in 'Trees'.'

'Cos I almost wasn't. I was flying above it, looking over heads bobbing, lost on the ocean. I flew across them and kept going. It was too fucking good; the music, the moment, the power. I flew on because I was afraid to stop. I still am but the air's getting thin.

'Got a bit carried away.'

Philip stares at me with proud blue eyes, pupils wide and dark from the coke. The come downs are steeper. The climb back up heavier. Coke thumps against my heart, battering it with a steady rhythm. Every blow could shatter the glass.

'Tell me you didn't cost me a couple of fucks to talk about the gig.'

'Nah. Let's go outside. I could use some air.'

Philip's face shifts in confusion but he follows me onto the balcony.

The outside air is weighed down with a sickly, damp heat that sticks to my skin. I long for the cold clean air of home. Wherever the fuck that is these days.

Below us the world keeps moving. People dart and scamper;

cars and trucks shunt backwards and forwards. Even the lights are alive, winking coded messages to each other. The movement is overwhelmingly tiring. I'm knackered.

'Do you ever feel like it's not real?' I ask him.

'Has that coke gone to your brain?'

Maybe he's right. Shit. I shake my head, trying to tip the buzz out my ears. I'm going about this wrong. I've rehearsed this talk so many times in my head but now it's happening I've forgotten the lines.

I wave my hand at the restless world. 'You know what I mean: that. Doesn't it seem like it's a movie playing on the reel?'

Philip shrugs.

I stare down at it. What do I mean? How can I explain? If I jumped I wouldn't die. Because it's not real. I'd fall through the film, out of the screen and land on the other side, in a heap, on the floor of the shabby cinema that's playing the biopic of my life.

My brain stutters. I grapple with a line of words. It flicks past with the hypnotic sameness of an endless procession of railway carriages. Instead of the train's chugging I hear words. It's not what I planned but it'll do the bloody trick.

'Why did you sleep with her?'

'What?'

'Anna, why did you sleep with her?'

Philip moves his lips but there's no sound.

'I wanna know.'

'That was years ago. I barely remember it. I'm fucking surprised you do. She was just another shag.'

Is he trying to convince me or himself? He flicks his cigarette end over the railings. I follow the red embers as they scatter on the pavement.

'Not Anna.'

'Does it matter now? Forget it.'

His off-handed dismissal is what pisses me off. Pushes the big red button.

'What d'ya think I've been trying to do? Tell me why the fuck you did it. That's all I wanna know.'

Philip stares at me. Son of a bitch is trying to think of a reason that'll get me off his case. My heart pounds faster and louder. I worry it'll shut down while I'm waiting for him to think of something.

'Just 'cos I wanted to.'

It's the only answer that makes sense in our fucked up world. It justifies everything. ''Cos I want to.' Right now I wanna hurt him, to push him onto jagged rocks, watch the pain rip through him and let the tide take his body. I want to hate him but I don't. I want to kill him. But I can't.

'Jesus Christ, I think you owe me more than that after everything I've given you.'

'What's that mean?' Anger distorts his faces. 'Ya know, Mickey, I'm getting pretty fucking sick of you lording it over us like you're the bloody king.'

'That's not what this is about. It's not even true.'

'Yes it is and yes it fucking is. You really wanna know why I slept with Anna? 'Cos I wanted you to know what it feels like to have no control over the things that mean the most to you in the whole world.'

Philip stalks away through the doors. I double over the railings, trying to catch my breath. I look down and back: towards the end. If I jump I'll rip the film but at least I'll fall out of this fucking horror movie.

The Tower

Tonight's the award ceremony. I stand on the stage admiring the room. The tables are draped with white linen. Crystal glasses sparkle and twinkle as the swinging spotlight glances on them. The cutlery is sharp, the napkins blood red. Black figures circulate, adjusting: perfecting. A fist grips my intestines. Twists mercilessly. The lighting rig throws a beam over me. The world is annihilated in a violent white explosion. I pray for a painless death. The light sweeps on.

'One-two, one-two. We'll try that.'

Philip is sound-checking with his personal brand of anally-constricted fastidiousness. I'd forgotten what a pretentious tosser he is about that. If I'd remembered I might not've been so keen to do this. Yeah, right. 'Cos his fannying with the vocal levels are my main problem tonight. Not the five hundred-plus music dignitaries that will, in four hours time, be taking their seats and turning their ears to the stage for our spectacular come-back performance. Or our miserable, piss-off-back-where-you-came-from performance. Whichever it turns out to be. It's been over thirty years since we played together for an audience. The half-dozen rehearsals in various secret locations have not been inspiring. Truth is, I've hardly touched our music since Crown & Kingdom went extinct and we returned to being four separate blokes. Three. I'm still not convinced. Worse, I'm still not fucking convincing. My impersonation of Mickey Hunter, legend-in-his-own-lifetime-rock-guitarist is piss weak. Middle aged spread and a delayed mid-life crisis have done for him. For me.

'Mickey, you ready?'

Pete, bass on and plugged in, is standing where he always did, left of Philip, leaving me the space to the right. Philip scowls at me. He's not convinced either. Something's missing. Someone. Where's Ronsey? He's probably out back, draining the dregs from a bottle of Newkie Brown. James strolls onto the stage. Dickhead. What's wrong with me? James, not John, sits amongst the drums and drags on his cigarette. Seeing he's being watched, he grins, throws me a cheeky wink. And it is John after all. It's not now. It's then…

*

This is the U.K.'s biggest festival and we're the headliners. The field is packed with a solid mass of fans that carpets the grass completely. I could step onto their shoulders and walk out and back without getting my boots muddy. Colours merge into one massive pattern. I'm blown away by the idea of what's gone into making this night.

'Man, look at that lot. How many d'ya think there are?' Ronsey asks.

We stick our heads around the stage siding and sneak a look, two cheeky school boys clustered around a hole in the wall of the girls' toilets.

'Don said a hundred thousand but that's just the official number. A lot've jumped the fence so could be more like a hundred and ten, maybe even twenty,' I say.

'Fucking hell.' He squeezes my arm. 'This is the best. It's gotta be, it's fucking got to be.'

'How d'ya figure that?'

'I don't give a fuck about the States, or the Japs, or the I-ties. This is what I care about: the home crowds. Reckon I can die happy knowing we've made it here. And this—' Ronsey waves his hand over the heads of the waiting audience like the bloody pope giving a mass blessing— 'fucking proves it. Never mind what other shit's going on. This is all that fucking matters.'

He raises a fist to the blackening sky. 'Go on, ya son of bitch, take me now. I'm as fucking ready as I'll ever be.'

*

Returning James's wink, I cross the stage and take my place. I pass closer than necessary to Philip and glare at him. Show no fear. Show no pain. Show your teeth, even though half mine are false these days. I pick up my Les Paul. It's piled on the pounds since our last, strained rehearsal and drags down hard on my shoulder with the weight of the sixty-four years that have propelled me here.

'O.K.,' I say, 'let's go.'

James counts us in. We hit uncertain notes. The end starts again.

*

I toss down my cigarette. Grab the Les Paul by the neck, throwing it easily over my shoulder. Ronsey takes a final swig of beer. Philip gargles with a mouthful of brandy and spits it at my feet.

'Waste of fucking good brandy,' Ronsey moans.

Pete returns from his emergency, pre-show, nerve-induced shit. We're ready now. Out front the compére is baffling the audience with a rant about the current political situation, some governmental bollocks up. No one's listening. They shout him down with warrior cries. The clamour is a blizzard in my ears and, as white flakes fall, I pick out the pattern of my name chanted louder and louder:

Hunter

Hunter

Hunter

Finally he gives up and introduces us with the words, 'So where the fuck have these guys been for the past two years? Crown & Kingdom.'

We step into a rush of heat as the crowd's energy erupts: the down-draught of fighter jet engines; the white-hot cloud of the H-bomb; the blaze of Hell's fires. I warm myself in the flames, charging the front of the stage, firing a flurry of notes from my guitar. They spit, buzz and crack through the air, machine gun bullets loosed into the crowd. The field, with its troops massed thousands deep for the forward push, falls at my feet, razed by half a dozen precisely aimed notes. I'm alive again, feeding off their energy, sucking them dry. Sating myself. Behind me three others do the same and the music soars aimless and purposeful, filling the night sky with starbursts of sound.

*

We trudge through the three numbers we've planned to open the ceremony with. Actually it's a medley, the three biggest hits from the first three albums rolled into a giant wall of sound. So said the prick musical director at the meeting three weeks ago. I hate it. It's too bloody manufactured. I limp to the end of the production line. We used to play what we felt. We used to feel what we played. It stung, stabbed, seared, right in the gut; a raw, raging fire stoked by a yelling crowd. It was the pain that made me feel alive. Any pain in my gut these days is bloody indigestion. I need to stand in that fiery heat, burning alive, martyred at the stake. I want the agony of playing like it's fucking life and death and the euphoria of surviving.

'What do you think?' Pete asks.

Philip says, 'I'm happy with that.' He's referring to his vocals.

'I'm bloody not.' I stroll over to James. 'Gimme a fag.'

James offers me his pack and lighter. Cigarette in hand, smoke swirling around my head, I feel a smidge more like Mickey Hunter, legend-in-his-own-lifetime-rock-guitarist.

'What's wrong with it?' Philip asks.

'There's no fucking life in it. What the hell happened to that?'

'What happened is we grew up. At least most of us did,' Philip scoffs.

We face off. How much would I love to smack him right on the nose, self-righteous twat.

'And some of us never made it past middle age,' I snap. It hits lower than his nose. Philip flinches.

'So what d'ya wanna do?' Pete asks.

'I wanna do what we used to do. Play like we fucking mean it. Like we want to do this,' I say.

Pete blinks. Philip raises his eyebrows. James balls his fists.

'Why don't we open the way you guys always opened?' he suggests. 'If your voice is up to it, Uncle Phil.'

Dunno if it's the accusation, the reminder that he's old enough to be an uncle or the irreverent use of 'Phil' but inside Philip a switch is thrown and the ignition sequence engaged. Batteries to power; turbines to speed.

'O.K., if we're all up to it.' He throws this to me. I stretch up and catch it.

*

The sun sets in a swathe of passionate reds and acid oranges over the festival field. The world bends to darkness. We'll light it with our music. The crowd start their chanting worship: all hail the kings. It's the incantation that summons us, a spell that conjures the miracle they crave. We are the divine; here to answer your prayers.

Notes spin off, sparks from a devilish blacksmith's anvil. They thicken as the beat speeds up, forming rays more brilliant than the sun's, penetrating the impenetrable night. Each song is the sweeping beam from a lighthouse. We are cliff-top, illuminating the way with pulses of sound. Follow the music. Step into the light. Come with us to a newer, better world. Riffs thrum. Notes shriek. Beats throb. Licks curl and dive. We drive hard, plunging the crowd into the sublime, taking them from quiet to loud, high to low, light to dark: pain to pleasure. Songs bleed into each other. We plunder and pillage, wielding our weapons, whooping and wowling our victory cries. I play so fast the sound struggles to keep up, my fingers scorched by the frenzied movement. A string snaps. Someone hands me another guitar. The rhythm doesn't break or bend. The music is inside me, streaming from every pore, bursting my eardrums, gushing, bloody, from my nose, forcing its way up my throat and spraying from my mouth. I fight to contain it but it expands, notes gyrating off into deep space in gravity-defying arcs. My lungs sting as I inhale the crowd's heat. The fire of this crowning moment, that devoted mass, our maniacal music, is all-consuming.

Ronsey crashes the cymbals in a thunderous synergy of power. The harsh wavering sound bounces around inside my head. It runs out over the surging mob, leaps the fence, plunges down the hillside and escapes into the green and pleasant English valley that has been scorched by our inferno. I drop to my knees at the front of the stage. My guitar smoulders with hot-coal ferocity. I am deflated, evaporated: incinerated. It's over. I crawl about in the ashes. Thousands of tiny flames, held aloft by our devotees, twitch on the breeze: light a Zippo for the dead.

Crown & Kingdom have left the stage, the country, the planet, the galaxy: the whole fucking universe.

*

We are finally ready to rise like the phoenix.

'In five, four, three…' The last two digits are mimed by the fingers of the runner who has us lined up in the wings, ready to go out the moment the cameras start rolling and the broadcast is live.

The lights go off, as I instructed. I allow myself a further count of two before moving. There's no introduction, also as I instructed. We stroll on in almost complete blackness to the cries and clatterings of diners groping to feed themselves in the dark. At the same moment, in living rooms around the country, TVs go dark and viewers grope for remotes. By the time the swirling peel of red and blue illuminates the stage we're in place, four as one again. The shock is an icy, saltwater blast, the cheering a fiery wave. I haven't played a single note and already I'm bowing and waving to a crowd high on the thrill of anticipation. It intoxicates me as utterly as it always did.

Aware that the world is staring at us through the barrel of a camera, we break the line up. I carry out the mentally rehearsed steps, lifting the waiting Les Paul and shouldering it, striding into the space to Philip's right. Pete mirrors me. James sits behind the drums. Philip leans towards the microphone.

'Good evening.'

I dive into the music once more. The peel of my guitar drags me in a resonating riptide. I stroke chords, pulling myself free of the current, swimming through the storm I conjure.

*

I haven't seen my mother for a long time. Not since I breathed new life into Crown & Kingdom. Not since I killed what I had with Anna. Not since I emerged from my chrysalis as Mickey Hunter, rock legend. Not since Philip and I started trying to demolish each other. I should go back, see her again. I don't want to. Am afraid to. But I should go. Will go.

I'm on the doorstep. Dunno how I got here. I stretch for the door knob. It's too high. I can't reach it. I beat my fist on the door. Let me in. Let me in.

The door swings open. The hallway is dark. Hands outstretched for seeing with, I step inside. The house is quiet. Mebbe she's sleeping. I tiptoe over the cold hall tiles.

The kitchen's empty. The living room's empty. It's all gone. I circle vacant rooms, double back on myself, can't find my way out. I shouldn't have fucking come. But I have to see her. Make sure she's O.K.

I climb the stairs. Which is her room again? There're too many doors. I open one. See a cliff-top vista, white waves foaming against a ragged shoreline. I look behind me. At the hall, the peeling paper, the threadbare carpet, the other doors. I'm here and not here. Dunno where the fuck here is.

I open another. See my old acoustic guitar. It's been here all along. I sit on the floor with it cradled in my arms and play a chord. It crashes. I try another. It screeches. I try a third. There's a muffled thud. I stare at my fingers. Fuck, I'm doing it wrong. I fight to remember but my mind's empty. There's nothing there. I've lost everything. I cry.

I find her in the third room. She's sitting on her pink chair. I'm a terrible son. I should visit more often. She's my mother. From now on. I promise.

I go over. Start apologising. She doesn't reply. I stop. Start again. Tell her I've missed her. She stays silent. I get right up to her. Put my hand on her shoulder. She's cold. I shake. Her head rolls back. Flops over her shoulder. Her eyes are large and bulging. Red lipstick is smeared around her mouth. Her tongue protrudes, bloated and swollen. Upside-down and backwards, she glares at me.

Why didn't you come home sooner?

Because you were dead all along.

I haven't come to see you.

I turn. Anna's in the doorway.

I came for you.

She smiles. Her green eyes sparkle. She holds something out. It's for me. A present. I rush to her. Reach out. I'll take whatever she gives me. I fix on her face. This is right. My hands touch hers. I feel something warm and soft. I glance down. She's holding a baby. Tiny, pink and squished up. I'm afraid. Pull away. It's not why I came back. I came to see my mother. I turn to her chair again. It is empty.

Anna?

Too late.

My mother stands in the doorway, her head tilted awkwardly to one side. It might drop off. The room stinks of vomit and death.

I wake up, the triumphs of yesterday's festival performance ringing in my ears and a spew of vomit on the pillow beside me. I sit, grope about on the bedside table, searching for the needle. Pleasure is my life raft. Fucking blissful, essential, words-can't-describe/can't-get-enough/never-had-it-so-good pleasure. Give the son of a bitch who first cooked up poppy seeds a Nobel fucking Prize.

'Here's a good one.' Don thrusts another magazine at me.

My photographic reflection stares back, contorted in the final throws of orgasmic pleasure as we bring the festival, and its adoring audience, to climax. I glance over the page. Words grab me; magnificent, awe-inspiring, flawless: nothing can slay these gods of rock. I don't bother reading on; I know how it ends.

We're gathered around the oak table in Don's office. It's not the office he used to have. It's majestic, as it bloody well should be for the manager of the world's most adored and acclaimed musical ensemble. As quoted in August's issue of *Melody Maker*. I've stopped hunting for words to label us. Since *The Slain Gods* went platinum in a week it's fucking pointless.

'Pass it here.' Ronsey stretches out his fingers.

I slide the magazine across the smooth table-top. John palms it, stopping it before it dives off the end.

'Look at that.' He taps his finger at his own face in the picture. 'Your old man's a hero.' James looks at it then Ronsey.

'Dad, you can't be a real hero because you haven't got a superpower.'

'Sure I have. What about this?' Ronsey grabs two pens and taps out a complex six-eight beat.

'That's not a superpower,' James insists. 'A superpower's something only you can do, like spidey-sense.'

But Ronsey won't be outdone by an imaginary dude in a leotard.

'Who else do you suppose can do that?' he demands.

'I can.' James takes the pens off Ronsey and imitates his dad's rhythm.

'Proper chip of the old drum stool, aren't you.' Philip ruffles James's hair. He scowls. I remember hating it when someone did that to me.

'He's got you there,' I say to John.

'Well, gotta be someone to carry on the family business.'

We smile but I'm faking. Trying to hide my jealousy. I want what John's got: hope for the future. I want a fucking hit, a drink at least. I pull the coffee pot towards me, throw some into my cup and, getting a bottle from the cabinet in the corner, top it up with brandy. It's 9.30 on a Wednesday morning.

We flick through the festival press cuttings for a while. My fingers wander over the pages but I don't take much in. The approval of others means fuck all to me now. It's everything I ever wanted. And I've got it. Now I want another something. Dunno what the fuck I want anymore. My eyes are drawn to James as he continues to tap out a drum beat, one he's heard his dad play. James is so fucking lucky; he has the whole world to explore and conquer. Starting right now.

I wander into the next room, pluck my old acoustic from its hook on Don's wall, where it hangs between our first gold disk and a framed copy of our debut *Rolling Stone* cover, and return to the main office. James stops drumming to watch me. I play, something quick that I make up on the spot, a riff with bass notes separated from the trebles of the chords, in four-four but with a syncopated pattern so it's harder to follow. I stop for the count for two bars before coming in again, repeating the pattern. James listens, his head turned away as if seeing stops him hearing clearly. I put the stop in again and this time when I start back up James comes in, at exactly the right moment but with the syncopation half a beat behind. His brow darkens and he screws his face up. The physical effort he's putting in to working out what's wrong and how to put it right, it's blood awesome. Giving up isn't an option for him. Giving up means admitting you can't do something. He hasn't yet learnt that some things are impossible.

'Here.' Ronsey reaches to take the pens from James.

'Don't,' I snap and Ronsey jerks his head up. 'Let James work it out himself. He can do it, can't you, mate?'

'Let me do it, Dad,' James says and moves out of his dad's reach.

I resume playing. James takes up the beat, getting it smack on, and we jog through the progression four times.

'Now keep it going,' I say at the last stop as I leave off the chords and go into a brief but racy lead break. James drums his way through it, slick like oil, even puts in a couple of rocking fills.

'Christ, Mickey, give it a rest, will ya.' Philip whacks a magazine against the edge of the table, dragging attention back in his direction.

Ronsey tears his eyes off his little drummer boy. Flicks a glance between me and Philip. Philip glares at me. He's angry, not about my game of follow-the-leader with James but 'cos he's deciding he's had enough of being second lieutenant. He wants captain's stripes. Thinks he deserves them more than me. I put the guitar down. Light a cigarette and drain my coffee cup. The pot's empty now so I refill with neat brandy and find myself stared at from all sides. I catch Pete's eye. He looks away. Don tuts.

'Anyone else?' I wave the bottle around.

'You're turning into a right pisshead, Mickey,' Philip says.

'And you're turning into a right…'

James stops drumming. 'Can we go soon, Dad?' he asks.

I'd like to leave as well. The silence simmers.

Philip and I scowl at each other. I wish for a pair of twisted antlers, to lock into his. I've dodged this long enough. Maybe it won't be as bad as I think. Maybe I'm ready for it. Maybe I just don't give a shit anymore.

'Dad?'

Philip won't start anything in front of James.

'Dad?'

'In a minute, son,' Ronsey says.

A scream wells up. I stand. Stride to the door. Head down the corridor. Take the lift then the stairs. Emerge onto the roof. My boots crunch across the gravelled surface. A hundred feet below me London sprawls, crawling like an ants' nest. I want it trampled underfoot. Razed to the ground so I can start again. I've done it before. Can do it again. A howling wind cyclones up around me. It squeezes, suffocating, twisting away into the grey sky, a reverse-running tornado. I yell to the goat on the cloud. 'Accept all that is created by others.' How the fuck am I supposed to do that when the music's not enough to hold us together? It's breaking down. I want it to break down: collapse. As soon as that happens

I'm gonna crawl outta the ruins and start again.

They're talking as I enter but shut up when they see me. I sit opposite Philip, my intentions clear as glass. I'm going to give Philip Crown & Kingdom. If he wants it, let him fucking have it. When it goes wrong it'll be his fault, not mine.

'Everything O.K., Mickey?' Don asks.

'Dunno.' I glance across the table. 'Phil?'

He looks at his hands. The cigarette between his fingers tremors. A moment ago he was ready to tear into me, rip flesh from bone, but now that moment's gone. Another, different, moment's here. He can't do it. But I fucking can.

'Give us a minute.' I keep my voice flat.

Don hesitates. 'Mickey, we…'

'Ronsey, take James downstairs, show him our gold disks,' I suggest. 'Pete, go with them.'

Fuck off the lot of you so we can have this out.

Grimaces are exchanged and words muttered. Like a mob of disturbed starlings, they rise together.

At the door James tugs on Ronsey's hand. Turns to me.

''Bye, Uncle Mickey. See you later.'

'Yeah, see ya, mate.'

They're gone. It's me and Philip. Winner takes all. Looser leaves it all behind. That's the fucking hope, anyway.

I pace the room.

'Well?'

'What?' Philip barks.

'Are you gonna tell me what the hell's eating you?'

'It's not me; it's you.'

'Oh?'

'It's always been you. And I'm sick of it.' He gets to his feet. Faces me.

'What the fuck d'ya mean by that?'

'It's all yours.'

'What's mine is yours, brother.'

'I don't bloody want yours. I want mine.'

'You leaving?'

Philip switches to mute, dropping his eyes off mine.

Yeah, thought not, you pussy.

''Cos you can, if that's what you want. Fucked if I'd try to stop you.' Go on, Philip, get some balls. Fuck off and leave me the hell outta it.

'It's not.'

Fucking coward.

'I just want more of a say, some bloody control over it,' he mutters. 'Pete and Ronsey, they're happy doing their thing but I'm not like that. I'm fucking tired of you telling us what to do. After all this time you're still treating me like I don't know my way around this. Album sleeves, tour schedules, running orders, what key to fucking play in, even the bloody lyrics, the one thing that's mine: everything needs your O.K. even though you don't give a shit about anything other than the next goddamn high.'

'I don't recall O.K.ing you shagging Anna.'

Philip laughs. I shudder.

'You're still on about her? I guess that's understandable since it's the only time I've bested you,' he taunts. 'Hard to take, is it?'

I fight to pull myself together, let myself fall apart.

'Is that what you want? To beat me?'

He slumps into a chair.

'No.' He raises his head. 'But this whole thing, it's yours; your songs, your ideas, your music, your set up, your design, your fucking band.'

I wander towards the door.

'Where're you going?'

'To tell Don.'

'Tell him what?'

'That you're in charge from now on. You want it you can have it, have it with fucking pleasure.' I spin back to him, spread my hands. 'Crown & Kingdom's yours now, man. Good luck.'

Things are going wrong. Fucking good. That what I want, isn't it? Hell, I'd rather die flying into the sun than falling to earth. I get high, stay there and love every fucking minute. The right mixture of smack, booze and pills keeps me up so I can watch from above, outside the fallout zone, where I'm un-fucking-touchable. Gomez makes daily deliveries.

Don calls me. I know what he's gonna say. I instruct the cheap blonde I'm shacked up with to make excuses and get rid of him. She does. When she comes back to bed I fuck her brains out.

Pete pops round.

'Man, you look awful,' he says.

'Thanks.'

'Have you spoken to Don lately?' he asks.

'Why?'

'He wants to know what we are gonna do next.' Pete's voice is dulled by worry.

'Did he send you?'

Pete peers shiftily into shadowy corners, dodging my question. I follow his gaze as it fall on the side table, the array of needles, bottles and bags of powder there.

'Shit, Mickey.'

'You want some? It's really fucking awesome, ya know.'

He shakes his head.

'C'mon, why'd ya think it's forbidden? Doesn't do to have the masses enjoying themselves,' I laugh, ''cos who's gonna do all the fucking graft while they're blissed out?'

Pete sighs. 'Philip's got some new material. He's booked studio time. Wants us all there.'

'I'm busy.' The cheap blonde slithers onto my lap.

'He says...'

'What does his lordship say?'

'If you're not there...'

I run my hands underneath her thin smock. Edge my fingers over each rib 'til I reach her smooth, firm breasts.

'Honestly, Mickey, I think Philip's had enough of waiting for you. If you don't show up next week I think he'll go,' Pete says.

'And you? Ronsey? Will you go with him?'

Pete doesn't reply.

'Fine. Good. Fuck you. Fuck him. Fuck everything. I don't give a flying fuck what you do, or Philip. Fuck all of you.' I reach round with my other hand. Grab an empty whisky bottle. Chuck it nowhere near Pete. It strikes the wall. He flinches as it shatters. Shards of glass sink into the shag-pile, bedding down.

'Get fucked. I'm not interested in any of it anymore.'

I want that to be the truth but part of me's still frightened of what'll happen when it is. I get the blonde to show Pete the door while I load up again. She comes back as I submerge into the mind-razing oblivion that thrums through me as poppy-reddened blood rushes to my brain. Her thin smock swings around her spindly figure as she stands mute in the doorway. She drifts across the room, a glowing wraith. I close my eyes before she reaches me. Feel her hair brush my cheek as she bends over to draw the empty needle from my arm.

Later I tell her I hope Philip destroys this monster I've created. She doesn't understand. Doesn't even answer. We lie on the living floor on a heap of cushions. She rolls a joint. Holds it while I take a drag. I picture James, his face balled up as he struggled to get the rhythm, his pure joy when he did, in the end. I grab at that feeling. Try holding it but it floats away from me. Along with everything else.

I wake up a week later; the blonde is gone. Dunno who's idea that was. I totter into the bathroom. Snarl at the face in the mirror that isn't mine. Throw my guts up in the sink. Lose my balls. Ring Gomez.

'Mickey, what can I do you for?'

'I need a ride.'

'Red head? Blonde?'

'In a car.'

'Where to?'

'Wherever the fuck Philip is.'

'I'll be round in ten.'

The studio isn't the one I use. Three cars and a van are parked outside. Gomez pulls up.

'What ya got on ya?' I ask him.

He fiddles in the deep inside pocket of his jacket, producing one of his trademark bottles; brown glass, unlabelled. He unscrews the top. I offer up my hand like a good boy. He tips an assortment of multi-coloured pills into my cupped palm. He never says what they are but I trust him and he's never disappointed. Anyway, it adds to the thrill. I choke down two. Pocket three more for later. If nothing else they'll keep me awake.

I stroll in. The receptionist flutters false eyelashes.

'Where are they?'

She points a purple talon.

When I enter they're deep into something, Ronsey banging out a rapid rhythm, Pete running after it on his bass. They stop as Philip spins round to confront the interruption.

'Hey, Mickey. Good to see you.' Pete comes forward, hand outstretched.

Ronsey waves his sticks at me. Philip scowls.

'Yeah, right.'

We roll through the Philip's songs. I make some undisputed essential changes. Philip seethes silently. I'm here playing his shit;

that'll do him for now.

We work on the new album; I know it's our last. Philip's moved as far away from my sound as he dares; eight tracks all more melodic, less aggressive, than the music I write. He's too far up his own arse to realise that whatever he does, from now 'til he croaks, he'll always be compared to me. I leave him to his King-of-the-Kingdom fantasy.

At night Gomez drives me home. Inside, alone, I crawl into a den of cushions on the living room floor, stab a needle in my arm and lie in the darkness waiting for a silence I struggle to hear. After enough time's passed it's morning and Gomez is braying on my front door. He drives me to the studio where the clock hands move too slowly. My fingers bend and pull on the strings. My eyes scan the lines and dots that Philip throws down in front of me. My ears absorb the sounds I make, water blotting into paper, but it's a process, nothing more. Finally the clock hands reach seven. I go home again. Get high and let the blackness take me. Hear a pounding fist. Get up again. Stagger towards something I can't see. And repeat. And repeat. And repeat. I'm doing it but it doesn't feel like I live through any of it. And I'll never play this music live because this music's not alive. Neither am I. I give up. Wait for the end, the final high. It's all I'm fucking capable of now.

It's the last session of the last day. I'm trying to put the last lead guitar track down. Everything else is done. There's only this one song left. It's called 'Over the Edge'.

'Mickey, are you O.K.?' Pete asks.

Am I? What's that buzzing sound? I check my amp. Is it knackered? Not sure. I reach round unsteadily. Flick the switch off/on. The buzzing persists.

'Mickey?'

'Can't you hear that?'

'What?' Pete crouches next to the amp. 'Sounds fine.'

'It's buzzing.'

'Don't think so,' he says.

Philip flings open the studio door. He's been in the control room, listening to the mix on the play back.

'What the hell's wrong now?' he snaps. 'We've only got a couple of hours. We've gotta get this done.'

'It's this thing. Can't you hear it buzzing?'

The sound's louder. It's everywhere I turn. I'm following it or it's following me. Whatever, it's getting fucking hard to hear anything else.

'There's no buzzing. Stop pissing about, Mickey.'

I turn on Philip. 'The bloody thing's hissing like fuck. Can't you hear it? What's wrong with you?'

'What's wrong with you?' he retorts.

The buzzing drowns out all other sounds. My ears are bloated with it. Philip's voice shrinks, vanishes. Philip starts shrinking too. Blood red light, flecked with blue sparks, speckles my vision, whirling into a tight vortex. A nebula storm cloud, it hurtles towards me. I fix on it with the realisation that when it's consumed everything else, I'm next. Philip's arms flap. His lips move. I can't hear him. He's so far away, rapidly compressing into a blinding speck of dense light. I can feel energy building. Heat. Pressure. A star getting ready to go supernova. Blue light obliterates everything. There's no sound. I'm dead.

I wake up in a strange bed. Everything's too white. My eyes hurt. Dunno where I've been or where I am now. I close eyes again. I wanna go away from here.

This time when I open my eyes things are less bright. I'm in a hospital, thank Christ, not hell. I remember the session, the supernova, 'Over the Edge', and laugh out loud. A passing nurse hears and comes into my room. She's young and pretty. Her soft brown hair is flecked with gold. Her eyes are blue and steady. I think about starting a new collection: women in uniform.

'Are you alright, Mr Hunter?'

I stop laughing. 'Yeah, bloody marvellous. How long've I been here?'

'Two days.' She comes close. Checks something on the chart suspended at the end of the bed, then examines the drip that's plugged into my arm. When she does that it hurts.

'Can I get you anything?' she asks.

'You can get that fucking thing out, for a start.' I point at the drip.

'I'll need to check with the doctor,' she says.

'Fuck that.' I rip it out.

'Mr Hunter!'

There's blood throbbing out of my vein. She snatches a dressing off a shelf, presses it to my arm.

'Hold that there, please.'

'Get me a phone,' I say, squeezing my palm against the dressing and trying to sit up at the same time.

'Mr Hunter.'

'I wanna get out of here.'

'Really you should—'

'Get me a fucking phone.'

She whirls around. Grabs the phone off the table behind her. Thrusts it at me.

'Keep your bloody voice down, you'll wake the whole ward. You're not the only person here, you know, and some of them are actually ill.'

Slapped by her words I mutter, 'Sorry.'

'You should be,' she says. 'I'm on my own tonight and the last thing I need is some egotistical rock star who thinks he's God making more work for me.'

She turns to go but I catch her wrist. Her mouth opens. Surprise? Fear? I think she might scream and let go, feeling the warmth of her skin echoing in my palm. She steps back but the terror fades. I scan her face. She's nice. Sweet and genuine but not a pushover. I like her. She reminds me of someone.

'What's your name?'

'Meg.'

'That's nice.'

She rolls her eyes.

'I really am sorry.'

'You really should be,' she hisses.

'How about I do us both a favour and go quietly?' I suggest. 'If you'll give me a hand?' I repeat my smile.

It takes a second but she smiles too and it's really fucking beautiful.

'You sure you want to do that? I don't know if you'll be up to it.'

'You don't need to worry about me, darlin'.'

'I'd be a pretty crap nurse if I didn't worry about my patients.'

'I don't think that applies to egotistical rock stars who think they're God.'

'I'm sorry, I shouldn't have said that, it was unprofessional, but I wasn't expecting you to rip a hole in your own arm.'

'I wasn't expecting to wake up in hospital.'

'Then you should take better care of yourself.'

I know she knows what landed me in here.

'Or next time I might not be waking up at all?'

'You should get some help.'

'The only help I need is to get me out of here,' I say.

She shakes her head, regret rather than refusal.

'At least have the decency to tell me you'll think about it, the help, so I don't go home with a guilt complex as well as blisters and back ache,' she says.

'For you, darlin', anything.'

The door mat is strewn with three days' post. I stride over it. Gomez clumps in behind me. In the darkness he stumbles but I'm so used to it that I weave and dodge smoothly; down the hall, step out to avoid the side table, bend right behind the staircase, hook left into the living room, dead ahead and collapse on the floor. I'm sitting comfortably while Gomez blunders around, cursing, clattering into the record cabinet. I pull out my lighter. Spark the flame into life. Touch it to a candle. A circle of weak light ripples across the room. Gomez looks around. I spark a cigarette off the candle; the light splutters.

'You want anything 'fore I go?'

'Nope.'

'Sure?'

'Yep.'

Gomez leaves. I hear him tripping over something in the hall and cursing again. I wait 'til the front door bangs before laughing out loud. The sound bounces round the room. Returns to me with the hollow, inhuman quality of an echo. I blow out the candle. Drown in the darkness. Let myself sink.

Meg. Nice. Proper twinkle in her eyes. Flecks of gold in her hair. Yeah, nice. Got me out of there. Probably did that for her own sake. One less to see to. Does it matter why she did it? She did it 'cos she liked me. Wanted to help. A good sort. And real. Was she? Really real? Not sure I know the bloody difference anymore. Thought Anna was real but she was gone when the smoke cleared. Soon everything else'll be gone. There'll be nothing left. But nothing is something. If there's nothing there's nothing to fuck it up. Nothing is better than something. Somethings go wrong. Nothings can't. Nothing is perfect. Nothing is everything. That's what I want. Pure and orgasmic: nothing...

The brown door is the same. Thank God some fucking thing is. I bang on it, praying it'll open like it did before. It does.

'Who's there?' Ade's scarred face appears in the crack between door and frame.

'Hey Ade, it's Mickey.' I hope to hell he remembers me. 'I was a friend…'

'It's O.K.,' he cuts me off, 'I know. Long time no hear.'

'Yeah, been kinda busy.'

'But not tonight?'

'Nah. Tonight I'm gonna do nothing.'

He smiles his broken smile at me. Opens the door fully. I squeeze past him in the narrow corridor and am heading down the passage when a thought halts me. Ade bangs into me.

'It's O.K.,' he says, 'she doesn't come here anymore. Haven't seen or heard from her in a bloody long time.'

I nod then remember that's no fucking good to him.

'Cheers.'

Opening the inner door I travel back to one of the beginnings. The same red glow hangs in the air, a bloody mist. The place is littered with the same ramshackle collection of tables and chairs. On the floor are two bodies, knotted together. I convince myself it's the same couple who were here before. Nothing else has changed. Well, hardly nothing. Nothing that matters. I go to the bar. The barman looks at me with unblinking eyes.

I ask for a Scotch. He pours it silently. I loiter at the bar, studying the scene. Nobody pays me any attention. It's soothingly cool to be anonymous. Anna was right. I was lucky before.

'What've you got that's good for oblivion?' I ask the barman. Still without blinking he pushes a small bag towards me.

I pay him, take the bag and my drink to an armchair in an empty corner and sit alone. No island is an island. She said that. Even in space there's no such thing as a void. But there can be the illusion of a void. And illusions are as real as reality. I peer into the bag. In the redly burning light the powder has a sickly ochre hue.

I've no idea what it is. It doesn't matter as long as it does the trick. I lick the tip of my finger. Dip it into the bag. Wipe the power off on my tongue. It tastes bitter. I drink some more of the whiskey. Take a second dab of powder. And wait…

'Mickey?'

The sound of my name reels me in. Ade's leaning over me, hand on my shoulder.

'I'm awake,' I mumble.

He straightens up.

'What time is it?' I ask.

He laughs. 'Never mind what time, what day's more like it.'

For a night and a day and another night I've done nothing, felt nothing. I remember nothing. I was nothing. No thing.

It's Monday morning. The club's empty 'cept for a wasted blonde in a heap in the corner. Ade senses me staring at her.

'She's alright, I'll kick her out later. You want breakfast?' He walks to the bar and with freaky accuracy pours two exactly equal measures of vodka, tops them up with exactly equal amounts of orange juice.

I lean against the bar. My legs haven't returned with me. I'm in pieces. But, as the vodka burns down my throat, feeling floods back. It fucking hurts. Still, means I'm alive.

'Hope I haven't outstayed my welcome.'

'Not possible here, man. Thought you knew that.'

Maybe I did. Maybe that's why I came.

'Feeling better?'

'Now? Nah,' I say, 'but it was good while it lasted.'

'The problem is it doesn't last,' Ade says.

'Yeah, but I can always come again.'

'Course. Anytime.'

I finish my breakfast drink. Head out.

The unopened post on my doormat is now a mini Everest. I have to push hard against the door to move it aside. The last two nights haven't really helped 'cos everything's still here. But I clench the thought of those blank nights in my fist. It was great, that dive into nothingness. Feels like I've slept well for the first time in a decade.

I open the living room curtains. Sunlight rushes in. The place is a proper mess. I scramble amongst the rubbish, searching for cigarettes. Something bites my finger. I snatch my hand away, see blood dripping into my palm. I comb through the carpet. Find a sharp piece of shattered glass. Others glitter with cruel intensions among the long, thick pile. It's the bottle I chucked the day Pete called round. I'll clear it later.

I wade through the post. On top of the pile are half a dozen telegrams. I know what they'll say. What I've been trying in some half-arsed way to do for too long is finally done. It's been going on so long. Since Anna? Nah, 'Trees of Eden' says not. Or maybe it started then but stalled. Anyway, it's behind glass now. Stuffed and mounted. From out of my ruins rises a single sweet fact: it's over.

Annihilate and regenerate. Burn it back and start again.

I shove the telegrams aside. Beneath them is a pale blue envelope. I flip it over. See my name and address written in unfamiliar neat lettering. I tear it open. A card slides out; peaceful meadow scene, thin blue ribbon of water winding through blossoming trees, sun shining warmly in the clear sky. It's done with the faded softness of water colours. I want to fall into that picture. Christ, who the hell do I think I am, Mary fucking Poppins?

The phone rings. I snatch the receiver. Let it drop from my hand. It swings like a body on a gibbet. I open the card. Inside are the words, 'Hope things are O.K. and you are feeling better.' There's also a scribbled number at the bottom, cramped in a corner as though it was an after thought. My eyes fix on the looping signature: Meg. Getting rid of her guilt complex? I grope for the phone. Hover it over my ear.

'Hello? Hello? Mickey, you there?' It's Don.

I could hang up again. Walk out, down the street and keep

walking 'til I reach that brown door. Bang on it 'til Ade lets me in. Gives me whatever he's got that'll take me back to nothing.

Nah. Not this time. I need this fucking finished off. Then I can get myself sorted. Annihilate and regenerate.

'Yeah, Don, I'm here.'

'Thank God for that. Where the hell've you been? I've been calling and sending messages for days. Didn't you get any of them?'

'I went away for a bit.'

'Was that a good idea?'

'I'm bloody fine.'

The silence says Don doesn't agree with my self-diagnosis.

'I hope so because we've got a lot on in the next few weeks. The final mix is finished, there are preliminary cover designs to be approved, I've got a tentative tour schedule worked out but we need to go over that, there are press releases to finalise and I've got three requests for interviews.' His words are shrapnel. They bury into my flesh. Annihilate and regenerate.

'No.'

'What?'

'No.'

In his silence I hear the emptiness of a land after the H-bomb dropped. There's nothing left. Sweet Nothing.

'O.K., you need some time, I understand that. We all do. Maybe I can put a few things off for a bit. Give you the chance to—'

'I don't need you to put things off. I don't want you to put things off. I don't want 'things' anymore. It's over. I'm done.'

'Mickey, you can't be serious. What about Pete, Ronsey, Philip? They'll be devastated.'

'They'll be relieved,' I snort.

'You can't quit like this.'

I study Meg's card. I like how the swirling tail of her 'g' coils back round on itself. I close the card and admire the picture on the front. That's were I'm heading next. I'm going find a stream to sit by, listen to the music of the birds and lie on the grass instead of smoking it.

'Yeah, I can,' I say. I'm the legendary Mickey Hunter.

'I hope you don't expect me to tell them. This time you can do your own fucking dirty work, Mickey.'

The phone goes dead.

The Star

The crowd of musical big-wigs has got over the shock of our onstage appearance and finished applauding us simply for showing up. It's time to play. I strike the strings with my plectrum, igniting a match. The notes sing out with exuberance. The pleasure of their gorgeous sounds thrills through me. I'm young again. I live again. The audience gives off a heady mixture of surprise and exhilaration. When something burns it's not destroyed; energy's released and zooms off on another mission. That's what I'm drinking in as I play for this crowd of suits and evening dresses who are on their feet, jiving around the tables, cheering us crazily. They're still those kids in denim and beads that used to come for a wild musical ride. They've grown older, yeah. But not up.

Behind me Pete is plucking the strings of his bass fervently. There's a real danger he might snap one. James is lost in heat of the crowd, the moment and the music. His sticks flail thc skins without mercy. The beat races on. I chase it, catch up and power ahead. Even Philip is enthralled by the rapture of the music and the moment. He answers the call of my guitar with those high wailing screams of his and means every words.

John's here too. God knows where he's been all this time. He wasn't in any of the places I looked before; not in the bottom of a shot glass or at the end of a line of coke. Not even in the vapours of the heroin that smelt so pure every time I cooked up and got ready to chase the dragon. He certainly wasn't in that bloody cemetery. But he was around. Energy in the air. Latent. And tonight he's returned to us, helping us play like we used to and remember why we loved this so fucking much. The music is everything.

As the song rolls on I think of a piece of time-lapse film from a nature show on the Arctic freeze that Meg made me sit through. It showed streams, in free-flow for the summer, slowing, becoming dense motionless ice masses for the winter. It's been a long hard winter for Crown & Kingdom but the fucking thaw's come at last. Philip catches sight of me. I grin at him. He starts a charge across the stage. I gallop towards him. The audience vanishes. There's only the two of us, knights on horseback, lances raised, riding each other down. We clash. Play to each other in a frenetic orgy of screeching notes and screaming vocals, battling with sounds that tow us skyward. I pray for a long hot summer of good times and dancing days.

The song ends with pealing cymbals, a thunderous drum roar, raging guitar chords and Philip's yell of defiance and majesty. Out of the darkness a million twinkling lights come at us, not the familiar flicker of cigarette lighters but the stuttered flashing of digital cameras. Whatever, they're stars in the Milky Way, a million infinite universes alive with limitless possibilities and I'm so fucking glad to see them again.

It's the old formula: $one^4 = one$.

*

Like soured milk we've separated out. It's not common knowledge yet. But it's happened. Philip and Ronsey are coming round. I don't know why 'cos it's done. We're finished.

I'm trapped in my own living room 'til they show. It makes my skin itch, my guts twist, my head throb. It's late. Or early. Depending on whether you're looking forwards or backwards. Right now I'm looking down so everything's slewed, off-centre.

Someone bangs on my front door. I drain the half inch of

Scotch in my glass. Heave myself up.

Philip and Ronsey are on my step. There's a wild wind. It whips at Philip's hair, making it dance around his face. What is there to say? I let them in. At least Pete's got the sense to stay the hell out of it.

I plonk down two more glasses. They help themselves to the bottle of Scotch on the coffee table. Ronsey drains his glass quickly, twice. Philip doesn't touch his. His eyes flick around the room. What's he looking for? After a few seconds, with a shrug, he gives up. He didn't really expect to find it here but he had to look in case.

I feel twitchy, empty the bottle into Ronsey's glass and go into the kitchen, grabbing another from the cupboard then raking through the drawers. I find one of Gomez's familiar brown glass bottles and twist off the top. Multi-coloured pills hop up and down as I shake it: pick me, pick me! I promise myself when this is over I'll pack in. But I can't go cold turkey on everything all at once. I tip out a handful of the gaudy tablets. Down two white ones. Pocket three more, two pink and a yellow, for later. The pills joggle around in my stomach. I leave the bottle on the side of the sink and go back to the lounge.

Philip's in the red wing-backed arm chair with the rip in it. He sits upright and rests his hands on the arms of the chair. His crown is missing.

They're talking in low voices, stop as I enter.

'You look like you've seen a ghost, man,' I say to Ronsey, plonking on the sofa next to him.

'Mebbe you should look in a mirror.' He forces a smile. He doesn't want to be here. Dunno why Philip dragged him along.

'No point, no reflection anymore,' I say.

'Oh?' John raises his eyebrows, waiting for the punch line.

'Sold it. For an immortal soul. Pretty good deal, don't you reckon?' I joke. Ronsey laughs but it's edgy.

Philip studies us. Under his piercing stare I feel exposed, here, in my own fucking house. I plump for a smoke screen, start rolling a joint.

'Don said things are really moving ahead with the new album,' I say.

'They are.' Philip's enjoying a bloody good gloat. Maybe that's why he came.

'Well, there's no reason anything should change for you.' I light the joint. Drag deeply then pass it to Ronsey who does the same. With a slight stutter of hesitation he passes it to Philip who accepts. A peace pipe? Maybe we can get through this alive.

Philip pulls on the joint. Hands it to Ronsey who is appointed go-between. Yeah, that's why he came, even though he didn't want to.

'That's a bit naïve, isn't it?' Philip says. 'You really think we can go on as we were without you?'

I seriously fucking doubt it but that's not my problem, man.

'I thought that's what you wanted,' is what I say.

'I wanted some bloody control, some input: a say, that's all. I didn't expect you to…'

'Abdicate?'

'Fuck off and leave us in the lurch with a finished album and no bloody band to tour it,' Philip rages. 'It makes everything we've done in the studio null and fucking void.'

'If you've come to change my mind you're wasting your time.'

Stalemate: I won't stay; he won't let me go. This is gonna be a long night. Least the pills are kicking in. There's a hop-skip feeling settling around my heart.

Ronsey tugs at his beard. 'Hey, lads, let's have a toast, eh?'

'What the fuck are we toasting?' Philip demands.

'How about the good times? We've had plenty of those. If nothing else, that's worth a toast,' Ronsey says. 'To the good times.' He raises his glass.

I do the same. We wait for Philip. He lifts his drink too slowly to mean it.

'To the past,' he says.

I tip the whisky into my mouth but it's hard to swallow. My head feels light-weight. A flick-book of jumbled images, the events that have led me here tonight, blur in my memory. In the night sky a star falls out of sight.

Ronsey's on one now, though. He reminds me of the time he threw me fully dressed, guitar in hand, into a hotel swimming pool. Of the night we pitched five TVs from our balcony. Our narrow escape from the dreaded L.A. plaster casters. That mad moment when all four of us streaked down the Vegas strip in just our boots. How, on a flight to Calgary, we got booted out of first class for being well loaded only to get booted back to first 'cos we kicked up such a fucking racket in cattle the entire section nearly lynched us. The Phoenix gig where Lenny roughed up some guy he caught with a microphone and tape deck, thinking he was a bootlegger only to find out he was from the fucking volume police. The night Ronsey and Pete kept Jagger talking in one room while I banged his old lady next door...

'And that journo, the one you nearly tipped over the balcony. Man, that was fucking hysterical,' Ronsey howls, 'dunno who's face was the prettiest picture, yours, his or Don's when he realised what'd almost happened. I thought he was gonna chuck you over himself. He was proper fuming.'

'I'll have to take your word for that, it's kinda hazy,' I say.

'At least we can say we've definitely done it,' Ronsey adds.

'What, trashed every hotel from New York to Frisco?' I ask, pouring the dregs of the whisky out of the now nearly empty second bottle and passing him the dog end of a second joint.

'No, you know: It. Haven't we, Phil?'

Ronsey takes a drag. Passes it to Philip who's stayed quiet through Ronsey's jag. It's like he wasn't there for any of it. But he goddamn well was. I wonder what he remembers. Crown & Kingdom, the greatest hits? He takes the joint from Ronsey, holds it between his fingers and stares at it for a second before smoking. When he's done he holds it out, directly to me. I shake my head.

'Nah, finish it, man. I need a proper hit.' I drain the whisky in my glass, fire up a cigarette and dig in my pocket for a pill. Chance of one in three. It's yellow. Acid yellow. I swallow it. Philip shakes his head and tuts.

'You'd rather watch me shoot up?'

'Oi, I'm talking.' Ronsey pulls us together again.

'What's that, mate?'

'I was saying how we've done it, cheated death.'

'You've lost me,' I say.

'I can't believe it. You don't remember? My most eloquent and moving speech of all time.'

'Since when've you done moving and eloquent? I thought coarse and dirty were more your line?' I quip.

'I remember,' Philip says quietly.

'Thank you. Ya see? Best mates all these years.' He reaches across and slaps Philip's leg. 'I knew you'd remember, man. I can always count on you.'

'Remember what?'

'He means, don't you, Ronse, that we've done enough to leave something behind so we'll be remembered: our music, our legacy. Our way of living forever,' Philip says.

And now I do remember. The ultimate hustle. Beating Death at his own sick game.

'Shakespeare.'

'Exactly,' Ronsey says. 'We've showed that fucker, haven't we? Never mind reading Mac-bloody-beth, kids'll be listening to our records and analysing the shit out of that for years to come. Reckon they'll get a canny bit of mileage from some of your trippy lyrics too,' he says to Philip.

'Have we though?' Philip ignores Ronsey's last remark.

'Have we what?'

'Done enough.'

I stare through the cloud of blue-grey smoke that lies in thickly spread layers between us. His face shimmers through the vapours as though he's bobbing about on a choppy, sunlit sea. I want to trap him in one place but the image floats in and out. For real or drug-induced? Each time I see him he's a different Philip: the young, raw one; the cocky, full-of-it one; the real, talented one; the selfish, arrogant one; the angry, bitter one. I try to pin him in place but my hand's not steady enough.

'Hey, if not, there's plenty more where that came from,' Ronsey says, nudging me, 'i'n't there, Mickey?'

'I'm sure there is. You're all great musicians,' I murmur. I can't take my eyes off Philip as his face swims tantalisingly close before slipping away again.

'Hell,' Ronsey mutters, 'you're really going then?'

I nod.

'Why?'

Yeah, why? Why would you want to give up everything for nothing? Because I've gorged myself on everything and I'm sick, totally fucking sick with it.

Philip jumps into my silence.

'Because he can't stand seeing me do a better job than him. Honestly, I'm glad you're going, Mickey, 'cos I was gonna have to ask you to leave after we'd toured the album. You're timing's shit but at least you've saved me one job.'

His matter of fact tone and sheer bloody-minded egoism light the fuse.

'For that to be true there'd have to be someone doing my job better than me.'

Philip leans forward, taking careful aim.

'You arrogant son-of-a-bitch.'

'Takes one to know one, Phil. If you think you're better than me then you're not. 'Cos I never thought that about you.'

'The hell you didn't.' Philip gets to his feet, fists clenched. 'You always thought that. We might as well've been The Mickey Hunter Band, nothing but a cast of extras propping you up, making you sound good, helping you polish your gold disks and your gigantic ego. And you know what the worst thing was? You actually had me buying that Mickey Hunter, king-of-the-world bullshit. How fucking stupid must I've been? But I'm here for a refund now.'

I struggle to my feet. The ground shifts and I feel myself slithering on an oil slick. 'Hey, if you thought that then it's on you, not me. I never thought it and I don't know how the fuck you can stand there, telling me I treated you like an extra. I fucking made you.'

'Did you fuck. You just showed up, right time and presto.' He snaps his fingers.

'Bollocks. You'd still be singing in working men's clubs if I hadn't come along. You got everything because I fucking believed in you and when you stabbed me in the back I still kept faith with you. I'm the fucking idiot.'

'What's he talking about?' Ronsey asks.

'Here we go a-fucking-gain,' Philip groans.

Ronsey wobbles up on whisky-soaked legs. 'C'mon lads, settle down.' He flutters the matador's cape between us.

But Philip hurls hard words at me. 'That bloody whore. Wish I'd never touched the slag. She wasn't that good a shag anyway.'

But he's only partly right. It's still poison to me, him and Anna, the fact that he slept with her to settle a score with me, costing me everything and not even getting anything out of it himself. But it's not the real reason why I don't wanna do this anymore.

'You think that's what this is about? If that's true how the fuck did we write 'Trees of Eden' together? How did we go on for another eight years? You can't see it, can you? It's over.'

'Because the great Mickey Hunter says it's over, it's over?'

'For Christ sake, Philip, it's over 'cos it's over. You keep trying to best something that can't be bested.'

'So what was that legacy bullshit about? Reaching higher, climbing to the top, your words, Mickey, not mine.'

'Fellas, cool it,' Ronsey says, yanking on his beard.

'We're at the top. There's no where left to go, Philip…'

'Like hell there isn't.'

I'm crazed by rage and on the edge of a trip, the world warping around me. Now of all bastard times. I struggle against the acid.

'…'Cos you're not good enough to take it any higher and I'm too fucking spent to keep dragging your sorry arse around with me.'

The three of us sway in the pre-bang silence. Philip blows up first, grabbing me. We struggle together, fingers jabbing and stabbing, hair pulled, clothing torn, flesh bruised. Am I trying to hold on to him or get him off me? Booze, weed and acid blurs and brightens, tearing me apart. When I feel hands gripping me I don't know if they're mine or Philip's 'til they close round my throat.

I step out, to the side and up, floating somewhere near the ceiling, looking down on us wrestling together, grappling with each other, awkwardly: desperately. It's the most fucked up trip ever. All I can do is watch. I see Philip aim a punch at me, me duck to avoid it and the blow glance past my ear. I fire one back at him, catch him on the side of the head. He jabs an elbow into my stomach but there's no stab of pain. I throw another punch, miss, and kick out instead, getting him on the knee. Ronsey jumps in, snatching at me, missing and trying instead to untangle us with one hand while holding Philip at bay with the other. I watch myself fall backwards, stumbling over a side table. I see myself lying on the floor and try to make myself get up, move, open my eyes but nothing happens. I fight but there's no response, nothing to push against; I'm disconnected from myself. The real me is numb, full body pins and needles, and the out-of-body me is powerless. I look at the others. See Philip shove; Ronsey fall. In my silent sideways dimension he crashes noiselessly into the wall, drops down it, lands bent on the carpet, eyes open. He stares at me. Not the me on my back with my legs sticking up over the side table but the me hovering around the ceiling light. He's absolutely fucking terrified.

Time jumps, the skip on a record where there's a scratch. I'm whole. I sit up. The room swirls hypnotically. In my ears there's a high pitched blaring tone, blocking out all other sound. I'm dizzy, sick, my arms and legs feel like they're rusty. I pull the table on top of myself trying to get to my feet. I stand. Philip comes at me. I throw him off and turn to Ronsey. Philip reaches me again, grabs hold and yanks me. I wrestle frantically but can't fucking make him let go. I shout but my own words are lost to the ringing that blocks my ears. I yank and tug and thrash, jabbing my elbow in his stomach. His grip loosens; I break free and try again to reach Ronsey who's still in a twisted heap on the floor. My legs are lead weights that refused to move. I glance down. Water surges around my knees, white foam and blue waves that swirl and eddy, spinning into a tight whirlpool that starts sucking me under. It's the trip's second wave coming. The room expands. Ronsey's carried further and further out, dragged by the acid tide, his eyes wide and fixed on me. An angry sea swells around me, flooding the whole room, transforming it into a storm-rocked ocean. Water breaks over my head in a torrent, soaking me, forcing me under, holding me below the surface, dragging me down and down. I can't breathe. My chest burns. I open my mouth to inhale cool, clear air; taste only salty water. I'm being crushed by this mad sea. I try to peer through it. Everything's blue and green.

Ronsey's too far away; I can't reach him. The current tows me along. I swim into it, fighting to shorten the ever-expanding distance between us but don't get any-fucking-where near and start sinking. Grey. Greyer. Blacker. Black.

Black. Grey. Whiter. White. My head breaks the surface. I gasp a breath and doggy paddle. The water keeps dropping; I fall with it. My feet hit the floor. I stand and watch the tide go out and down; chest, waist, thighs. I wade through it. It's a puddle at my feet. It's gone completely. Ronsey lies cast up on my carpet barely two feet from me.

I drop down beside him. His eyes are closed now. His head is at a weird angle. Forcing acid traces away, I lean over, touch him, trying to move him, sit him up, make him more comfortable. He's too heavy. My lips form the word 'Philip' but all I hear is that fucking ringing. I say it again, louder, shout it. 'Philip' echoes faintly back to me, a ripple buried under the droning wail in my ears. If there's a reply I can't hear it.

I slap Ronsey's bristly cheek; say his name without hearing that either. His eyes stay closed. He doesn't move. If I can lift him, maybe get him onto the sofa, he'll be alright. Then I'll call an ambulance. I put my arms round him. Feel the warm, wet patch that has spread beneath him. Snatch my hands back. They're covered in red. I wipe them on the pink and red swirls of my shirt; the stains bleed into the pattern. I tug at Ronsey. Everything goes watery. I blink. Realise I'm crying. Draw my hands away again. Everything's red.

'Philip. Philip!' I scream his name, feeling my throat crack under the strain but hearing only the tinniest shadow of the word. He must've heard. Where the fuck is he? I wrench and pull and heave and wrestle. Finally I get Ronsey rolled over. I don't know what the fuck good that is but I can't do anything else. There's a dark spreading pool underneath him, soaking into my shag pile.

A million twinkling lights dazzle me through my tears. I reach for one. It spears my finger. I bring my hand closer to my eyes. It's a piece of glass. I stare at the floor. It's covered in jagged bits of broken glass. One of them's buried deep in the top of Ronsey's leg. There's more blood. A lot. Too much. It's sticky. Still warm. He's still warm. It's a mistake. A fucking mistake. It should be me. Or maybe Philip. Not John. Me.

What the fucking hell have I done?

The Moon

Did you see the NIME awards last night? I couldn't believe it when I realised who it was. I never thought they'd do it again. Do you think they'll tour now? Hope so. It's been too long. Wasn't it fantastic though? Hearing them play, tight as they ever were. Young James, the way he beat those drums, just like his dad. Philip's not let his voice go, still can scream in top A. Pete, solid as ever, no one can keep the beat like him. And Mickey! What can you say about Mickey? A fucking genius; the speed, the energy, the power. The way he controls it but makes it look like it's running away with him. When they tore into that first track I felt like I was seventeen again. And they say you can't go back☺.

We were bloody brilliant. Everyone's saying so. People cluster around us, congratulating, praising, drooling at the prospect of future successes and future earnings. We're euphoric. James particularly. He's certainly a chunk off the Ronsarno granite. But I always knew that.

First Pete then Philip go to James. Philip throws a fatherly arm around James's shoulders and sings his praise to the nearest gaggle of journalists, all of whom hold out digital Dictaphones, listen and nod; no need for red hot pen nibs and cryptic shorthand anymore. I remember my old collection and smile the way normal grown ups do over the toys they once loved. Seeing Philip showering in the attention we loved and loathed in equal measure I can't remember why I even started collecting. He, at least, still enjoys having his arse kissed. In the glare of their adulation he morphs into Philip Hall, aged twenty-two, ego on max and sex drive set to warp speed. He's almost pulling it off. There must be something to that healthy living bollocks because, in the half light of the wings, he doesn't look bad, for a pensioner. I suspect the furtive aid of modern medical methods too but can't blame him for that. He's had to stay young and beautiful 'cos he still wants to be loved.

I'm tired now, a shaky old dog who's been walked too far. Time to sit, rest and lick old aches. A grinning Keira materialises from the throng. She thinks she's done me a good turn. She kinda has; I knew it was the right thing to do. Not the same as good though. Good's about pleasure; right's about duty. I blame and thank her in the same breath.

She reaches me.

'That was magnificent.'

'I know.'

'Are you O.K.?'

'Tired. Can you get me outta here for a bit?' I glance around at the exits, all covered by circling journos, waiting to dive-bomb me.

'Sure.'

Keira leads me through the maze of people and into a corridor lined with dressing rooms. I head in the direction of my own but Keira pulls on my arm.

'Go in there.' She points to a door that says Britney or Courtney or something, I can't quiet get the words into focus. 'She's on stage for the next thirty minutes so you won't be disturbed.'

'Good idea.'

'I'll get you in a bit.' Her parting reminder that I'm not to wander off before the presentation. Bollocks, I keep forgetting about that. The gig was the thing, not cocking it up. And we didn't. We fucking sold it. I feel the smile deep inside me. I replay the music in my head, note for note. It wasn't perfect but it was dynamic, heady: real.

Apart from the weakness in my legs and the ache in my shoulder from the weight of my Les Paul, I'm alright. But I'm not in my twenties anymore. Sitting at the dressing table I face myself in the mirror. The wrinkles and the grey hair don't look any worse. If I wake up in the morning breathing on my own, well, anything else is a fucking bonus these days so tonight's an absolute ball-busting triumph.

In search of cigarettes I open a drawer.

There's a needle, surgically clean, resting on a gauze pad. It's been a long time since I held one but when I pick it up it feels instantly familiar, a lost toy, the muted warmth of the plastic tube and the contrasting metallic cold that clings to the hair-thin tip. I rotate it in the light from the bulbs around the mirror and feel it come to life in my fingers, stirring a past of days and nights lost to artificial oblivion. Christ only knows why I was spared permanent oblivion when so many weren't.

What's her chosen poison, then? They cook up some really whacky shit these days. Scientific name, un-fucking-pronounceable but known as Fairy Dust or some other euphemistic bullshit. Play up the pleasure; play down the pain, that's how it is now. At least 'smack' tells you it's gonna fucking hurt: eventually. Not physically, not in your body. All that bullshit about drugs killing you, even if it's true it's a fucking sweet way to go. It's your mind that gets hurt, throbs with it in the end 'cos it's never as good as that first time but you keep hoping, trying: chasing.

In the drawer there's a bottle. I pick it up. The label is neatly typed but the words blurry. Damn, I really will have to start carrying those bloody reading glasses. Remembering the anonymous brown bottles Gomez used to carry in deep pockets, each filled with a multi-coloured assortment of highs, I hold this bottle at arm's length and squint 'til I get the distance right then I make out: Botox – to be administered directly to the required area under medical supervision.

While I was watching the eastern sky for the sun a black moon rose behind me in the west.

*

I sit on the floor with Ronsey 'til we're both cold. Dunno what else to do.

My first sane, conscious thought is that I need a hit, a fucking proper one, the dragon that chases all other monsters away. I dial Gomez's number. There's still that ringing in my ears. I strain through it and catch a single, distant word.

'Hello?'

'Gomez?'

Nothing but that damn ringing.

'Gomez?'

'Mickey?' It's faint, underwater.

'Gomez.' I form the words slowly in my mouth and breathe them out, 'Listen. You gotta come over. I can't hear anything. You've gotta come over. Something's happened.'

There's a low rumble of words. I can't pull them up to me.

'I can't hear what you're saying. Look, get your fucking arse over here. Now. Bring me some gear. John's dead.' Even though I can't hear them, those two words sound fucking dreadful. I slam the receiver down. My bloody handprint is wrapped around it. I race from the room.

In the kitchen, I go to the sink to wash my hands. See that bottle of magic pills still sat on the side. I hurl it at the window; it bounces off the sash, falls in the sink, cracks and spills its gaudy guts. I pace round the room. Where the fuck is Gomez? What's taking him so long? The ringing refuses to shift even when I shake my head. Everything I do's missing a bit 'cos I can't hear. I'm totally fucking detached. Part of me is numb. No matter how hard I prod it I don't feel a fucking thing.

The kitchen door flies open. It's Gomez, his shirt done up wrong, the laces of his tennis shoes tangled, his hair ruffled. He's speaking. I see his lips moving.

'I can't fucking hear you. Something's up with my lugs,' I yell.

He keeps talking at me. It's fucking pointless. I jab a finger in each ear. Shake my head. He mimes it for me, pinching his nose, screwing up his eyes and puffing out his cheeks. I get it and do like you do on a plane when the pressure makes your ears fill up. I blow down hard. The shriek pitches up a tone. There's a pop and a fizzing sound. I do it again to be sure. Another pop. Warmth gushes into both ears. I stick a finger in. There's red on the tip when I check.

'Can you fucking hear me now?'

'Yeah. Did you bring it?'

He reaches into his pocket. Produces a tightly folded square of foil. I open my hand. He snatches it out of reach.

'What the fuck did you say on the phone? About John.'

I shiver. Fix my eyes on the living room door. Gomez swing around, charges down the hall and falls through the doorway.

'Shit. Fuck. Jesus. Fucking fuck.'

I stay in the kitchen. He comes back.

'What the hell happened?'

'Gimme the gear, will ya.'

'You've gotta be fucking kidding. What the shitting hell's gone on 'ere?'

I think about the fight, the acid, Philip: what I said to him. Why the hell did I say it? Christ, it's not even fucking true. He is good enough. Ronsey. If I hadn't been off my face maybe I could've... It's nobody's fault but mine. And there's no fucking way I can tell Gomez that. There's no way I can tell anyone. Ever.

'Dunno. I was outta it.'

Gomez shakes his head. 'Shit. Christ's sake. Bollocks. Fuck. Mickey.'

We scowl at each other.

'Give me the bloody—'

'Here.' He flings the wrap at me and stalks out.

I light one of the gas rings, grab a spoon, tip the whole wrap onto it and cook it 'til it bubbles. A needle lies ready on the counter. I suck the brown liquid up in it and make a fist but my veins refuse to surface. They've packed up. Folded. Failed, like everything else, from too much too often. I swap hands, hold the needle clumsily in my left and bunch my right hard enough to crush coal. Nails, grown long for finger picking, cut into my palm. I keep the fist squeezed tight, bullying a pale green line into appearing on the back of my hand. Grip trembling and uncertain, I jab the needle at it. Miss. A tiny red bead swells up out of the needle prick. Fuck sake. I re-aim, jab a second time. Score the hit.

Heroin rushes through me, warming my arm, spreading soothing heat across my chest. I urge it on. It races eagerly, a flood soaking dry ground, calming a universe of pain. It reaches my brain. Relief, pure and empty, finishes me. I slump against the cooker.

Aaaaaaaaaaaaaaaaaauuuuuuuuuuuuuuuuuummmmm mmmmmmmmm 𝄇 'Mickey?'

I'm sleeping. He's trying to wake me up. I'm not going to let him.

aaaaaaaaaaaaaauuuuuuuuuuuummmmmmmmmm 𝄇

'Jesus, Mickey!'

I'm heavy all over, even my eyelids feel weighted down. I force them up. Gomez is in the kitchen again. He reaches past me to switch off the gas then puts his face to mine and looks through me, watching the heroin dancing behind my eyes.

'You've got a fucking nose bleed,' he says. ''Ere.' He jerks a cloth off the counter and shoves it at me. 'We have to get rid of everything. I mean, every fucking thing.'

He snatches the kitchen bin and tosses in the needle, spoon and empty wrap then starts tearing open drawers, binning anything doubtful. I float and twirl, spinning the hit out further and further, trying to hold onto the slippery swirl of euphoria.

Aaaaauuuuummmmm

He retrieves the colourful mess of pills in the sink. Goes out. I hear the toilet flush. Twice. And he's back in the kitchen.

'Where does ya neighbour keep their bin? Round the back?'

'What?'

'Their fucking bin, Mickey. Round the back? Shed? Garage?'

'Garden.'

He goes through the rear door. The patio security light flashes on. His arse is lit up, disappearing over the fence. Two minutes later he reappears, minus my rubbish. He opens the freezer and retrieves a bottle of black label Smirnoff, takes a swig and passes it to me. I swig too. He lights a cigarette. Gives it to me before lighting another for himself. Then he slaps me across the face.

'You here? 'Cos I gotta call Don now, and the cops.'

aum

'Yeah.'

'Fucking pull yerself together, Mickey. Try not to sound like an incoherent smack-head for fuck sake.'

He calls Don from the hall phone. I picture the bloody handprint on the one in the living room.

'Don?... It's me... Yeah, it's bloody urgent. Would I be fucking ringing ya at this hour if it wasn't? Ya better get over to Mickey's. Something's happened...'

I stagger forward. Kick the kitchen door shut. Now I can hear I don't fucking want to. I sag down into a chair. Blood drips onto the table and lands in thick spatters. I don't know where it's coming from. I don't try to stop it.

By the time the police arrive, along with the ambulance crew, Don and our lawyer, are already here. Dennis Isaacson, QC, is a boiled-dry, sour-lemon faced school friend of Don's who's driving desire is to clear his clients. At the sound of the doorbell I remember the two pink pills I put in my pocket for later, before. I throw them into my mouth before Don can stop me. He has to be content with a warning shake of the head. Gomez hisses into my ear.

'You wanna get arrested? I said every fucking thing.'

'That is every fucking thing,' I snap.

The police take us outside. We wait in the garden in full view of the street. I remember another time, in a different but equally fucked up universe, when I stood in a different garden while different cops crawled over a different house, taking different photos, leaving with a different body on a stretcher while different neighbours gawped and gossiped. My mother's bloated face swells up in gory detail: smudges of war paint, greasy-streaked; bulging, bloodshot eyeballs; tongue purple and rotten, protruding from her mouth.

A senior officer stomps over to us. I shake down my mother and make myself listen. Don does the talking. I huddle behind him. Light another cigarette. It's my last one. Hope to hell Gomez has more. A window across the street lights up. A human silhouette appears. The cop turns to me. Where was I last night? What was I doing? What time did I come home? The window opens. The figure leans out for a better view.

Bloody Mrs Henderson. Always lurking, spying, gossiping about me and my mother. Mind your own fucking business. Nosey bitch. She's like the Stasi. I know it's fucking her who rings the coppers about the comings and goings at ours. Well, she's getting a bloody good show tonight, cops everywhere and me standing out here like a prick. She's gonna get a fucking shock in a minute. When they bring my mother out, her face purple and bloated. Serves her right, silly cow.

'Hope you're enjoying the show, Mrs Henderson, you daft bitch. Stick around for the second half, it gets better, I guarantee it,' I yell to the figure in the window. The light snaps out.

'Mickey, who are you talking to? Who's Mrs Henderson?' Don's face materialises.

What's he doing here? He shouldn't be here. He wasn't here before. Why's he here now?

'Mickey?' He shakes my arm but I can't answer; my thoughts are wordless. I'm choking. The world's turned an odd grey colour. He faces the cop. 'He's clearly in shock. You'll have to ask your questions later. I need to get him to a doctor.'

An invisible hand slides the fader down; voices trail off like the end of a studio track. I let myself fade too. In the distance there's a cracking sound somewhere between the shattering of glass dropped from a height and the crunching of gravel as you walk over it. I hear it then feel it, hard on the back of my head. Now I'm lying in the drive, underneath a night sky full of stars; a million twinkling lights that dazzle me. They hurt my eyes; I stop looking.

The funeral is tomorrow. I don't want to go. Don says I have to. He sends Gomez to make sure I don't do a runner or something even stupider. Gomez is smart enough to know there's only one way he can deal with me tonight. He dopes me up. I lie on my bed, enjoying a careless stupor, while he rakes through my wardrobe.

'Where's your suit?'

'Dunno.'

I hear the clattering of hangers as he wades from one end to the other.

'Shit.'

'Try the other room.'

He pounds across the landing. I stare into the wardrobe's colourful belly. If he can't find it fuck knows what I'll wear. He pounds back.

'Got it.'

'Cool.'

'You want some grub?'

I shake my head. Close my eyes. Keep them closed until the insides of my lids fade from black through burgundy, red and finally, orange and it's time to open them again.

He's hung my suit outside the wardrobe. Flat arms and legs dangle miserably, a hanged man waiting to be cut down. I drag myself off the bed. Force myself to do the cutting. It weighs sod all. I nearly collapse under the load but manage to haul it to the bed. I put the trousers on sitting down. When I stand to fasten them there's a lot of swaying. And they're too big. I sit again. Wait for Gomez.

'Mickey, you ready?' he calls through the door.

'No.'

He comes in. 'Car'll be here in a minute.'

'I need a belt.'

'What?'

I point to my jeans, dumped on the floor. He picks them up.

'It's brown,' he says.

'So the fuck what?'

He shrugs, yanks it off the jeans and brings it to me.

'Tie?'

'Don't have one.'

'Christ's sake. Why didn't you say so yesterday?'

My turn to shrug.

'I'll ring Don.'

He goes out. I hear him on the phone, telling Don to bring a tie. I pull the jacket on. It's too big as well. This isn't my suit. Can't be.

I pass the living room door with blinkers on. It's closed; I keep my head down anyway. From the kitchen comes the thick smell of frying sliced through by sharp coffee vapours. Gomez follows me in.

'Said he'll bring a tie.'

'Fan-fucking-tastic.'

'Have some of this.' He pours a coffee.

'And?'

''Ere.' He chucks a packet at me. It drops on the counter. I pick it up. It's white.

'What the fuck's this?'

'Coke.'

'Yeah, right.'

'Don said…'

'I don't give a fuck what Don said. Since when does Don pay you?'

'There's gonna be cops and press every fucking where today,' Gomez warns. 'Can't have you zombiefied. You need to keep it together.'

'With this? It's a fucking joke.' I yank open one of the drawers.

'Don't waste yer time, man. That's all there is.' Gomez takes it off me and cuts it into lines. Hands me a tightly rolled twenty. Outside a car horn beeps. 'Hurry up.'

The four white lines on the counter-top are four strikes: marked time. One, two, three, four. I need one more slashed through them to cross the whole thing off and reset to zero. One and one and one and one is four. I snort one of the lines. And then there were three. But it has to be all or nothing. I can't leave three standing alone, a man down. The car horn beeps again. I knock back the others with only a breath between, then pocket the twenty.

'Christ, Mickey, what've you been doing?' Don asks as I scramble into the limo. 'We're going to be pushing it to get there on time.' He throws me a tie.

I slump in the seat next to Gomez. The leather upholstery lets out a small, sad sigh. Don knows perfectly fucking well what I've been doing. I sniff down the answer.

Gomez takes the tie, puts it round his own neck and wraps it deftly into a loose knot before taking it off and handing me the noose.

'Where'd the fuck you learn to do that?'

'Eton.'

I put the tie on. Tighten it. 'Eton? Bullshit.'

Gomez eyeballs me.

'Mickey, you need to be on your best behaviour today,' Don says, bobbing forward like a jack-in-the-box to interrupt. 'There's going to be a heavy press presence. Don't say anything to them. Not a single fucking word. I mean it.'

'Christ, Eton, really?'

'Shit, shut up about Eton,' Don snaps. 'Did you hear what I said?'

'I fucking heard you.'

He slides back inside his box. I watch the buildings scroll past; house, house, house, newsagents, house, house, post office, house, house, house, house, petrol station, house, house, house, off-licence.

'Pull over.' I open the door. Put a foot out before the car stops. Before Don stops me. Gomez is a bit quicker. He jerks my arm.

'No yer fucking don't.'

I whirl round. Punch him on the nose. He falls against Don. I charge across the pavement into the shop.

It takes a minute for my eyes to adjust to the dark interior. I scan the shelves behind the till. The shopkeeper's a little man in a bobbly beige cardy. He peers over half-moon glasses.

'Gimme a bottle of Scotch.'

'Anything in particular?'

'Whatever.' I fish in my pocket for Gomez's twenty. Hand it over still rolled up, traces of coke on one edge. The shopkeeper unrolls it suspiciously. Holds it to the light. Satisfied, he plucks a half bottle of Bells off the shelf. On the counter next to the till is today's *Daily Mirror*. Before I can stop myself I've read the headline: King of the sticks laid to rest. Blood congeals in my veins. The shopkeeper puts the bottle on the counter beside the paper. I snatch it up and dash for the door.

'Don't you want your change?'

The door clangs shut behind me. On the street I unscrew the top and swallow a mouthful. It lands in my stomach with a crash, bounces, comes up and out, all over the pavement. I down another mouthful, make sure it's staying put, and clamber into the car. Gomez is clutching his nose.

Don leans forwards.

'No more pit stops,' he orders, handing Gomez a hanky. The limo pulls away. I hunker down with my bottle. It's something to hold on to.

The church is in the suburbs. Three more black limos are parked in the road outside. And a hearse. There's a coffin in the back. Flowers cover it completely, one clump arranged to spell the word 'Dad'. I drink the last mouthful of whisky.

Philip's by the church gates. It's the first time I've seen him since That Night. He'll know by now what my story is. Don'll have told him; Ronsey and me were having a few drinks, I passed out, when I came round he was already dead. Philip's blue eyes are dry and empty as he stares me down. He doesn't know why I've lied for him. Doesn't know both us should've saved Ronsey but neither of us could: did. I'm not giving him the satisfaction of knowing I'm as much to blame as he is, the fucker. Why the hell should I? I owe that son of a bitch nothing.

A series of explosions blind me, camera flashes going off. Questions are fired at us. Don flanks me on one side, Gomez on the other, his nose purpling from my punch. They steer me up the church path, towards sanctuary. I swivel my head to keep Philip in sight and see a bloke in a full mourning suit joining him, saying something. Philip breaks our locked-tight gaze to listen to him. Don and Gomez keep me moving 'til I'm too far along the path to see Philip anymore.

Inside the church black shadows drift about in private trances. I'm one of them. We sit. Two rows in front James's dark head rises above the pew. His mother sits next to him. Her shoulders are hunched and shaking. James's are held back: still. He turns. His face is rigid and numb. What the hell's he thinking? He smiles at me, a tiny smile. The sort you give to someone who needs it more than you.

Six pairs of footsteps echo round the chapel in perfect sync with each other. Don stands. My legs're too weak. Gomez hooks a hand under my armpit, heaving me to my feet as they reach us and glide down the aisle. Philip's in the middle, on my side. His hands are clasped in front of him. He leans out awkwardly to counter the weight on his shoulder. He doesn't see me. Thank fuck.

The minister, leading the procession, mounts the pulpit.

'In the midst of life we are in death.'

I close my ears. It's the hardest thing I've ever done, not listening to him: not listening to anything. I conjure a hum, in F♭, a note that doesn't exist, and allow it to drone through my head. I can't use any other note 'cos it's always gonna be the sound of death.

By 1:30 I'm home again: high again. We're in the kitchen. Don and Gomez are here, drinking my brandy.

'They're taking him up north, eh?' Gomez asks.

'A private interment, the church in his home village,' Don says, 'tomorrow.'

'Is he going?' I ask.

'Who?'

'Philip.'

Don frowns at me. 'Why?'

'Is he?'

'I don't know,' he says. I think he's lying.

'Anyway, it's over,' Gomez says.

'There's the inquest,' Don reminds him. Me. 'A fortnight tomorrow. Hang on to the tie, Mickey.'

'Cheers.'

The inquest is tomorrow. I've been called as a witness: summoned. There's no getting out of it. Gomez has copped for baby-sitting duties again. He's got me some Valium. I feel pretty mellow. It's O.K. shit, not much of a come down but it doesn't properly bliss me out. No pleasure for the wicked.

My suit's back from the dry-cleaners, hanging inside the wardrobe, buried. I lie on the bed with my eyes open, watch all night for the monster lurking in the cupboard.

There's no limo this morning. Gomez is gonna drive me in my old TR4. He can't get it started. He swears and sweats. I sit in the passenger seat, half-catatonic.

'Fucking thing.'

'Have you got some choke on it?'

'Course I fucking have. Think the battery's knackered. Jump leads?'

'Christ knows.'

'Jesus, we're gonna be fucking late.' He turns the engine over again and stamps hard on the accelerator. It coughs and splutters then fires. 'Halle-bloody-lujah,' he mutters as he swings out of the drive, splitting the shoal of waiting journos. Disorientated, they dart about in our wake before giving chase.

The building's square and grey, the windows precisely spaced, some with dark blinds closed. The journos have re-massed on the steps, ready to swoop. Don's arranged for us to park around back, in the secure car park, but to get to it Gomez has to drive through the shoal again. This time it doesn't break so easily. He thumps the horn and barrels forward. It tightens around us. Flashbulbs blow off everywhere like fireworks. I keep my head down but the white lights flick on/off through the window, scorching my eyeballs.

We go in the rear entrance, into a private waiting room, beyond the reach of hungry press piranhas waiting to slay me for good.

Don's already there, and Dennis Isaacson, QC. He has a briefcase, looks like he knows what he's doing. Fucking hope so.

'Mickey.' He greets me, hand out, like he's a mate. 'Remember, this is a formality. The coroner will be asking you to tell him the events of that night as you remember them. That's all you need to do.'

'Fucking marvellous.'

'If any other interested party decides to ask you anything, their questions must be directly relevant. The coroner will advise you if he thinks the questions are not relevant or if you might incriminate yourself by answering. If you're not sure look at me; I'll nod if it's O.K. to answer,' he explains.

'Bloody great.'

'There's no need to be nervous. Inquests are to establish cause of death only, not to apportion blame. You're not on trial.'

What do you call a lead guitarist in a suit?

'As we discussed the other day, they'll likely record a verdict of accidental death.' He pats my shoulder. 'That'll be officially noted and the case closed.'

Un-fucking-likely.

'There's nothing to worry about. This was a tragic accident.'

'Gimme a cigarette,' I mutter to Gomez. He passes me his pack.

'I'm not sure you're allowed to smoke in here,' Isaacson

mumbles.

'Let me know when you're absolutely sure 'bout that,' I reply and keep smoking. He shrugs, says something in Don's ear and heads through the door to the inquest room.

The other door, the one we came through, is behind me. It bangs open now. Don's jaw locks. I turn. See Philip, James and his mother. Three pairs of eyes drill into me. Ronsey's missus takes James's hand. Philip puts an arm around her shoulders. They're some kind of fucked up, unholy trinity come to dish out vengeance. I think I'm gonna puke.

'Philip,' Don says, too calmly.

'Don.' But he keeps his eyes on me, shuffling his place in the triad so he can rest a protective hand on James's head. James screws his face up in annoyance. Rage ripples through me. Nothing matters more at that moment than charging at Philip and punching his lights out. Don grips my arm.

'What's 'is fucking problem?' Gomez hisses in my ear.

'Me.'

'What the fuck for? 'S not like it's your fault.'

'He thinks it is.'

'Mickey, for Christ's sake, don't start something,' Don warns.

We face off to each other, three on three, the scales seesawing up and down, waiting for the load to stabilise. James breaks ranks and rushes me. I cringe, brace for the impact of tiny, angry fists. Fuck knows what Philip's told him. James throws himself at me: round me. Clings to me, hiding his face against my chest. I'm left standing there, wondering what the fuck to do, while James crushes me. I look at Don. He mimes a comforting cuddle. I chuck my fag end on the carpet and do my best to give James his hug back. It's a piss weak attempt, not surprising given my shaking-like-a-dog-shitting-bones state. His tousled curls tremble. He shakes deep inside. I know I should say something but there's nothing in my head. I want to say sorry but the word lodges in my throat. James tries to fold himself into me. I can't help him. Or myself. Isaacson reappears, mutters to Don.

'Mickey, we need to go in,' Don says.

'Shit. Now?'

'Yes,' Isaacson barks.

'James, mate.' He looks at me with bright eyes. 'I gotta go.' He nods grimly and untangles himself but stays rooted to the spot, giving me that smile again. 'Cos I still need it more than he does.

We're ushered in. The public gallery's full. One side is press; the other fans. A single flash bursts. Christ knows which side fires first but it triggers a volley of shots. The clerk showing us where to sit stops abruptly.

'The use of cameras is not permitted in this inquest,' he warns. 'Anyone found using such a device will be escorted out.'

I slide weakly into my seat and try to be grateful for too-late mercies.

The coroner slithers into position behind a large desk at the front. Another clerk opens the proceedings. I listen as the coroner explains the purpose of the inquest: to formally identify the deceased and record the cause of death. My right leg starts hopping. Don jabs me with his elbow.

'Sit still,' he mutters in a strained whisper.

'I can't fucking help it.'

Gomez produces a bottle of pills and passes them to me. My hands are shaking now, too.

'I can't get the damn top off.'

'What the hell?' Don mumbles.

Gomez twists it open and hands me two. ''S O.K.,' he tells Don, 'they're legit: Valium.' He shows Don the label but doesn't say where he got them.

My mouth's too dry to swallow. I crunch the pills. Am still chewing when the coroner calls me to the stand. It's a long way away. I walk slowly, shuffling like an old man, and ease myself into the chair.

He asks. I answer, keeping to the facts as known by everyone. Everyone except me and Philip.

'Me and Ronse were having a few drinks. I fell asleep—' I've been warned not to say 'passed out'— 'and when I woke up John was on the floor, dead.'

'What, to the best of your knowledge, had caused his death?'

'There was a broken bottle on the floor. He musta fell on it and cut himself, bled to…'

'Were you aware there was a broken bottle on the floor?'

'No.'

'And when you awoke it was clear to you that Mr. Ronsarno was already dead?'

'Yeah, his fucking blood was all over my carpet.'

'Mr Hunter, please refrain from using obscenities at this hearing.'

'Sorry.'

'Did you make any attempt to save Mr Ronsarno?'

'…'

'Mr Hunter, did you hear the question?'

'…'

'Mr Hunter?'

'… Yes, I did.'

'Thank you. Does anyone else wish to question this witness?'

A man jumps to his feet.

'I do.'

The whole room swivels to gape. He's tall, stocky, an old grey suit stretched across broad shoulders; thick greying hair and a salt and pepper beard mark his age. He tugs at it. There's an icy burn in my chest.

'Please state your name and relation to the deceased for the record,' the coroner instructs.

'John Ronsarno, senior. Father.'

The coroner nods. I didn't even know John's dad was alive and here he is, striding over no man's land towards me.

'Please ask your questions.'

'I only have one. Isn't the real reason my son's dead because you were off your head on drugs and couldn't help him when he fell?'

Panic claws at my throat. Yes, it is. Yes, it fucking is. I see the lawyer shake a very definite 'no' at me. The coroner interrupts.

'Mr Ronsarno, our purpose here is only to establish the medical cause of death. Your question is not relevant. If nobody has any relevant questions…?' He challenges the room. Nobody else speaks. 'You may step down.'

'It is bloody relevant. My son's dead because of him.' John's dad points an accusatory finger at me. From the press pen I hear the furious scratching of nibs.

'Mr Ronsarno, I sympathise with your grief at this difficult time but your question is of no relevance to the purpose of this inquest. Mr Hunter, please step down.'

I get shakily to my feet and stagger for my seat.

'Look at the bloody state of him. He can't even walk straight. He's probably on something right now,' John's dad shouts.

I make it to Gomez, fall into the chair beside him.

'Clerk, will you please escort Mr Ronsarno outside,' the coroner orders. 'The next witness is Dr William Morelle.'

'It's your fault, you bastard.' The words leap over to us as John's dad is forced from the room between two clerks. Philip's in my eye-line too, his face stone. The door bangs shut on Mr Ronsarno. The coroner begins to question the post-mortem quack. I pray for the end.

He's dead. So's she. It was my fault. Both times. I could've made it come out differently but I fucking didn't. Tried to save John, wanted to, fought to: failed. Didn't even try to help her 'cos I thought she deserved it, silly old cow. She was my fucking mother. I should've helped her. Not walked away. Left someone else to deal with it all, even her bloody funeral. I don't even know where she's buried now. That's what all this is for. What goes around comes a-fucking-round. I'm getting what I deserve. It's long overdue. But not John. It's not fucking fair. He shouldn't've had to stump up for me. And James. Jesus fucking Christ.

Gomez slaps my leg.

'He's gonna say the what's-it.'

'Verdict,' Don prompts.

The coroner gets to his feet. Launches into a great long spiel I'm incapable of following. Finally I hear the words 'accidental death'. There's a whoop from some of the fans. Don tuts.

'Anybody would think you were on trial the way they're going on.'

I should be. Me and Philip.

'Can we please get the fuck out of here?' I beg.

Pinned between Don and Gomez I'm steered back the way we came. We're almost out of the room when we're waylaid.

'Mr. Hunter, any comments about the inquest? The verdict?'

Don's programmed to respond; it's a reflex. His body turns before his brain registers what he's doing.

'We'll be issuing an official statement later today.'

We will?

The journo pushes harder. 'Mr. Hunter, what about the accusation of Mr Ronsarno, senior?'

'The poor man is clearly, and understandably, distraught,' Don says, 'but his grief has made him jump to inaccurate conclusions.'

'So you weren't using illegal substances on the night in question?' The journo bores into me with a pair of steel-grey eyes that see the truth.

'No more questions. This is a difficult time for all of us,' Don says and pulls me away.

'Of course. This inquest must have brought back painful

memories for you, Mr Hunter,' the journo says, 'of your mother's murder. You were a witness at her inquest, too?'

Gomez clamps both hands on my shoulders and shoves me through the door into the waiting room.

'I'll go bring the car round,' he offers.

'No.'

'I thought yer wanted to get outta 'ere.'

'Let's leave it 'til that fucking lot've cleared off.'

He sits beside me. Gives me a cigarette.

'Yer old lady was bumped off?'

'I'll tell you 'bout that if you tell me 'bout Eton.'

He cackles. 'No chance, man.'

We sit there smoking. I fix on the door: the way out. The handle rotates down slowly. I press my fingers into my eyes, take a deep breath and look again. It's still pointing down. I sit up. Dig Gomez in the ribs.

'What?'

I nod at the door. 'Someone's out there. Might be that reporter.'

Gomez stands. 'If it is I'll punch 'is fucking lights out.'

I grab his shirt, holding him back. Gomez frowns at me. I shake my head. Behind him the door inches open a crack. Stops. We freeze. Nothing moves for a long ten seconds then the door edges a bit wider, the gap growing. I steel myself for whatever the hell's behind it. I kinda expect to see a gaunt figure in a black cloak, shouldering a scythe. James fills the doorway. Hysterical laughter starts bubbling in my gut. I manage to smother it to a single guffaw by the time it reaches my mouth.

'James. Christ, you scared me. Where's your mother?'

'Dunno.' He shrugs and comes into the room.

'You'll cop it for wandering off.'

'Don't care.'

'Gomez, go find his bloody mother, will ya?'

'Now?'

'Yeah, now.'

He slams out. I light a cigarette. Take a drag. James watches me with his father's eyes.

'Come an' sit down, mate.' I pat the seat beside me 'cos I don't wanna have to look him in the eye. He sits.

'Were you in there, James?' I jerk a thumb at the inquest room.

'Mam wouldn't let me. It's not fair. I wanted to hear what they said. I'm not too young.'

'She's trying to look out for you, that's all. Anyway, you didn't miss much. It was boring grown-up stuff.'

'It was about Dad.'

'I know, mate, but what got said in there, it doesn't make any fucking difference. Shit, sorry. Don't you dare repeat any foul language in front of your mother. She'll know you got it off me. Promise.' I throw James a quick glance. He agrees with a nod. 'Cheers, mate. Look, what I mean is, yeah, there's this stuff going on, about your dad and that, but it doesn't change anything. He's still…'

'Dead. I know.'

'Yeah, and this, it's stuff that has to be done when someone…'

'Dies?'

'Yeah.'

'Why?'

''Cos people are always looking for answers. But knowing why or how something happened doesn't make it hurt less.' Out of the corner of my eye I see James frown. 'Have you ever had any fillings, James?'

'Yep.'

'And the dentist said why he was gonna have to do it and told you what he was doing?'

'Yes.'

'Bet it still hurt like hell though?'

James nods.

'So knowing why something's happened doesn't always make it better. Sometimes it makes it worse. That's why your mum didn't want you in there.'

'O.K.'

'I know how much this hurts, mate.'

'Is your dad dead?'

'Dunno. Never knew him. My mum is though.'

'Were you sad when she died?'

'Yeah. And, you know what, that's the first time I've ever told anyone that.'

'Why?'

'Maybe 'cos I didn't want to admit it. But there's nothing wrong with feeling sad and missing someone when they're gone and wishing they were here.'

'O.K.' James kicks his legs under the seat and out again, like he's swinging.

'And ya know what else? Your dad is here, kinda.'

'How come?'

''Cos you're here, mate.' I aim a playful punch at his arm. 'Chip off the old Ronsarno block, remember?'

He nods.

'James, d'ya know what a legacy is?'

'Is that like when you leave someone some money in your will? I heard Mam say something about that.'

'Yeah, but it's something else, too. Something more important. It's what you leave behind when you're gone, for other people to remember you by, like if you do great things with your life.'

'Like you?'

'Fuck, no. Not like me. But like your dad. He did great things. He was a great bloke, James. Don't ever let anyone tell you different. And you're gonna be like him. You're his legacy. That's special. You should be proud of that.'

He nods again. I don't know how much longer I've got so I push on.

'There's something I want you to promise me, James.'

'What?'

'That you'll look after your mother. Make sure she's O.K. and stuff, yeah?'

'O.K.'

'Promise?'

'Yeah.'

'Cross your heart and that?'

'Yeah, cross my heart.'

'Cool.' I get up. 'Dunno what's happened to Gomez. Reckon we better look for your mum.'

James stands too. 'Will you come and see me? So we can jam like we did that time.'

'I'm not sure I'd be welcome round yours, mate.' His face goes a pinched shade of white. 'I'll try. Maybe not for a while, though. But you've gotta keep playing, right? 'Cos I will come, promise. I'll come and we'll play together.' I hold out my hand. 'Deal?'

He puts his tiny hand in mine. His grip's good and strong. We're shaking on it as the door opens. Ronsey's missus is standing there. She pretends she hasn't seen me.

'Come on, James. We're leaving.'

James lets go of my hand. 'Thanks, Uncle Mickey.'

What the fuck for?

I replay what I said to James, trying to convince myself I didn't arse it up. By bedtime I'm so drained with it that I feel completely empty: sucked dry. I send Gomez packing. He drives off in my TR4. I hear the horn beeping angrily as he fights through the mob of journalists hanging around my wrought iron gates. When the sound dies away I know it's over at last. All I want now is to close my eyes, go under and come up again a long way from now, when this is buried deep. I don't know any other way.

The next morning I thrash out a plan and put it into gear. I don't wanna see Gomez anymore. I don't wanna see any of them anymore. I stock up from Ade, barricade myself in, locking the doors and windows, closing the curtains and dragging the hall stand against the front door. For the first time since That Night I go into the living room, the scene of the crime: the departure lounge. I haul the sofa across the door and settle down to get high. Only the emergency exit is signed.

I travel far, far away…

I don't know if it's night or day. It's permanently dark. Some dumb cunt forgot to bring the sun with them. That'll be me, I suppose.

Animal smells fill the air; sweat, blood, shit.

Mysterious voices mutter around me. I don't know whose they are. They're here somewhere. Trust me to people my own world with shadowy strangers.

I start walking. Fuck knows where to. I'm afraid of falling off the edge but I keep going.

Once, as I'm walking, I glimpse something, right at the limit of the blackness. I stop to search for it but it's gone too quickly. I saw enough, though, to know what it was: a quiet, shady glade with leafy trees and a winding stream, a clear sky overhead, tiny and far away. That's where I'll head. It's something, sweet something. I trudge on blindly.

Every now and then I stop, revolve slowly and stroke the empty air that surrounds me. I'm afraid of touching something sharp that'll slice through my skin. I'm afraid of feeling something warm, wet and sticky on my hands. I keep my eyes open, hoping to see my glade again. I wanna know if I'm going in the right direction. There's nothing. Just a whole lot of black. Night. Winter. Death.

After a lot of walking, when all I've seen is darkness and all I've heard is the buzz of phantoms muttering, something flutters across my face. I think it's a bird, flown too close to me in the darkness and I'm relieved. I brought birds with me, song birds, hopefully. Please, not crows. I stretch my hands up, try to catch it but it darts free. Later it flutters past me again. I come closer to it or it comes closer to me. I miss every time. But I know it's here. I keep reaching into the air, grabbing for it and missing.

Finally, I catch it. Trapped in my praying hands is the rapid beating of a heart that's not mine. It struggles against my fingers. The pulsating quickens; I press my hands more tightly around it, not wanting to let it go. I hold it against my chest so that its heartbeat and mine fall into step, a heavier thumping interspaced with a light, trembling patter. I hold it for as long as I dare. It struggles to escape. Feeling it live I know I'm alive. But I can't keep it alive in my hands forever. I should kill it. I tell myself to kill it. That's what I wanted. That's why I exiled myself in this fucked up fantasy kingdom of eternal night with enough smack in my veins to do for ten mortal men. But I've been lost too long to get out or to stay here and that shady glade is light years away. The tiny trembling grows fainter and fainter. I hold it to my ear, straining to hear the sound that can barely be felt now. It struggles feebly, driven by futile instinct. The time is coming when I'm gonna have to do something. If I don't decide, if I do nothing, it'll die anyway and I'll be alone. I wait. I'm afraid. I wait. I decide, opening my hands. The tiny, fragile thing floats away, taken by the wind like the white-green clock of a dandelion. I close my eyes. There's a red glow everywhere.

I sit up. Look around. An empty needle's stuck in my arm. I yank it out. I'm on my own, in my living room, on the floor. This is real. So was wherever the hell I've returned from. I remember Ronsey. Where he fell there's a big blank space. Clean up was taken care of fuck knows when, when I wasn't in any fucking state to pay attention, and now it's just there, threatening me, this big fucking space of fucking nothing. The floor cleared, the carpet shampooed. No tidal wave. No broken glass. No Ronsey. Nah. I've made a mistake. A really fucked up mistake. Should've gone all the way. Let that fluttering thing die in my hands. I fumble among the refuse surrounding me. Every pill jar's empty. There are only crumbs in the folds of all the foil wraps and plastic bags. I dig up a bottle with half an inch of whisky in the bottom, down it in one, retch and gag. I crawl across the floor, clambering through more rubbish. The smell of something rotten and rancid poisons my nose. I find bottle of gin, clear liquid sloshing around inside. I hate the bloody stuff but knock it back. My stomach heaves. I choke on the bile in my mouth before spitting it on the carpet. The room swims. My brain feels like it's trying to crack through my skull. There has to be something here somewhere that can make this stop. Half hidden beneath the chaos I see a sliver of pale blue. I pull it towards me. Flip over a printed picture of a peaceful countryside scene where a thin blue ribbon of water winds through a glade shaded by leafy, green trees. Hope in a 6 x 4 greeting card. I reach for the phone. A dark brown stain materialises on the recently scrubbed-clean receiver. I have to get out of here. Now.

I tug at the sofa, pulling it clear the door, and squeeze out the gap, tip the hall stand aside and escape.

A wan dawn drips liquid gold onto rooftops. Down the road's a phone box. Inside it I realise I don't have any money and reverse the charges, getting the operator to dial the number on the card. It rings for a long time. She's not there. Fuck it. I'll go back to Ade's.

'Hello?' The voice is sleep-slurred.

'Meg?' My tongue's stiff, my mouth dried-out.

'Who's this?' The voice sharpens.

'Mickey Hunter.'

She's not replying. Shit, she doesn't remember. Then:

'You got my card?'

'Yeah. Thanks.' I don't know what else to say; I didn't think I'd get this far.

'It's early,' she says.

'I didn't mean to wake you. What time it is?'

'Seven-thirty but it's O.K. I've been on nights and fell asleep in front of the telly. If you hadn't rang I'd have probably woken up here with a crick in my neck just in time to go back to work,' she says.

'Oh, good. That I helped by waking you, I mean.'

Another pause.

'Is this a pleasant chit-chat or do you want something?'

Fucked if I know.

'Do I dare hope you've been thinking about that help I recommended?'

'Honestly, I haven't been thinking 'bout much of anything for a bloody long time.'

'Well, what the hell is this?'

'I think I'm gonna kill myself.'

'I see, and you're after some tips from a medical mind.'

'I didn't mean it like that.'

She cuts across me. 'You want me to get you some drugs, is that it? What's wrong, your usual guy out of town?'

'No. Look, it's not, like, a plan or whatever. I'm scared it's what's gonna happen next. Soon. Suicide by instalment. Please. There's no one else I can ask. I'm properly fucked here.'

The silence is heavy. I don't try breaking it 'cos I'm scared of finding she's gone.

'O.K.,' she says, 'I'll come round.'

I think of the stench in the living room, the rubbish of my life and sitting down with her at the crime scene. 'Can I meet you somewhere instead?'

'I suppose. There's a café near me.'

We make the arrangements, me swinging enough time to change and clean up first. On the way home I pass a young lad taking three empty milk bottles to a waiting float. I ask him what day it is. He gives me a weird look and says it's Monday but that's no bloody good 'cos I can't remember what day it was before. I daren't ask him anything else. Back inside I put the radio on, find some early morning news. I have to sit for a moment, remembering, counting on my fingers. It's hard to find a point to start from but when I do I realise I've been spaced out for days.

The wreck that used to be my living room testifies to the timeline; bottles, cans, fag ends, food wrappers and scraps, dirty clothes, newspapers, letters: needles, sticking up everywhere, rapidly spreading weeds. One newspapers is front page up. I've scanned the headline before I can stop myself: **Crown & Kingdom guitarist accused at inquest**. I have to get it all outta here.

I get black bags and rubber gloves from the kitchen and return to the living room. The gut churning stench of shit hits me again as I go in. I start sweeping as much of the surface crap as possible into a bag, gagging with every breath. When I find the source of the stench, a bucket behind the armchair overflowing with a watery yellow-brown stew of shit and piss I'm hurl my guts up, gin and stomach acid gushing outta my mouth and splashing into the bucket, the bag and onto my shoes. Stumbling around the room, hand clamped over my nose and mouth, holding my breath, feeling faint, dizzy, eyes watering, gagging and retching, I scoop more rubbishing into the bag and drag it to the kitchen door. With a wet tea-towel as an improvised gas-mask I return for the bucket. Fumbling and juggling I get the door open and dump the lot onto the patio. There's a can of petrol in the shed. I tip it over the mound and light a cigarette. Smoke fights the flavours of shit and vomit in my mouth. After two drags I toss it onto the pile. It whooshes up in cheery oranges and reds, the petrol blazing merrily. Flames dance. I watch it burn, feeling the heat on my face. It's good and hot. Glass bottles pop. Paper and plastic crinkle and wither in the flames. The smoke becomes black and carbolic. The fumes are charred remains. I pour on more petrol when the flames start fading and watch them leap up, engorged with pleasure.

'What the hell do you think you're doing now? We're all bloody sick of your crazy antics. You're going to have every house in the avenue on fire.'

My neighbour is craning over the fence, red-faced and freaked out. He's a banker, bald, middle-aged and sensible. I'm his worse goddamn nightmare. Wonder if he found the present Gomez chucked in his bin the other night. Nah, that was weeks ago. It'll be landfill by now.

'I've had enough. I'm calling the police.'

'Don't you think this is a job for the fire brigade, man?'

He puffs. His face gets redder. He stabs a finger at me and splutters wordless outrages.

'Hey, take it easy, man.' I pick up the hose pipe. I don't wanna be late for Meg and I don't need any more fucking cops hassling me. I wind on the tap. The flames are shrinking now anyway. I spray the lot with an icy jet. It's tempting to spray it at him, his face needs putting out, but nah, not today.

'There, man, no harm done. Think of it as an early bonfire.'

He splutters some more but leaves. I retreat inside and, with dread, upstairs. What the fuck's that gonna be like?

It's a bit dusty and untidy but otherwise O.K. 'cos I've been hibernating in my downstairs den, in the midst of my own shit and chaos, the upstairs abandoned to dust and spiders, three of which lie belly-up in the bathtub. I scrape their corpses into a beer glass that's been left on the windowsill and flush them down the bog. Then I take a bath. Lying in the clear water I examine myself. The outline form of my skeleton is visible in X-ray precision beneath pallid skin. The detail fascinates and horrifies me. I wash and dry quickly, find clothes cleaner than the ones I was wearing and, an hour later, run-down but presentable, head off to meet Meg.

The cabbie drones on about the government or religion or some shit. I'm not listening 'til he says, 'It's the kids I feel sorry for, growing up without a dad. My dad died when I were a nipper and it was right hard.'

Our eyes meet in the rear view mirror. Is he talking about Ronsey? Christ, why wasn't I listening? We're at a set of lights and they're on red. I dump a handful of notes on the seat and scramble out.

Meg's waiting for me when I find the café. She lets me come to her. I flop down opposite her. A waitress appears. Meg orders. I'm still shaken by the confrontation in the taxi and the come down's starting to hit me. I'm numb and shivering. Hot coffees arrive. Trembling, I take mine to my lips. Meg watches.

'You need some of this.' She stirs two heaped spoonfuls of sugar into the creamy brown liquid. 'When did you last eat something?' She sounds like she cares. Force of professional habit?

'Can't remember,' I say as I pick up the cup again, gripping it in both hands to keep from slopping.

'I heard about…'

'Yeah.'

'It was in the papers.'

'I know.'

'They said it was a tragic accident,' she continues.

'Yeah…'

'It must be hard, especially for his family. For you too,' she adds, seeing me recoil and splash coffee over the Formica.

'Yeah.' Christ sake, that's the third time I've said that. My brain's empty.

'But in your house…'

'I know. I was fucking there.'

We drink the coffees. Order two more. My hands shake out a jagged rhythm. My lungs feel solid; breathing hurts. My body begs another fix. My heart's running like a cheetah. A cold film of sweat coats my back. Best case is that I'll pass out. Dunno if I can do this.

Meg eyes me up. She knows what's happening.

'Do you want that help now? Or are you going to run back to the booze and pills and God knows what the first chance you get?'

'I called you, didn't I? That's the first step, isn't it? Asking for help?' I push the rest of the coffee away from me. I feel like puking again.

'But you have to want to do this or there's no point.'

'Fuck, are you trying to put me off?'

'No. I'm giving you a reality check. Something I doubt you've had for a long time. There's no easy way out of this. Being rich or famous or talented, none of that's going to help. You've got to do it long hand, the same as anyone else.'

I sit there, the coffee skinning over in front of me.

'Well?' she challenges.

'I'm still here, aren't I?'

She raises her eyebrows at me.

'I'm sorry but the way I feel right now that's all I can fucking give you.'

'O.K.,' she sighs. 'There are places that do rehabilitation programmes. They can help you. I'll get you some numbers. You can check into one.'

'Like a hotel,' I joke. She scowls. 'Fine. How soon?'

'I don't know. It might take a few days to find somewhere with space. There aren't a lot of places here like there are in America.'

'Dunno if I can wait few days.'

She raises her eyebrows again.

'I'm not trying to be dramatic; I'm telling you what I feel. If I don't do this now, while you've got me here I'm probably gonna go home and call for a special delivery. Christ, I feel like I'm gonna… I meant what I said on the phone before.'

She stares at me. Her eyes are cornflower blue, not that I've seen a fucking cornflower but that's what colour I imagine they are. I want to cry. Everything throbs.

'O.K. I'm still working at that private hospital. Maybe the chief consultant there can help us.'

'Now?'

She frowns at first then nods. 'Fine. Now.'

Her blue Chevette is parked around the corner. She drives me there. Gets me a consultation with her boss. He's in his fifties. Old enough to have seen too many people in all possible states of self-annihilation to be surprised by me and my attempts at spontaneous deflagration. He asks a lot of questions: What I am using? How much am I using? How do I feel on it? How do I feel right now? In the middle of the consultation I puke coffee over his beige carpet where it pools like a shadow. He calls the cleaner who wordlessly mops it away. It'll be hard, he tells me. I fucking hope so 'cos life's been too easy for me. He agrees to admit me. I sign some papers. Get a private room. Money won't fix me but I might as well be fucking comfy on my way through hell. A nurse gives me a hospital gown. Takes my clothes. I'm trapped now. I get undressed and into bed, between crisp white sheets. It's almost lunchtime. The doctor reappears. Wires me to an IV drip. Gives me some pills; I fall asleep.

I stay in that bed a long time, leaving it only to use the en-suite bathroom, which I have to do a lot. Meg comes to see me sometimes, not when she's on duty. She's seeing if I can do this by myself. I find out from the other nurses what shifts she's working so I know when she might come. Then I count down the hours. I don't want to see anyone else. When they try I get the nurses to make excuses. Eventually they get the message and send flowers and cards with silly get well notes. I'm not sick but I am an invalid of sorts. I'm in-valid, unable to function without a load of smack or booze or pills. I'm fucking pointless. I shake and shiver, smoke too much and turn myself inside out. When I can keep my hands steady enough I roll my own; it gives me something to do, a familiar, reassuring action. But most of the fucking time I've got no control of myself. My body tortures me in revenge for my attempted purge. Toxic waste gushes out of me, both ends. I shit hot, yellow, molten eruptions, then my guts back up like a knackered toilet. A nurse appears with a length of rubber tubing. It's the worst humiliation of all. When she's done my business for me I feel like a bin that's been emptied and tossed aside. I wish I was dead, think of leaving, fantasise about a hit. But Meg shows up. She smells of freshly cut lawns. I stay.

My mind's fucked too. During the day I pull reality in as close as I can and try to stock up on it before nightfall. It's never enough. Weird things fly at me from out of the darkness; faceless, inhuman forms, monsters from trips past. I keep my eyes closed, the hospital issue blankets over my head. They're out there, waiting for me to stick my head up. It's so fucking childish and so fucking real. I'm scared into the corner. Then the monster I've been dreading the most appears.

The first time it's sleep that propels me into the nightmare memory of it. It's That Night. Philip lunges at me. There I am, floating out of it. We're fighting while the other, astral me is hovering safely off to one side. I fall over a table. Hit the shag-pile deck. Don't get up. The action jerks sideways. Ronsey comes at us, spreading his hands out, trying to save us. I shove him and he falls, lies crumpled on the carpet, among the rubble. I see myself get off the floor. First I think I'm still astral me, watching from above but as I see myself stand I realise I'm eyeball to eyeball with me. Or rather me is eyeball to eyeball with Philip. Because this time round I'm Philip, wrestling with Mickey who throws me off and staggers across the room towards Ronsey, lying there still and silent. Panic strangles Philip-me. Shit. Did I do that? There's a second when nothing happens. Mickey is frozen in his stride. Philip-me is frozen in a half-turned stance. Neither of us does anything. Then Mickey breaks the moment by taking another step. Philip-me moves too, sprinting for the door, into the hall, out the front, down the drive and into my car. His car. Not a yellow Triumph TR4. A silver soft-top Alpha Romero. I start the engine and drive as fast as I can. I'll leave Mickey to sort it. He's the king after all. Ronsey'll be O.K.

I wake up screaming. A nurse appears. An orderly follows hot. I'm thrashing around on the bed, a beast with its leg in a trap. He has to restrain me while the nurse sticks something in the IV. Sleep creeps back over me. I fight it; I'm terrified of the dream coming again. I lose.

The next time it happens I'm awake. I watch it like a fucking private viewing at the cinema. I try switching it off before Ronsey dies but can't. It comes again and again. I'm stuck watching 'til it plays out, in every possible permutation; me as me, me as Philip, me as Ronsey, Ronsey as Philip, Ronsey as me, Philip as Ronsey, Philip as me: me as all of us. The director's cut. None of us never fucking manage to stop drowning in time to save John. When Barmy Barswarmi, the head-shrinker, asks me how I'm sleeping I limit myself to, 'Fine, thanks. How 'bout you?' Sleeping's not the problem. My nightmares come when I'm awake.

One day a nurse brings me a radio. I listen to the strained and discordant notes of mindless, musicless pop tunes. They're soothingly crap. Sugar for my ears. But the D.J.'s a malevolent bastard. He catches me out. 'From their number one album, *Return of the Kings*, 'Trees of Eden' by Crown & Kingdom.' I make it through the first four bars before hurling the radio at the wall. It smashes. A jumble of plastic and metal parts scatter on the carpet tiles. I cry and cower, a kicked dog. When she comes back with lunch neither of us says anything about the broken radio. She sends in an orderly to sweep up my mess. When he's finished I open the window, it only swings out three inches, and press into the gap, listening to the world outside; the steady hum of traffic, the babbling of people in the grounds, the drone of planes overhead: the light musical birdsong, sweeter than any melodies I could come up with.

The doc pops in most day. Asks the same bloody questions: How do I feel? Am I eating? Are my bowels normal? He takes my bloody pressure, freezes a stethoscope to my chest and listens. Looks in my eyes and ears, down my throat. Scribbles on my chart. I try reading it but his handwriting's pissed-up spider tracks. He comments disapprovingly on the things I've said to Barmy Barswarmi. They're obviously in cahoots.

'Mr Hunter, we're only weaning you off the drugs in this room. If you want to stay off them when you get out you need to explore why you take them and work with the psychologist to understand what's going on in you head.'

I take them 'cos they keep my head empty. But fucked if I'll admit that.

'There's nothing going on in my head apart from a constant throbbing.'

'Dr Barswarmi says you won't co-operate.'

'That's not true.'

'He said you answered every question last time with either 'yes' or 'no'.'

'Because those were the bloody answers.'

'If you don't try this is never going to work.'

'It's a load of bollocks.'

He shakes his head. Studies my chart. 'We'll get you down to 50 milligrams by the end of the week.'

I'm glad when he's gone. I can retune in on the birdsong.

A little before 3:30, when I'm expecting the head-shrinker any minute, the door opens. I don't look round 'til I smell her.

'Meg?'

'Hi.' She smiles.

'What're you doing here?' She's wearing her uniform. I check quickly. No rubber hose. Thank God.

'I'm on at four,' she says, avoiding my stare, 'thought I'd pop in before my shift.'

That's fucking off.

'You don't usually come before work.'

'Dr Clayton says your dose is nearly down.'

'Fuck, what is it really?'

She flashes her eyes on me. 'Mickey, are we wasting our bloody time or what?'

'What d'ya mean?' I hope playing dumb might get me out of bother.

'If you're not going to do it properly you might as well leave now. Here.' She flings a buff coloured folder onto the bed. 'Discharge papers.'

I flick through them. All I need to do it sign.

'Got a pen?'

She pulls one from her top pocket and spear-throws it at me.

'Ow.' I pick up the pen. Scribble on the form.

'You're a bloody arsehole,' she says and turns to go. Stops. Turns back. 'I knew you couldn't do it. You're totally bloody pathetic.'

'Don't you want this?' I wave the form at her.

'Drop it off on your way out.' She wrenches opens the door.

I race round the bed and grab her arm.

'Get off or I'll scream.'

'Read it.'

'Piss off.'

I hold on. Shake the form at her. 'Read it.'

She snatches it. Glares at the paper. Next to the X, under the line that says, 'I, the patient, hereby declare that I formally wish to discharge myself and agree to the immediate cessation of all medical treatment at my own risk.' I've written, 'No thanks.'

'Oh, God. You bastard.' She whacks me on the arm with her fist, the form crushed between her fingers.

I nudge the door closed. Take the form. Shred it and drop the bits in the bin. When I glance up I catch Meg pressing her fingers into her eyes then wiping them on her uniform.

'All I need,' I say, 'is an incentive.'

'Being sober, that's your bloody incentive.'

'Of course, but there should be a reward. Something to aim for.' I close in on her. She watches me warily. 'Meg.'

'It's not a good idea.'

'Some of the best things that've ever happened to me started off as the worst of all possible ideas.'

I'm really close now. She's backed-up against the door. Reckon this is my one chance. I lean down. She doesn't move or pull away so I kiss her, gently. I haven't kissed someone so carefully for a long time. Maybe not ever. I'm afraid of hurting her. I keep it brief; I've pushed my luck too far already today.

I step back. She looks up with eyes darkened by sudden pleasure.

'I'm not getting involved with you until you sort yourself out properly,' she warns.

'Fine.' I retreat a bit further. 'It's nearly 3:30. You better go and leave me and Dr Barmy, I mean Barswarmi, to it.'

'So Mr Hunter, you seem pleased to see me today. It appears that you're more open to what psychology can do for you. Can you tell me what made you change your mind?' Barmy asks.

I don't want to tell him it's Meg. But I better tell him something. 'Just wanna get myself sorted, whatever it takes.' He nods understandingly. 'But I can't help thinking this psychology stuff's a load of bollocks,' I admit. 'Hell, my brain's been fried by all kinds of shit and I'm not talking about the stuff I've shoved up my nose or in my veins. There's loads of stuff buried in my head. I don't get how digging it up's gonna make things better. In fact, I'm pretty sure it'll make things worse.'

'It sounds like you're saying the reason you got into drugs was to help keep things buried. Have I understood that right? Is that why you think you do drugs?'

He's asked me this before. Why do I do drugs? ''Cos I want to,' has been my stock reply. That's been the only reason for anything for a bloody long time. I remember the taste of strawberries in my mouth after kissing Meg.

'Yeah, maybe. Partly.'

'Partly?'

'It goes with the job. Like an occupational hazard, man.'

'You say 'hazard'. It makes it sound like you're thinking of the risks involved in taking drugs. I suppose that's something a lot of people think about given the number of high profile deaths, Jimi Hendrix, for example.'

'You don't think that when you're high. You don't think anything. You just feel it and it's bloody fantastic. I mean awesome, sublime. Shit, there's not a fucking word big enough for it. And that's why you do it. Why I did it,' I explain.

'Hmm.' He scribbles something on his notepad.

Upside down I read, 'pleasure principle'. But that's wrong, it's not just a nice taste, a brief buzz. It's some kind of spiritual bliss, utter contentment, the memory of it lingering, urging you to chase down an eternity of it. That's why no one ever does heroin only once.

'You'd understand it if you'd tried it,' I say. 'Maybe you should, ya know, so you can get on the same wave length as your patients. I could fix you up.'

Barmy puts his clipboard down. Regards me over the top of his bi-focals. The light glints off the dark brown dome of his bald head. I wonder what's hidden in there.

'Unless you have tried it before?'

'You feel, perhaps, concerned that I won't be able to understand your experiences because I haven't shared in them, that only someone who has taken drugs can help you. Is that what you're trying to tell me? I wonder because, you see, Mr Hunter, sometimes when people ask a psychologist about themselves it's because they feel the psychologist doesn't appreciate what it's been like for them. But other times it's because they are uncomfortable talking about their own difficulties and I get the sense that you're asking me personal questions to make me feel awkward because you don't want to talk about yourself,' he says.

'Yes, I do. It was a joke. Look, I am trying here. Honestly. I wanna sort myself out. I'm not gonna lie and say I'm convinced this is the way to do it but everyone else reckons it's a good idea so I'll give it a go.'

He raises his eyebrows. I've fucked with him so many times in these sessions there's no way he's going to bend over again.

'How 'bout I tell you something that I've never really told to anyone. I mean, people know about this, know it happened, but I've never talked about how it made me feel,' I say.

His ears prick up like a dog's at the shout of walkies.

'It's about my mother. You know she was murdered, don't you?'

He asks about my childhood, how I do I think it's effected me not knowing my father? The kind of relationship I had with my mother, how I felt about it then, how I feel about it now. What role do I think her death has played in my experiences, in my turning to drugs and booze to keep afloat (my words, not his)? I tell him I hated her, thought she was a sad old whore who deserved what she got. And why should I give a shit about some random bloke I never knew? What's he to me? Fuck all. I fall back on my stock response: drugs make me feel great and who doesn't want that? It's got fuck all to do with her. She was a pain in my arse. I was glad to get shot of her. Barmy tentatively suggests I have feelings of anger towards my mother, that maybe I'd like to talk about those. I say I wouldn't, thanks very fucking much. Then time's up and he leaves me with the parting shot that he thinks I've made some real progress today.

It's not progress. It's regress.

I shrink down to twelve year old me. I sit on my narrow, saggy bed, glaring at my newly acquire second hand acoustic guitar, wishing I knew what to do next. She comes in. Her hair's up. She's in her navy dress. She looks like a normal mum today. She holds out a brown paper package. It's a used copy of Bert Weedon's *Play in a Day*. She smiles at me. Ruffles my hair. Tells me I'm a good boy. That she loves me. I don't say it back. I pray for her to go. She does. I'm glad.

I'm sixteen. I've got the chance to go on the road with a proper band. I'm packed and in the hall, waiting for my lift. She comes home, catching me in the act of going, abandoning her. We row. She thinks I'm wasting my life, I should get a decent job. I tell her least this is better than hers, opening her legs for every Charlie. I chuck my key at her. Call her a slag. Leave.

I'm taller, older. Not wiser or kinder. I drive out to rescue her late one night. A smarmy sergeant tells me what she's been up to. I try not listening but hear it anyway. She's brought out. She's a mess. I can't bear to touch her, see her. She sits in my car. One of her stockings is missing. Her nails are tattered and torn. She tries to hold my hand. I pull away. She says she's sorry. I don't forgive her.

I'm not even there. She lets a stranger into the house. Into the bedroom. Into her bed. He thanks her by wringing her neck. I'm not even there.

I break everything breakable in the room; the shaving mirror in the bathroom, the print of Van Gogh's 'Sunflowers', the plate and mug left over from lunch, the vase of dried flowers on the windowsill. I rip the curtains down, tear the sheets off the bed, flick the mattress over, pull the drawers from the bureau and throw them around the room. I make as much fucking noise as I can. A nurse comes. Two nurses. They try to reason with me. One goes for an orderly. Meg arrives. I punch the window. A cobweb of cracks spiral out from my fist. The orderly races in. He wrestles me to the floor. I put up enough of a fight to make it look convincing. Dr Clayton arrives. He looms towards me, armed with a sympathetic needle. The room goes bright and blurry for a few euphoric seconds. A soft peace settles on me.

When I wake up I'm in a different room. The bed's on the wrong wall. The view's reversed. There's no vase on the windowsill, a tide-mark of dirt surrounds a square of cleaner paintwork where I'll bet a print of Van Gogh's 'Sunflowers' used to hang. If I go in the bathroom there won't be a mirror. Doesn't fucking matter. It was worth it, to make it go away again. Make her go away again. My mother. My problem. My guilty secret. One of. My hand feels heavy. There's a thick bandage wrapped from finger tip to elbow. Cautiously, I flex my fingers inside it.

'You're lucky you didn't break it.' Meg's in the doorway in her civvies.

'Reckon I'll be able to play again?'

'You'll have to ask the doctor. Does it hurt much?'

'Yeah.'

'Good.'

'Any chance of some morphine?'

'None.'

'Fair enough. You coming in?'

She puts a hand on the door handle ready to pull it closed on her way out.

'Any reason I should?'

'I wanna tell you something.'

She inches into the room.

'Close the door.' She does. 'What time is it?'

'Ten. It's Friday, by the way.'

My yesterday was Wednesday.

'I'm sorry.'

'Why the hell did you do it?'

I swing my legs off the bed. Stand unsteadily. 'For you.'

'What does that mean?' Her face creases.

I take three baby-steps over to her. Reach out with my good hand for hers. She steps back sharply.

I retreat. 'O.K. O.K. Don't go, please. Look, there's a lot of stuff you don't know. Stuff from years ago. Stuff I think it's better you don't know. Hell, stuff I wish I didn't know. I thought I was handling it. Now I know I'm not. I bit off too much and choked on it. Sorry I lost it like that.'

'Does this mean you're really trying now, with the therapy, I mean?'

'Yeah.'

She shakes her head. 'You're running out of chances, Mickey.'

'One more, please. I won't fuck up again.'

'Alright.' She offers her hand. I take it gratefully. Squeeze lightly.

'I'm gonna do whatever I have to, to make this work,' I promise.

She looks through me, scouring my innards, searching for the lie written in capital letters. It's O.K. though 'cos this time I'm telling the truth. I will do whatever needs doing to get across this and out the other side.

Turns out that what needs doing's me re-imagining myself. Bloody Barmy and his therapy, it's not a can of worms he wants me to open; it's a can of vipers. And I'm not poisoning myself. So I get creative. Memory and imagination, they're both just thoughts, mind pictures. He won't fucking know. Thinking he can fix me just 'cos of his fancy-lettered qualifications. I took the risk, fell off the wall. I'll put me back together.

At night I lie awake, concocting tomorrow's story. I rewrite the mythology of Mickey Hunter, legendary rock guitarist, keeping in the shadow of reality, making it sound authentic. Sometimes we sail perilously close to the rocky truth but I manage to steer round it and dock safely after each session. At first I'm worried he'll catch me out. But I'm smarter than he is, keep beating him. It's a good game. I don't feel victorious.

'Well, Mickey.' I couldn't let him keep calling me Mr Hunter; it was aging me by the syllable. 'It feels like it's got easier to talk about your issues and to think about what the earlier experiences meant for your life.'

'I agree.'

He smiles. 'I know it was difficult at first. People often find it a challenge to talk about their difficulties but it seems talking has been useful for you.'

'Yeah, it has.' Talking, lying: whatever, man.

'You've worked hard and I've noticed a positive change in you. What do you think? How would you feel about being discharged?'

I resist the urge to jump up, punch the air and whoop.

'Reckon I'm ready.'

'Good, because I think you are. Of course, it doesn't stop here. You'll have to keep working on this for the rest of your life. As I've said before, there's no cure. You'll always be an addict, but not a practicing one.'

This, he thinks, is pricelessly funny. I humour him with a smile.

'I spoke to Dr Clayton this morning. He tells me you've been off medication for over a fortnight, and that you're otherwise a fit and health young man.'

I'm not so sure about the young bit. Feels like I've lived three lifetimes already.

'I'd like to see you as an outpatient, once a month, at my practice office. How would you feel about that?'

Damn. Thought I was free. I shrug. 'How long's that gonna go on for?'

'I don't think it's necessarily helpful to set a period of time but the usual is six months. It depends on the needs of the individual. After that I might see you once in three months and then six. It's a process of gradually withdrawing support as best fits your needs,' he explains. 'Here's my number. You can contact my secretary to book the first appointment.'

I guess my doubt's writ large because he adds, 'It's important to keep up the good work you've done.'

I take his card and nod. I can chuck it away later.

He holds out his hand to me. I take it. His grip's firm.

'With your permission I'd like to write up your case for a medical journal. It would be anonymous, of course, but I think it would be an interesting example to have in print for therapists who are struggling with patients who, well, who think it's 'a load of bollocks'.' He takes off his glasses, regards me keenly with eyes large enough to see me properly.

Fuck, he always knew it was a game but he wasn't playing it. He was the ref.

'Er, yeah, whatever,' I mumble.

'Excellent. Don't forget that appointment,' he says as I stand.

'Don't worry, I won't,' I lie.

We're all just chasing our own dragons, wanting our own unending bliss-out.

Meg comes to see me that afternoon.

'How do you feel?'

'Fine.' I'm surprised to realise I mean it. Despite Barmy's attempts to exhume the terrors in my brain and my body's efforts at sabotage I actually am A-1.

'You're going home?'

'I guess.' Home? I shudder. That's a fucking joke. I should have torched the whole damn place.

'You could stay with me, if you like,' she offers, adding, 'on the couch, just temporarily.'

'Don't you trust me to be let loose on my own?'

'You know this is the hardest bit? It's easy in here where there are no temptations. Out there you have to be strong enough to make it without the safety net of the medical staff beneath you.'

I smile at her.

She catches my grin. 'What?'

'I'm thinking of making a highly inappropriate joke about having a member of the medical staff beneath me,' I say and before she has time to bollock me I grab her wrist, pull her towards me and kiss her. It is the warm, soft sensation of chocolate mousse melting on your tongue. It's gone too quickly.

'Mickey, I meant it. On the couch.'

'Sure.'

'I'm not going to let you wreck this now. You've got to promise me you'll keep clean.'

'I'll be on my best behaviour, scout's honour.'

'You were a boy scout?'

I shrug. 'I promise I'll be good.'
'I hope you intend keeping that promise,' Meg says.
I kiss her again. 'Yeah, I fucking do.'

THE SUN

We got married in June, on the brightest day of a very white summer. I wanted to do it the way Meg wanted so we ended up in a quaint church, in the town where she grew up. I was a long way from home and loving every clean, real moment. She walked down the aisle to me in an ivory satin dress. The lines of it gave her the flowing shape of slowly poured water. She held a small bouquet of pink and yellow roses. I stood beneath the cross and felt at home in a world where I'd always thought I'd only ever be a trespasser. We said our vows under the gentle guidance of the vicar. When we'd finished he leaned over, whispered:

'Congratulations, Mr and Mrs Hunter. Erm, would you mind... Could I possibly get your autograph? I'm a big fan.'

I had to sign his Bible. If nothing else, I'm fucking sure I'm going to Hell for that. Afterwards we walked back down the aisle holding hands, a new, pure unity born out of the violent destruction of an older, more malevolent one. I thought the past was finally buried forever.

'Mickey?' Keira's head and shoulders are sticking through the dressing room doorway. 'It's time for the presentation.'

'O.K.' I drop the bottle of Botox into the open drawer. 'I was looking for cigarettes,' I explain.

'I'll find you some. Come on. They're about to announce your award.'

The party's swinging. Whispering Bob and Johnny Walker sip

champagne by the buffet table. Bowie swans around, arm-linked with a leggy blonde. The starlet whose dressing room I was hiding in is flirting with Chris Evans. Keira buzzes around with her Blackberry, speaking to people, tapping in numbers and dates. I go to stop her but she flits off. Oh well, suppose I can worm out of things later. Danny Baker and Mark Radcliff are tête-à-têteing with Roger Daltry. A skeletal Keith Richards is slumped in a chair. These are the post-ceremony celebrations. Post-post celebrations because everything's over now. Again. The total of my life's achievement is a gold-plated piece of tat mounted on plastic. Some fucking legacy. People creep up to me. They say things like, 'brilliant,' 'stunning,' 'awesome.' A young lad approaches, face raw pastry white, coal black hair hanging in matted waves over puffy cheeks and bruise-shadowed eyes. He's dressed in red and white, candy-cane colours. Speaks in a soft American accent. Says his name's Jack. I brace for more sycophantic praise. He loved the raw attitude, he says, and walks off. I'll have to ask Keira about him later.

James sidles over. I've been avoiding him. He's where he should be but he's not who I want him to be. That's my fault though. And Philip's.

'Think I did O.K.'

'You did great, mate.'

'Really?'

'Drummed like a god.'

'So what next?'

'You can start by giving me a cigarette. Keira said she was gonna get some but looks like she's busy.'

James follows my gaze across the room. Keira's talking to some bloke, neat hair and sharp suit, a big important nobody.

'Looks like she's taking care of business,' he says, passing me his pack, 'Who's that she's talking to?'

I take a cigarette. 'Some exec.' I shrug it off but James keeps watching her as she lightly moves her hair off her face then, in a flowing gesture, rests her hand on the man's arm for a second.

'She's a real...' James stops himself. 'So was the old magic there, Uncle Mickey?'

'Even better: it was new magic.'

'Glad you enjoyed it,' he says, draining his glass, 'I'm off to get another. You want anything?'

I inspect my own glass, still half full of clear brown liquid. 'I'm fine.'

James shrugs. Heads in Keira's direction.

'James.'

He glances back.

'You're right. She's a real... Be careful, won't you?' I'm a hypocrite, doling out warnings like that, but I have to say something. Shit, don't wanna to lose a bloody good PA.

'Sure,' he says as he merges into the party's white noise.

I feel a light touch on my shoulder. Meg's arrived. I hold the cigarette behind my back as she plants a kiss on my cheek.

Laughing, she says, 'Don't bother, I could smell it as soon as I came in.'

'Sorry.'

'No lectures tonight,' she promises.

I hug her tightly. Over her shoulder I see Philip on the other side of the room. James has skirted around Keira and emerged next to him. Philip reaches out a hand, stretching up, not down, this time, and ruffles James's hair. James laughs. They could be a proud father and trusting son. It's like That Night never happened. The sight, the thought, the fucking awful, in-my-face reality of it revolts and repulses me. This is my fault. But it's Philip's fault too. So how come he can stand there laughing, brimful of pleasure and pride while I feel like I'm gonna puke at the memory of That Night and James being here instead of his old man? It's wrong. I was wrong. Should've told the truth 'bout what happened That Night: to Meg, I owe her everything I've got now; to James, he should know what a fucking bastard I am. Christ, maybe even to that head-shrinker Barmy-whatsit, he might've have some 'coping strategies' or some bloody thing. But mainly I should've told it to Philip. But I haven't 'cos I'm a fucking coward.

I hold Meg at arm's length. 'I am sorry.'

'As you said before, you're old enough to make your own mistakes.'

I crush the cigarette with underfoot. 'That's not what I'm apologising for.'

'What then?'

'Meg, we gotta go.'

'Why?'

'I need to tell you something.'

'Just tell me here,' she says, frowning.

'I can't. I'm sorry. Am probably gonna to be a hell of a lot sorrier after I tell you but not as sorry as I'll bloody be if I don't tell you.' I rush out the words, take her arm and start tugging her towards the door.

'Mickey, you can't leave like this. It's your party.'

'If it's my party I can leave when I want to and, yeah, I may even cry later,' I add, dishing up half-cooked humour.

We slip out throw a side door, unchallenged. I scan the car park for Meg's BMW.

'Where did you park the damn Beemer?'

'I came in a taxi. Mickey, what is it?'

'Taxi?' I think about the horde of hungry fans prowling out front. 'We'll go round the back. We can get a cab on the main road,' I say, still pulling Meg's arm.

She protests but follows. The bemused watchman guarding the delivery entrance lets us out after I offer him a bullshit story about Meg being my girlfriend and we're trying to avoid my wife who's inconveniently showed up. I don't know who's more startled by how easily such a plausible lie comes to me, me or Meg. But on reflection I've been a practiced liar all my life so why the fuck I've surprised myself I don't bloody know.

We can't find a taxi so walk, take a tube, another tube 'cos they're doing more bloody maintenance, then a bus and finish up walking again. It's further than I thought. Meg limps on her heels and that's a good excuse for me to slow down, avoiding any suspicious puffing and panting. It's a cold night. I give her my jacket. Tell her everything on the way.

We stand for a few seconds in our mosaic-tiled Victorian hallway.

'Are you all right?' I ask.

The silence stretches out.

'My feet hurt. I'm going to bathe them.' She turns away.

Definitely time for a drink: large Scotch, cheers. I sit with the glass in my lap, waiting for her to come down. When she does she's wearing a pair of squashed, faux fur-lined booties beneath the fleecy dressing gown with a faux-fur trimmed hood. She looks like an Artic explorer ready to head out for the night. She flops in the armchair opposite and surveys the coffee table.

'Only one drink?'

I pour another Scotch. She swallows a mouthful and grimaces.

'But I thought it just you and John that night? You were both drinking, drunk, I suppose, and, no doubt, high on God knows what.' The words 'drunk' and 'high' are black-underlined with blame. 'He fell over in his stupor. You found him later, when it was too late. It was an accident. Philip wasn't even there. At the inquest they said…'

I shake my head. 'Philip was there. It happened like I said.'

'But you said he knocked you out, you were unconscious. How can you have seen him push John?'

'I told you, it was some weird of out-of-body thing. I saw it. Sorta, I dunno, a near death experience. You must've had patients who've told you stories like that.'

'Yes, but I never believed…'

'Well you should,' I interrupt. 'It was a real to me as this is right now.'

She holds my fierce gaze for several seconds, X-raying me for a fracture in my truth. When she doesn't find one she glances away, picking at a loose thread on her dressing gown.

'O.K., fine,' she says, 'but—' she looks up again— 'why didn't you say anything at the time?'

'You know what a mess I was afterwards. I couldn't 'cos I didn't even wanna think about it never mind tell anyone. Plus, it was my fault too. I provoked Philip into that fight, got him wound so tight with anger he was crazed, ended up shoving Ronsey and…' I stop. It's gotta be the whole truth. I know it but I'm terrified of it.

'Mickey? Are you O.K.?' Meg stares at me.

What the hell is she seeing? It can't be the Mickey Hunter she thought she'd married. That twat never really existed. He was my alter-ego, a phantom persona. The real me is the one who should've saved Ronsey. My eyes fill up. When I drop my head the tears seem to shimmer about my feet like a rising sea. I fucking have to tell her.

I blink. Hot droplets run down my cheeks.

Meg kneels in front of me. Rests a hand on my leg. 'Tell me.'

'I'm trying to.' In more than thirty years I've never wanted a hit as badly as I do right now. The memory of that warm, comforting wave of blissful contentment beckons me. But this has to be done without any anaesthetic. I drag a long breath deep inside me. 'I didn't save John.'

'It was an accident. You and Philip got into a fight and, tragically, John got caught up in it. Philip didn't mean to push him, hurt him. He probably didn't even realise John was injured. And you couldn't have done anything if you were knocked out cold.' Meg rubs my leg, like there's a graze on my knee she's trying to sooth.

I shake my head. 'Don't kneel. Sit up here.' I pull her onto the sofa next to me. 'You saved my life, you know.'

She laughs. 'That's a bit…'

'It's not 'a bit' anything. You saved my fucking life. If you hadn't helped me, that day when I called, I would've, yeah, that would've been it. You saved me, Christ knows why, 'cos I sure as hell didn't deserve it.'

'Everyone deserves a second chance.'

'Ronse didn't get one, did he? It should've been me, not him.'

'Mickey, listen: you couldn't have saved him.'

'Yeah, I could.'

'What?' Meg pulls her hands away from mine. If I look behind me right now there'll be a big black vortex waiting to suck me in.

'I came round before… John was still alive, I'm sure of it. He looked at me but I couldn't do anything. I was…' My heart pounds too fast. I drag another ragged breath towards me. 'While they were there, I dropped some acid. I didn't know that's what it was 'til it was too late. When I came round I saw Ronsey, knew he needed help. Then I started tripping and that was it. I couldn't get to him. Couldn't do fucking anything. I must've blacked out again and the second time it really was too late. If I hadn't been so outta it I could've saved him but I was too busy getting high to think about anything else. Anyone else. And Philip. He must have known too, that Ronsey needed medical help. And known there was no way I was in a state to provide it. But he fucked off. Abandoned us. We're both to blame. That's why I never said anything. I could've saved John. But I didn't. I couldn't deal with that. Still can't.' I brace myself for her yells, a slap in the face, the banging of the living room door as she flees from me in horror. Feel only a soft fump as she leans against the cushions like she's winded.

'Yes,' she says finally, 'you are both to blame. As much as the drunk who gets in his car. You didn't mean to do it but it happened because of what you did.' Her words are steady. 'You've had to live with that. I'm not going to tell you it's all right. It's not. But Mickey, don't forget, hindsight's twenty-twenty every time. You can't change what happened.'

'I know.'

'So why are you telling me now?' Her eyes meet mine and hold them without hesitation.

'I need you to know what really happened. I can't keep it buried any more. It's wrong. It's not fair to you, for a start. You deserve to know what a bastard I am. I have to take the consequences, whatever they are.'

'You think I'm going to leave you?'

'You bloody well should.'

'You can't get rid of me that easily. God, Mickey, don't think I didn't know what I was getting into with you. I was never naive enough to think life with you would be easy. It hasn't been, in case you were wondering.' She flashes me a wry grin. 'But loving you has.'

'I don't see how.'

'No,' Meg muses, 'love's too complicated for anyone to understand, even the legendary Mickey Hunter.' She takes my hand. 'Mickey, love is unconditional. But that's not to say there aren't times when I'd like to slap you in the face for being a bloody berk.'

'Is now one of those times? I'd like to know so I have time to duck.'

'No. Yes. Maybe. I don't know. My God.' She pulls her hand away again. 'But what's the point now? Does Philip even know you saw him?'

'No. I'm gonna tell him. Make him face it. We both need to face it and, I dunno, try and put it right. No, I don't mean that.

Try to make up for it. While we can.'

Meg sips her whisky.

'I'm not after a prosecution or anything. I just wanna stop hiding from my past, and try to make amends for it.'

'How are you going to do that?'

'I want a proper reunion for Crown & Kingdom, with James on drums. It'll get his career going. Be a pay back, best I can do for him now.'

'And Philip's agreed to this, has he?'

'Not yet.'

'I see. So either he does the reunion or you'll tell James the truth?'

'Something like that. Anyway, isn't one of the first steps in righting a wrong admitting that you did wrong in the first place?'

'You think James needs this dropping on him?'

'What else can I do? I have to do this, Meg. I have to get Philip to do this.'

'So it's a bluff? One you're hoping Philip doesn't call you on?'

'No, it's not a bluff. I'll admit what I did. And Philip'll have to, as well.'

'Do you want to hurt James all over again? I'm not going to tell you what to do, Mickey, Christ knows that's a waste of time, plus I understand you wanting to deal with this in your own way, but think about the consequences. You've got the opportunity to do that this time. Don't add another regret to the list.'

We're lounging in Pete's palatial garden. I remember his pre fame-&-fortune garden, dry, bare, withered, me sitting in it one afternoon several lifetimes ago, with the thick, yellowed pages of an old, brown hardback upturned to the sky. This garden's nothing like that one. Red brick walls and vivid green ivy shelter us. The lawn's neatly striped and runs away to the trees and bushes that cluster in the boarders, wild colour bursts. There are pinks, yellows, whites and purples. The sky's dreamtime blue, the sun strong enough to thaw the bone-snapping frost in my chest. It's a day from an idyllic childhood I never had with jugs of homemade lemonade I never drank, sherbet dips I never ate and a kite I didn't fly with the father who wasn't there.

Everyone's here 'cept Meg. Susie swishes between us in her floral print dress, a butterfly amongst the flowers, serving crustless triangular sandwiches; salmon mousse and cucumber, honey roast ham and crisp iceberg, creamy Emmenthal and sweet onion relish. Pete tops up our long, cool glasses of Pimm's from a fruit-floating jug. James sits beside Keira. She wasn't sure about coming. It's social gathering, not a business meeting. But I didn't want to come alone. Plus, James wanted me to bring her. I hope he's not going to fuck with her. He's leaning in a bit closer than he needs to. She looks O.K. about it, though. She looks really good, actually, in her faded 501s and a pink and white chequered shirt. It's all very chilled.

Philip's on their other side with his latest conquest: Nancy from Bolivia. Her skin's the colour of caramel and her hair's dark and wavy. Not his usual big-tits-and-cow-eyes selection. I can't take it in because, I realise, I'm stuck on picturing him in bed with Anna. I keep forgetting she was never more than another shag to him and he's way beyond that now. Yeah, we're all more grown up these days. Maybe he'll settle down with this one, have kids. She's young enough. She keeps close to Philip, holding his hand, large sunglasses hiding darkly exotic eyes. When she speaks there are musical intonations in every word. Like how Anna spoke. I wonder if Philip hears it too.

So we're all gathered. 'Cept Meg. She's leaving me to it, like when I was in rehab. Fair enough. It's my mess. I have to clean it up.

We sip our fizzy drinks, nibble mouse-like at the sandwiches, talk about the award ceremony, the performance, the party and the publicity that's the fallout after the main blast. The interviews we gave are in print now and we amuse ourselves with the cuttings, laughing at how the journalists have twisted what we said. Even James, who's pretty new to this, takes it easily.

'Fucking hell, have you seen this picture of me?' he laughs, 'I look like I've been lined up for the firing squad.'

He holds the paper to Keira who laughs too.

I lean over.

'You've definitely got that I've-never-done-this-before-and-I'm-shitting-my-pants look going on. Once you get used to cameras pointing in your face you'll start posing. You might even manage to look like you're enjoying it.'

'This from the man behind this picture,' scoffs Keira, picking up another magazine and waving a glossy full page print of me looking only marginally less terrified than James.

'I'm out of practise,' I mutter.

'Me too,' Pete confesses, 'but I wonder if it's worth while getting back into shape.'

I catch Philip shaking his head. The silence is filled by the soft buzzing of bees going about their micro-cosmic world that knows nothing of the complications and catastrophes of human existence. One settles on Keira's arm.

'Oh,' she says.

'Just sit still. It'll fly off in a minute,' Philip advises.

The bee snuggles down on her warm skin.

'It's taken a shine to you,' James teases.

Keira wriggles uncomfortably. Her breathing speeds up. She bites her lip, her face rigid with fear.

'It's only a bee. Christ sake,' Philip mutters as all attention focuses on the black and yellow fuzz-ball on Keira's arm.

'I'm allergic,' she murmurs.

'Here.' James kneels at her feet. Philip reaches for his drink, bored with the drama. No one else moves. James rests his hand, palm down, on Keira's arm and nudges his fingertips against the bee. With James's encouragement it crawls cautiously onto his hand. He stands, blows softly and the bee takes flight. I follow its path, see it land on a red bloom, ignorant of its starring role in a mini-saga.

Keira laughs but I know her well enough to tell it's backing onto hysteria.

'Are you O.K?' James asks. He kneels again. Lays a hand on her knee.

'My hero,' she jokes.

'Is it serious, your allergy?' Susie asks.

'Oh, you know, the usual gasping for breath, turning blue and dying,' Keira flips the words but they send round a further ripple of horror.

'Why didn't you tell me, Mickey?' Susie scolds. 'We could've sat in the conservatory.'

'I didn't know,' I reply defensively.

'Well, I think we should move inside now,' Susie says.

'It's not necessary,' Keira insists, 'I'm fine. That's never happened before, having a bee land on me like that.'

'It could probably tell how sweet you are,' James says.

'I really think we should go inside,' Susie repeats, 'I don't want your death on my conscience.' She begins loading a tray with our plates and glasses.

Keira gets up. James too.

'Are you really O.K.?' I ask Keira. 'You should have told me.'

'Why?' She stares at me with her very green eyes. It's not defiance. It's a rare kind of weird fearlessness that doesn't see the point in giving a shit about possiblies and maybes. Anna had it too.

'What if one flew into the office. Stung you and that's it, game over?'

She just shrugs.

'Well, nice save, James.' I stand and pat him on the shoulder unnecessarily exuberantly.

He grins it off. 'No big deal.'

'I disagree. Man, good assistants are too fucking hard to find these days.'

'And excellent ones just about impossible,' Keira adds, her smile restored.

They follow Susie up the garden, James taking Keira's arm as they walk. Pete lifts the second tray and heads off too. Philip doesn't move.

'Aren't you going up to the house?' I ask.

'Too nice out here.' He stretches his legs, a cat unfurling in its own private sunbeam.

I sit again. He looks at me. Here's my fucking chance. For a second we size each other up. My heart races. That fucking Night is projected, a hologram, revolving in the summer day, translucent and shadowy. I shudder at the memory of Ronsey's blood soaking me but keep my eyes locked on Philip's.

He breaks away first, patting Nancy's arm. She turns huge sunglassed eyes on him.

'Pass me my hat, darlin',' he says.

She reaches into the large canvas bag at her feet, magics out a white Stetson-style thing. Philip dons it. Mumbles to her, something I don't hear 'cos there's suddenly a loud, shrill tone ringing in my ears. I back away 'til I'm standing on a deserted street. It's hot and dusty. Tumble weeds blow by. We're alone, me and Philip. Time for the show down. Shoot first. Shoot last. Leave neither of us standing. I reach for the gun that I know'll be there.

Nah, it's a trick of my fucked up mind, the ghost of an old trip jumping out of the cupboard in my head. I struggle back to reality, tune out the ringing, retune the hush of the wind through cherry trees. Nancy heads for the house.

'Aren't you?'

It takes me a few seconds to realise Philip's returning my question of only a minute ago.

'I'll keep you company.'

'Bullshit.'

'What?'

'You heard. What're you doing, Mickey?'

Is he reaching, unseen, for the same gun as me?

'Dunno 'bout you but I'm having a pleasant drink with some old mates. Cheers.' I raise my glass.

Philip studies me from under the brim of his hat. He too reaches for his glass.

'Fine, Mickey, whatever.' He slumps lower in his seat.

I need to see this through. But carefully.

'Just like old times, isn't it?' I say. 'All of us here, talking about the gig, flicking through the press cuttings. The heydays.'

He laughs harshly.

'Well, 'cept it's James, not John,' I add.

'I was thinking more of the fact that you're not stoned out of your tree this time,' Philip smirks.

'He's a bloody good stand-in, though. I lost count of the number of times it threw me when we were on stage, I looked up and realised it was James not John. Bet Ronsey's dead chuffed, wherever he is. Course, he should be here, with us. Don't you miss him, Philip?'

'Course I bloody do but…'

'What, Philip? Was it so long ago that you don't give a shit about it anymore?'

'Hey, Ronse was my best friend. I don't know where the fuck you get off talking to me like this.' Philip sits up. Tilts his hat off his eyes. They are two ice-sharpened flints.

'So why'd you do it?'

'Do what?'

'Fuck off and leave him to bleed to death on my shag pile.'

A thick cloud eclipses the sun.

'You're crazy.' Philip lengthens the 'eee' sound until it's a word on its own.

I nod slowly. 'Sure, I'm crazy. But not wrong. We both know what happened That Night.'

There's a dark silence. The cloud drifts, leaving us drenched in searing light.

'And you're totally innocent? Always smacked out of your brain, lording it over us, king of the fucking castle, with your 'fuck you' attitude. You didn't give a fuck either. You wanted what you wanted and to hell with the rest of us when we'd kept it together all that time.'

'I'm not pretending to be whiter than rice in this, you bloody shit. Don't think I don't know I'm as much to blame as you.'

'Anyway, what fucking difference you think this is gonna make now? There's no proof I was even there,' Philip says.

'What the hell do I need proof for? You think I want you arrested for something that happened over thirty years ago?'

'Then what, Mickey?'

'The point is, I know. I've always known, Philip, but I've kept my mouth shut all these years.'

'For Christ sake, stop fucking around.'

'I think, if Pete's agreeable, which I'm sure he will be, we should reform properly, with James on drums, of course. We should take whatever we're offered. Do a tour. Start with the UK. Maybe onto Europe and the States.'

'What the fuck for?'

'For James. He's a bloody good drummer but he could use a boost, get himself out of the shadow of the past. And for...'

'You expect me to do that?' Philip cuts in.

'... Ronsey. Legacy. That's what's at stake now. So, yeah, that's what I expect.'

'And if I say no?'

'I tell James the truth about good old Uncle Phil.'

'Like fuck you will. You've got too much to lose yourself if you do that.'

'Nope. I don't.'

'You're full of bullshit, Mickey. You care too much about your precious image to go through with it.'

'Mebbe, but when I'm dead I won't give a shit anymore.'

'You gonna top yourself?'

'Apparently, I already have. Life fast; die old from a fucked heart.'

He raises his eyebrows.

'You wanna see my doctor's letter? Chronic heart failure. I'm going out soon enough so…' I spread my hands. 'Nothing to lose, Phil. Best I can hope for now is to die on a fucking slow news day and get a decent obituary from 6Music.'

'You'd really tell James?'

'Worried I might go through with it? 'Cos you should be, you arrogant son of a bitch.'

His eyes flick over my face. Then around the garden. And back behind him. Into the past.

'Yeah, it'll fucking hurt but James is his father's son. He'll handle it. Can you? I'm not shitting you here, Philip, I will do this.'

'You said one show, for old times and memories.'

'And that's why you agreed to it? C'mon, how fucking stupid d'ya think I am?'

'Since you know everything suddenly, why don't you tell me why I agreed to it,' he snaps.

''Cos you know that without Crown & Kingdom you're nothing.'

He sits forward, leaning towards me. 'Bollocks.'

'Hey, don't worry about it, man, neither am I.'

He shakes his head in protest.

'Philip, give it fucking up, will ya? It's the truth. That's why you were happy to get up there with us and accept the award: the glory. That and you thought it'd keep me quiet for another thirty years.' I stand. 'So? You gonna do it?'

'Jesus, it must be pretty fucking lonely, up there on your throne, only your mighty morals keeping you company. Don't pretend, you're any different to me, Mickey. You're only doing it for yourself.'

'Of bloody course I'm doing it for myself, Philip. Christ sake, I'm fucking dying and I'm gonna go out with a blast. But that's not the only reason. If I wasn't sick I'd still be doing it.' I think of Meg's caution and draw up short. Once, long ago, Philip was my friend: my brother. 'There's something else you should know, another reason why I have to do this.' I sit back down. Philip watches me warily. 'When you left us Ronsey was alive. I saw him looking at me, waiting for me to help him. But I started tripping. Was too fucking wasted to save him, just like his dad said at the inquest. We both left him to die, Philip. That's why we both have to make this right.'

Grief warps his face.

'Let's not make this about what'll happen if you don't do it. Let's make it about what'll happen if you do. James is the legacy of all that we were. This is about him. And for Ronsey.'

Philip pulls his hat down over his eyes. Presses his fingers into the sockets. You have to destroy before you can rebuild. This is my last chance. I've got to get it right.

The Aeon

Right now the world's missing something we can provide. I can't fucking fathom it, try calculating out the problem that we're the answer to, assigning different values to the unknowns of X and Y. I get closest to the solution by multiplying the two factors.

X is the past: a point on the map of history. People remember what they want: Woodstock, not Altamont; peace and love, not Vietnam; Kennedy and King but not their assassinations; full employment, not union strikes; drugs that opened minds, not coffins. They live in a memory land where the young cursed their elders (no longer their betters). That's the flag we're bearing back to them and right at the point when they're waking from the dream to a nightmare reality. One they brought on themselves. One we brought on ourselves. Fucking bollocks. Serves us right.

Y is for the now generation to whom X is just that: a cross on a map marking a place they've never been to, can't even find, so they haven't wised up to the fact that we're from somewhen that's already been. They think we're from somewhere that's never been. Sick to fuck of hiphop-popidol-primo-emo-postgrunge-postmodern-poststructural-postpost they're onboard for the ride. Judgment Day's coming so fuck everything; it's rock, paper, scissors, hope for the best and get blind drunk if it goes to shit. Luckily for us Y balances X making the equation is what it should be: equal.

We've got the old following, disciples of the past, returned, relieved, to the sanctuary of their church, and new converts tagging along, not to worship, but to gape at the holy relics.

There's also a shit load of baffled journalists who can't work out how we're doing it and are pissed off that we can when they said we couldn't. Then and now.

It's better once I've done the maths for myself. It's no good having some other prick telling you two and two's four. Or one and one and one and one is.

What I'd really like from this last blast is a rerun of the properly old days: touring in rusty vans and staying in cheap, dirty motels; trashing rooms and groping drunken groupies; playing 'til midnight and partying 'til dawn. Might as well go out in a blinding flash of euphoria.

But three-quarters of us are too old to endure five hours on a rickety bus with hangovers. We fly or get chauffeurs and limos. The hotels are overpriced but the sheets are clean. I sleep alone, calling Meg from every city to say goodnight and remind myself that, anyway, it was always about the music. We play hard, flaking rust from our fingers, oiling seized joints, retuning wax-clogged eardrums. We play in cosy clubs where a few hundred punters cluster round the stage, close enough for me to see the sweat on their foreheads. At one gig I think I see Aoife. I hope it was her. An eleventh hour rescue. One tragedy side-stepped. Another night a young lad gets hauled out by security for recording the gig on a portable mobile device no bigger than my palm. Bootleggers are still the same free-ride jockeys but their gear's smaller, harder to find. I tell the clubs not to bother about it. We couldn't stop 'em then and we won't now so why fucking try? We're here to be had; let them take us.

Keira suggests an arena tour, venues that'll seat tens of thousands. I tell her she's fucking insane if she thinks we can sell out gigs that size. She tells me I'm the mad one if I think we can't but to appease me she suggests a support act, knife-edge modern, and arms herself with CDs by bands whose names are initials, misspelled words or self-invented lingo. I listen to some gangster shit about fuckin' ya bitch up and hangin' in da crib wid nigga bros. There's even one tosser called J-Zee yacking on about regrets. In order to survive, apparently, you've gotta learn to live with 'em. What the fuck would he know about it? I put the disks to better use as coasters. Keira rearms.

'Try this,' she says, feeding the stereo a candy striped titbit.

A bare drum beat pounds from the speakers, chased by a stinging guitar riff: duhr-duhr-de-duh-de-dee. My ears wake up. A lick replaces the riff, tasting of the '60s but reseasoned, 'Heart Full of Soul' with more salt. Then it morphs again, seesawing between two chords, heavy, dark and angry before the screeching vocals pierce through. It's crude and incredibly fucking powerful, not a song but an energy.

'Who's this?'

'Good, aren't they?' Keira grins, 'twenty-first century rock.'

'Yeah, but who are they?'

She tosses the CD box onto my desk. 'You met him.'

The red, white and black cover shows a couple, her in a red dress clutching a white boa, him in white t-shirt and red trousers, dark hair in his eyes.

'Book them,' I say, 'and tell him I love his raw attitude.'

We sell out every date on the arena tour. The White Stripes open every US show for us and most of the UK ones too. Watching them on stage, her perched on a high stool thumping a hard, simple beat and him thrashing a plastic red guitar bought from a department store, I'm really fucking relieved by the realisation that rock is capable of reincarnation.

A few months into our reunion regime a new being rises from the union of four individuals, just as it did once before. It's alchemy: the right combining of molecules resulting in a new substance. One with the iridescence of a musical rainbow that gleams and sparkles with polished brilliance. One we decide to capture while we can, making a live album, the combination of audio tracks recorded at three different gigs spliced seamlessly in the studio. We sit in the control room listening to the playback, twiddling the EQ knobs as though we remember what we're doing, ordering and re-ordering the songs. We bandy technical jargon; reverb, distance miking, vocal presence, and go home at night with smug-bastard grins, leaving the sound engineer at his desk, correcting our cock ups with precise keystrokes while a computer programme runs a musical model and balances the sound with automated accuracy. We agree, mostly.

Next we're cocky enough to have ourselves filmed, our arthritic antics recorded in high definition and burnt onto shiny silver disks. Movie reel is dead. I don't mourn: life is progress, rebirth. Let someone else wipe the baby's arse though. I'm more worried about what to wear. This is my final portrait; I don't wanna look a complete tosser. Keira recommends black, it's slimming, and something simple, jeans and a T-shirt. It's sensible. Practical. Not the flamboyant stage rig-outs of Mickey Hunter, legend-in-his-own-lifetime rock guitarist. When I try the outfit on I feel like I'm wearing the understudy's costume.

So, on the first day of filming, once the sound checks receive Philip's grudging approval, I head out on a shopping spree. We're in Amsterdam. The trees flanking the canal banks sway in a stiff wind. Tall, narrow houses crowd over me. Some of them are brightly painted and cheerful. Others are grim-faced and dowdy. I move through the city, enjoying the energising wind, mulling over our recent achievements. We've done pretty bloody well in the last few months, playing with conviction, keeping it civil, friendly even, onstage and off. Since Philip resigned himself to his penance the way's been smooth and easy. But it doesn't feel right. We were closer to it at the award ceremony: angry tensions, conflicts bubbling, that's what pushed us to our limits before, made us all we could be and more. It was the crude power of four young bucks ready to conquer the world. Now the danger's past we're flaccid. In need of a right kick up the arse. As the Amsterdam wind charges through me it draws up residual energy, kindling an almost spent ember.

I pass a shop. See what I need in the window. Stop too suddenly and stumble. A young woman, beside me as I stagger, catches my arm. Speaks to me in Dutch.

'I'm alright, thanks,' I say.

'Are you sure?' she asks, switching to English.

'Yes, thank you.'

She lets go and stares at me.

'You are Mickey Hunter,' she says in an accusatory tone. 'You are playing at the,' she pauses, 'auditorium tonight.'

'Yeah.'

'My father, he is going. He has been looking forward to it for weeks. He has told me he saw you play here a long time ago, when he and you were both younger.' Her words are fluent and but the accent causes my hearing to stutter. 'He says you are a, erm, talented guitarist.' She smiles.

'I hope that's still true,' I say then, feeling I owe her, I ask, 'Do you have a piece of paper and a pen?'

She produce a notebook and a blue-black fountain pen.

I write a furious scribble of words. Give her it.

'Tell your father to show that to the security guards when he comes to the theatre. I have invited him to sit backstage to watch the show from the wings.'

'Thank you. He will be very happy.'

She tucks the note away. Pats my arm again. 'You are alright now?'

'Yes, I am.'

She smiles and moves on.

Now she's gone I turn to the cause of my stumble, stepping up to peer through the window at the dusty black Stetson. I remember a hat just like it. Seeing it invokes its grubby white twin, me and Philip facing off, quick draw on Main Street. I shot him, killed myself. It's the memory of a trip, as real as it is imaginary, illusory but not less illuminating for it. Thoughts are things. I go in and swoop, exchanging my Euros for an anonymous brown paper bag of goodies.

I should head to the venue now. Nah, fuck it. I let the wind blow me in a different direction. It leads me along the other side of the canal, down a side street and into a cobbled square. In the far corner is a building with a green door and matching windows, the kind with lots of little panes that are busily being replaced everywhere with large-print double glazing.

Inside everything's wooden; no bloody plastic or chrome. Simple, square-topped, straight-legged tables. Stiff, round-seated, upright-backed chairs. I pick a table by the window. Its surface is covered with scars; people's names, significant dates and other stoned doodlings.

The waitress drifts over. She's young and bored. I scan the menu and order a local beer. She seems surprised. In heavily accented English reserved for stupid tourists she asks if I want something from the other menu. She jabs the chewed end of her pencil at a second card wedged between the sugar bowl and a vase of brackish water that is slowly poisoning one red tulip. I take the second menu.

'What do you recommend?'

'This is good. Organic. Not too strong. Is best for you, I think.' Her pencil hovers over a familiar name.

'Organic? Shit. Yeah, O.K.'

She goes behind the counter. I sit waiting. What it'll be like? How much hell will I cop if Meg finds out?

When the waitress returns I'm lost in memories.

'You pay now,' she says, putting the bill down.

I hand her the last of my Euros. She set a tray before me. Goes back to the counter. Takes up position next to the barman. A flurry of Dutch follows then, in clear English, 'Crown & Kingdom'. I raise my glass to them. The barman salutes. The waitress grins. I light the joint. Its sweet smoke releases mad, childish rebellion. I take out my hotel key. Score the words, 'Mickey Hunter was stoned here,' and the date, among the other graffiti on the table top.

When I leave the café the world outside's smaller, older, more chewed-up than I remember leaving it. I walk slowly, focused on each step. With the homing instinct of an old drunk, I find my way back, slip into the theatre through the side door and go to my dressing room to get changed.

I'm admiring my inspired purchases when there's a banging on the door.

'Mickey? You in there?' It's James.

'Yeah.'

He opens the door.

'You O.K.?'

'Yeah.'

'Philip said he couldn't get any answer from you before.' James frowns.

'I went shopping.'

'Oh? Buy anything good?'

'Might have.'

'Besides wacky-backy?' James laughs.

'You'll see.'

'Well, hurry up, we're on in fifteen minutes.'

I emerge dressed completely in black, the jeans and T-shirt Keira suggested plus the leather trench coat and the black Stetson I've just bought, the perfect prop for my planned re-enactment of the battle Philip and I fight evermore. My flame coloured Gibson hangs at my crotch, a firework exploding against a midnight sky.

I am officially a rock cliché, worn out by overuse. It's perfect. I stride into the wings and am greeted by James's amused, Pete's slightly awestruck and Philip's mildly pissed off stares.

'Ready to rock?' I ask.

James grins. 'Nice topper, Uncle Mickey.'

'Cheers. Now, c'mon, what're you pussies waiting for?'

I lead them onto the stage. The crowd explodes, their cheers and screams cracking concrete, buckling brick and warping wood as the sound of their roared greeting fills the theatre. They start the familiar chant like the words haven't been off their lips in three decades: all hail the kings.

James rushes past me, dives for his drum stool and peels off a roll, crashing cymbals and thumping tom-toms. Pete strides into place, taking up a confident, wide legged stance, bass slung low, and fires out a series of canon-booming notes. Philip leaps from the wings, sweeps the mic off its feet and sings a cappella, 'We're gonna rock around the clock tonight.' That just leave me.

I move forward, edging towards the edge, plectrum poised over those six strands of wire that come alive with my touch. The chant dies away. Yeah, too fucking right, 'cos they wanna hear this. I whack once through the riff from 'Ride Out', off our fourth disc: da-da-dada-di-dada. And wait.

Mickey. Mickey. Mickey.

I repeat the riff, faster, harder.

Mic-key. Mic-key. Mic-key.

I crank the volume to ten, stamp onto the gain channel and launch into the riff again, keep it going this time, straining to hear myself over my own name yelled by every one of the five thousand people crammed into the auditorium: my people.

Hours later their cries are still in my head, stretching off into infinity like the images in two facing mirrors.

While we're out on the road we manage the occasional party,

gatherings populated by worn, tired versions of ourselves and those who used to flock to us in the past. Ronnie Wood's a regular and Townsend shows up a couple of times, Clapton once and Pagey on a different night, a first for him but since Plant suffocated any possible Zep reunion he's been left clinging to the crash-landed wreckage. We sip champagne, smoke the occasional Cuban, have our egos greased by pretty young things, try to outdo each other with lurid anecdotes and laugh over past high-jinks but no fucking way are we up to reliving them. If I could would I even want to? Hell, yeah, but I'm not that young god anymore. Hey, though, I was once and that's pretty fucking special.

One night I come back to the party from an urgent, bladder's-not-what-it-used-to-be break and see James climbing onto a table. Breath held, I wait for the riot to erupt but all he does is pull on the silver string of a balloon that's drifted to the ceiling. He draws it down, passes it to Keira who stands beside him, watching. She laughs. He laughs too, leaps down, making her a low, gallant bow once his feet are on solid ground. I breathe again. Shit, there are plenty of moments from the past I don't wanna fucking relive.

It's better when we're left having a quiet one. On these nights James often joins me. We sit in our hotel suites alternately reminiscing and forecasting. There's beer, wine, and the good Scotch. Sometimes there's weed. But that's where the line's drawn. He's too smart for anything else and I've been there, bought the T-shirt and puked down the front of it too many times to wanna wear it again. Jesus, I've finally grown up.

We're doing this one night, towards the end of the year, when time's winding tight around me, constricting my movements to the nth degree. It's gone midnight but we're enjoying trying to talk the world right while smoking a soothing spliff too much to head to bed. I'm reminded of the night the first Crown & Kingdom aeon ended. How it started with Philip, Ronsey and me splitting one last joint, looking for a desperate peace. For the first time ever I'm able to stop myself from thinking of how it finished and remember why it started.

James and I chew over the gig, the tour, the DVD release, which has been pushed back again 'cos the cover design's still under angsty debate.

'What's wrong with it, anyway?' James asks.

I grin. 'What's wrong is it's my idea, not Philip's.'

'Was it always like this with you two?'

'Yeah. Nah. Mebbe. Fucked if I can remember now.'

'But you guys must've been close to work together all those years.'

'We were welded metal tight, 'til it came loose.'

'I remember Dad coming home at the end of a tour. He'd be buzzed to be back, canoodling Mum, dragging me out to play footie, cooking us massive fry-ups. But it'd last a week. Then he'd start moping. Think that's why he started teaching me to drum. He couldn't cope with not playing, not being with you guys.'

The day of Ronsey's inquest rears up: me squaring off to Philip for round thirteen, or a hundred and thirteen or fuck only knows; a young James charging across to me, throwing himself at me and clinging on like I was the last finger-tip grip on the cliff face; me not being able to bring myself to say it.

'I'm sorry.'

'For what?'

'For taking your dad away from you.'

James frowns. Jesus, I can't do this. Not 'cos I'm scared of him but 'cos I'm scared for him. I can't watch him fall.

'I mean, we were on the road a lot when you were a kid. And then…'

'Crown & Kingdom was his life. He wouldn't've wanted it any other way. You shouldn't feel bad about that,' James says.

For a time the only sound is the tiny crackling made by the burning joint.

'Why did you want to do this?' James asks.

'Thought it'd be nice for the fans. I'd nearly forgotten how much they gave us. Thought I better give something back while there was time. And I wanted to see if I could still cut it. Plus, I wanted you to have this. I hoped it might make up for, well, at least you're getting to see what it was that stole your old man from you.'

'You don't owe me anything,' James says fiercely.

'Mebbe. I do know that I owe your dad. He saved my arse more than a couple of times. James, I mean it. I'm sorry.' I meet his gaze and this time he accepts without protest.

Yeah, I'm right not to dump on him the terrible shit that happened That Night; it's not his mess. I needed to say it Philip and Meg, for different reasons. But what I need to do for James is protect him. This is mine to carry. I've managed it this bloody far so reckon I can limp to the end. Nearly there anyw…

'I think I'm gonna ask Keira to marry me.'

I sit up in of my self-dug pit. 'What?'

'I thought you should know first.'

'Why the hell d'ya think that?'

'She doesn't have any family, and you're her, well, I dunno,' James shrugs, 'I thought it'd be right.'

Anna's face appears as clearly as if she was inches from me. She stares at me with emerald green eyes set in creamy-white skin, framed by a dark bob of hair. She stares without accusation or reproach. I feel guilt and shame. I never thought of marrying her.

'Are you in love with her?'

'Why else would you marry someone?'

I married Meg for love, but also for salvation 'cos only she could save me. There were no reasonings with Anna.

'Then you should bloody well hurry up and ask her.' I flash

him a grin.

There are a hundred or more moments of pleasure in our revival year: headlines proclaiming our return to the throne of rock; gig reviews that praise our power and marvel at our undiminished potency; encounters with fans new and old, living or reliving the thrill of our music; concerts where we stand onstage, looking out over thousands of indistinguishable faces, listening to them shouting our names, baying for our band: my band. I try to savour each moment, rolling them around my mouth, melting them slowly on my tongue. I know this time it's not an endless supply. One of these delicious morsels will be the last. In the end all that's left's an empty wrapper.

Tonight we're playing the 100 Club in London. It's the last gig of the last leg of our 'Bring it on Home' tour, clubs and halls dotted around the UK, the places where we started, places that really mattered to us, especially Ronsey. After tonight there's a break planned. After that, fuck knows.

I'm at the breakfast table stirring my espresso, alternating sips of it with drags on a cigarette. I've had some really good coffees and pleasant smokes on the road. I'll be home tomorrow, drinking camomile piss and wearing a frigging nicotine patch, for Christ sake.

'Mickey.'

Philip enters. For the last two weeks he's been arriving a couple of hours before the gig to set up then vanishing again, reappearing right before for we stride out. He's not even staying in the hotels with us, preferring to trek home from every corner of the country. He's keeping outta my way, sticking up for himself when he can't leave it but there's this line he doesn't wanna cross. And I'm starting to get why. Over the years the power dynamic between us has swung back and forth, a metronome on 180 bpm. In the beginning I was in charge 'til things equalised, mebbe 'cos of

Anna, that's why he fucking did it. But I pulled back my power share when I carried on despite him, her: it. Couldn't hold on, though, and lost it properly when I let the highs matter more than the music, searching for a permanent ecstasy that doesn't exit. Now we know each other's worst secrets it's even again but not the way it used to be; it's thinner, more brittle. Don't touch 'cos the slightest vibration'll shatter it into a million unglueable pieces.

He sits opposite me. I keep stirring.

'Have you had enough?'

'This is my first cup today.'

'I'm not talking about the bloody coffee. I'm gonna take Nancy away for a while, she wants to see her family. After that I thought a tour to the east would be nice. When I come back I want…' He gropes in the dark. 'To know we're squared up here.' His words are more honest than any I've heard from him in this lifetime.

'A cleaned slate deserves a clean break.'

He holds my gaze. 'Really?'

'Yeah. Reckon we've done what needed doing.'

He accepts with a nod. 'It's for the best, Mickey. We're not young any more.'

'James is.'

'James wouldn't wanna think you're killing yourself doing him a favour.' His words are too true.

'Yeah.' I sip my coffee. It's still too hot. 'Thanks for not saying anything, to James or Pete 'bout my health.'

Philip shrugs. 'You kept quiet for me long enough.'

I splutter coffee. Jesus, is he really gonna pick up that rod of uranium 320?

'Why did you, Mickey?'

Wish I could tell him there was some noble motive. But the old reason for everything's still the truest one: I just wanted to.

'Were you planning this?' he presses when I don't answer,

'saving it 'til you needed it, to use against me?'

'No, but I'm flattered you think I'm that savvy.'

'So why?'

''Cos I didn't want the whole world and his fucking dog to know what a bloody balls I'd made of everything.'

He drops into a deep silence, finally surfaces with, 'Me too.'

'Christ knows how I remember this but didn't you once say Crown & Kingdom was my band?' Philip nods. 'Guess I thought that was true so when I'd had enough I reckoned I could kill it easy.' I snap my fingers. 'But when I tried…' I shake my head. 'We've been waiting to die from that fuck up ever since.'

He stares at me. His baby blues are shot through with red.

'Yeah, we have.'

Philip and I agree we'll part amicably, duty done, as long as he lets me stage manage the end. I guess being King of the Kingdom wasn't how he thought it'd be.

That evening, wearing my dusty black cowboy crown one last time, we mount the narrow stage and face off to fewer than two hundred people who've each forked out a ton for this intimate show, Philip and I sharing the secret that it's the last time we'll do this. The crowd whoop and cheer. 'All Hail the Kings. All Hail the Kings. All Hail the Kings.' I strike the opening chord with violent energy. Philip takes up his sultry stance at the microphone, cries out the first words. We're off.

James's pounding drums shake the floor. Pete's steady bass, our heartbeat, thrums in my chest. The first three numbers are bold and defiant. We toss them to the audience who grasp at them with eager fingers, starving masses scrabbling at the first food thrown to them after a famine. Philip pauses only to greet the crowd with his trademark, 'Good evening,' before we move on through three more hits, playing our anthems, letting the music speak for us. The lights flicker on and off, splashing a kaleidoscope of colours around us.

At the last note of the last song of the trio the lights darken. I replace my Les Paul on the stand; take up my seat on a stool brought out by a well trained roadie. Philip sits next to me, clutching the mic. We do two acoustic numbers, both from 'Twilight Manoeuvres', the Crown & Kingdom album Philip wrote and produced. I've had to add them to the set to appease him. And so I can catch my breath, literally. Tonight I also use the slowed pace to watch myself at work for the final time. I follow my fingers as they pick rhythmically through the strings. The movement's flowing and graceful. I can't believe it's me doing it, making these elegant harmonies that lilt and chime. The melodies float about the club, encircling me in a warm breeze.

When they're sung out I'm counting down song by song. Only ten more to go. We up the tempo. Play back-to-back five numbers that make the audience throb with eardrum-bursting joy. For the next four numbers I extend the guitar solos, going free-form. I've got nothing to lose so throw everything away. In the middle of 'Moving On Under' Philip looks over at me. I feel his stare. Meet it. Challenge. Push him to be all he can for one last time. He screeches and screams the notes, howling senseless sounds that match my guitar's cries. James bangs at his kit with furious energy, the snare drum quivering and cringing under his relentless fury. He's picked up the pace, is running along side us, desperate to keep us together. Pete too is struggling to stay in the race. I glance at him. See him bent low over the neck of his bass, fingers running through a familiar pattern at an unfamiliarly ferocious speed. His grim concentration warns me I've taken this as far as it can go. I step off unexpectedly, leaving Philip singing against a naked drum beat with only bass notes for pitch. The song clatters to the end with the chaotic sound of the hooves of four horses who've run together for so long they're unable to stop together. That's the last but one. The audience reinstate their imploring chant, 'All hail the kings.' Fresh adrenaline pumps through my body. Philip crosses the stage to me.

'You O.K.?'

'Yeah. You?'

He breaks into a grin and sprints to the mic.

'This is an old one but I know you still like it: 'Trees of Eden'.'

It's our song. Without it there would've been so little of us left I doubt it would've been worth sweeping up the pieces. I pick the strings with tender ease. The single notes ring out clearly and crisply. Philip joins me, singing with a clarity and elegance that wasn't necessary before. James adds the drum beat at the moment I switch from picking to strumming while Pete lets the bass notes flow. For one last time we fly together, over the hills and far away. This time I know I won't return.

> ♪ We flew higher together
> Than I ever dared dream
> Rode the wind up to heaven
> And left the world far below
> Found paradise together
> Above the green trees of Eden ♫

Philip nods to Pete and James. They both stop playing and Philip stops singing. I shake my head to him but he smiles encouragement so I keep playing. The crowd take up the words, repeating the final refrain for him.

> ♪ Beneath the trees of Eden
> Under the trees of Eden
> Beyond the trees of Eden ♫

Shit, he's letting me have this last moment: the only way he can thank me.

There are two encores, double what we normally do but they

don't count. The end is there, with the last note of the song that was both a beginning and an ending. The lights darken. I take off the Stetson, the brim damp with sweat, and drop it. Leave it. We slip off stage. Time to go home.

It's late when I get in. Meg's asleep on the sofa. There's a book, opened face down on one arm of the chair, on the other, the TV remote. A mug, emptied of cocoa, and a wine glass, also empty, are at her elbow. Two magazines are tossed on the floor at her feet. Wonder if I'm still strong enough to carry her upstairs? Then our arsehole neighbour heads out on another moonlit drive, slamming his car door. She sits up, her eyes wide.

'Meg, darling, it's only me.'

'You git, Mickey.'

'What?'

She rushes me. There's a sharp, crisp snapping sound as her palm slaps my cheek.

'You bloody bastard. All this time you were out on the road when you should've been in hospital. You fucking...'

The rest of her words are lost as she crumples under her own impact.

'Meg?'

'Don't even think about giving me that dumb act of yours. Your doctor rang. Wanted to know when you were going to reschedule the appointment you missed last week.'

'Oh.'

'Is that all you're going to say? For Christ's sake, Mickey, you need medical treatment.'

'Nah, I don't. I need you,' I say, 'come here.'

I reach for her hand. She recoils.

'I couldn't tell you. Knew you'd never let me back on the road if you found out and I had to.'

'So that's what this business with Philip was about, that stuff about putting the past right?'

'Yeah, and I have now and I'm home.'

'Well, don't think you're bloody going anywhere else.'

'I don't wanna go anywhere else.'

I go for her hand again and this time she lets me pull her in, throwing her arms around my neck, holding on to me in a way she hasn't had to for a long time. I feel my neck getting wet. I keep her closer. Breathe her into me.

'I love you.'

'I love you too,' she says, her voice muffled by the collar of my coat. 'Promise you're going to take care of yourself now.'

'I promise. In fact, I'll start right away by having you fix me a soothing cup of tea. Camomile, maybe?'

She smiles, dries her eyes and heads to the kitchen. When she brings me the tea we curl up on the sofa together. Her body's warm and soft against mine. It's selfish but I'm glad I'm leaving the stage first.

The Universe

'Morning, Keira.'

'Can you believe it? Those idiots are digging up the high street again. Two sets of temporary lights this time. I thought I was going to be there all bloody day.' Keira bustles about the office; dumping the post, hanging her coat, throwing her bag down, taking my empty cup. 'Can I get you another tea?'

'God, no. Don't suppose there's any chance of a coffee, is there?'

'Hmmm,' she studies me, 'O.K.' And heads for the kitchenette.

I'm gonna have to tell her about this heart thing soon. Every morning for the last fortnight I've been daring myself to do it. Keep putting it off 'cos telling people makes it real. When I tell her, there'll be one less place where I can pretend things are fine. Now Meg knows home's far too fucking clinical. Keep expecting to find her in a starched apron, watch in hand, demanding to be called Matron. The office is my refuge.

'Coffee.' Keira sets the cup down beside me. 'With sugar.' She smiles, 'You might as well be hanged for a loaf as a slice.'

'Yeah.'

She sits at her desk. I take the opportunity to slip my hand inside my top drawer and withdraw a small white pill. I force myself to swallow. Of all the pills I've downed over the years these are the least joyful but the most important. Keira works through the post.

'Oh.'

'What?'

'This year's NIME nominees.' Her face is paler than a moment ago.

'Let's see.'

She passes the letter. I scan the list. There we fucking are, towards the bottom, in the 'Best Live Album' category.

'Christ sake. Wonder what our chances are?'

Keira takes the paper back. Discards it amongst the leaf litter on her desk. It's awkward 'cos this time we know it isn't another beginning.

'Have you heard from James recently?'

'He rang last night,' she says. 'They've got another three weeks of rehearsals then it's off to California for some publicity then a week's break so he's hoping to fly back for a few days. They're meeting in New York on the fourth, the first show's the sixth, I think he said.'

'And he's enjoying himself?'

'Yes. Says he gets on really well with the bass player and he's pleased with the music.'

Thank fuck it's working out for him. Was worth tugging on a few old strings to get him set up like that.

'A month, that'll soon pass,' I say cheerfully, catching a flicker of pain in Keira's green eyes. 'When are you two gonna set a date?'

'Maybe when he comes home. He should have an idea of the touring schedule and we'll be able to see when we can fit it in.'

'That doesn't sound very bloody romantic.'

'You don't see me as the white dress and vicar type, do you? I'd probably turn to stone if I set foot on holy ground.'

'Yeah, me too.'

'Anyway, we'd rather have something small and quiet. It's a private thing, marriage. It's not about the rigmarole. It's about being happy. Which we already are.'

There's her pragmatic logic. Shit, hope she can turn it on when

I finally get the balls to tell her I'm dying. Maybe I should say something now…

'Keira…?'

'Can I…?'

We speak at the same time then fall into a unanimous silence.

'Normally I'd say 'ladies first' but if you don't mind…' I force myself to edge nearer the precipice.

'Of course not.'

'There's something I need to tell you. Should've mentioned it before but it's a bit, well, it's just…' I feel my heart running hard. Christ, at least let me tell her first before you fucking kill me off. 'I'm not well.' You chicken-hearted bastard.

'I know.'

'What?'

'At least I guessed. You were either taking medication or you'd reacquired a nasty habit. So I checked in your drawer. Meg'd never forgive me if you were using again and I didn't…' Keira rushes the words in her attempt to waylay a bollocking I'd never give her. 'Sorry but I had no choice.'

'Fancy going through an old man's drawers.' I smile. 'God knows what you might've found.'

Keira tries to smile too but her eyes give her away. Her face crumbles. She gulps down sobs.

'Keira, hey, there's no need for that.' I feel an overwhelming urge to hug her but it's so strong I'm afraid of it and don't let myself obey it.

She yanks a tissue out of the box on her desk and furiously rubs her face dry, turning the skin a raw shade of pink. Her reddened eyelids make her green eyes glow.

'Keira, please. What is it?' I inch towards her.

'I couldn't make up my mind to tell you. I always thought there'd be time so I just put it off but I'd never thought about you… getting older. Then I talked to James, told him and he said

I should tell you, but I still wasn't sure. Thought it might seem like I was trying to get what I could before… but that's not why.' She shakes her head. 'Part of me thinks you should know and the other part thinks 'why complicate things?' I wish sometimes I hadn't found out because things were easier before.'

Her breathless jumble of words fires the thrill of panic through me.

'I found out by accident, after I'd been working here a while. I thought about telling you then but I didn't know you that well, wasn't sure how you'd take it. So I hesitated, then couldn't say anything because I was afraid it would seem like I'd kept it from you out of some ulterior motive. Then I figured maybe she didn't want you to know, that was why she never told me. Oh, hell, it's such a bloody mess.'

'Who? What are you talking about? What is it?'

Her eyes are filled with a pleading uncertainty.

'Keira, whatever it is, it'll be alright.'

She goes to the filing cabinet. Takes out a photograph.

'This is how I found out.' She offers me the picture.

It's a snap, from one of the many lifetimes I've survived, of me and Philip and, sandwiched awkwardly between us, Anna. It's familiar but in that backwards way only photographs have. You remember the reverse image, the one from your side, looking into the camera. I stare at the three of us. Remember posing, the photographer pressing us closer together so he could fit our trio in the frame. Anna was trying to break free 'cos, I thought, she didn't want to be in the spotlight. Only later could I've figured out the real reason she didn't wanna spend eternity trapped in a 4 x 6 between me and Philip. But by then I was thinking of other things. Or trying to not fucking think at all.

'Where d'ya get this?'

'I found it when I was sorting through old press cuttings. You asked me to catalogue them.'

I stare at the photograph.

'This is me and Philip, God this must have been seventy, I don't know, maybe one or two?'

'The woman…?' Keira half prompts, half asks.

I consider dumping her in with all the others, 'Dunno, just some groupie,' but it's one thing I can't lie about.

'That's Anna. She was my…' Jesus, I don't even know.

'She was my mother,' Keira says.

Air jams up in my throat. I look at Keira's green, green eyes. In my hand, the photograph sags under the weight of its own revelation.

'First I thought it was a funny coincidence. But it didn't feel like that was it. So I petitioned the registrar, got a copy of my full birth certificate.' Keira stops.

I sink into my chair, legs quivering, and lay the photo on my desk. There's a damp thumbprint on the corner where I've been holding onto it. The things I thought I'd achieved swirl up in a foamy cloud. Tiny shimmering bubbles carried by the wind, they pop and are gone.

'I have a copy if you'd like to see it. Of course there are other ways to check, if you wanted to be sure: DNA.'

'That's not necessary.'

She sits down, weakly? with relief? We're silent a bloody long time. It's not like it is in the movies: 'Daddy?' 'Darling?' And a rushing of bodies, arms outstretched, hair cascading, tears of joy streaming.

'Why didn't she fucking tell me?'

'I don't know.'

'Did you ask her, about me?'

'Yes, when I was old enough to realise you were missing. Maybe she thought I was too young, was waiting 'til I was older but she never got the chance.'

'Does that mean…?'

'She died when I was seven.'

'Oh.'

'A car accident. I was brought up by my aunt and uncle, my mum's sister. They had my surname changed to Martin: theirs,' she explains. 'I guess it was easier that way, for all of us.'

Memories, daydreams, nightmares of Anna have haunted me so many times since I exiled her from my life. I've raged at her in anger, clung to her in despair. Now she's a shadowy ghost and I'm betrayed a second fucking time.

But she's flesh and blood, too. She's standing right in front of me.

'I don't want anything. It's not because you're, well, I hope you don't think this is about money.'

'You're too much like her for that to be it.'

Keira smiles. Fucking good, I meant it as a compliment.

I never thought there'd be a beginning at the end. I was thinking of it as a line between two fixed points; start at A, travel along the line, arrive at B: mission accomplished. I should've been thinking of it as a loop; start at any point and you're done when you get back to where you started. Then you start over again, going round for another turn. Now I'm at the end I know I'm at the beginning again; the same but different.

I go for a walk. It's a Saturday afternoon in April. The wind blows in squalls of rain, dumps them down then blows off to reload. Just about fucking perfect for the mood I'm in. I trudge down the street, eyes fixed on the ground, stepping into grey pavement squares, some childish superstition. I turn from a side street onto a busier main one and get engulfed by a platoon of men and boys in their battalion colours; red for United and blue for City. They jostle and bustle, singing outta tune, marching to a mistimed beat.

'Mind out, Grandad,' one yells.

Prick.

We come to a junction. They turn off.

At the next cross roads I wait for the lights, using the delay to suck in some air. It's harder than it should be. The wind gusts, strikes me on the left side of the head, a sharp blow, pushing a few faint notes into my ear. At first I think the sound's inside my head and it's probably always there but I've stopped noticing it, like a minor tooth ache. But it gets louder so I head towards it, tracking it to the doorway of an abandoned shop.

He's flanked on either side by gaudy posters proclaiming 'Final closing down sale' and 'Everything MUST go': a young man, about twenty. He stands defiantly, guitar over his shoulder, and plays the blues. An anaemic crowd has gathered to listen, exhaling the enjoyment and envy of those who watch while others do. I join their ranks, my habitually critical ear grading the notes he plays. I can't find anything to slag off other than his lack of sincerity; he's too young for true blues. So was I, once.

The song ends. There's some half-hearted applauding and the tinny chink of low-value coins thrown into his case as people move away.

'Do you do requests?'

'If I know them,' he says, rubbing the stubble on his chin.

'O.K.' I fish for my wallet. Don't usually carry much cash but today there's sixty-five quid in notes. I release them over his case. They land, silent as snow, on the purple velvet interior. 'Play me your favourite song.'

He stares at the money, then buries his face in his guitar and finger picks the opening of 'Trees of Eden'. I burst out laughing. He stops. Glares.

'Are you serious 'bout this?' I jab a finger at his guitar.

'No, that's why I'm out here every Saturday freezing my bollocks off for £3.80, sweet wrappers and left over holiday change.'

I meet his youthful anger with ancient fury. 'Well, here's some good advice for you, take it or don't, I couldn't give a fuck, if I've passed it on that's my job done: never give your audience what you think they wanna hear. Give 'em what you want 'em to listen to.'

We scowl at each other then he smiles. I smile too.

'Thanks.'

'You're fucking welcome.'

He starts playing Led Zeppelin's 'Kashmir'.

'We've decided. The 25th.'

'What?'

'For the wedding. While James is home, before his tour starts,' Keira explains.

I snap, 'Don't do this quickly and spoil it 'cos of me.'

Today's a bad day. I'm tiring too easily which pisses me off, driving me to do more than I can in some macho attempt to prove I'm fine when I'm not, leaving me even more tired and narkish. It's a fucking bad day.

Keira perches on the edge of my desk.

'It'll spoil it more if you're not there. And, if you're up to it, I'd like you to walk me in. I know it's a low-key thing but it'd be nice to observe something traditional.'

'Bollocks.'

'O.K.,' Keira lashes out. 'How about this instead? I'd like you to do it because you've done sod all else for me in the role of dad. Or is that bollocks too?'

Her anger's not real but she's an expert manipulator. Not in a vindictive way but she's awesome at getting things that need doing done. I'd never ask for it but this way she can force me into it. I'm quietly fucking grateful, as always.

'If that's what you want,' I say sulkily, keeping up the pretence that I'm doing this for her, not me.

'It bloody is.'

I savour the pungent irony of giving away something I've only just realised is mine. It tastes like lemon pith.

'Does that mean you'll do it?'

'Whatever.'

'Music,' says Meg one night over a dinner of steak and chips. A dying man's last meal? Not quite but she's relaxed the rules a bit on healthy-eating crap.

'Pardon?' I say even though I heard her perfectly, as usual.

'For the wedding. Keira didn't want to ask, but I said, 'What's the point of keeping a dog and yapping yourself?', so I'm asking.'

Before I told Meg the truth about Keira I was shitting it at the thought of them playing mothers and daughters, too fucked up even for me. But it's cool. They've always been co-conspirators, looking out for me. Now they're just a bit less business-like about it. I'm glad Meg'll have someone to share the grief when I've kicked over the stack. And Keira.

I cram in a mouthful of salty sweet chips. 'Ask me what?'

'If you'll play at their wedding.'

'Just me?'

'I think James would like it if you all played.'

I put my fork down.

'You mean one last gig? The four of us?'

'Yes.' Meg looks at her salad; chips are still more than she can stomach, 'Do you think Philip will do it?'

'I'll ask.'

I go to the office early. Root around on Keira's desk 'til I find Philip's number. I've done this before so I know I can do it again. I dial. It rings. Is answered by a woman. Nancy?

She gets Philip. I hang in mid air, a sky diver who's forgotten to plummet to his death.

'Hello?'

'Philip?'

'Mickey.'

There's an uncomfortable pause.

'Sorry, man, I need another favour.'

'I thought we were settled up now.' Philip's voice is husky with dread.

'We are. This is something different. James and Keira are getting married.'

'Oh.'

'They'd like us to play at their wedding. All of us.'

'We said no more.'

'I know. I wouldn't ask if it wasn't a big deal but it is.' As the words come out their weight crushes my chest.

'You don't need me for this.'

'Yeah, I do. I want it to be perfect for them. It's my only chance to do something for them, for Keira especially.'

'Christ, she's only your bloody secretary.'

'Actually, Philip, she's a bit more than that. She's my daughter.'

'Daughter? Anna.'

Those two words are the apology I've waited three decades for. He'll fucking do it, alright.

Tomorrow I have to give the daughter I didn't even know I had to someone else. It's cool, though. James'll take care of her. Something I never could. Never can. I roll over gently. Meg's sleeping at last. Hope she finds someone to take care of her.

I creep out of bed and pad down to the basement, grope the wall for the switch and flick on the bare bulb.

Down here's all the crap I never need but don't wanna get rid of. I'm gonna have to sort through it before… soon. The walls are lined with shelves. Two of them are filled with magazines that ran Crown & Kingdom articles back when that mattered too much. A lot of them are not flattering, especially the early ones when people didn't get us. Another is filled with the bootleg C & K LPs I've collected over the years. Hope there'll be time to add the bootleggers' latest batch but I'll be trawling cyber stalls, not market stalls, for them. There's also a rail, covered with a dust sheet, on which hang my pretentious stage costumes. I kept them for playing dress-ups with phantom children. Keira's too old now. Maybe her kids… Stacked in the middle of the floor are five packing crates filled with things I bought after I stopped wasting money on smack. Somewhere, lost amongst the shit that never meant anything to me, is an anonymous, brown, hardback book, that, one day, an aeon ago, gave me the answer I needed when I needed it most.

I wade through a hundred bits of junk, mostly a miscellany of tour souvenirs and gifts sent by fans. Half way down the third crate I find a shabby copy of *Play in a Day: Bert Weedon's Guitar Guide.* The front cover is tattered, the pages well-thumbed, corners folded to mark those showing simple blues for guitar, chord shapes and skiffle rhythms. My mother picked this off the shelf, carried it to the counter, took it home, wrapped it in brown paper and gave it to me. It's the only thing she gave me that I could bare to keep, even then I had to bury it down here. What the fuck am I gonna do with it? What do people do with the things from their past that they want to survive them? I put it aside and resume my original search.

At the bottom of the fourth crate I find what I came for. As I flick open the brown jacket and yellowed pages the hopes and dreams I had for Crown & Kingdom when we were an undefined collective of musicians trying to collect ourselves flood over me. 'Find thyself in every star; achieve thou every possibility.' And we fucking did.

I take the tarot book and dear old Bert into the lounge. Setting Bert on the coffee table, I hunt for a pen and my reading glasses. Wanna make sure I do a neat job. I sit and, resting the tarot book on the arm of the sofa, hover the pen over the fly-leaf. Words were never my thing. I go simple.

'To Keira. All my love…' One word to go. A signature. My name. C'mon, man, you can fucking do it. I scribble. It's done. In ink. Can't undo it now. '… Dad.'

It's a bright, blue-sky day. Reminds me of my wedding to Meg. She's thinking about it too, as she ties my tie, pins the cornflower button-hole she's insisted on. My swollen feet are tight in my best shoes. Meg wanted to buy me a new pair but what's the point? I won't get the wear out of them.

We drive to the registry hall. Keira didn't want a fuss so there isn't one, just four cars pulling up outside a red brick building with heavy grey doors barring the entrance. A handful of people are gathered on the pavement. Some are menacingly armed with pro cameras, notepads and tape recorders.

I get out of the car. Turn to help Meg. She takes my hand with a frown; she thinks she should be helping me but not today. Keira emerges from the next car with James's help. She's wearing a pale green dress, lightly beaded and ruffed. It's beautiful. James is in a suit; the top button of his shirt isn't fasten and…

'I told you I didn't need a bloody tie,' I hiss to Meg.

She shushes me through a smile.

'Bury me in a tie and you'll be sorry,' I caution her. She scowls with her eyes, keeping the smile on her lips.

I go to Keira and take her arm. Everyone else hurries into the building as the flashbulbs start popping.

'Mr Hunter, a picture, sir?' Before I can refuse we're snapped, father and daughter, arm in arm, a dusty Ford Focus in the background. 'You must be proud today,' he comments, hoping for something he can caption the photo with.

'Pride's bad for you,' I tell him and rush Keira through the doors.

We pause in the vestibule. I gulp down air. Keira fans her flushed face and patiently waits for me to recover.

'Before we go in I wanna give you something.' My words come in breathless gasps. 'I know you're not that into traditions but I've got you something old and something borrowed.' I reach into my pocket, pull out Bert and the other book. She takes one in each hand. 'I thought that might useful if you and James ever have a kid and he wants to learn guitar.' I tap *Play in a Day.* Keira raises an eyebrow. 'You never know and, Christ, if you're gonna bother learning an instrument it might as well be a proper one. Bloody drums, that's not music; it's noise.' I grin at her.

'I'll tell James you said that.'

'No, you bloody won't. You know I'm kidding. Anyway, mebbe you could have two. Drummer and guitarist.'

'You want me to knock out a twelve piece orchestra or something?'

'Drums and guitar'll do, cheers.'

Keira runs her finger over the dog-eared cover.

'Sorry it's a bit tatty. My mother gave it to me, donkey's ago. It's had a hard life.' Like the person who bought it. And the person who's giving you it.

'Don't worry, I'll take care of it.' She examines the other book. 'What's this?'

'It's nothing really. Was Pete's. Well, Susie's, actually. It was useful a couple of times, when I was looking for answers.' I shrug. 'Dunno what to do with it now but I can't bring myself to chuck it. Will you take it?'

'Of course.'

'You don't have to read it but hang onto it for me, eh?'

'O.K.'

Keira turns it over in her hands, looking for an explanation. The cover's blank. She does the obvious: opens it.

'Don't do that now,' I say but her eyes are already scanning the six words that are all I have to give her. 'You can't cry today. I won't allow it,' I add.

'Oh, you won't,' she teases, closing the book. Then she smiles at me, a smile golden and pure. A smile I never thought I'd see again. 'Thank you.'

'Jesus, you're so beautiful.'

'Like my mother?'

'Yeah.'

'If you promise not to crumple me I'll submit to a hug.'

'Oh, you will.' I return her teasing. She nods. I gratefully pull her into my arms. Her hair tickles my cheek. She smells so sweet, flowers and honey. I try to muffle choked sobs but do a piss-weak job.

'I thought you said no crying today?'

'That only applies to you.' I hold her at arm's length for another look, one moment that I want to last for ever but that's gone in a heartbeat. 'You ready?'

'Yes. You?'

I rub my fingers around my eyes. Glance to the door that leads into the main room. I'm glad to be going out through the in door.

'Yeah.'

Keira tightens her grip on my arm. 'I hope you won't be mad.'

'At what?'

She opens the door as the third verse of 'Trees of Eden' plays out over the sound system.

> ♪ Nirvana forever
> It was too good to be true
> Branches couldn't break our fall
> Golden days were too few ♫

Ronsey was right. Legacy is everything.

FIVE SHORT PIPS FOLLOWED BY ONE LONGER PIP

JOHN MARSH: This is the BBC news at seven o'clock on Sunday the ninth of January with John Marsh. Tony Blair and Gordon Brown have given interviews calling for unity in the Labour Party. Two weeks since the Indian Ocean tsunami, officials are continuing to identify victims. There is fresh hope for peace in the Middle East as Palestinians prepare to go to the polls. Guitarist Mickey Hunter has died aged fifty-six. (BEAT) Tony Blair and Gordon Brown have appealed to Labour Party members for unity within the party. In an interview with BBC One's *Breakfast with Frost* Mr Blair said he and Mr Brown were concentrating on issues that concerned the country. Mr Brown, speaking to BBC political editor Andrew Marr, added, 'The only reason we are in government is to get on with the job in a unified way.' There has been speculation of a rift between the two following their separate responses to the Asian tsunami. Tory leader, Michael Howard accused the Prime Minister and Chancellor of, 'squabbling like schoolboys.' (BEAT) Two weeks since the Boxing Day tsunami that caused widespread devastation throughout south east Asia, officials are continuing efforts to identify victims. An aid worker told the BBC bodies now being washed up are so badly decomposed that confirmed identification is becoming impossible. Across the region thousands remain unaccounted for since a 9.0 magnitude undersea earthquake forced a wall of water reaching heights of twenty meters to crash into coastlines as far away as east Africa. Estimates suggest that more than two hundred thousand people have lost their lives in the disaster. (BEAT) There are renewed hopes for peace in the Middle East as Palestinians prepare to elect a new president following the death of Yasser Arafat in November. Exit polls suggest that Mahmoud Abbas is on course for a landslide victory. Mr Abbas, regarded as a moderate, has said violence is not the way to resolve the conflict between Palestinians and Israelis. (BEAT) The death of legendary rock guitarist Mickey Hunter has been announced today. The Crown & Kingdom lead guitarist died at home in the early hours of this morning. He had been diagnosed with chronic heart failure in 2003 and his failing health became apparent during the recent Crown & Kingdom reunion tour. Philip Hall, Crown & Kingdom lead singer, told the BBC that they decided to call an end to the reunion when it became clear the punishing workload was taking its toll on Mickey's health. Speaking from his Hertfordshire home he said, 'I feel privileged to have worked with Mickey for so many years. He was a massively talented guitarist and a good friend.' Lauren Lavern of 6Music looks back over Mickey Hunter's extraordinary career.

LAUREN LAVERNE: Mickey Hunter fell in love with the guitar at a young age. Self-taught, he proved himself to be a guitarist of exceptional standard during the early days of his career. Finding fame in the seventies with Crown & Kingdom band members, Philip Hall, Peter Smith and John Ronsarno, Mickey Hunter became one of the most acclaimed guitarists of his generation. The band chalked up a string of platinum-selling albums but were never far from controversy, with drink, drugs and rock excess taking their toll. The band split following the accidental death of drummer John Ronsarno in 1979. Crown & Kingdom's 2003 NIME lifetime achievement award triggered renewed interest in their music and fans were treated to a full scale reunion. Joined on drums by James Ronsarno, son of John, the band proved that, if they were the 'dinosaurs of rock' some quarters of the music press accused them of being, it only meant they were leaving big footprints for others to follow. They delighted fans globally with performances as good as those during the height of their notoriety. Mickey Hunter's daughter, Keira Ronsarno, recently married to drummer James, spoke on behalf of the family, saying, 'We are devastated by the death of my father but his legacy lives on through the music that will be enjoyed by future generations.' Following news of Mickey Hunter's death, Crown & Kingdom albums are occupying the top five slots in the Itunes download chart. It is expected that the group's classic rock anthem 'Trees of Eden', from their seminal album, *Return of the Kings,* will be played at the funeral which takes place on Wednesday.

JOHN MARSH: The death, announced today, of guitarist Mickey Hunter aged fifty-six. And that's the BBC news at five minutes past seven. More news at eight.

D.J.: And in memory of Mickey Hunter here's Crown & Kingdom's number one single, 'Trees of Eden'.

<u>MUSIC PLAYS</u>

<u>END</u>

'Trees of Eden'

from *Return of the Kings*

Intro:

(Arpeggio)

| Am | Am | Dm | Dm |
| Am | Am | Em7 | Em |
| C | Dm | Am | Am |

Am Am
An empty void of darkness
Dm Dm
A world of ice and pain
Am Am
Waiting out an endless night
Em7 Em
A moon always in wane
C Dm Am Am
Beyond the trees of Eden

C Dm Am Am ×2

Am Am
The dawning broke at last
Dm Dm
You came and brought me light
Am Am
We rode to Shangri-La
Em7 Em
A place beyond the night
C Dm Am Am
Above the trees of Eden

C Dm Am Am x2

Am Am
Nirvana forever
Dm Dm
It was too good to be true
Am Am
Branches couldn't break our fall
Em7 Em
Golden days were so few
C Dm Am Am
Among the trees of Eden

C Dm Am Am ×2

Guitar Solo

| Am | Am | Dm | Dm |
| Am | Am | Em7 | Em |
| C | Dm | Am | Am | ×4

E5 E5

F F
The hope of Hell
G G
And fury of the gods
F F
We couldn't see the trees
G G
Hidden by the woods

E5 E5

Am Am
Together we flew higher
Dm Dm
Than I ever hoped to go
Am Am
Rode the wind up to Heaven
Dm Dm
Left the world far down below
Am Am
Found paradise together
Em7 Em
How did we fall this low?
C Dm Am Am
Beneath the trees of Eden
C Dm Am Am
Under the trees of Eden
C Dm Am Am
Beyond the trees of Eden

C Dm Am Am ×2

Mickey Hunter: Chronology & Discography

1948
2 August: Born in Nottingham.

1953
Family moves to London.

1957
Play in a Day: Bert Weedon's Guitar Guide first published.

1960
August: buys second hand guitar with saved pocket money and, aged 12, begins to learn to play the guitar.

1964
July: Joins Davy Wilson Quintet, on rhythm guitar.

1964–6
The Davy Wilson Quintet tour the UK club scene.

1966
March: Davy Wilson Quintet split; joins Three Bob Band on lead guitar.
June: TBB release *Take Three*, the band's first album with Mickey Hunter on lead guitar; first single release, 'Keep Playin', Baby', reaches no. 1 in the UK singles charts.
July–December: TBB tour the UK, Europe and America; second single release, 'Rock and Roll Daze', reaches no. 1 in the UK and US singles charts.

1967
May: TBB release *Black and Blues*; 'Nothin' but the Truth' reaches

no. 2 in the UK singles charts and no. 5 in the US singles charts simultaneously.

June–November: TBB tour the UK and Europe.

1968

January–April: TBB tour America; 'Black and Blues', the title track from the album of the same name, reaches no. 1 in the UK and US single charts.

July–December: TBB tour the UK and Europe for the final time.

1969

February: Quits TBB.

Spring/summer: Forms C & K. Mother murdered.

August: First C & K gig; meets Anna Litchfield.

November: *Crown & Kingdom, vol. 1* released; C & K complete first UK tour.

1970

February: C & K perform at Royal Albert Hall as part of second UK tour.

August: *Crown & Kingdom vol. 2* released and goes straight to no. 3 in the UK album chart and no. 4 in the US album chart; *Crown & Kingdom vol. 1* becomes C & K's first gold-selling album.

August–December: C & K embark on first US and European tours.

1971

March: *Crown & Kingdom vol. 3* released; all three C & K albums occupy the top three spots in the UK album charts for a record-breaking twelve weeks.

March–September: C & K second European and US tours.

Late September: Breaks up with Anna Litchfield after she has affair with Philip Hall. October onwards: C & K on hiatus.

1972

April: C & K hiatus ends.

May: C & K begin writing and recording new material.

21 May: Keira Litchfield born.
June–August: third UK tour.

1973

January: *Four Kings Ride Out* released and becomes fastest ever platinum-selling album.
March–July: Fourth UK tour including headlining at the National Jazz Blues and Rock Festival in Reading; third European tour.
September–December: Third US tour.

1974

February–April: C & K write and record *Return of the Kings.*
May: *Return of the Kings* is released and goes straight to no. 1 in both the UK and US album chart.
June: Single 'Trees of Eden' is released, becoming the only single release by C & K during the lifetime of all original band members. It goes straight to no. 1 in both the UK and US singles charts, knocking ex-Beatle Paul McCartney's new band Wings off the top spot. The song goes on to become C & K's anthem.
July–September: Fourth European tour.
October–December: Fifth UK tour which included three nights at the Alexandra Palace, gigs which are recorded and later released as a live album and concert footage.

1975

February: *Crown & Kingdom Storm the Palace—Live at Alexandra Palace* is released, becoming the first live album by a British band to go straight to the no. 1 spot in the US album charts.
April: Concert footage of *Crown & Kingdom Storm the Palace—Live at Alexandra Palace* is given a US cinema release in lieu of an American tour and plays at picture houses across American for two month.
March–November: C & K write and record *Long Live the Kings.*

1976

January: *Long Live the Kings* is released and reaches no. 5 in the UK and no. 7 in the US album charts. The album is heavily criticised in the music press for being unoriginal.

February–April: Sixth UK tour.

July–September: Fourth American tour.

November: C & K record a BBC session album of traditional blues covers in direct response to criticisms levied at *Long Live the Kings*

1977

March: *In the Presence of Royalty*, the blues cover BBC session album, is released.

June: C & K headline the Stonehenge Festival.

August–December: C & K write and record their ninth album, *The Slain Gods*.

1978

February: *The Slain Gods* is released and C & K become the first band to have all nine of their albums in the UK Top 40 album chart.

June: C & K headline at the Knebworth Festival. This performance becomes the last ever live performance with John Ronsarno on drums.

July–December: C & K on hiatus

1979

June: Anna Litchfield killed in car accident, Keira, the daughter from her relationship with Mickey Hunter, is sent to live with relatives.

July: Hiatus ends. C & K begin writing and record *Twilight Manoeuvres*, which includes the song 'Over the Edge'. The album is their tenth and final and the only one written and produced entirely by Philip Hall.

11 November: C & K drummer John Ronsarno dies at the home of Mickey Hunter. Following a coroner's enquiry the cause of

death is recorded as accidental.

15 December: C & K's management issue a statement confirming the break up of the band.

21 December: 'Over the Edge' is released as a single, in tribute to John Ronsarno.

1980

January: Admits himself to a private hospital in central London for drug rehabilitation treatment.

1981

May: Marries Meg Collins, a nurse he met during his hospital stay.

1982

January: Officially retires from public life.

February: Secretly founds Hermit Productions which is subsequently credited with producing several award-winning original film scores between 1983–1995.

1996

April: Establishes the Fortune Foundation, a charitable organisation which funds grassroots music opportunities for inner-city youngsters.

2003

March: C & K are honoured with a lifetime achievement award by the UK music industry body NIME (National Institute for Musical Excellence); C & K reform with James Ronsarno on drums and perform live at the awards ceremony in London.

June–December: C & K, with James Ronsarno on drums, embark on an extensive tour which includes the UK and Europe. Amsterdam gig is recorded for later release on DVD.

2004

January–May: C & K tour America, returning to the UK in April where they perform their last ever gig at the 100 Club in London.

July: *Ace of Kings—Crown & Kingdom Live in Amsterdam* is released on DVD.

28 August: Keira Hunter marries James Ronsarno. C & K are rumoured to have played at the wedding reception.

2005

9 January: Dies of chronic heart failure aged 56.

Author's Note

This novel has waited a long time in the wings. I started writing it in 2008. Now, published over a decade later, *Rock God Complex* has lived nearly as many lifetimes as its fictional protagonist. It is on its third title and 'auditioned' at several publishers before, in 2015, Cinnamon Press said they would be happy to produce it. At that time I was already under contract with Cinnamon for the Celtic Colours Trilogy, the release of which was time sensitive as I wanted part one, *Green Dawn at St Enda's*, to appear in 2016 to coincide with the Easter Rising centenary. Knowing we couldn't interrupt the publication of the trilogy by bringing out *Rock God Complex*, this novel had to wait its turn in the spotlight. Ladies and Gentlemen: *Rock God Complex: The Mickey Hunter Story.*

Unlike all three parts of the Celtic Colours Trilogy, I can't pinpoint when and where I came up with the idea for *Rock God Complex*. First I got into rock music, not until my twenties I'm afraid to admit. Then, as a writer, someone who loves stories, it wasn't enough for me to play the CDs and go to the gigs: I needed to know the stories. So I started reading band biographies, watching documentaries and listen to interviews. From this grew a fascination with that magical entity — 'The Rock Band' — and, in particular, how most bands start off so tight and end up so fractured, barely able to talk to each other let alone create music and perform together. I wondered what could drive a band apart so violently and what it would take to reunite them. Coupled with this was a curiosity about what becomes of those rock stars who live beyond 27, who outlive their notoriety and achievements. This book is a fictional exploration of those musings.

As I've said, I didn't consciously research this novel. But the real life stories I encountered through my interest in rock music were helpful sources of information for writing this book. Although Crown & Kingdom are entirely fictional as both individuals and a group they are based on the multitude of actual rock stars I read about, particularly those who rose to fame in the late 1960s and who rode the rock wave during the 1970s. If some of C & K's antics seems familiar it's because I was inspired by several infamous anecdotes associated with bands of that period.

Supporting C & K in this novel are some real rock stars, in cameos, all fictionalised in my usual manner who, had C & K actually existed, would certainly have interacted with my four kings of rock. But I remind readers that C & K are not real and neither is anything that happens in this book, to them or their entourage.

So, having listened to the music, attended the gigs, bought the T-shirts, read the books, even learnt to play guitar and had the occasion minor foray on stage myself, axe in hand, I wrote the novel. For me the best thing about being a novelist is being able to live someone else's life in the pages of the story. And who wouldn't want to live the life of a legendary rock star?

Tracey Iceton, 2020

ACKNOWLEDGEMENTS

This book owes its existence to the following people:

Anne Coburn, who, in her role as Royal Literary Fellow at Newcastle University, offered me the first professional reading of this text and generously continued to support and help me long after her official duties had ended.

The Creative Writing department at Newcastle University who helped me through my creative writing MA, for which I submitted sections of the book for assignments and, through feedback given, enabled me to make improvements.

Dr. Aayesha Mulla, my 'oldest' friend, who in her professional capacity as a psychologist, helped me with writing up Mickey's therapy sessions as well as for giving me encouragement and support not just on this writing project but for over three decades and also for writing one of the most 'laugh out loud' comments on the MS that I have ever had from any feedback!

My good friend, poet, Natalie Scott who took precious time out from her own writing to read *Rock God* and make valuable suggestions.

Fellow author Guy Mankowski for the interesting chats we had on how to write about music-making and the trappings of fame that accompany it (see *How I Left the National Grid*) and for offering words of praise for this book.

Dr Adam Hansen of Northumbria University's English Department who found the time to read the finished text and generously added his endorsement.

Fred Gardner who helpfully acted in the capacity of 'ordinary reader' for this book and kindly said he had enjoyed it, giving me much needed encouragement at an early stage of my writing career.

Anthony Iceton, Philip Bage and Ken Smith, all of whom made sterling efforts down the years to teach me to play the guitar so I sounded like I knew what I was talking about in relation to guitar music.

The Invisible Friends, experience of playing bass guitar for whom gave me a tiny taste of what being in a rock band might be like, allowing me to do what writers are always being told they should do: write what they know (well, sort of).

Jan Fortune and Adam Craig at Cinnamon Press for helping me develop *Rock God* into a publishable work, for continuing to support my writing dream by publishing me for a fourth time and for an amazing, as always, cover design. Also to Ian Gregson, fellow Cinnamon Press author, who mentored me through the final draft of this text, whose insight into writing about rock 'n' roll was invaluable and who so generously put forward words of praise for the book.

My family who continue, always, to support and champion my writing in any way they can.

The headline act: my husband John who not only read and reread this book, put up with my endless agonising over it and never tired of doing any of that but who also introduced me to rock music in the first place, without which I would never have been able to write this. ('That sounds like a whale being murdered!')

Mickey Hunter for coming to me, in the way only he could, and sharing his story with me. There were many the highs and lows during the writing journey but the destination, this book, was worth it all.

And finally to all those musicians who rolled the rock, from Aerosmith to Zappa, AC/DC to Zeppelin and everyone in between. Thank you!